Until All Curses Are Lifted

Tim Frankovich

WARPSTEEL
PRESS

Dedicated to all the guys who have attended a Men of Valor retreat.

N
Ch'olan
Mandiata
Drusa's Crossing
Djatan Desert
Efesun
Tenjkidi
Great Plains
Trebi's R.
Woqan
Arazu
Reman
Zes Sivas
Annis R.
Varioch
Sandu- Emuq
DISPUTED
Lake Litanu
Kuktarma
Rasna
Raeton
Simbala
the Six Lands of Antises

(((1)))

"It's coming for you, Curse Boy."

Marshal scowled but ignored the taunt. He crouched in the snow and reached a hand out to trace the footprint in front of him. His fingers shook and he drew the hand back, hoping the others hadn't noticed.

Titus, the young man who had spoken, walked around Marshal and whistled. "Look at how far apart the footprints are," he said. "That thing must be huge."

Marshal nodded. The footprints, three-clawed like a lizard, were as wide as his handspan, and at least a yard apart.

"Not so huge," said Victor, the third member of their group. He pushed his way past a small pine tree to get a look from a different angle. "From what I hear, their legs are spread out from their bodies. Look, you can see where its stomach dragged through the snow a little." He pointed.

Marshal craned his neck to see. As the only cursed individual in their village, his interest was more than curiosity. If these tracks really belonged to the creature known as a curse-stalker, he needed to be wary. According to his mother, curse-stalkers weren't actually drawn to curses, but to magic itself. But since curses were the most obvious manifestation of magic most people would ever see, the idea persisted.

"It looks like Balaes is ready for us," Victor said. All three boys looked back toward the blacksmith's home and ruined workshop. The blacksmith, Balaes, gestured toward the ruin, saying something to the woman beside him.

Marshal and the other two hurried back. As they approached, Balaes bent and reached down through the snow. He pulled up an iron ingot, and tossed it into a pile next to the wall of his home. Snow had piled up this winter, both in the branches of the surrounding trees and on the roofs. It had only been a matter of time until one of the trees collapsed. Unfortunately, it had happened directly above the roof workshop.

A hand held Marshal back. "You aren't wanted here," Titus said. "We can handle it."

"I think you'll find that you need his help." Aelia, Marshal's mother, stepped away from the blacksmith. "With half of the town's men laid up with the fever, and the rest gone to check the pass…"

Balaes scowled, a common expression for him.

"Got to clear everything out of the way before we try to lift the trunk," Balaes said. He waved at the young men. "You three get busy on that, and then we'll work together."

Marshal stepped away from Titus and pulled at a fallen branch. Balaes was the biggest and strongest man in Drusa's Crossing. If he needed help lifting something, it must be enormously heavy. He eyed the tree trunk.

"Maybe when we're lifting it, we accidentally let it slip on Curse Boy here," Titus said.

Victor helped him lift a larger branch and glanced at Marshal. "He can hear, you know," he said. "He just can't speak."

"It's more than that!" Titus made sure the older adults were out of earshot. "I hear he has a sign up in his house to remind him about the difference between nodding and shaking his head! We could talk about anything in front of him and he wouldn't know half of what we're saying."

Titus' lowered eyebrows and half-smile irked Marshal almost more than his words. Aelia did have a sign in the house. It read, "Nod is yes. Shake is no." Marshal repeated it to himself constantly. Truthfully, he had no trouble whatsoever understanding other people. His problem, caused by his curse, came in communicating for himself. He couldn't speak, and struggled just to remember nodding and shaking. Aelia had tried throughout his life to teach him hand signals, but every time, the knowledge just slipped away from his mind. After eighteen years, she had finally given up.

Victor looked at Marshal again, then frowned and tried to shift a piece of timber from the fallen wall. "He understands more than you think," he said.

"Just because you're Bonded to him doesn't mean you have to

defend him, you know," Titus said.

"Shut your mouth!" Victor's face tightened. "You think I like it? I can't ever leave this place unless he does! I hate it. I hate him."

"So…" Titus inclined his head toward the tree trunk. "Like I said, maybe an accident happens, and you're free from that."

Victor's gaze shifted between the other two, but his eyes had narrowed. Marshal tried to focus on the work. He knew that Victor resented the Binding between them, even hated him for it. And like so many other things, it wasn't Marshal's fault.

Actually, he did own some fault to that one. When the boys were only eight summers old, Marshal had saved Victor's life, stopping him from plunging over a cliff. By the Laws of Bindings and Cursings, Victor became bound to Marshal until he could repay the debt. Marshal couldn't feel it, but he knew Victor could. Any time Marshal stumbled into the slightest bit of danger, Victor felt compelled to rush to his rescue.

Since the village already considered Marshal a freak due to his curse, Victor's discomfort grew over the years. Now that both boys had grown into men, discomfort had turned into hatred. With the Binding in place, Victor could never fulfill his own dream of joining the army, no matter how often he practiced with the worn-out flail he often carried on his belt.

Victor yanked the piece of timber out from the pile of debris and threw it, barely noticing where it fell. "Breaking a Binding like that… it's not good. That's what they say, anyway. So let's just… just work here. No more talk."

Titus shrugged. All three of them continued at their work. The sun rose higher, at times making things too bright as it reflected off the omnipresent piles of snow. Despite the cold air, all three worked up a healthy sweat by the time midday arrived.

Balaes' oldest daughter, Careen, brought the boys some bread and cheese. Several of the other young women of the village joined the gathering, laughing and talking together.

Marshal sat apart from the others. The girls were all near his age, but none of them spoke to him. Victor, with his rugged physique and sandy blond hair, drew most of their admiration, especially Careen's. Titus was somewhat skinnier, but his dark eyes and hair worked wonders with his lopsided grin and smattering of facial hair. The girls loved his company almost as much as Victor's.

Marshal knew that his looks weren't the problem. A stranger would have considered him fairly well-built, muscular, and somewhat attractive, with his light brown hair and eyes. But the stranger wouldn't know about his curse, wouldn't know that he couldn't communicate, and wouldn't know about the shaking.

He took another bite of bread and looked at his hands. Both felt like thousands of tiny needles poked them all over. He dealt with this feeling daily, sometimes all day. He was used to it. But sometimes the buzz from the needles led to the shaking. He hated the shaking most of all, because he couldn't hide it.

Victor and Titus took great delight in showing the curse-stalker's tracks to the girls. Most of them glanced at Marshal throughout this conversation. He knew they were talking about him, wondering if this creature was coming after him.

Aelia emerged from visiting with the blacksmith's wife. She started toward Marshal, but the girls intercepted her and crowded around. They had always been drawn to Aelia, perhaps because she was younger than their mothers. She had been younger than these girls when Marshal was born.

"Mistress Aelia, did you see the tracks?"

"What a monster it must be!"

"Should we fear this creature, or is it only after… him?"

Marshal looked up in time to see the girl look directly at him. Some slight color came to her cheeks as she shifted her gaze away. Aelia took a breath, briefly closed her eyes, and then smiled at the girls.

"You all know the thrummers, yes?"

"The bugs? The ones that bite you?"

Aelia nodded.

"The only good thing about winter is that the thrummers are all dead!" Careen said. Victor and two of the other girls laughed.

Aelia smiled. "The thrummers will bite anyone, as you know," she said. "But they are especially drawn to anyone with magic in their blood. When they taste it, they glow and thrum louder than ever."

"I've never seen one glow!" Titus proclaimed with narrowed eyebrows.

"I'm sorry for you," Aelia said. "When they do, they're amazing to watch. But the curse-stalkers are the same as the thrummers in some ways. They will attack anything that moves, but they are especially drawn to those with magic in their blood."

She looked around the group. "So yes, we should be cautious. While the old tales might make you think this creature is only interested in my son, the truth is that it is dangerous to all."

The young people looked around at each other. A couple of them glanced briefly at Marshal again.

"I thought you boys were here to work!" Balaes called from the front of the house.

Marshal, Victor, and Titus jumped back to their tasks. By now, they had cleared almost everything out of the way. Balaes brought an axe and chopped off the tree's remaining branches and its narrow top. The boys dragged them out of the way. At last, only the trunk remained. The four men together rolled it on top of a few boards to give them a gap underneath.

Balaes looked over his helpers and the trunk. He rubbed his scruffy beard and twisted his mouth as he appeared to think it over. He blew out a long puff of mist.

"I'll take this end," he said, pointing to the thickest part of the trunk at its base. "Victor, you stand here." He pointed to a spot a few feet further down. He placed Marshal near the middle, and Titus close to the top. All four were staggered on opposite sides of the tree.

Balaes bent down and wrapped his huge arms around the tree trunk. "Use your knees, not your back," he grunted. The other three followed his example. Marshal found that Balaes had placed him in just the right position that his arms wrapped all the way around the trunk. A quick glance at Victor showed it to be the same for him.

"Now!"

All four men groaned as they strained. Marshal gritted his teeth and lifted. He felt like he was lifting the heaviest object he had ever handled in his life. But because of Balaes's massive strength and the balancing he had arranged with the other three, the tree trunk rose into the air.

"They did it!" Careen exclaimed from the side.

"This way." Balaes took a step forward. The four men shuffled together, moving the tree bit by bit out of the ruins of the workshop.

And then Marshal's hands began to shake.

Not now. Not now. He looked back and forth. His breathing accelerated. He had no way to tell the others he was having problems, and the tree still needed to move another dozen feet or more.

Another step. The shaking spread up into his forearms. He would not be able to hold on much longer.

Victor noticed his discomfort. Or maybe the Bonding alerted him. "Marshal? What's going on?"

He couldn't answer. He struggled to maintain his grip on the tree, but he couldn't do it.

"Don't you let go!" Victor shouted. "I can't hold the center alone!"

"What's going on?" Titus asked.

Balaes turned his head to see.

Marshal looked at Victor's face, pleading in his eyes.

"No!" Victor said. "Don't--"

Marshal's arms vibrated apart and he staggered several steps backward, releasing the tree.

"Arrrghh!" Victor's neck bulged as he strained, but it was futile. Without Marshal, the tree was unbalanced, and the remaining three men's strength could not handle it.

As the weight shifted, Balaes and Victor let go and scrambled back. Titus attempted to do the same, but did not succeed. The tree trunk rotated as it fell, catching him by surprise. He backpedaled and fell. The trunk came down on his right leg.

Marshal collapsed in the snow, his arms still shaking. Behind him, Titus screamed. Racing footsteps and cries of dismay surrounded him.

"Get it off him!"

"What happened?"

"Stay back!"

"Hurry, Victor!"

Aelia, the town's only healer, grabbed Titus's hand as Balaes and Victor lifted the trunk off him. "Oh, this is bad," she whispered. Titus shifted from screams to loud moans.

Marshal felt the shaking subsiding. He stumbled while standing again, then turned to see the others.

A powerful blow struck his face and sent him sprawling back into the snow. Balaes stood over him, his face twisted and jaw set. "What is wrong with you?" he shouted.

"Balaes! No! He can't help it!" Aelia said. "Help me here! I need you!"

The blacksmith scowled down at Marshal and turned back. Aelia instructed him on holding Titus while Careen and her younger sister ran for supplies.

Marshal climbed back to his feet. His eyes darted from the frightened looks of the girls to the accusatory glare from Victor. He took a step closer and looked down at Titus. Even from here, Marshal could see that the leg was shattered. Even with Aelia's skill, it might never heal straight.

As he often did, Marshal struggled with conflicting thoughts. Unable to discuss these feelings with anyone, he could never quite resolve them. Looking at Titus, he felt both sadness and pleasure. Part of him mourned harm being done to anyone. But another part of him celebrated the injury of his tormentor.

"You did this!" Titus's voice was ragged. He stared right at Marshal. "You did this!"

"He's right," Victor said. The girls murmured.

"I hope that monster gets you!" Titus shouted. "I hope it eats you alive!"

Marshal ran.

(((2)))

Seri hated the sound of her own name. It wasn't a bad name in its shortened form, but she had heard her full name, Seri-Belit, so many times that *Seri* suffered by association.

Her parents and teachers all assured her that her name held rich historical significance. Ordinarily, that would have excited her, as she loved the study of history. But in this case, it didn't matter. "Seri-Belit" might be a fine name for someone who lived hundreds of years ago, but not for a young woman on the verge of major accomplishments. It was far too… old fashioned. Stodgy. Mired in old traditions.

Like this man pulling at the oars right now. Hauk was his name. A perfectly acceptable name for a person in his position. Simple, but with a bit of strength to it. Hauk ferried people across Lake Litanu from larger ships to the shores of Zes Sivas, island of mages and Kings. A simple job requiring a bit of strength, but mired in old traditions. Just like his name.

"Can't remember the last time I took a woman across," Hauk said, proving her point.

Seri sighed. He was baiting her and she knew it.

"Do y' think they'll let a woman become a mage?" Hauk asked, chewing on something. He strained a little harder at the oars.

Seri fixed her gaze on him. "I have the full confidence of Lord Enuru and Lady Lilitu," she declared.

That was not the entire truth.

For all she knew, Lord Enuru hadn't even heard of her. Lady Lilitu, on the other hand, had given her a hand-written note which she kept stowed in her satchel on the seat beside her.

Hauk shrugged and kept rowing. Seri's temper flared, but she wasn't sure whether it was at Hauk for his attitude, or at herself for reacting to it. She kept her mouth shut. Her mother had often chided her about speaking too much at the wrong times. She considered her efforts to abide by that warning to be supremely admirable.

A lump rose in her throat as her parents flooded her thoughts. She knew the pull, the homesickness, was caused by the Binding that everyone bore toward their native land and people. Yet another thing she had to fight.

A few moments later, the early morning fog cleared and Zes Sivas came into view. Yesterday, she had seen it from the ship, but only as a vague mass in the distance. And drawings could never do it justice. The island rose thirty or forty feet out of the water before leveling off, the sides rising steeply, but not into outright cliffs. Moss clung to many of the surfaces. A few haphazard cypress trees dotted the top of the banks, extruding knees in a myriad of directions around them and down the sides.

Seri paid little attention to the flora, so focused was she on the island's structures that covered most of its surface. Two massive fortresses stood side by side with walls and towers so intertwined it was virtually impossible to tell where one structure ended and the other began. Seri knew this was intentional, symbolic, representing the union of sovereignty and magic. Most of the stone appeared to be either grayish limestone or reddish marble. None of it was native to the island itself. The task of ferrying that much stone across the lake had to have been immense.

The Citadel of Kings sat northernmost on the island, built to house Akhenadom the Great and his descendants. It stood empty now, as far as she knew. There hadn't been a King over the six lands of Antises for over seventy years.

The second fortress, the Citadel of Mages, had been built to house the Conclave, the greatest magic-users of all six lands. Together, sovereignty and enchantment were supposed to work for the good of all within the realms. Seri wondered when that had last been true.

Hauk continued rowing, not sparing a glance for the fortresses. "We have to get around to the southeast for docking," he said, turning the boat with expert strokes.

Seri ignored him, her eyes fixed on the citadels. She felt her heart beating faster. She was here at last. The one place in all the lands that she had longed to see her entire life.

"This is so amazing!" she exclaimed. "So much of our history took place right here! Akhenadom and the Conclave crafting the Bindings and Cursings. The Lords' Betrayal. The Loss of the Last King. The yearly Passing. I can't wait to--"

She cut herself off.

The rowboat drew parallel to the island, veering south. Seri took a deep breath to calm herself. Master Hain, the current head mage of her homeland, would be waiting at the dock. Five years ago, he had seemed disdainful of her chances at the Conclave. Yet he had accepted her application to become an acolyte. She hoped that meant his opinion had changed.

A small wave swept across the surface of the lake, running counter to the normal waves. Hauk noticed it too, and frowned. "What's that?" he mumbled. A second wave flowed past the boat.

"It's coming from the island," Seri said, leaning forward to get a better look. A chill wind struck her face as the boat rocked.

"Watch it!" Hauk warned.

The island shuddered. Seri saw rocks and clods of dirt tumbling down steep banks. The citadels themselves seemed to vibrate, as the ground on the nearest slope cracked open, dirt and water both pouring down inside.

Seri caught a glimpse of a tall figure in purple robes at the top of the slope, looking down at the crack. He looked unsteady, as if he were having a hard time keeping his balance.

And then, to Seri's open-mouthed horror, one of the citadel pinnacles began to tilt. Slowly, as if time itself decelerated, thirty feet or more of the tower began to fold over on itself. Bricks separated. Windows shattered. Roof tiles slid in every direction. The entire conglomeration plunged toward the water only a few yards away.

Seri leaned further, trying to discern from which citadel the pinnacle had fallen, and if the man she had seen was safe. The collapsing tower struck the surface with a tremendous impact, splashing ice cold water over the rowboat. Hauk pulled with all his strength, trying to get them out of the chaos, but the boat's rocking intensified, catching Seri by surprise. She lost her grip on the gunwale and plunged into the lake.

The glacial temperature of the water rendered Seri insensate, turning her muscles into ice. Her heavy clothes sucked her under the waves. The cold penetrated straight through her clothes, her skin, and her very bones.

Seri's thick gown, so rooted in current Arazu fashion, tangled around her legs. Even if she could manage to tear part of it off, it would be too late.

Her mind comprehended all of this in an instant, even as it screamed out at the injustice of losing her life when she was so close to achieving her greatest dreams.

And then, a rope came toward her. No, the rope *swam* toward her, moving back and forth as if it were a sea serpent skimming through shallow waters in an oasis. Seri assumed it must be some final hallucination, perhaps due to the lack of air in her burning lungs.

In spite of all that, she seized the rope, but her fingers struggled to entwine. It yanked her back toward the surface. She lost it for a moment, grabbed it again, and found herself dragged upwards into the light of day.

Bursting out of the waves, she gasped, choked, and spewed water. The rope continued to pull up onto the nearest slope of the island. The tall man she had glimpsed before stood waiting at the top.

"Welcome to Zes Sivas, Seri-Belit," he announced.

As she collapsed, shivering uncontrollably, Seri's couldn't help thinking that if all the mages already knew her full name, she might as well have drowned.

(((3)))

The earth shook on the day Marshal's life changed forever. It wasn't much of a shaking, like thunder from a distant storm, but strong enough to be felt. Marshal looked around Drusa's Crossing uneasily. A couple of nearby villagers murmured. One touched his index fingers to his palms and whispered. But nothing changed and the shaking did not repeat itself.

Aelia emerged from a cottage, pulling on her gloves. "Titus's leg is knitting," she announced. "But it will be some time before he can walk again." She handed her bag to Marshal, who had been waiting outside for her. She cocked her head, noticing the look on his face. "What is it, son?"

He grimaced and pointed toward the ground.

Aelia nodded. "I felt it," she said. "It was far away, whatever it was. I'm sure it means nothing to us."

Marshal started to nod, but stopped. That wasn't right. He shook his head.

"Skeptical, are you?" Aelia started down the central road through town. "The wider world leaves us alone. Let us do the same for it."

Aelia flipped her hand in the air and looked at him expectantly. Marshal frowned. He knew she had used this gesture many, many times, but when he tried to decipher it, his thoughts seemed to dissolve in his head.

His concentration broke at the sound of hoofbeats. He turned to look at the same time as his mother. Five riders emerged from the forest and rode into Drusa's Crossing. A single rider would be unusual here, especially before the mountain pass opened. Marshal couldn't remember seeing five at once.

"Theon's wings shelter us," Aelia whispered. Marshal glanced at her, but his attention returned immediately to the strangers. The riders passed right in front of him.

Three appeared to be guards or soldiers of some kind. Their long swords hung in practical sheaths at their belts, while two also carried bows and quivers full of arrows on their backs. The third had a flail on his back, something sure to draw Victor's attention. Their red and gold-trimmed cloaks marked them as part of Varioch's military.

The other two were not soldiers. A woman, thin and severe, ignored everything around her. Her small, upturned nose, sharp eyebrows, and long, dark hair screamed haughtiness to Marshal. But it was around the final rider that the guards formed a protective circle. This man wore an air of elite nobility that radiated in every direction. His tailored clothes fit tightly to his muscular frame. As Marshal watched, the man threw his hood back, despite the chill, revealing short blonde hair and a carefully groomed short beard. His cold blue eyes settled briefly on Marshal before moving on to Aelia. His eyes sharpened at the sight of her, and he glanced back at Marshal.

"This way, your Lordship!" one of the guards called. After one more glance back at Marshal and Aelia, the noble continued on.

"I should have known," Aelia said. She gave a great sigh. "I just hoped we'd have more time…"

Marshal frowned, but Aelia smiled at him. "Don't be concerned, my treasure. Whatever happens today, remember what I have told you every day of your life. And--" She stopped and laughed. "I almost said not to tell them anything. I'm getting old, son."

He shook his head. No matter how old he grew, his mother always seemed young. He knew she had been very young at his birth, barely old enough to have a child of her own. No one could use the word "old" to refer to her.

The riders dismounted in the center of town. The nobleman gestured and one of the soldiers returned down the road on foot. After a few steps, he looked with dismay at his boots, coated now in thick mud, and growled something incomprehensible. He shook his head and approached them, head down as he tried to avoid the muddiest spots.

Aelia spoke first. "Good day to you, sir."

"Good day," he answered, looking back up at them. "His Lordship would like a word with you." He gestured toward the town center, really nothing more than a wider space in the road.

The mother and son followed him dutifully. Marshal studied the longbow slung across his back, the fine thread of the red cloak, and the erect posture so different from the average villager around them. A crowd of townspeople gathered around the horses and their riders.

As they approached, Marshal saw the nobleman talking with several locals, including Balaes and the village major. Marshal almost laughed at their expressions. He couldn't tell if they were honored or frightened. Maybe both. The woman had not dismounted, and continued to stare off into the distance.

Upon seeing them approach, the nobleman gestured the other men away with a small but insistent gesture. He strode to meet Aelia and bowed to her. The act shocked the other townspeople. Marshal couldn't hide his smile this time, but he was just as confused as everyone else.

"My lady," he said, "I'm sure you can guess who I am, but I do not know your name." He spoke loud enough to be overheard some distance away. Marshal frowned.

"You are Varion's son," Aelia answered. The crowd almost exploded over this information. As one of the six Lords of Antises, Varion ruled over the land of Varioch.

The young man's eyebrow twitched. "I am," he said. "My name is Volraag, heir to the Lordship of this land." He lowered his voice so the other townspeople could not hear. "Though not the eldest son of Varion, if I am right about your identity."

"What do you want from us?" Aelia demanded.

Volraag looked taken aback. "I came to meet my brother and speak with him." His eyes turned to Marshal.

Marshal's smile vanished and he took a step back. Brother? Of this nobleman? That couldn't be right.

The townspeople started to move closer, but the three guards stepped in the way.

"If you know what you claim to know, then you also know that my son is cursed because of your father. He cannot speak." The last three words came in almost a whisper. Aelia's face hardened and she swallowed.

Marshal's mouth went dry. Aelia had never told him the name of his father, the man who had raped her and passed a curse down on his son. Lord Varion was that man?

Volraag's eyes narrowed by a fraction. "Then we shall communicate in other ways. What is his name?" His voice returned to its normal levels.

Aelia looked back at him, breathing hard. She opened her mouth, but didn't say anything.

The town major stepped forward nervously. "His name is Marshal, your Lordship," he said. "He sort of helps out in odd jobs around town. He doesn't…" He trailed off.

"When I want to hear from a blathering side of beef, I will ask for it," Volraag said without turning around. The major blanched and stepped back.

Volraag's eyes blinked to Marshal and then back to Aelia. When she still did not speak, he glanced around again and sighed.

"Otioch, make sure we are not disturbed," he said to one of the soldiers. He pointed at Marshal. "You, come with me." Without waiting for a response, he stalked away past the framework of Balaes's new workshop.

Marshal looked to Aelia for instructions, answers, anything. He needed to know something more from her. She glanced at him and only nodded. Without any other guidance, Marshal frowned and followed the Lord's son away from the crowd.

He caught up to Volraag next to the fallen tree beyond the workshop. Balaes and Victor had rolled it some distance further. Upon seeing it, Marshal could think only of Titus. Volraag sat on the trunk, folded his arms, and studied Marshal with a sharp eye.

Marshal stood still under the scrutiny, not knowing what else to do.

"You are different than I expected," Volraag said after a moment. "I can see our father in your face and hair, but your eyes definitely come from your mother." He glanced back toward the village. "It's easy to see what Varion saw in her, by Theon. I've rarely seen such a beauty in such a… rustic locale."

Marshal scowled. What Varion saw in her? He had raped her! His fist clenched.

"Before I arrived, you didn't know your father's identity, did you?"

Nod is yes. Shake is no. That he could remember. Usually. Marshal shook his head.

Volraag snorted. "Well, I never thought I would be the one to give out such news, but congratulations. You're the firstborn son of the all-powerful Lord Varion." He paused. "You're also a bastard, conceived by rape." He shook his head. "To be honest, muteness seems like a relatively minor curse for the crime of rape, compared to others I've seen."

Marshal found himself growing angrier as he considered this information. He wondered why Aelia had never told him, but the full weight of Lord Varion's actions was almost unbelievable. Most people who bore a curse bore the consequences of their own actions. But the Lords of Antises had exempted themselves from the magical laws. Any curses of their actions fell on their children. Marshal had known that his father must be a noble, but Lord Varion himself?

And a "minor" curse? What did Volraag know of him? Muteness was only the beginning. As if in response to his thoughts, his right hand began to tremble.

"There it is!" Volraag whispered. He rose from the fallen tree and took a step toward Marshal. His eyes had widened, but not with surprise. Marshal had seen the same look on faces at the town's annual thawing feast. He had seen it on Victor's face a time or two when he looked at Careen and she wasn't looking back. Volraag's face held… desire?

Marshal took an involuntary step backward and grabbed his right hand with his left.

"Does it do that often?" Volraag asked, never taking his eyes off the trembling hand.

Marshal shrugged. That was the right gesture, wasn't it?

"That is not a part of your curse, brother. That is something… much more."

Marshal looked at him with narrowed eyes.

Volraag tore his eyes away from the shaking hand and looked Marshal in the face. "Do you at least know of the six Lords and their magical power?"

Marshal nodded. Who didn't?

"Varion is one of the six Lords. That means he holds a vast portion of this world's magic within him. He wields unbelievable power when he chooses to…" Volraag trailed off and looked away, as if thinking of something unpleasant. He shook his head and looked back.

"Despite the fact that the… circumstances of your birth led to you being cursed, your birth also entitles you to this inheritance. When Varion dies, or surrenders his power at the Passing, that power will move on to you."

Marshal released his trembling hand and looked at it. Magic power? The power of a Lord? He had nothing like that. He had shaking, trembling. He was "Curse Boy," not "Lord's son."

"Yes, you already possess a tiny fraction of the power within you."

Volraag took another step closer. "It's like a lodestone calling out to metal. When Varion releases his power for the last time, it will be attracted to that. It will come to you, and there's nothing anyone can do to prevent it."

Marshal found himself breathing hard. He could feel the trembling spreading through him. It had done that before, but he hoped it didn't happen now. He didn't like the way Volraag looked at him, and he didn't know how to think about these revelations.

Volraag started to turn away, then rotated back, a long, thin dagger in his hand. "Actually, there is one thing that can prevent it: your death."

Marshal stumbled and looked around. The guards still kept everyone else in the town center.

Volraag looked down at the dagger. "I could kill you myself, right here and right now. Based on what I can guess of your life in this pathetic dungheap, I doubt anyone would be very upset, other than your mother."

Volraag casually pushed the point of the dagger a full inch into the fallen tree trunk. Marshal's eyes remained fixed on it.

"But since I'm not a Lord yet, if I were to do that, I would be cursed. And I won't be a Lord until my father dies. At which point, you would already have the power." He spread his arms wide. "You see my dilemma."

Dilemma. Marshal's existence was a dilemma to this man.

Volraag sighed and leaned back against the tree without actually sitting. "This is not going as I expected it to," he admitted. "Out of all possible curses, I had not anticipated muteness. I was relying on my own persuasive ability here, but it's impossible to tell if you're sufficiently grasping what I'm saying."

He studied Marshal again. "I've been searching for you for a few years now. Obviously, I knew Varion had a bastard child, but I didn't know where. I've had spies out all over Varioch and even across the borders." He paused and gestured toward the south. "That's not easy when we might be going to war with Rasna any day now.

"A few days ago, I heard about a cursed, fatherless man in a secluded village, and I knew." He tapped his own head. "I just knew that my search was over."

He pushed away from the tree and stepped forward. Despite his own admission that he was the younger brother, Volraag stood a full span taller than Marshal and appeared far stronger. Marshal's hand continued to shake, and he swallowed. If Volraag really did choose to kill him, he could do nothing about it. The only thing protecting him was Volraag's fear of cursing himself.

"Let me put it this way," Volraag said. "Lord Varion's power will be mine one day, one way or another. In fact, it's really just one of two ways."

He held up two fingers and pointed to one. "The simplest solution for all of us is that you kill yourself. No one gets cursed, and I get what I want." He looked into Marshal's eyes. "If Varion's power came to you, after all, your curse would prevent you from fully using it. Besides, who would miss you? Your mother is still young. She'll get over it. And I would think, with the life you live here, it would actually be a… relief."

He pointed to the second finger. "And she is the reason why you don't want to wait for the second solution. Should you fail to kill yourself, I will have to arrange for your death in other ways. More specifically, I will send someone to kill you, someone who isn't worried about curses."

He leaned in so close Marshal could see the moisture in the corners of his eyes.

"And he will also kill your mother."

•••••

Volraag spun on his heel and walked back toward the town, leaving Marshal shaken and alone. He started to follow but stopped to pull the dagger from the tree. It took more effort than he had expected. When he finally got it free, Volraag was far ahead. He frowned, concealed the dagger in a pocket inside his coat and hurried past the workshop.

When he reached the town center, Marshal saw Volraag already mounted. "Let's move!" he called to the soldiers. "I want to be back in Reman before the new moon!"

The five horses and their riders departed as unceremoniously as they had arrived. The townspeople watched them go, then almost without exception, they all turned their eyes back toward Marshal.

He was used to people staring at him from time to time, but this was different. Instead of the usual hostility, they were curious. They were all dying to know what the Lord's son had to say to their Curse Boy. They could go on wondering, for all he cared. None of them had heard the revelation of his identity, and couldn't imagine why the two had talked together.

Aelia hurried to his side. "Are you all right?" she whispered. He nodded. She hugged him, but he felt stiff in her embrace.

"I didn't want him to talk with you, but the guards kept me back." She led the way past the staring eyes of their neighbors. Past the edge of the town, they arrived at their small cabin.

"I don't know how much the lordling told you, of course, but he probably told the truth. Mostly." Aelia looked back at the town and sighed. "Varion is your father. I've thought about telling you many times, but your life has been hard enough. I didn't want to complicate it any further. Now... well, things are about to change. Did that-- that pathetic excuse for a man back there threaten you?"

Marshal did not respond. His thoughts were chaotic.

Aelia turned to face him. "Did he threaten you?" she demanded.

Marshal nodded.

She frowned and looked around. A chill breeze swept past them, but even so, the air felt warmer than it had a few days ago. Spring would be coming soon. Marshal wondered if he would be alive to see it.

Aelia came to a decision. "Then it's time," she said firmly. "I want you to go find Victor and get him to come to our cabin as soon as possible."

Marshal obeyed, glancing back to see Aelia enter the cabin. So many strange things in the past few days. The curse-stalker. Titus. Volraag.

He found Victor still in the village center, discussing the brief Lord's visit. He had to pull on him and point repeatedly until Victor understood enough. "Yeah, all right. I'll be there shortly," he answered, scowling.

Marshal returned to the cabin. When he entered, he found his mother moving about their tiny living space, and sorting through her meager collection of clothing on her bed. "Some of this will be useless to bring along. Winter won't last much longer, and too many heavy outfits will only weigh us down." As was her habit throughout Marshal's life, she talked aloud as she worked. "I'll have to strip down my healing supplies, too. I'll leave some with the major. I've instructed a couple of the young women over the past few years, so they should get on well enough without me."

Marshal doubted that. Aelia's healing skills had kept them fed for years. The village would not be the same without her. Without him? They'd be fine. They probably wouldn't even notice much. He had no real job, no purpose here. Aelia worked hard just to persuade people to give him any extra jobs that needed doing. Usually, he took on the most menial of tasks.

Despite his promise, Victor didn't show up at the door for another half an hour. Marshal let him in. Victor stared at the cabin's interior, which now looked ransacked. His eyes glanced briefly at the sign still hanging on the wall: "Nod is yes. Shake is no."

"What is going on?" he asked.

Aelia tossed her bag back on the bed, and faced him. "Victor, I am very, very sorry about this, but there's no way around it. We have to go."

He shook his head a little. "Where are you going?"

"You aren't hearing me, Victor. We're leaving Drusa's Crossing, and because of the Bonding, that means you have to come with us."

Victor opened his mouth to protest, but said nothing. He scowled.

"As I said, I'm very sorry," Aelia said. "If there were any other way, I would take it. But the young Lord wants Marshal dead, so we need to leave right away."

Victor shot a look at Marshal, eyebrows raised. "But why?"

Aelia told him. Marshal wished he could laugh. Victor stood stunned, his eyes frozen and his mouth hanging open.

"I know, it's ridiculous, and if you think too hard about it, you'll have another dozen questions," Aelia said. "Just go make your goodbyes to your family and Careen. Gather your things. I don't know how long we'll be traveling."

"Careen," Victor repeated. His face fell as he realized what he would be leaving behind.

"Give her an extra-long kiss," Aelia said. "You may not see her again for a very long time."

"But… but… where are we going? What will we do?"

"There's only one thing we can do, something that I've put off for far too long." Aelia looked at Marshal and her eyes took on a strange glint. "We will find a way to remove Marshal's curse."

(((4)))

Seri shivered, wishing she could return to her room and the fireplace. She stood facing a semi-circle of raised seats in which six mages looked down at her. They were the Masters, the highest-ranking mages of the Conclave, and she stood within their audience chamber, a circular room that seemed far bigger than it needed to be.

"Do you, Seri-Belit, swear before this Conclave that you are free of all curses and have done nothing worthy of a curse within the past two days?"

"I do." Seri relaxed. She knew this oath was the most important part of gaining her official position on Zes Sivas. As the island was the only place in Antises where magic could be practiced freely, those with curses could not be allowed. Only the pure could take part. Any more questions after this would be mere formalities, no doubt. She glanced at Master Hain. The wisps of white hair that framed the balding top of his head made him stand out among the other Masters, most of whom had shaved their heads entirely.

"Explain the origins of magic in Antises."

Seri bristled. Did the Conclave of Mages think her an infant? Any child's basic education included this. Why not ask her something more difficult?

She took a deep breath and began to recite.

"In ages past, all magic was wild. From what little we know of that time, people of all kinds became attuned to the magic, using it as they pleased, some for good and some for evil. Thus, in a time lost to memory, the Conclave of Mages was formed, its purpose to study, quantify, and ultimately understand and control the magic of our world."

Seri could recite this in her sleep, but she tried to emphasize individual words and phrases, to show how much she believed this history. She did not want to appear bored over a rote memorization, even if that was how she had learned most of her history.

"Then came the Great Cataclysm. Though its true nature is often debated, the importance of the cataclysm is not the event itself, but the effects of the event. The people of the six nations came together under the leadership of Akhenadom the Great, most revered of all men.

"Akhenadom led the six nations across a wasteland devastated by the cataclysm. In time, they arrived at a body of water and saw an island at its center. Through careful negotiation, the six nations agreed to settle around the body of water, creating new nations and borders. Each land was ruled by a Lord, and all six swore fealty to Akhenadom as the high King over all six lands, now known as Antises.

"The island was named Zes Sivas, and became the home of the new King and his family, as well as the Conclave of Mages. But by this point, the Conclave had reached the height of its study and was ready to implement a radical change."

Seri paused. The next bit tied into religion, which could be a tricky subject. The mages before her came from all six lands, each of which interpreted religion somewhat differently. Seri wasn't completely certain of her own beliefs, but she did say a short prayer to Theon each morning. Best to keep things as generic as possible.

"While he led the nations to Antises, Akhenadom also introduced the people to the worship of Theon, the one true god. When he took his throne, Akhenadom revealed Theon's Book of the Law, which would form the basis of his government. While the Law covered many, many issues, it did not address the use of magic. And this is where the Conclave stepped in."

Seri felt rather foolish reciting the Conclave's history to the Conclave itself. When she had arrived on the island yesterday, she had been forced to spend the rest of the day recovering from her swim in the lake. The cold stone structure of the citadel had not helped with her recovery. She had stayed close to the fireplace in her room all day. Otherwise, this meeting would have taken place immediately.

"The Conclave summoned the King and the six Lords and explained their plan. They would unite all of the magic of Antises and place the majority of it in the hands of the Lords and King himself. Thus, their authority could never be questioned by any others.

"This they did, but not before the Lords insisted that magic must be linked to the law. Together, they created the Bindings and Cursings. The magic of the land linked everyone to the law and to their homes, creating curses for lawbreaking and Bindings to hold the people together in community. The remaining magic of Antises was bound and given to each of the six Lords, with the greatest power being given to the high King himself.

"The Conclave did keep some magic centered in Zes Sivas itself, for continuing study, and there are always rumors of wild magic cropping up now and then…" Seri broke off when she noticed one of the Masters scowling. His pale skin indicated he was from Rasna or Varioch. Master Hain also frowned. Perhaps mentioning wild magic wasn't appropriate.

"Sadly, the Conclave and high King were both soon betrayed," Seri hastened to go on. "The Lords united their power in secret, and attempted to alter the Bindings and Cursings. They prevented any curses from falling on any Lord or King for his own actions. But being unable to alter the magic completely, the curses fell on their children instead. They lacked the power to eliminate the curses, but managed to divert them."

Seri gritted her teeth. She still had trouble fathoming the unbelievable selfishness of the Lords' Betrayal. It twisted everything the original Conclave had been trying to accomplish.

"And what of the Passing?" one of the Masters prodded. Seri realized she had been quiet for too long.

"Ah, um, soon after the Lords' Betrayal, the Conclave discovered their… oversight." When she had memorized this history, the word had been "error," but Seri felt a little uncomfortable using that word in the present company.

"With most of the magic of Antises contained within seven men," she went on, "the land itself eventually began to fall apart. It seemed that the magic was required to literally hold things together. Whether this was related to the Great Cataclysm is unknown, though many theories have been proposed." Seri wasn't entirely sure what "fall apart" meant in this context. Her education had been lacking in that particular bit of history.

"The solution to this problem came about through the once-a-year Passing. At that time, the Lords assemble here on Zes Sivas and willingly lay down their power for one day. The magic restores and binds the land before returning to them. Also at that time, the Lords may choose to pass the power down to their eldest child. If not, the power passes automatically upon their death."

"Given that all this is true," Master Hain intoned, "how would you explain what took place yesterday at the time you arrived? If the Passing keeps the land restored and bound, how did it shake so?"

Seri's brow furrowed. They were asking *her*? This must be a test.

"I would suppose, Master," she said with care, "that there are several possibilities."

"List them, then."

"First, it could have been wild magic."

"Ridiculous!" the Master from Rasna snapped. "Wild magic has never been that powerful, nor would it be centered on Zes Sivas!"

Seri winced. "Second, I suppose it could have simply been something natural, not related to magic at all. But that seems highly unlikely," she hurried to add.

She took another deep breath. "Finally, there is the most likely and most troubling answer. Since Antises has been without a high King for so many years, his power has not been a part of the yearly Passing. Perhaps that lack is having an effect that, while foreseeable, has no immediate solution that I can conceive."

Silence fell when she finished. Her eyes darted from one Master's face to another. They all seemed almost made of stone.

"There is a fourth possibility," one of them said. Was he from Kuktarma? All eyes turned toward him.

"It could have been the Eldanim."

● ● ● ● ●

Master Hain stalked down the hallway with Seri in tow. "Eldanim!" he snorted. "The shaking earth has clearly addled Master Simmar's brains."

Seri hastened to keep up with Master Hain's quick pace. His narrow frame could move surprisingly fast. "Was he being serious?" she asked. "I couldn't tell. You all seemed so grim in there, it was impossible to tell anyone's mood."

Hain snorted. "Serious? Not really. Your explanation, as simple as it was, is undoubtedly the truth behind the matter. He just doesn't want to accept it. And he's not the only one."

"So he blames a fairy tale?"

Hain came to a stop and looked at her with raised eyebrows. "Fairy tale?"

Seri almost blushed under his scrutiny. "I mean, isn't it like, that is, isn't it just the same as blaming the Lilim or Gidim?"

Hain almost rolled his eyes, but stopped himself and started down the hallway again. "Your education, girl, is clearly lacking in some regards."

"I-- I had the finest education in Arazu!" she insisted. "The University of--"

"The university does well enough," Hain said, "for what they believe. However, speaking of a local fantasy such as the night spirits, the Lilim, is a far cry from speaking of the Eldanim."

"I don't see how," Seri said. "They're both imaginary creatures blamed for all sorts of mischief and difficulty."

"The Eldanim are not imaginary."

This time, Seri stopped. Hain took several more steps before realizing she no longer followed him. He turned back with a bemused look on his face.

"But... but how can that be?" Seri said. "They're... they're..."

"Fairy tales?" Hain asked with a raised eyebrow.

"Yes?"

"The Eldanim are no more of a fairy tale than you or I, acolyte. You would do well to remember that. They wandered Antises long before we arrived."

"Are you going to tell me they steal one shoe at a time if I leave them out?"

"Don't be absurd. Just because the Eldanim are real doesn't mean the silly tales that have evolved around them are anything remotely close to the truth. The only reason such stories have arisen is because the Eldanim avoid us, for the most part. They are far more intelligent, far more sophisticated, and far more dangerous than most humans you will ever meet. You would do well to keep that in mind." Hain began walking again.

"You didn't mention the Gidim. Are they real too?" Seri asked, following in his footsteps.

"Ah, good. You caught that. I didn't mention them because they're... complicated."

"Why?"

"Because I have yet to establish proof of their existence." Master Hain paused at an intersection as if he weren't entirely sure which way to go. He glanced to the left and turned right. "Stories about these apparitions show up in all six lands, by various names. But since I've never seen one myself or met anyone who has, I can't speak to that. Yet."

"But you have met someone who has seen the Eldanim?"

"Indeed. But I'll let you judge that for yourself."

"How so?"

"Because it may not be long before you meet one of them."

This time, when Seri stopped, Hain kept walking.

• • • • •

Master Hain led the way to a nondescript door in yet another nondescript hallway within the Citadel of Mages. Just learning her way around this place would be one of Seri's most difficult tasks, as far as she could see.

As if reading her mind, Hain said, "I realize we haven't had much time to orient you yet, what with the shaking and the Conclave meeting. You'll get used to this place in no time, I'm sure."

Seri doubted it would be "no time," but she determined to make it work.

Hain led her into a small room with a window facing the East. He looked out of it. "On a clear day, you can almost see the coast of Arazu from here," he observed. He turned back to find Seri examining the small desk beside the window. "Yes, well, this is where you will work, for starters," Hain said. "It's only mid-week, so you have four full days of labor ahead of you before the next Rest Day."

Seri looked up. "What will I be doing?" she asked.

Hain pointed to the opposite wall. A lattice rack holding dozens of scrolls filled it from floor to ceiling. "Many of these scrolls are getting old," he said. "Your job, for now, is to copy them onto fresh papyrus, so as to preserve them."

Seri tentatively touched one of the scrolls. "Are they instructions for magic?"

"Oh, no, no. These are records. Histories of the six noble families. The line of Kings. And, of course, all of the mages who have gone before us."

"So… I'm copying the names of dead people? This is my job here?"

Master Hain nodded and looked back out the window.

Seri found herself fighting a growing anger. "But I… this…"

Master Hain turned back. "Yes?"

"I came here to become a mage!" she insisted. "This is a recorder's work. Why am I being treated like this? Is it because I'm a woman? Is it--"

"Devouring fire!" Hain exclaimed. "Is that what you think? Oh, my. We have work to do, I see."

"What do... I..." Seri stopped, afraid to go any further. Four days of this before the next rest? Ugh.

Hain moved to the door. "You are being treated this way because you are the newest acolyte within this building. There are others, you know," he said. "You'll meet them this evening at supper, I assume. Each one of them has possessed this job before you, just as I had it when I first arrived. In time, you will be given greater tasks. For now, I have seven words of advice for you." He stopped at the doorway.

"What are they?" Seri couldn't help asking.

"Careful of the ink. It dries quickly."

(((5)))

Kishin found darkness comforting at this stage. Bright light had been agony to him for many years, but now even average daylight could send spikes of pain through his eyes. Fortunately, it had not yet affected the clarity of his vision. The day it did would be the day he put a knife through one of those eyes and ended it all. Without his vision, he would be useless.

Between jobs, he usually sat in a room with no windows. The door had a curtain over it, shielding even the light that seeped in around the edges. It also muffled the sound when Aapo knocked with his customary insistence.

"Come," Kishin said in a guttural rasp. He could still speak, but sometimes found it difficult to form the proper syllables after lengthy periods of disuse.

The door opened and Aapo pushed aside the curtain to enter. Kishin winced as the light streamed in, but his eyes adjusted. They always did.

Aapo shifted his balance from one foot to the other. He looked in every direction but at his master. Kishin frowned. Aapo had only been with him a few days, but it was surely long enough to avoid this kind of nonsense.

"Look at me!" Kishin commanded.

Aapo's eyes focused on Kishin's face and a visible shudder ran over him.

"What is it?"

"A, uh, a message has arrived," Aapo said, "from Reman. A job, I think."

Of course it was a job. Why else would anyone send a message?

Aapo seemed to be lacking in basic logic. Kishin nodded at him to continue.

"The message said 'Cursed man. Marshal of Drusa's Crossing. Usual rates.'"

Kishin considered for a moment. The job must be from Volraag. The young Lord grew more ambitious. Drusa's Crossing - a village far to the north of Varioch, almost on the Ch'olan border, if he recalled correctly. How could a cursed man there have angered Volraag enough to hire Kishin? Ultimately, it didn't matter, of course, but Kishin found it curious. He scratched the back of his hand and a long piece of dead skin fell off.

Aapo cringed.

Kishin moved with shocking speed. One moment he sat cross-legged on the floor. The next, he had Aapo pinned to the wall with his left hand around the servant's neck.

"Two things I will not tolerate in a servant," he said, his voice sinking even lower. "Disgust. And pity. I am Kishin the Untouchable. Men call me pariah, leper, outcast. But do you know what I truly am?"

Aapo shook his head, eyes full of terror.

"I am cursed. I have the worst curse imaginable, a living death. Do you know what that does for me?"

Aapo continued to shake.

Kishin leaned in closer. "It sets me free."

He drew back his right hand and an obsidian dagger suddenly thrust out from his sleeve. He guided the blade up to Aapo's face and traced the point around each eye.

"I could cut your eyes out right now," he said. "And I do it without worry. No other curse can touch me."

He leaned back in, his face almost touching the other man's. The dagger nicked Aapo's ear as it slid down the side of his face.

"Tell me your curse."

Aapo trembled. "I… I have no curse."

"We all have curses. Without exception. Now. Tell me your curse."

"I don't have a curse!"

Kishin let him go and turned away. The blade slid back into its housing within his sleeve.

"Pack my things," he ordered. "Make sure there's enough food and starshine. I'll be gone for some time."

Aapo rushed out of the room as quickly as he could. Once he finished packing, Kishin would ask him one more time. If Aapo proved unable to name his curse, Kishin would have to kill him. It was a shame, as it would have been nice to have someone take care of the household while Kishin was gone. But everyone must be shown. Everyone had a curse.

He shoved the curtain aside and stepped out into the light. The pain that struck his eyes felt almost welcoming this time. It was one of the only things he could genuinely feel. It reminded him that despite the curse's best efforts, he still lived. Despite the mages, despite the Lords, despite even Theon himself, Kishin still lived, flouting all their laws.

Perhaps that explained why they found him so useful.

(((6)))

"This is ridiculous!" Victor said for about the fourth time. The three travelers had been walking down the road from Drusa's Crossing for less than an hour, traveling south down the same road by which Volraag and company had ridden away.

In time, this road would lead them down from the mountain foothills. Eventually, it would wind all the way to Reman itself, the capital city of Varioch. Marshal doubted they would be heading in the direction of danger itself. He suspected they would be leaving this road before too long.

"What do you want from me, Victor?" Aelia asked. "I've told you why it must be done. There's no other choice."

"Sure there is! We just don't go anywhere!"

"And when the assassins come to kill Marshal? How will your Binding affect you then? When you fail to protect him and he dies? Do you know what that does to someone?"

From the look on Victor's face, he clearly didn't, but he pushed on. "But that'll give me a chance to save him! And then the Binding will be removed!"

Aelia sighed. "Lord Varion's son is the second-most powerful person in the land," she said. "Do you know what he is capable of?"

"Not really."

Marshal looked from one to the other as the conversation continued. Despite the dispute, all three kept walking.

"Think about it this way," Aelia went on. "With the Laws of Bindings and Cursings, how would you go about killing someone?"

Victor furrowed his brow. "I... wouldn't. No one would. The curse that would fall on you for murder is too much. It wouldn't be worth it."

"To the Lord's son, it is worth it… but not for himself. He wouldn't risk getting cursed, or he would have killed Marshal this morning. So think about it: what kind of man would he go to… who would he be able to find, with his resources, that would be willing to do that?"

"He would have to be insane!" Victor walked on in silence for a few moments. "Do such people exist?" he wondered.

Aelia nodded, her face grave. "They do. They are extremely rare, obviously, but they deal in death and are not concerned with the consequences. Such men are beyond your ability to protect Marshal. You would fail. The Binding would be broken. And you would suffer for it the rest of your life."

There was another solution, of course, but no one spoke of it. Marshal felt inside his coat for Volraag's dagger. Maybe his brother had been right. If Marshal killed himself, neither his mother nor Victor would have to suffer. But even if he wanted to, did he have the strength to do it? Marshal hated his life, but he wasn't so sure he wanted to experience death just yet.

Aelia's final words back at the cabin echoed through his mind. Could his curse truly be lifted? The traveling priest who came to their village once a month spoke of a time when all curses would be lifted, but Aelia didn't seem to be referencing that story. She spoke of lifting only Marshal's curse. If that were possible, why hadn't she done it sooner?

Just before nightfall, they reached an intersection and Aelia took a right turn. The new road, smaller and less used, led southwest, while the main road they had abandoned curved to the southeast.

As night fell, the temperature dropped. While they had been walking, Marshal had almost been able to ignore the cold. But now all his warm clothes seemed useless. The chill sank into his bones.

Aelia found a small clearing a few feet away from the road. The level ground and a ring of stones showed evidence of its previous use as a campsite. "Gather some firewood," she told the boys. "Let's try to warm up."

Marshal walked in a widening circle, picking up every stick he could find. He heard Victor griping nearby while doing the same. He smiled in spite of himself. Truthfully, Marshal didn't know when Victor was being serious, despite having known him for most of his life. Victor always told people that the Binding between the two of them was the worst thing that had ever happened in his life. But when they were alone, when Titus in particular wasn't around, Victor treated Marshal almost normal.

He tried to look at the situation from Victor's point of view. He had been dragged away from home, from his family, from his girl, and forced into a journey with companions he never would have chosen on his own. No matter how he considered it, Marshal couldn't see anything positive for Victor.

His curse continued to find new ways to hurt others.

Back in their chosen campsite, they worked together to get the fire started. Victor grumbled some more during the process, which took far longer than any of them liked. Finally, the fire grew large enough to provide significant warmth. All three of them stood as close as they dared to the flames, rotating their bodies from time to time.

"We'll have to feed it throughout the night," Aelia said. "That curse-stalker might still be about, but the fire should keep it away."

"Should we take turns staying awake?" Victor wondered.

"We can try. I'll sleep first. Wake me when you're too tired to stay awake."

After spreading out their blankets. Aelia wrapped up and closed her eyes. Victor pulled a deck of cards out of his pack. "How about a game of Mages and Lords before bed?" he asked. Marshal shrugged. He tolerated the game, though he knew Victor loved it. Maybe that's why he almost always won.

Victor flipped the first card from the top of the deck. "Lord," he said, taking the card and placing it in front of him on his blanket. Marshal flipped the next one. A wild mage. Useless this early in the game. He returned it to the bottom of the deck.

The game was simple enough. The deck held only twenty cards. To win, you had to assemble all six Lords or all six Mages. The other cards in the deck could affect the deck's order or imprison some of the other cards. The King card was fun to play, as he could release all of the prisoners. Marshal liked that part, though he wondered why the General could do practically the same thing. He also enjoyed the artwork. Each of the Lords and Mages appeared like they would in their native lands.

Victor won, of course. When Marshal declined a second game, he put the cards away and left to retrieve more firewood.

Marshal remained sitting.

He took out Volraag's dagger and looked at it again.The hilt's wrapping was the finest he'd ever seen, tight bands of leather cord.

The pommel held an engraving of a bird in flight. The dancing fire reflected from the shiny blade, so beautiful and so deadly. What would it feel like to thrust that sharp point into his own chest?

He had felt the pain of being stabbed before, though not by something like this. Some years back, he had been helping his mother with her tools when his hand shook. He dropped a dozen different items all over the floor. When he tried to salvage the situation, a large needle pierced straight through the palm of his hand. He still remembered that particular pain. A stab from this dagger would be like that, only worse.

What would happen if he stabbed his own heart? Would it stop beating? Aelia said the heart pumped blood throughout the body. Would all of his blood stop moving? Drain down into his legs? What would that feel like? The thoughts pursued him into slumber.

Marshal awoke to find Victor and Aelia sound asleep and the fire almost dead. He shivered and stood. The only solution to the early morning cold was a bigger fire, and that needed more fuel. He tossed the last few sticks onto the tiny flame and pushed his way through the snow to find some more.

Not far from the fire, he found a large dead branch barely clinging to a tree at his chest level. His hands shook, but he managed to break off large chunks of it. As he worked on breaking off the largest piece, a blur of movement caught his eye.

Something wrapped around his left ankle, yanked hard, and jerked him to the ground. He took the branch with him, but struck his chin on the ground and nearly bit his tongue.

Marshal rolled into a sit-up, somehow keeping hold of the branch. Not much of a weapon, but it would have to do. The dagger was back at the campfire.

He found himself face-to-face with the curse-stalker. The creature hissed at him. Though he had been warned about them all his life, Marshal had never seen a curse-stalker before. Bigger than a man, it resembled a giant lizard with a massive head, shaped like a half circle. Its enormously wide mouth opened, revealing double rows of serrated teeth. Behind the teeth, Marshal saw something begin to move.

He shoved the branch into the creature's mouth and scrambled backward. He found another stick and grabbed it, wishing he could shout or scream or do something to attract attention. Anything at all.

"Ha, ha! Finally!" Victor's cry shattered the silence.

He leaped into view, attempting to strike a dramatic pose between

Marshal and the beast. The attempt was ruined when he slipped on the snow and almost fell. When he regained his balance, he spun a flail above his head and shouted a challenge at the creature. He glanced over his shoulder at Marshal and grinned.

The curse-stalker hissed again and circled this new foe, eyes darting back and forth. Marshal took the opportunity to back farther away. Out of the corner of his eye, he noticed a shadowy figure standing inside the tree line.

With a grunt, Victor leaped forward and swung his flail. The rusty iron ball at the end of the chain bounced off the curse-stalker's head. The monster snarled and charged.

Victor tried to get the flail spinning again, but the beast moved too fast, rushing past him, intent on Marshal. The beast's tail whipped around and slammed into Victor's chest as it passed. The impact flung him half a dozen feet through the air before he landed and rolled through the snow.

Marshal waved the remaining branch as the curse-stalker charged him. The creature slid to a stop a few feet away, its eyes watching the branch as Marshal moved it back and forth.

Victor shoved snow aside, and his eyes met Marshal's over the creature's back. He wasn't holding the flail. Victor yelled, and charged at the creature bare-handed.

The curse-stalker lunged at Marshal, who swung his branch at its head. The creature snatched the branch from his hands and snapped it in pieces. At the same moment, Victor launched himself in a full-body tackle.

Victor wasn't a huge man, but his tackle took the curse-stalker to the ground. They both slid through the wet snow and mud. The creature thrashed, legs and tail whipping around in every direction. With no other options, Victor held on. "Get out of here!" he yelled at Marshal.

Marshal scrambled toward the campsite. The wet and slippery ground, torn apart by the conflict, slowed his progress. His hands shook. Not now! Once again, he caught a glimpse of the shadow. It had moved closer, still watching.

The curse-stalker bleated a strange sound, something between a goat's cry and the call of a large bird. Marshal glanced back and saw it roll on top of Victor, crushing him into the mud. When it got back on its feet, Victor punched at the creature. It seemed not to notice.

This time, nothing stood between it and Marshal.

It moved with surprising speed on the uncertain surface, closing the distance between them in moments. When Marshal turned to face his pursuer, the beast's mouth opened wide. Two long, slimy tongues shot out with blinding speed, passing by either side of Marshal's face, then wrapping around his head from both directions. The sticky tendrils yanked at him and covered his nose, ears, and one eye. Marshal grabbed at the tendrils with both hands and pulled.

Through one eye, he saw Victor get to his feet, head twisting back and forth as he searched for his flail. He lunged at a nearby snow bank and extracted it just as Marshal's mouth opened in a silent scream.

Where the beast's tongue touched his skin, it burned, dropping Marshal to his knees. The pain worsened, searing into his entire skull.

He could barely see Victor. A short sword appeared out of nowhere, severing both of the curse-stalker's tongues. Marshal and the beast fell backward at the loss of their connection. The curse-stalker shook its head, keening a horrible sound.

Marshal looked up at his savior with his one uncovered eye. Aelia stood poised for action. She cut a strange figure, clad in her warm peasant's clothing, while wielding a vicious short sword. A fog descended over Marshal's uncovered eye.

"Help him!" Aelia yelled to Victor. She took two more purposeful steps toward the curse-stalker. It continued to shake its head, keening and knocking its mouth against the ground.

"Stupid boy," Marshal heard her grumble. "What use is a rusted flail against this?"

Victor scrambled toward Marshal and tried to remove the remains of the tongues. "Ugh," he said. "Let me get a knife."

In a haze, Marshal saw Aelia lift the sword high and stab it down in one smooth motion.

The sounds of the curse-stalker ceased.

Victor pulled his glove off and fumbled at his belt, while Aelia landed on her knees next to the boys.

"Marshal! Are you all right?"

Victor found his knife and cut the tongues loose from Marshal's head. "I can't… These things are stuck to him. What was it doing?"

"The curse-stalker feeds on magic," Aelia answered. She reached in and guided Victor's hands. "The tongues draw the magic out. Without help, it would have drained Marshal of both magic and life, leaving him a dead husk. I've seen it before."

Victor shot her a quick look. "You've seen it before?"

"Not now." Together, they pulled the final piece of tongue loose from Marshal's face. The pain erupted worse than before, like liquid fire pouring through his head and down into the rest of his body. He tried to look for the shadow in the trees, but his vision swam.

Victor made a sound of disgust. "That's not going to help his looks." He got to his feet and looked back at the carcass of the curse-stalker.

Marshal felt the pain and his vision dimming. He heard his mother whispering words of comfort, but his last clear memory was of Victor looking down at him and saying, "The Binding is still there. I hate you so much."

(((7)))

"It's coming for you, Curse Boy."

Titus had been right. The monster had come for him.

Marshal pulled himself up and blinked several times. A moment passed before he felt throbbing pain all over his face and palms. He lifted one hand and saw bandages. He didn't remember that happening.

He glanced around at their campsite. Victor sat across the fire from him, watching. He opened his mouth to say something, then closed it. His face looked more empathetic than Marshal ever recalled. No, that wasn't the right word. He looked... pitying.

Marshal felt drained, as if he had been working hard for several days straight. It wasn't a new feeling, but he was surprised at its intensity.

Aelia entered the campsite, still carrying the short sword. She sheathed it and set it beside her pack. Then she knelt beside Marshal.

"Hello, my treasure." She reached up for his face, hesitated, then brushed his chin with the gentleness he had always known from her. "Are you in much pain now?"

Marshal reached toward his face. Aelia stopped him. "Wait." She dug in her pack, and pulled out her looking-glass. Marshal had often admired the glass as a child. Its value must have been far higher than anything else in their small village. Aelia never talked about where it had come from.

Then he saw his reflection.

Bright red wounds criss-crossed his face where the curse-stalker's tongues had latched on. Aelia had treated them with some kind of ointment, but the blood looked brighter, closer to the surface on every wound. In places, he could even see blood flowing through his veins. It was like the tongues had pulled all his blood to the outer layer of his skin.

That seemed strange. Aelia said the curse-stalker fed on magic itself. Did it also suck blood? Or did blood itself contain the magic? Did his curse permeate his blood?

He felt the back of his head. Where the beast's tongues had wrapped around him, his hair had been ripped out. He wasn't overly concerned about the scarring, but it felt wrong that he might have hairless spots back there.

The shadowy figure that had watched troubled him even more. It wasn't the first time he had seen it. The villagers called such things eidolons or apparitions. Some claimed they were spirits of the dead returned to roam the earth. Others thought they were creatures of the underworld. But only one or two villagers claimed to have ever seen one. Marshal had seen them five times now that he could remember, all within the past three years. They always seemed to be watching him.

Victor took Marshal's hand and dropped several serrated teeth into it. "From the curse-stalker," he said. "You might be able to... um... never mind." He scrambled back to the other side of the fire and looked away.

Marshal stuffed the teeth into his pocket. The thought of Victor smashing the creature's teeth out, probably with his flail, almost made Marshal smile. Instead, he winced as a throb of pain startled him with its power.

"Look at me, Marshal," Aelia said.

Marshal didn't move. He didn't want to do this in front of Victor.

Aelia frowned. She gripped his shoulders and looked him full in the face.

"Look at me," she commanded.

He tried to look away, gritting his teeth against the pain.

"Look at me."

Finally, he met her eyes. He had admired those eyes, full of golden warmth, for all his eighteen years. No one else in the village had eyes quite like hers.

"You are greatly loved, Marshal. Do you believe me?"

Nod is yes. He never questioned her love. Of all the people he knew in Drusa's Crossing, he couldn't imagine any of them raising a cursed child alone for all these years.

"You are valuable, Marshal. Do you believe me?"

That one was harder. He nodded again.

"You have a purpose in this world, Marshal. Do you believe me?"

Purpose? Cursed men had no purpose. He scowled and shook his head.

Aelia sighed. "Two out of three will have to do for now, I suppose. But whether you believe it or not, Marshal, it doesn't change the truth. We all have a purpose, and yours..." She trailed off and looked away for a moment. "Yours is greater than most," she finally whispered.

A long silence followed.

"I... didn't know you had a sword." Victor said.

Aelia smiled and touched the sheathed blade. "It belonged to my father," she said. "That's all that really matters."

"And that you really know how to use it."

Marshal smiled in spite of his pain. His gentle mother had charged into battle wielding a sword on his behalf, killing a monster all on her own.

"We're only a few hours away from home," Victor said. "Should we turn back?"

"No." Aelia looked down the road. "We can't go back. And we're losing time, but Marshal is exhausted. We'll have to wait here a few hours. This afternoon we'll try to make some progress."

Victor stood. "Then I'm going to go break off a few more teeth from that monster. I want to have plenty of proof when I tell the story."

Aelia chuckled. But as Victor stepped past the fire, she frowned. "Did you happen to notice the most troubling thing about it?" she asked.

"Most troubling? Besides the teeth and the freaky tongues?"

Aelia pointed to her own neck. "It had rope burns around its neck. Someone captured it and it got loose... or was let go."

(((8)))

Seri took the tray of food from the chef and made her way to the nearest open table. Everything looked edible, if somewhat boring. It couldn't be easy to keep up with food supplies on a small island. She felt that Binding pull toward home again, where she enjoyed much more elaborate meals. She allowed herself one sigh and then firmed up her resolve. She would have to get used to simple fare.

She had barely taken two bites when two young men sat down across the table from her. "Welcome to Zes Sivas!" exclaimed one with the biggest smile she had seen since leaving home. Their light orange robes, like her own, marked them as her fellow acolytes. Seri had difficulty getting used to the flow of the thing while at the desk today, not to mention the color. It still made her feel awkward. These two seemed perfectly at home in them. They both let their hoods fall back, revealing heads that had been shaved almost to the scalp. Seri whispered a quick thanks to Theon that no one had asked her to do likewise. She enjoyed having hair that reached her shoulders.

"Thank you," she said politely. "I am happy to be here."

"Aren't we all?" said the second acolyte. His skin, a little darker than Seri's own, looked smooth and creamy. An irrational desire to lick it popped into her head, which she suppressed with horror. "I'm Dravid, from Kuktarma." His voice had a slight lilt to it, adding to his exotic appeal. He gestured to his friend. "This is Jamana, from Mandiata."

Jamana, the one with the huge smile, had skin darker than the table on which he rested his hands. Of course he had to be from Mandiata. No other people group had skin that dark, as far as Seri knew. She found it quite beautiful in a way that almost embarrassed her. Her own olive-colored skin seemed ridiculously pale in comparison.

"We know who you are," Jamana said. "You're Se--"

"I'm Seri," she interrupted before he could blurt out the full version. "I was wondering when I would meet any of the other acolytes. I am very pleased to meet you both." She felt safe within formality. Though it seemed the most normal thing in the world, talking to someone her own age thrilled her. Everything else had been so bizarre since she boarded the rowboat to reach the island.

"I assume they have you copying scrolls?" Dravid asked. He pushed a couple of green vegetables to the edge of his plate and scowled at them before looking up for Seri's answer.

"Yes!" she exclaimed. "So the other acolytes really have done that job? It's not just me?"

"Jamana had it last," Dravid said. His friend rolled his eyes while chewing. "Everyone gets stuck there at first, apparently. I had it before him."

"But only for a few days!" Jamana said. "It's hardly fair."

"So you're the two newest besides me." Seri looked around the dining hall. Less than a handful of other people occupied the tables. "How many others are there?"

"We're the only ones," Dravid answered. "New acolytes are very rare. The Masters don't train new people until they start thinking about their own departure."

Seri thought about that a moment. "One doesn't go directly from acolyte to Master, though," she said. "Aren't there other stages?"

"Oh, yes," Jamana said, speaking up before Dravid could finish chewing. "You move from acolyte to apprentice to journeyman to Master."

"No one calls them journeymen!" Dravid chimed in. "They're just mages. They serve in the Lords' courts and sometimes travel a lot, before they become Masters. Didn't anyone tell you all of this?"

Seri shook her head. "This is what I have wanted all my life, but the doings of the Conclave of Mages is kept in strictest secrecy from the people, at least in Arazu." She glanced around. "Are there any apprentices here, then?"

"Four, I think." Jamana looked to Dravid, who nodded. "Four, yes. We don't know them very well. They're always busy about something. Far busier than the Masters."

"I think they're only busy when it's time for the Passing," Dravid said. "It's like the only thing they have left to do." He pushed his tray away, clearly not pleased with the remaining food. "So, Seri. What can we do to help you get settled in here?"

"I need help finding my way around," she admitted. "This place is a maze!"

"We can do that!" Dravid said. "In fact, we'll--" He broke off and looked at Jamana, who grinned even larger than before. "We'll show you some secrets we've discovered."

Jamana nodded. "You have much to learn." He tried to say it in a grim voice, but couldn't erase his smile.

• • • • •

Dravid and Jamana's promised tour did not happen that evening. Master Hain showed up as they finished eating and instructed Seri to come with him. He led the way to his quarters, substantially larger than Seri's. The first of his two rooms appeared to be an office of sorts. Seri assumed the Master used the the second room, which she couldn't see, as his actual bedroom. The Master mage gestured for her to sit at his desk, an oak construction significantly newer than the one she had been using.

"I saw your work today. Your handwriting is very neat and precise," he explained. "I'd like you to take down my letters to the court. Lord Enuru often complains that my writing is too difficult to read."

Seri agreed and took up the pen, reminding herself to write a letter of her own to her parents later. At the thought, she felt the pull of the Binding toward home. Master Hain made sure she was ready and then began dictating, walking about his quarters with aimless movements.

For the most part, Master Hain filled his letter with procedural exposition and observations on politics throughout the six lands. Seri found most of it intricate but boring. Rasna and Varioch were threatening war with each other, though the causes were confusing. Ch'olan had broken off some of its trade with Mandiata and no one entirely knew why. One of Lord Meluhha's sons had gotten married in Kuktarma. And so on.

Seri only found herself interested when Master Hain discussed the earth shaking event from her arrival. "As you well know, the loss of the King and the Heart of Fire make the annual Passing incomplete," Hain said. "It is the concern of the Conclave that this is causing a systemic breakdown in the very fiber of Antises." He paused to let Seri catch up. "We urge once more that strenuous efforts be made to locate the heirs of the kingship. They must be out there somewhere.

"Warmest regards to the Lady Lilitu and your household, your loyal servant, Hain."

Seri finished the writing and looked up. "The Heart of Fire?" she asked.

Master Hain seemed distracted. Seri was beginning to recognize that as one of his default positions. "Eh? What's that?"

"You mentioned the loss of the Heart of Fire," she repeated. "What is that?"

"The power of the King, of course," Hain said, as if he couldn't believe the question. "It's the very thing you talked about before the Conclave yesterday."

"I've never heard it called that before."

"Genuinely?" Hain appeared taken aback. Then he seemed to reconsider. "I suppose… yes, hmm. It is the term used among the mages and Lords, but I suppose there is little reason for it to have spread elsewhere."

"I don't understand," Seri said. "Why would you have a term that isn't used, um, elsewhere?"

"It's the appearance," Hain said. When he saw her uncomprehending expression, he went on, "The way it looks when… ah, yes. I see. Of course you wouldn't know. You would have no reason to know."

Seri waited patiently while Hain tried to illustrate a shape of some kind with his hands. Finally, he gave up.

"When the rite of Passing takes place in the Inner Sanctum, the Lords surrender their powers one by one," he explained. "On the central dais, the powers each have a visual representation as they flow back into the land. There are six lands, six Lords, six matrices of power. Each matrix forms one side of a large cube of… light. That doesn't describe it anywhere near well enough, but it's suitable for present purposes.

"When the King would surrender his power, last of all, it filled the cube. It was a fire, a brilliant, pulsating fire. And thus, the term became 'Heart of Fire.'" Hain made a gesture as if to communicate the rest should be obvious.

Seri frowned. "I thought all the power passed back into the land, to heal it," she said.

"And so it does," Hain agreed. "As I said, the Heart of Fire is just the visual representation of it happening. I'm not entirely sure why the original Conclave thought a visual representation was necessary, but that's the way they set it up. I suppose it helps prevent falsehoods."

"How so?"

"You tell me," Hain challenged.

Seri thought for a minute. "I suppose if a false Lord or King were to pretend he was Passing, or if a real one only pretended to pass on his power, the visual representation would not happen," she said.

Hain nodded approvingly. "And thus, if a true heir to the Kings returns to us, he will be known by the Heart of Fire alone. No one else can make it appear."

Hain swept up the letter Seri had transcribed and began reading it over. After a moment, he waved over his shoulder. "You may go now."

Seri returned to her own modest quarters after only two wrong turns. Along the way, she tried to visualize the Heart of Fire as Master Hain had described it. Yet the only way she would ever see it for herself is if the King returned... and she became one of the Masters herself. Acolyte. Apprentice. Journeyman Mage. Master. She had a long way to go. Unless she did so well she skipped one of the stages. A new resolve took its place in her heart - not just the first female Master, but the fastest to achieve that status.

(((9)))

Marshal felt well enough to travel after lunch. The rest of that day and the following progressed much the same. The three travelers hiked down the road at a brisk pace, pausing only when necessary. The sun shone warm, but only just enough to keep the air from being too chilly. When it began to set, the temperature dropped rapidly.

Toward evening on the third day, Victor stopped in the middle of the road and looked back. Marshal stopped and watched him. He looked troubled.

"I don't understand this," he said.

"What is it?" Aelia asked.

"I've never felt like this before. All day long, this ache inside" --he patted his chest-- "has been growing. I keep thinking about home and wanting to go back. It's almost as if I… were being pulled."

"Is it like what you felt when Marshal was in danger from the curse-stalker?"

Victor frowned. "Yeah, a little bit like that, but not as strong. When Marshal's in danger, it's almost as if someone yanks me and spins me around. It's impossible to ignore."

"It's the Bindings," Aelia said. "The Binding between you and Marshal is the strongest that can be formed, but everyone has Bindings to their home, their family, their friends. That's what you're feeling."

Marshal felt nothing pulling him back. He had no attachment to Drusa's Crossing or anyone in it any more. He supposed that was a good thing, at least now.

"Is it always going to be this way?" Victor's voice took on a plaintive sound Marshal didn't remember hearing from him before.

"Not always." Aelia patted him on the shoulder. "The Bindings are there to keep the people of Antises together, because our community is our strength. But… given enough time, the lesser Bindings lose their potency. I suspect you will feel it for a long time. But it will fade."

Victor didn't look comforted and Marshal couldn't blame him. The whole thing sounded horribly inconvenient. All his life, Marshal had hated the curses, but the Bindings didn't seem that much better.

As it grew colder, Aelia found a hollow not far from the road, next to a tiny rivulet. Marshal marveled at the flowing water, not frozen. The end of winter drew nearer than he had thought.

Practiced now, Marshal and Victor set about collecting firewood while Aelia took stock of provisions. "There's not much to eat," Victor pointed out.

"We'll have enough," Aelia said. "We should reach another village in a day or two, where we can pick up a few things. That should keep us going until… until we reach where we're going."

"Where's that?" When Aelia didn't answer, Victor snorted and kept working on the fire.

As they ate later, he tried again to get Aelia to reveal their destination, but she remained firm in her silence.

"I may as well be talking to myself," Victor muttered. "He can't talk, and you won't."

Marshal gave him a gentle shove. Victor looked at him and he grinned. It was the best he could do. Victor nodded with a half-smile in response.

Around half an hour later, they were beginning to prepare for bed when a man stepped into the circle of firelight. He wore rough clothing, like most of the men Marshal knew, and appeared quite muscular under his coat. He unwound a thick scarf from his face, revealing a heavy, dark beard and a jovial grin.

"Good evening!" he announced. "I do believe it's a very lucky thing that I found you."

"Good evening," Aelia said. "Thank you, but we would prefer to be left to ourselves."

The man took a step forward, not losing his grin. "Well, I don't think you really know what you want, milady," he said with a mocking tone to his voice.

Victor and Marshal both jumped to their feet. "The lady is defended!" Victor said, his eyes blazing. Marshal felt for the dagger inside his coat.

Aelia remained sitting. Her bearing betrayed no stress whatsoever.

"You may be uncouth," she answered, "but you will not harm us. You don't look like the type of man who would bring a curse down on himself."

"You're going to give me exactly what I want," the man answered, his joviality hardly diminished. He held his hands out to the fire. "I don't have to worry about curses."

Marshal started around the fire, but stopped when he caught a glimpse of movement just outside the fire's light. Another man came into view, holding a thick rope. A curse-stalker strained at the end of it. This one looked more muscular, though not nearly as big as the one they had fought before. Scars criss-crossed its back.

"I think you can begin to see the situation," the first man said. He pulled off a pair of worn gloves and clapped his hands together. "Mmm, nothing like a fire to warm your bones." He looked significantly at Aelia. "Well, except a woman, that is."

The second man came closer and the curse-stalker moved toward Marshal. He backed up and glanced at Victor. His mouth hung open and his eyes darted about. He didn't know what to do either.

The first man stood over Aelia and looked down at her. "Stand up," he ordered. She shot a look at Marshal and got to her feet.

"You look like you could warm me up right nicely," the thug said, looking her up and down. He reached out and took hold of her chin. "And you know why you're going to do so willingly, right?"

Aelia stared fire into his eyes and did not respond.

"You wouldn't dare!" Victor broke in. "You--"

"Shut your mouth, son!" the second man snarled. He let the curse-stalker's rope loose enough for the beast to lunge forward within a couple of feet from Marshal.

The first man looked at Victor, but didn't take his hand off Aelia. "You don't seem to grasp the situation here, boy," he said. "We don't have to hurt anyone and risk one of Theon's curses, thanks to our little pet here and your friend. Explain it to him, Marcus."

Marcus laughed. "You will give us what we want, freely and willingly, or I just let go of this rope. You know what happens then, right?"

"Of course they know," the first man said. "Look at his face. They already ran into the one that got away."

Marshal grasped the dagger's handle underneath his coat. He would not allow his mother to be harmed for him, not like this.

The first man ran his other hand down Aelia's side. "You look like you have quite a nice shape underneath those clothes," he said. "Let's take them off and see if I'm right."

"I want a turn when you're done with her, Jolin," Marcus said. "And then they can give us their food."

"Good idea," Jolin answered. "I think I'm about to work up an appetite." He pulled Aelia toward him and kissed her.

Marshal whipped out the dagger and took a step toward Jolin. But at that moment, his hand began to shake violently. He took another step and the shaking spread up his arm and into his torso. He'd never experienced it this bad. The dagger fell to the ground.

Marcus hooted. "Look a' this, Jolin! The little Curse Boy can't even hold his pig-sticker!"

Jolin pulled away from Aelia to see Marshal collapse on the ground, shaking all over. Both men stared in amazement as Marshal rocked back and forth, his body consumed by spasms. The pain from his facial scars flared with each violent tremor.

"He's having some kind of fit," Marcus said. "You ever seen a curse like this before?"

"Devouring fire," Jolin murmured. "That's..." He released Aelia and touched his index finger to his palm. "Evil is what it is. Maybe we should let the beast have him, after all."

"You're the evil ones!" Jolin looked back to see Aelia drop to the ground in front of him. He stared stupidly at her for a moment, then looked up in time to see an iron ball speeding toward his face.

"I told you the lady is defended!" Victor shouted as his flail smashed into Jolin's face and sent him reeling.

That beautiful, ridiculous flail. Victor found it rusting away in a field near their village when he and Marshal were only six or seven years old. Since then, he had practiced with it daily, resulting in many bruises over the years. As ineffective as it had been against the curse-stalker two days ago, it was devastating against Jolin. He crumpled to the ground and lay still.

"You asked for this!" Marcus cried, and he let go of the rope.

Marshal fought to control his body. His limbs thrashed around and every part of him seemed to be vibrating at once. From his limited viewpoint, he saw the curse-stalker leap toward him. To his utter astonishment, Marshal saw Aelia dive over him in front of the leaping creature. Somehow, she had snatched up the fallen dagger, and she slashed at the curse-stalker's face. The blade cut a small furrow across its snout, enough to redirect it while Aelia scrambled to her feet.

Marshal tried to roll away, but couldn't get enough momentum to flip his own body. Victor rushed past him, swinging the flail. Having learned from his previous encounter, he didn't aim at the beast's head, but at one of its upturned knees. He grunted at the satisfying crunch, followed by a cry of pain from the curse-stalker. It staggered to the side, its shattered leg dragging uselessly.

Aelia took one deliberate step forward and stabbed the creature through the eye. It reared back, fell on its broken leg, and began to crawl away, squealing like a wild hog.

Marshal's shaking began to slow. He rolled onto his side as Aelia sat down hard beside him. She stared at the thrashing curse-stalker.

"Over twenty years since the last time I saw one of these things," she said, "And now I've killed two in the same week."

"Ho!" Victor yelled. "Where do you think you're going?" He charged into the brush.

Aelia helped Marshal sit up. His shaking subsided. They both watched the curse-stalker continue to squeal and thrash about. Neither felt strong or motivated enough to do anything about it.

Victor returned, pushing Marcus in front of him. The once-arrogant thug seemed cowed. He gazed in shock at the dying curse-stalker and then at Aelia, who rose to her feet in front of him.

"Kneel," Victor ordered. "And beg the lady's forgiveness."

Marcus dropped to his knees immediately. "I'm so sorry, milady," he pleaded. "We was fools, no question about it."

"That's one way of looking at it," Aelia answered. "Take your friend and get out of here. He'll need help if he's to live beyond tomorrow."

Marcus scrambled to Jolin's side and shook him awake. He promptly began to scream and curse, putting both hands to his face. Marcus made feeble attempts to silence him.

Aelia flinched. She checked on Marshal to make sure he was all right, then moved to her pack. She found her bag of healing supplies and removed a small vial. She handed it to Marcus.

"Take this," she said. "Put some pressure on his face until the bleeding stops. Then coat it with this. It should stave off infection until you get him somewhere to be properly treated."

Marcus looked at her with wide eyes. "He don't-- we don't deserve this," he said.

"No, you don't. Now get him out of here before I change my mind and let Victor bounce his flail off both your heads a few more times."

Marcus hastened to obey. The two thugs left the ring of firelight and soon disappeared into the darkness. Their former pet went silent, but continued to thrash sporadically.

Aelia sat next to Marshal. Victor crouched nearby, but kept an eye on the spot where the thugs had left.

Marshal looked at his mother. His own shaking had passed, leaving him exhausted and sore. But Aelia seemed to be shaking herself. She looked down at the dagger in her hand and held it up to see better in the firelight. The curse-stalker's blood still dripped from it.

"This is a good blade. Well forged, very sharp." She looked at Marshal. "Did Volraag give it to you?"

Nod is yes. Then he wrinkled his eyes. Was that right? It wasn't a gift, necessarily.

"I see."

"Why would he do that?" Victor asked. "I thought you said he wanted Marshal dead."

Aelia's weary look made Victor stumble back a little. "What? I don't get it."

Aelia took a cloth from her pack and wiped the blade clean. She handed it back to Marshal hilt first. "If the Lord's son wants my son dead, Victor, what is the best way for him to accomplish that task?"

Victor gestured loosely. "Send someone like those guys after us, I guess. Someone who's not worried about getting cursed?"

Aelia looked into Marshal's eyes, but continued to speak to Victor. "And if no such person can be found readily enough?"

"I don't..." Victor looked at Marshal and the dagger and his eyes widened with understanding. "Marshal, you wouldn't!"

"Whatever he said to you, my treasure," Aelia said, continuing to gaze into Marshal's eyes, "he did not say it for your good, but for his. Killing oneself brings no curse in this world, but who can say what Theon will do in the next?"

She stood and dusted off her skirts. "We must fight on, until all curses are lifted," she whispered.

(((10)))

When Marshal woke up, he saw Victor sitting by the fire, idly stirring the coals with a stick. His eyes stared without seeing, and Marshal wondered if he had slept at all.

Victor spoke without looking at him. "I've been waiting to see what my curse will be."

Marshal raised his eyebrows.

Victor gestured with the stick. "I almost killed a man," he explained. "I smashed in his face. It's not the same as actually killing him, but I expect the Laws don't much care."

Marshal got up and began the morning preparations. He hoped Victor wouldn't be cursed for his actions. After all, he had tried to save people. To be cursed for that wouldn't be fair, would it? Then again, to be cursed for a crime your father committed against your mother wasn't fair, either. Fairness did not seem to have weighed heavily on the creators of the Laws of Bindings and Cursings.

Aelia sat up and stretched. "You won't be cursed, Victor," she said. "You did nothing wrong. In fact, quite the opposite."

She pulled her knees up to her chin and looked at him. "Because what you did was done to protect me from great harm, I am now bound to you."

Victor blinked and his mouth fell open.

"It's not as strong as the Binding between the two of you," Aelia said, "but I can feel it nonetheless."

Marshal grinned. They were now all bound together. He found it amusing and yet somewhat sad.

Victor got to his feet. "And of course, I didn't save Marshal again, so that Binding is still firmly in place."

"I suspect you'll have more opportunities," Aelia said. "Much that I wish it were not so…"

She suspected more danger. Marshal didn't know how to react to that. Volraag would be sending someone after them, probably nastier than those men last night. But what other dangers could there be?

He went to relieve himself, but was close enough to overhear Victor ask Aelia about the dagger again. Marshal strained to hear her answer.

"I could take it away from him, but what good would that do? If he truly wanted to kill himself, he'd find a way. A dagger is a useful tool as well as a weapon."

A long pause passed by and then Victor said, "Was… was that normal what happened to him? When he fell on the ground and was shaking so hard?"

"Marshal's curse strikes him in different ways at different times."

Volraag had told him the shaking had nothing to do with the curse. If so, maybe… maybe he could control it.

Marshal returned and joined them in packing their meager gear. When they finally set off down the road for the day, he dreamed of an end to his shaking.

●●●●●

He waited until the next day to put action to his thoughts. The three of them had stopped for a mid-day meal and rest. Aelia kept insisting they would reach another village any time now, but Victor remained skeptical. Neither of the boys had ever traveled this far before.

Aelia dozed off after the meal. Marshal knew she was having trouble sleeping at night, just as he also knew she would never admit it. He wondered what troubled her rest so much. Despite their current difficulties, he slept like a log every night. Walking all day left him exhausted and ready for sleep, regardless of any confusing thoughts.

Victor wandered off, muttering to himself and practicing with his flail. With no one paying any attention to him, Marshal slipped away and found a solitary spot several yards into the woods.

He sat with his back against a large oak and pulled off his gloves. The air already seemed warmer than yesterday, but still cold enough that he felt it right away.

Volraag claimed a magical origin for the shaking he experienced, his inheritance from Lord Varion. If so, Marshal reasoned, he should be able to access it when he wanted, perhaps even control it.

He focused on his hands. The bandages were long gone and the skin was healing. Both hands pulsed with the usual needle-like feeling. That was normal. But sometimes the buzz from the needles led to the shaking.

Nothing happened. Marshal took a deep breath, let his left hand drop into his lap, and focused on his right hand. He had no idea what to do, except to think about his hand and the shaking.

Still nothing happened. Marshal stared harder at his hand. He focused his concentration on the outstretched tips of his fingers and worked his way down them into the palm, willing each of them to start shaking. He imagined the needle-buzz pushing its way out of his skin, releasing energy as it did so.

His middle finger twitched. Then a second finger. A third. Soon they all vibrated, and he could feel it spreading down his palm, into his wrist.

But if he had caused this, then he should be able to stop it. He had no desire to experience a full body shaking like the day before. He gritted his teeth and willed the shaking to stop at his wrist and go no further up his arm.

To his surprise and delight, it worked. Only his hand continued to shake, though the tingling had already spread to his shoulder. He held his hand up in front of his face and watched all five of his digits continue to vibrate.

Marshal breathed the cold air in through his nose and let it out through his mouth. He lowered his right hand off to the side and lifted his left hand in front of his face. Once again, nothing happened at first. He concentrated as hard as he dared, while still trying to keep part of his focus on his right hand. He had to use the trick of running his concentration down his fingers to his palm twice before it worked. His left hand began to shake.

He felt a surge of glee. He could control it! He held up both hands and stared at them. They both vibrated hard. He could feel his bones and muscles beginning to ache. This was going on too long. He knew that after a significant shaking, like the one during the fight, his entire body could be sore for many hours. Time to put an end to this.

He hesitated. His hands vibrated differently from one another. Why hadn't he noticed that before? He drew them closer together for comparison. The difference grew more obvious, though still somewhat hard to discern. The more he perceived it, the less he could grasp its meaning. At first, he thought one vibrated faster than the other. But no.

They were just… different. His right hand twitched in ways his left hand didn't. And he had trouble straightening out the fingers of his left hand, whereas his right moved with ease. Why so different?

On impulse, Marshal brought his hands together with a sudden clap, to see if they would vibrate together.

He wasn't entirely sure what happened next. In his next moment of consciousness, a blurry Victor grabbed his coat and shook him. "Are you all right? Marshal? Mars?"

His consciousness returned gradually, along with a sharp pain in the back of his head and a terrible ache in both hands.

Victor looked away and called, "He's waking up! I think he's all right."

Marshal shook his head and his vision cleared. He still sat with his back to the oak. Victor stood over him. Behind Victor, he saw Aelia approaching with measured steps, looking around her in amazement.

Marshal stared. Everything had changed. The ground in front of him had been torn apart. Dirt and scrub brush and even some large tree roots had been shredded. The destruction formed a half-circle radiating outward from Marshal about three feet, then narrowed into a path that extended straight out for another ten feet or more.

"What could have done this?" Victor asked. "Did you see anything, Marshal?"

Aelia examined Marshal's face. "He knows exactly what happened," she said.

"What was it?"

"He did this himself."

"What do you mean?" Victor asked.

Aelia knelt beside Marshal and took his hands into hers, looking at them briefly before she held them tight. Marshal winced. "Volraag told you, didn't he?"

"Told him what?"

Aelia ignored Victor and looked at Marshal's right hand more carefully. "Bruises are beginning to form, my son. You were reckless. I think you will be in more pain for a day or two."

"What do you mean? What is going on?"

Aelia stood. "I don't think we'll be going any further today," she said. "Let's set up a fire and then I'll explain all. To both of you."

•••••

Once they had a new campsite set up, Aelia took out a salve and massaged both of Marshal's hands with it. He tried not to react too much, but her every touch of his fingers hurt. She also examined the knot on the back of his head. Apparently, it had slammed back against the oak tree.

"At this rate, you're going to lose both hands and your head on this journey," Aelia said. "You seem determined to keep injuring them."

Several hours remained until sundown, but Victor started a fire. It felt nice to receive warmth from both sun and fire. Marshal closed his eyes as Aelia began her story.

"Before the two of you were born, I came to Drusa's Crossing with my father. He was very sick, despite his own great skill as a healer. Everything I know, I learned from him in my early years. Unfortunately, we had very little time remaining together when we came here."

"Where did you come from?" Victor asked.

Aelia ignored the question and went on with her story. "One day, Lord Varion and his entourage came through the town. They were on a hunting expedition or something - I never learned the full story. The major offered them shelter and the best the town had to offer. And they took it.

"In fact, Lord Varion took everything he wanted, which included me."

"Oh," Victor responded in a whisper. He looked around uneasily.

"Now you understand," Aelia said. "My father, barely able to stand on his own, was furious and tried to confront Varion. The Lord killed him without a thought, blasting him with his magic. He did not even leave behind a body for me to bury. My father was simply gone."

Aelia paused and took a deep breath.

"Varion raped and murdered. And because the Lords of Antises twisted the Laws, the curse for this fell on his first-born son: Marshal."

Marshal felt uncomfortable for multiple reasons. He knew Aelia was explaining the truth, but to hear such horrible things said so calmly seemed unnatural. His mother had endured such hardships even before his birth. Yet somehow she had poured her love into his life for all his years and worked so hard to take care of him. Maybe she blocked the pain out by devoting herself to him. It didn't seem right.

"But because Marshal is Varion's oldest child, he also inherits the Lord's magical power, that which helps bind Antises together."

"So, the Lords' children get cursed for their actions, but then get the magic?" Victor said. "That's insane."

"It's not what they intended when they betrayed Akhenadom and twisted the Laws of magic," Aelia said. "But it was all they could do, I suppose, in their selfish quest to protect themselves from consequences."

"But what happened over there--" Victor gestured to where Marshal had experimented. "How can he have power already?"

"He does and he doesn't," Aelia said. "Lord Varion is getting old. The older he gets, the more the power bleeds away from him and toward his son. But Marshal..." She turned to him. "Because of your curse, there are complications."

Complications? It seemed a little worse than that. Even though he had magic flowing through him, the stupid curse would not let him use it.

"I cannot begin to explain, or even understand, how this all works," Aelia admitted. "I know some things about curses and some things about magic, but how this all combines in your body... that I do not know."

Marshal wondered, too. Something had felt different back there. The power in his left hand had felt good, but the power in his right hand had felt incredible. And they had been different from each other. Was that part of the magic? A complication of the curse? He wondered how many of his other infirmities through the years were caused by the curse and how many by the magic.

"Were you trying to control it?" Aelia asked.

Marshal tried to concentrate.

"Nod is yes, shake is no," she said gently.

Marshal nodded.

"I do not think that will be possible." Aelia sighed. "I have heard stories of past Lords who fathered cursed children who inherited the power. The Lords either arranged to have them die somehow, or else made sure they quickly fathered an uncursed child of their own, so as to continue the line. I have never heard a story of a Lord controlling his magic in spite of a curse."

Victor had that pitying look again. Marshal hated it. People always looked at him with either scorn or pity. He preferred the scorn. He could return that in kind. Pity? Yes, he had a horrible life. They were right. But pity did no good. Pity was nothing more than a variation of scorn that allowed people to feel better about themselves. Scorning people was morally wrong, according to the teachings of Theon, but pitying someone was morally acceptable. Yet they both said the same thing: you are worth less than me.

Marshal picked up a clod of dirt and threw it at Victor. He dodged out of the way.

"What was that for?" he demanded.

"He doesn't want your pity, Victor," Aelia said gently. "He wants to be treated as an equal. He wants your friendship."

"Friendship? He-- I'm only here-- Ahghhh!" Victor jumped to his feet and stalked a few steps away. He appeared to think for a moment and then came back.

"You said there might be a way to lift Marshal's curse," he told Aelia. "Does that mean he'll fully inherit the Lord's power and become the next Lord of Varioch?"

"He will inherit the power, yes," Aelia answered. "The Lordship is another issue. I don't know what will happen."

"This is just insane." Victor seemed to use that word a lot.

Marshal found himself growing sleepy again. Whatever he had done with the magic, it had taken a lot out of him. Aelia noticed.

"You should get some more rest." She handed him his blanket.

Marshal did not disagree. He curled up and pulled the blanket over him. The fire danced in his eyes until they lost their ability to stay open.

(((11)))

It had taken only two careful questions in the street to narrow down the home of the town gossip. Kishin waited until no one watched and then slipped through the door into the blacksmith's home. A portly woman stood beside a table, slicing meat while a pan of oil heated over the fire. She looked up at his entrance. Seeing a stranger, she peered at him uncertainly and stiffened.

Kishin knew appearances could speak louder than words. His own clothing, bearing, and even voice timbre were adaptable, depending on the identity he wished to convey at any given time. Simplicity itself in moments like this. He kept his hood up and stood with his back bent, shuffling his weight from one foot to the other. "Is this the blacksmith's?" he asked in a quavering tone. It communicated nervousness and weakness, just what the woman needed to set her mind at ease.

She relaxed. "My husband's shop is around the side," she said. "I'm sure he'll be pleased to help with your need, whatever it might be. Are you passing through?"

Kishin inclined his head in a slight nod. "I'm in need of some chains," he said.

The woman raised an eyebrow. As a request, it sounded uncommon enough to raise curiosity without being too strange. "Balaes doesn't get much call for that kind of job, but he can handle it," she said. She took a halting step away from the table to get a better look at him. "What kind of chain, might I ask? What do you need it for?"

Kishin made a weak gesture. The cold weather gave him legitimate excuse to keep his gloves on, hiding his skin. "My poor son. He's cursed, ya see." He let a regional Ch'olan accent drip through a bit stronger. "Sometimes he ha' these fits. Chains is all that can keep him from hurtin' us."

"You poor man." She tilted her head, trying to see under his hood. Kishin turned a bit to increase her curiosity and make it more difficult. "We had a cursed young man here in this town, too. Sad thing, it was."

"Had?"

"He and his mother left about a week ago, poor things. And that was right after that noble showed up. Such a commotion!"

"Cursings are never easy." Kishin turned back to the door. He had all the information he needed. "I'll talk to your husband now."

Before he even reached for the door handle, the door itself flew open and an immense man, dripping with sweat, stepped inside. "Here he is now!" the woman called out. "Balaes! This poor man needs some chains for his cursed son. Maybe that's what Aelia should have used, you think?"

Balaes stared down at Kishin with a curious expression. "How long a chain are you wanting?" he asked in a booming voice. "I have a couple forged a'ready that might suit your need." He stepped into the room, forcing Kishin to step backward as the blacksmith shut the door behind him.

"I would think four feet should be sufficient." Kishin took another step back. Suspicion radiated off the blacksmith like the heat from his forge. He must be used to looking his clients in the eye. The weak and nervous act would not suffice for him, but too drastic of a change would throw off the wife.

Before Kishin anticipated it, the blacksmith reached an enormous arm forward and flipped his hood back. His wife's sharp intake of breath split the silence that followed.

Kishin straightened to his full height, nearly the equal of the blacksmith. His eyes narrowed and he mentally prepared for what he might have to do.

The blacksmith touched an index finger to his opposite palm. "What are you?"

"Can't you see? He's the cursed one!" the woman exclaimed. "Theon preserve us! Look at him!"

Kishin knew what the sight of his face did to people, but it never failed to irritate him. He turned to the woman, reached up and peeled a long shred of dead skin from his cheek. She shrieked.

"That's no curse," Balaes said, a hoarseness entering his voice. "It's leprosy!"

Kishin hesitated, but he knew what he had to do. "Tell me your curse."

"We're not cursed," the woman answered, a baffled look crossing her face.

The blacksmith's face hardened instead. He took a step away, grabbed the knife his wife had been using and brandished it. Kishin glanced at the meat on the table. If he ended up killing them both, he could fry it up himself. He hadn't eaten well since leaving home. One of the frequent hazards of his occupation.

"Tell me your curse," he repeated.

"Why did you come into my house?" Balaes demanded. He took a step closer, knife at the ready.

Kishin's right arm flashed out. The blacksmith didn't even see the hidden blade that sliced across his outstretched forearm. The knife clattered to the floor. Balaes grabbed his forearm and sank to his knees, trying desperately to stop the spurting blood from escaping. His wife stood with mouth open, apparently unsure whether to scream or faint.

"Your wife has already given me everything that I wanted," Kishin said. "She has my gratitude. As do you." He bent over and kissed the blacksmith on the forehead. He found the horrified looks on the couple's faces immensely satisfying.

He pointed his blade at the wife. "Now. Tell me your curse."

The woman looked at her bleeding husband and back at Kishin. He took a step closer. She took a step back and her mouth moved without words. He lifted his blade.

Kishin left Drusa's Crossing certain of his course. His target had departed after a visit from a noble. Volraag himself perhaps? Since the road north had been clear, the target must have gone south, but not in Volraag's footsteps. It wouldn't take long to determine the correct road and catch up. Every so often, he lucked out into the simplest of jobs.

<h1 style="text-align:center">(((12)))</h1>

"Can't you just draw me a map?" Seri asked. Her third evening on Zes Sivas had been greatly improved by another meal with the other two acolytes.

Dravid and Jamana exchanged skeptical glances. "I don't know if anyone's ever done that," Dravid said. "At least not a full map."

"It took me twenty minutes to make it from my work space to the dining hall," Seri said. "And I've been here before! I need to get better at this. I don't even know when I've moved from one citadel to the other!"

"Well," Jamana said as if thinking carefully, "if you get to the gold-trimmed area, you've left the Citadel of Mages and moved into the Citadel of Kings..."

"Gold-trimmed?"

"Notice how everything here is trimmed in purple?" Dravid pointed to a tapestry hanging on one wall and then a set of curtains pulled back from the windows on the opposite wall. "Purple is the mage color, like the Masters' robes. Gold is the King color, I guess. So if you notice things trimmed in gold, you've crossed over. Usually, you would already know, because you can see where you cross a bridge between towers, but I guess there are places where it's more closely connected than that."

"That's something, I guess."

"We're on the ground floor here," Dravid went on. He attempted to draw shapes in the air to illustrate. "But there are a couple of levels below us. The Inner Sanctum, where the Passing takes place, is one level down. There are also the special quarters for each of the Lords. And there are storage areas below that."

"My work space is two floors up," Seri moaned. "How many levels are there?"

The boys exchanged glances again.

"Four above ground?" Dravid said.

"Three," Jamana argued.

"It depends on whether you count the towers. Or the center circle."

"If you count the towers, it's six."

"How do you get six?"

Jamana pointed up. "The library is on the top regular floor, and that's three levels up from here--"

"Then it's on level four!"

"No, I meant it's three levels up, not three above us now."

"Wait, wait, wait!" Seri interrupted. They both looked at her.

Her eyes sparkled. "There's a library?"

●●●●●

Seri did not love books for themselves. She loved them for the knowledge she could acquire from them. She had no interest in reading for pleasure, though she knew friends back home who did so on a regular basis. She wanted to learn everything she could, and the library of the Conclave was the perfect spot for that.

Master Korda summoned Jamana, so Dravid happily escorted Seri two levels up to the library. She caught her breath upon entering. Books of all shapes and sizes lined the walls. The shelves rose to slightly above her reach, but they wrapped into book-lined corridors in multiple directions. She took a few steps down one and stopped.

"You could get lost in here!" she exclaimed.

"It's like the citadels themselves," Dravid said, joining her. "But on a smaller scale. It's really not as big as it looks."

"How do you find your way around? How are the books organized?"

Dravid chuckled. "Don't ask me. I've only been up here a few times to fetch a book for Master Simmar. He always explains to me exactly where to find it."

"So there must be a system of some kind."

Dravid shrugged. "I'm sure there is, but the Masters don't seem too keen on sharing it with us yet."

"Then I'll just have to explore on my own."

"What are you looking for?"

Seri tried to keep her smile from showing too much excitement. "Everything. I want to know everything."

"That might take a while."

"What else am I going to do?" Seri pulled a book off the shelf and looked it over. "Copy names of dead people over and over?"

Dravid furrowed his brow. "You do realize that the copying job is kind of a test, right? To see if you're willing to do the work assigned to you?"

Seri rolled her eyes and put the book back. "Of course I know that. I'll keep up with it, but at the same time, I'll be learning more…" She scanned the titles and took another book.

Dravid looked at it. "About wild magic? Why?"

"*The Vicissitudes of Wild Magic and its Practitioners* by Master Sekou." Seri flipped to the first chapter and glanced at the opening line: "Wild magic can crop up anywhere in Antises, though it seems to favor three specific regions." She smiled and shut the book, though she wanted to read on right away.

"Because it's a start. I came here to learn magic and so far I've learned nothing. At least this way, I'll be educating myself. And maybe I can help figure out why the earth is shaking." Actually, Master Hain had gone on a big rant about wild magic earlier today. He seemed to despise the practice, which made Seri even more interested. She looked around. "Is there some kind of system for borrowing the books?"

"Not here," Dravid said. "I think they just trust to your honor. There's only about thirty people on this island total. As long as the books don't leave the island, I don't think anyone cares who has them or how long."

Seri moved to the next set of shelves and began perusing. Dravid glanced around and scratched his head.

"Look," he finally said. "I get that you want to learn, but I think your Master has a plan in mind for you."

"He hasn't told me anything."

"Yeah, mine didn't either, the first few days. But once I got settled in, he started hitting me with all kinds of assignments, reading, watching the apprentices practice, that kind of thing."

"Have you learned any magic yet?"

"Well… no."

"Then I'll read ahead and be even better prepared when he gets around to it," Seri answered. "I'm settled in. I don't need to wait."

"Well… um, good luck, then. I have a couple more chores to do before I sleep." Dravid made as if to move away.

"Goodnight," Seri said without thinking. She pulled another book down. She had a feeling she would not be getting to sleep any time soon.

(((13)))

Marshal stirred. That seizure had been a bad one. He glanced around and sat up. Neither Victor nor Aelia were in sight. They hadn't discovered him. Were they gathering firewood for a new night's camp? Had he been asked to get some too? He couldn't remember. He shivered, wishing the fire were already blazing.

A footstep crunched the snow nearby. Marshal looked up, expecting his mother. Instead, he saw an eidolon standing a few feet away, as if watching him.

He had no way of telling if this was the same creature that had watched the fight with the curse-stalker. Or had appeared to him several times before. It looked the same: just a shadowy man-shaped figure without discernible edges to its shape. This close, however, it looked more solid than he had noticed before.

Another footstep came from behind him. Marshal whirled in time to see Victor drop a pile of sticks and stare with open-mouthed wonder. He could see it too! Marshal wasn't alone. The thought filled him with relief.

"I got a pull from the Bond," Victor said, reaching for his flail. "But I never dreamed…"

Marshal got to his feet and pulled out Volraag's dagger. They both faced the apparition.

The creature tilted its head, as if curious. Then, as Victor began to spin his flail, it took a step back. It seemed to bow to them, then stepped to the side and disappeared. It didn't step behind a tree or anything else. It simply vanished.

Victor made a disgusted noise. "Saving you from that thing would have definitely broken this Bond!" he griped. He looked at Marshal.

"Still, never thought I'd see an eidolon. Wait until I tell Careen about this! She's always bragged that her uncle saw one from a distance once."

Marshal rolled his eyes.

At that moment, Aelia approached from the direction of the road. She carried an armload of wood. "Oh, good, you're both here already," she said. "Did you both get enough?" She glanced at the small pile next to Victor's feet and then at Marshal, who had nothing. She raised her eyebrows.

"We're on it," Victor promised. He and Marshal headed in opposite directions. Regardless of shadow creatures, they still had work to do.

•••••

Marshal woke sometime in the middle of the night. The fire had dwindled to embers, but warmth still radiated from it. Victor's light snores could be heard from the other side. Aelia was nowhere to be seen. Tomorrow was a Rest Day, but she had insisted they would keep traveling, anyway. Why wasn't she getting her rest now, then?

Curious, Marshal got to his feet and peered into the darkness around him. He saw no sign of movement or any other light aside from the myriad of stars he could glimpse through the tree cover. He closed his eyes and let his other senses work.

A soft sound came from off to the right, further away from the road. Marshal moved in that direction, as quietly as he could. As long as he didn't start shaking again, he could generally move without being detected. Years of trying to avoid notice had encouraged him to develop that talent.

He opened his eyes. A voice? Someone was saying something.

Marshal stepped through the trees, avoiding fallen branches and undergrowth. The voice grew clearer. It had a rhythm to it, as if it were repeating the same thing over and over. As he drew closer, he realized he knew the voice.

He reached a treeline and looked out at an unexpected sight. Aelia sat out in the open, on the edge of an embankment that ran down to a small stream. She looked up toward the stars and chanted. Something glowed with a soft orange light in her lap.

Marshal knelt and listened. "*...a curinir Eldanim. Curinir. Curinir...*" It made no sense to him.

Aelia lifted her hands as if beseeching the stars themselves. She continued with her odd chant, then broke off. She lowered her hands to her lap. "For the hope is almost lost," she whispered. The glow faded and disappeared.

Marshal took a step backward. As Aelia began to climb to her feet, he hastened away. He had no idea what that was all about. It added yet another layer to the mystery of his own mother, a mystery he hadn't even known existed.

(((14)))

Seri might have overestimated how much she had "settled in." After browsing in the library for some time, it took her a full hour to find her way out and back to her own room. After that frustration, she felt almost too tired to do any reading. She skimmed over a few pages from each of the five books she had borrowed. She got caught up in Sekou's *Vicissitudes* for over an hour and ended up getting far less sleep than she anticipated. She missed breakfast the next morning and rushed to keep from being late to her copying work.

To her further chagrin, Master Hain appeared almost as soon as she began and literally asked her how she was "settling in." Had Dravid tipped him off? Surely not.

"Fairly well, sir," she answered. "I'm still struggling with understanding the layout of the citadels here." She chuckled, trying to establish camaraderie over a shared experience.

Hain did not laugh or smile in return. "Well, keep at it," he said. "When you can find your way from one end to the other without any wrong turns, let me know. I'll have some more tasks for you, then." He left the room, leaving her blinking in astonishment.

Wrong turns? How did he know? The logical part of her brain tried to tell her that everyone must experience this difficulty at first, but the rest rebelled. She abandoned her work and went in search of Dravid.

Her explorations took a good hour, and she never found Dravid. Instead, she found Jamana cleaning up the kitchen for the noon meal's preparation. Seri stopped and bit her lip when she saw him.

Jamana gave her one of his enormous grins. "What is it, Seri?"

"I was going to complain about my work, but seeing you in here…"

Jamana laughed loud. "You think this might be a promotion from the copying?" He laughed again. His laugh seemed to come from deep inside him, almost like his entire body took part in the expression of humor.

"No, no, little Seri-Belit, that is not the case." His voice, so pleasant and deep and slightly accented, kept her from being mad at him over the use of her full name.

"I am here because I angered Master Korda. I spilled ink onto a scroll over which he had labored for many an hour. He yelled for many minutes. Now I work in the kitchen for three days."

"Oh."

Jamana hung a large frying pan from a hook. "What is it your Master requires of you today?"

Seri felt abashed. She had not experienced Master Hain's temper as of yet, if he had one, but Korda sounded much fiercer. "I'm sorry. It's nothing. I'm sorry you're having to work so hard."

"This?" Jamana spread his arms encompassing the kitchen. "This is not hard work. Time-consuming? Yes. But not hard." He pointed vaguely toward the northeast. "Someday, you will come to my city of Tenjkidi. There I will show you what is hard work."

Seri fought a blush. "I… I really need to learn my way around," she admitted. "When you are free, do you think you could help me?"

"I would be honored. Give me just a few more minutes here."

Seri moved aside and waited for Jamana to finish his work. It occurred to her that she would have to return to her copy work sometime later and work extra hard to make up for lost time. Master Hain hadn't given her a specific quota, necessarily, but she knew he must expect a certain amount of work accomplished each day.

The Conclave wasn't technically a school, but it was the place to be if you wanted to learn to be a mage. It had a system of apprenticeship and development. Yet there seemed to be no organized method of shepherding this development, no set curriculum, no designated instructors, no schedule. It had to be the strangest way of getting an education of any kind that Seri had ever seen.

•••••

"The Citadel of Mages is like a hand with three fingers extended," Jamana said, holding his up to illustrate. "It intersects with the Citadel of Kings in those three places. Sort of." He laced the fingers of his other hand together with the first. "Except it's really only the middle one that directly connects." He tried overlapping his middle fingers. "And the other two only connect via bridges from one section to the other…" He looked up at Seri's face and laughed, pulling his fingers apart.

"I will just show you. Come, we go to the outer walls."

Jamana led the way out of the Citadel, across the outer courtyard that encircled both structures and up a set of stairs onto the outer walls. Seri felt somewhat self-conscious as they stepped up onto the empty stone wall that wrapped itself around most of the island. In the early days of Zes Sivas, this wall would have had numerous soldiers on patrol, keeping an eye out for possible invasion. In later years, the number of soldiers diminished to a ceremonial force in service to the Kings. But once the King disappeared, the perceived need (or desire) for a military presence all but vanished. Seri didn't know if any soldiers still worked on the island.

A chill breeze swept down from the north shores of the lake. Seri wrapped her arms around herself while Jamana pointed at the structures.

"You see? The wall of the Citadel of Kings curves inward right there and appears to join with the Citadel of Mages. But it doesn't." He took a few steps toward the south. "From here, you can easily see that there is actually a gap between them there. But you cannot see it from other angles."

Seri nodded. She could see that much, at least. The breeze struck her in the face and she blinked. Immediately, everything changed. Day turned to night. A vast panoply of immensely bright stars filled the sky and lit up the island around her. The citadels lay in ruins around her. A narrow column of smoke rose from within a heap of stones where the Citadel of Kings had stood.

Seri blinked again and the vision disappeared. She staggered, her head spinning. Jamana caught her by the arm.

"Seri, are you all right?"

She blinked a few more times. The vision did not return, and her head cleared. "Yes, sorry. I… don't know what just happened." A vision, clearly. But of what? The future?

Jamana released her arm and started back down the stairs. "Perhaps it's too cold out here. Come. It's a long walk, but it will help you understand."

Together, they entered the gap between the two citadels. Jamana pointed up to where an enclosed bridge connected the two sections. She guessed it to be on the third floor. "This is the same on the opposite side of the island," he explained. "But it's the middle where it gets confusing."

They followed the open ground as it curved around to their right. The wind didn't blow here, and the height of the citadel walls meant almost no sunshine reached the ground. What little grass and scrub that still clung to life in this area climbed the walls, searching for the light.

As they rounded the extension of the mages' citadel, Jamana gestured with charismatic exuberance. "Now this. This is impressive." He frowned. "It is more than six. Dravid and I both were wrong."

Seri followed the strange construction upward and agreed. The first "floor" extended from the Citadel of Mages. She suspected it contained the primary living quarters of the Masters. Above it, a set of massive pillars held up an extension from the Citadel of Kings. This extension consisted of two floors in height. "The throne room of the King is in there," Jamana pointed out. Above that, a second set of strong pillars held up a top floor connected to both citadels and topped by a tarnished golden dome.

Jamana glanced up at the sun. "It is almost mid-day," he noted. "We should return and eat. Then I think we both have work to do. I know I will have to clean up after the meal. Master Korda was very specific on that."

Seri turned. "It's a long way back," she said.

"No, no. There is no need," Jamana said. "There is a side door in which we can enter." He led the way around the corner.

Jamana opened the door and allowed Seri to enter first. "Left or right?" she asked. The corridor looked exactly like all the other corridors that constantly frustrated her in the citadel.

"Left, I believe," Jamana said. "We can cut past the Masters' quarters. Not far from there to the kitchen."

The hallway curved toward the right, following the outer wall, from what Seri remembered. They reached a four-way intersection with another hallway. "Yes, this is it," Jamana said. "Left leads into the Masters' quarters. Right leads back into the main parts of the Citadel of Mages."

"What about straight ahead?"

"Up ahead is a set of stairs that lead down to the Inner Sanctum. I'd take you there, but I really need to get back."

"Another time." Seri started to follow Jamana to the right, but glanced back one more time.

Someone else had come into view down the hall. She frowned. He seemed to be having trouble walking.

"Jamana..."

The approaching figure wore purple robes. Not an acolyte or apprentice, then. One of the Masters? He stumbled toward them with halting steps.

"Master?" Jamana asked, taking a step forward.

The figure staggered and fell. Jamana raced to his side, followed by Seri. He took hold of the fallen Master and gently rolled him face up.

Seri gasped and stepped back. Jamana let go and lifted his hands, unsure what to do with them.

They stared at the unknown Master's face, wrinkled beyond anything Seri had ever seen. His skeletal structure stood out in bold detail against skin that looked ready to crack and fall off at any moment. His eyes were open and staring, though clouded beyond the ability to see. As they watched, one final breath escaped from the fallen Master and the body collapsed completely.

"He's dead."

"I don't know." Jamana reached out and touched the Master's face with a single finger. He yanked his hand back. "I think so." He looked up at Seri. "I'm afraid, Seri. Do we try to carry him somewhere?"

"I... I don't think we should move him."

Jamana stood. "You're probably right. I will stay here and you... No, that won't work." He looked at her face. "I am sorry, Seri-Belit, but I must ask you to stay with him. I will go find one of the other Masters."

She nodded. It made the most sense. Jamana knew his way around. She didn't. Still, the sight of him hurrying away made her chest tighten. A shiver ran down her body. She had never been this close to death before. Both her parents were alive and well, and her grandparents had died before she was old enough to understand.

This was insane. Master mages could die, of course, but what had happened to this one? She had stood before all six of the Masters only a few days ago and none of them looked remotely like this.

She swallowed and took another look at the emaciated face. The skin tone appeared somewhat dark, but she couldn't tell for sure. Whatever had done this to him could have altered the skin tone, as well.

What could have done this? She knew so little about life here, about what the Masters even did with their time. Had he been practicing some powerful magic and lost control? Her vision on the wall came back to her. Were they connected?

Seri took a few steps and peered down the hall in the direction from which the Master had come. Jamana had said this hall led down stairs to the Inner Sanctum. The Sanctum, the location where the annual Passing took place, was a mystery to her. Master Hain had talked about it a little bit in their discussion about the Heart of Fire. Did the Masters have to prepare the location? Many weeks remained until the Passing. What other reason could there be for going down there?

The sound of rapid footsteps made her turn back. Jamana returned, but two other Masters outpaced him. One was Master Hain. Seri thought the other one might be Master Tzoyet, from Ch'olan. Both uttered exclamations of shock as they drew near.

Master Hain knelt beside the fallen Master and placed a hand on his face. He held it there a moment and then released him. He sighed and sat back against the wall.

"Master Simmar," he said. "Quite dead, I'm afraid." Master Tzoyet muttered something too quiet to be heard.

Seri looked up at Jamana, who also had a pained look. Master Simmar came from Kuktarma. He was Dravid's Master.

"Master, what could have done this?" Seri asked.

Master Hain glanced up with a twitch, as if he had just noticed his acolyte standing there. "I'm afraid I don't know the answer to that just yet, Seri," he said.

Master Tzoyet folded his arms and closed his eyes. He seemed to have withdrawn from his surroundings.

Master Hain stood. "Well, we can't leave him here like this. You two acolytes find a pair of apprentices to help us. I believe you both have duties of your own to get back to."

Jamana nodded, flicked his eyes at Seri, and hurried down the hall. She hastened to catch up with him.

"What could have happened?" she wondered.

"If the Masters do not know, I cannot even guess," Jamana said. "It is most troubling."

Seri's mind tumbled through various possibilities. The most frightening concept involved some kind of disease. If so, they might all be in danger. They might have contracted it already.

But considering their location and the Master's identity, a magical source seemed far more likely. What did that mean? She recalled the similar discussion with the Conclave, debating the cause of the shaking earth. Three possibilities had been offered then.

Wild magic? She had learned a bit more last night, but it still seemed unlikely. One of the Masters had said wild magic would never be powerful enough to shake the earth. Did it take more power or less to kill a Master mage?

Could it be the magic of Zes Sivas itself? Since Master Simmar had been in the Inner Sanctum, it might be a strong possibility. But why? Had it been an accident? Had the Master been trying to control or channel the magic of Zes Sivas? Seri didn't know what that could even mean. Obviously, magic existed here, but what was the difference between it and wild magic? Or the magic of the Lords? Her education had barely begun. She knew so little.

Her mind drifted to the third possibility. She had thought it fictional, but Master Hain assured her the Eldanim were real. Could they have done this? Why would they have done this?

She almost stopped in her tracks at a sudden thought. Master Simmar had been the one to blame the Eldanim for the shaking earth. Had they retaliated against him?

(((15)))

"I don't know. I don't know." Dravid kept repeating the same answer to any questions related to how he felt, what he would do next, or anything else, for that matter.

Seri and Jamana did their best to encourage their friend, but nothing else could be said. After a few more platitudes that sounded worthless, they left him to his own devices.

"Do you think they'll send him away?" Seri asked.

Jamana nodded. "I don't think they'll bring in a new Master too quickly," he said. "Dravid will probably have to go home for a while." He looked downcast.

"Maybe they won't," Seri suggested. "Maybe they'll let him stay and work with us."

"Maybe." Jamana didn't look convinced.

Events unfolded as Jamana had predicted. Word came from Kuktarma that Dravid was expected back home as soon as possible. The remaining mages of the land would be assembled as soon as could be arranged, to choose a new Master. Unfortunately, the process could take weeks. There was no guarantee that a new Master would even be chosen by the time of the Passing.

To Seri's disappointment, she missed her chance to bid farewell to Dravid. One day he was there, and the next he was gone.

Seri occupied herself over the next few days with two major tasks: memorizing the layout of the citadels, and reading *The Vicissitudes of Wild Magic and its Practitioners* by Master Sekou. She also did her best to keep up with the work Master Hain had assigned her: copying the names of the dead. She managed to spend a few minutes with Jamana each day, but worry and nervousness colored their conversations.

Neither heard anything more about the mysterious death. Seri brought it up once with Master Hain. He told her to focus on her studies and not worry about such things.

Around a week after the death, Master Hain summoned Seri to his quarters. She hurried through the hallways, and congratulated herself when she arrived in record time. Master Hain greeted her at the door and stepped aside for her to enter.

She took three steps into the room before she recognized the presence of someone else. She turned to see the visitor and froze. A man unlike any man she had ever seen stood in the center of Master Hain's quarters.

He stood well over six feet tall, towering over her like a citadel himself. And yet he seemed even taller. She blinked, and for an instant, he became much taller. His head went through the ceiling, which suddenly… wasn't there. As quickly as it seemed that way, it no longer did. He stood there, smiling at her, with completely normal proportions. Except they weren't. It was as if she could see both versions of him simultaneously. She felt almost nauseated by the effect.

The strangeness of his appearance did not stop there. His tan facial features, framed by long white hair, were angular to the point of sharpness. His eyes - his eyes commanded attention in spite of everything else. The left eye shone with a crystalline green color. His right eye contained no white at all; only a pure orb of darkness with a sprinkling of tiny pinpricks of light, like a miniature star field.

"This is Curasir of the Eldanim," Master Hain said behind her.

Curasir stretched out a thin hand with knuckles so sharp Seri feared cutting herself. She offered her own hand in return. He took it and made a deep bow, a motion so smooth and gentle she almost felt he was dancing for her.

"This is Seri-Belit, the acolyte I mentioned," Master Hain said.

"Seri-Belit, it is a great pleasure to meet you," Curasir said. His voice commanded respect, but at the same time, he sounded pleased to meet her. As he lifted himself up from his bow and his head passed near hers, he spoke in a low voice that only she could hear: "You have a star in your eye."

Seri looked up at him and blinked several times. She had no idea what he meant, or if she had heard him properly.

Master Hain shut the door and walked around from behind her. "We only have the two acolytes here at present, due to Master Simmar's death, but both of them have shown great promise."

Seri blinked again, this time in surprise. Great promise?

"Unfortunately, like so many in Antises, she believed the Eldanim to be myths," Master Hain went on. "I am delighted that you have arrived to permanently dispel that notion."

Seri started to blush, feeling like an ignorant peasant. Curasir smiled in return, a smile without condescension. "How could she think otherwise?" he asked. "We do not interact with humans on a regular basis. The vast majority of you have never seen one of us."

Seri tried not to look directly at him. It was too disconcerting.

Master Hain moved to his desk and began sorting through some papers. "Indeed. Well, I'm pleased you have chosen to join us here. Should you need something more than a message sent, please consider my acolyte at your disposal."

"Master?" Seri asked, confused.

Hain turned back to her. "Curasir will be staying at the Citadel for the next couple of months, at least until the Passing. He is here to observe and advise. Should he need anything, I expect you to be accommodating, as you are for me. I believe it will be an educational experience for you."

"My people have been uninvolved with the proceedings of this land for too long," Curasir added. "That needs to come to an end. Perhaps we can assist with the current crisis."

"You mean the murder?" Seri said. She immediately regretted it.

"Murder?" Curasir cocked his head.

Master Hain rolled his eyes. "She means the unfortunate death of Master Simmar. With no obvious culprit, the younger people here have assumed foul play."

"Ah." Curasir nodded. "No, I was referring to the loss of the King and his magic."

Seri nodded in response, keeping her eyes down. "Of course." At least someone was taking things seriously, then. But perhaps the two problems were connected. Maybe she should say something.

"You may go, Seri," Hain said. "I will be by later to check on your current progress."

Seri dipped her head one more time and left the room in a hurry. The Citadel no longer seemed as familiar as it had a few minutes earlier.

•••••

"You have a star in your eye."

What had he meant? The statement plagued Seri all the way back to her room. She dug out a looking-glass and stared at her reflection.

She examined her eyes, starting with the left and moving to the right. They began to water from the attention. For a long time, she saw nothing. She wiped her eyes and closed them for a minute to stop the watering. She looked again.

Her eyes always seemed boring to her. They were brown, like most of the people she knew. They weren't a deep, rich brown, or a light, sparkling brown. Just an average, ordinary brown. Today, they still appeared average and boring.

Except… she stared closer. Was it her imagination or did the left eye sparkle? She glanced around to make sure it wasn't reflecting a nearby light source. She stared harder and her eyes began to water again. Frustrated, she kept staring. She was almost certain now that she could see a tiny pinprick of light in her left eye. A tear gathered from trying to focus on it. After turning away from the mirror and then back, it still stared back at her. Just beneath the pupil and slightly toward the left, her eye contained a minuscule star.

What did it mean? Did it have something to do with the way Curasir had appeared to her? Looking like he existed at two different heights, one that went through the ceiling?

She sat on her bed and considered. Curasir had a strange-looking eye himself. The light spots in it could be considered stars, based on his words. Would her eye change and become like his? That would be… strange. What did the world look like with an eye like that?

Seri bounded up and left her room. Master Hain had said he would come check on her work, but she needed to speak with Jamana right now.

She found him, as usual, in the kitchen. He had fulfilled his three days' labor, but had once again done something to annoy Master Korda. He still had three days left of an entire week's worth of kitchen duty now.

"Look in my eyes," Seri ordered.

Jamana grinned. "Pretty girls do not need to ask me this twice," he said.

Despite herself, Seri's heart skipped a beat. He had called her pretty. She swallowed and pushed on.

"I'm serious. Tell me if you see anything, um, unusual."

Jamana's grin faded a bit and he bent down to peer into her eyes.

His eyes radiated that deep, rich brown she wished for her own. He looked long enough that her eyes started watering again. She finally dropped her head from his gaze.

"They are very pretty eyes, like chestnuts," Jamana said.

Seri frowned.

Jamana lost his grin. "Was that not what you wanted to hear?"

Seri wiped the moisture away and pointed toward her left eye. "That one. Do you see a bright spot in it?"

Jamana looked again. He held one of his large hands up beside her face to block the light from the kitchen window. "Perhaps? Yes? Like a little star near the bottom."

Seri nodded. "That's what he said. That I had a star in my eye."

"Who said?"

"The Eldanim. Or would it be Eldani? Eldan?"

"You met one of the Eldanim?" Jamana took a step back.

"Yes, Master Hain introduced us. He's going to be staying here for a while." Seri paced several steps in a circle. "What does it mean?"

"Perhaps he is here to help us."

"No, not him. He said he was here to help. I meant my eye. I'm seeing strange things."

"Like what?"

"Like the Eldanim. Eldani. Curasir. He looked strange to me."

"I have not seen one before, but I am told the Eldanim look strange to all."

"No, no, not like that." Seri took a deep breath. "He looked... taller."

"Taller than what?"

"Than-- he-- argh!"

Jamana chuckled. "I do not fully understand what worries you, little Seri, but the star in your eye does not seem like it should concern you this much."

Unable to express herself, Seri stalked out of the kitchen and promptly ran into Master Hain.

"Acolyte. Would you care to explain why I did not find you at your assigned task?"

● ● ● ● ●

That night, Seri couldn't sleep for some time. To distract her mind from the star, she pulled out Sekou's *Vicissitudes* and read some more.

Sekou's explanation of wild magic fascinated her. Wild magic, as everyone with an education knew, consisted of "leftover" magic of the land that had not been consolidated when the Conclave of Mages united it. Though the mages had tried to unite all of Antises' magic, small bits and pieces remained here and there. Over time, individuals with an affinity toward magic had been able to tap into these pieces, with limited success.

He described three regions where wild magic appeared more often: one in the border zone connecting Rasna and Varioch, one in northern Ch'olan, and the third in central Kuktarma. Seri couldn't help being disappointed that Arazu wasn't part of that list.

Master Sekou argued that wild magic practitioners could only learn to use their magic for one purpose. That did not mean they could only perform one action or "spell," but that they could only work within a limited constraint. The magic itself was so fractured it could only be used in one particular direction. Thus, some wild magicians could generate various fire-related spells, though never in a powerful way. They could produce a small flame from nothing, light candles, and maybe even a torch, but nothing greater. And definitely nothing outside of fire.

Seri flipped through the pages at a rapid pace, skimming here and there. Sekou listed almost a hundred different wild magic specializations. Some appeared elemental, like fire or air, while some related to healing or other esoteric practices, such as minor levitation. She chuckled at the ridiculously useless ones, like the record of a farmer who somehow discovered he could alter his own hair color at will. Seri had looked through much of this already, but now she searched for anything related to eyesight.

She found record of a wild magician who could see through substances, but nothing thicker than clothing. He had not come to a good end once the women of his town discovered his ability. She also read about a woman who could focus her eyes to see great distances with precision. She found it interesting that the wild magic made no distinction of gender. Equal numbers of men and women seemed able to connect with it.

Seri skipped ahead some more. Eventually, she found a brief chapter about outward manifestations of wild magic. Sekou described one instance in which a wild magician's skin turned darker. But since his power related to clearing up skin diseases, Sekou could not determine whether he had done it to himself deliberately or even subconsciously, rather than it being an effect of the power itself. Overall, there seemed to be no definitive stories of the wild magic manifesting itself in someone's appearance.

Seri glanced at her looking-glass. She could immediately see the spot of light in her eye, now that she knew where to look. If this wasn't wild magic, what was it?

The Eldanim possessed their own magic, but all other magic in Antises came from the land. Since she was not of the bloodline of the Kings or Lords, Seri could not use their magic. Outside of wild magic, the only other source was Zes Sivas itself. Perhaps she somehow had tapped into the power of the island. Should she mention this to Master Hain? Should she mention it in her next letter to her parents?

And what did it all mean? She had no doubt the vision on the citadel walls was connected to this star, but visions were never mentioned in the books she read. Only Curasir seemed to know anything significant. He also was the only one who seemed concerned about the missing King's magic. She needed to talk with him before doing anything else.

(((16)))

As it turned out, Seri did not have to wait long before seeing Curasir again. At breakfast the next morning, Jamana joined her and seemed not to remember how she walked away from him the day before.

"You seem even happier than usual," Seri noted. "How is that possible?"

"Because I know something that you do not," Jamana said, his grin wider than ever.

"Oh? And what might that be?"

"It is a secret. I do not have permission to tell you yet."

"Then why mention it at all?" Irritated, Seri considered something more cutting to say when Curasir suddenly sat down across from her.

Jamana's eyes bulged. "You're…"

"Yes, I am," Curasir said. "And you must be the other acolyte. Jamana, was it? In service to Master Korda?"

Jamana nodded.

Curasir focused on Seri. She dropped her eyes, unable to look at him directly. "I would like to speak with you about your eyesight," he said. "Shall we go somewhere private?"

Seri shook her head. "Jamana knows about it," she said. She looked up at Curasir and grimaced. "I don't understand. I see you in two different… forms."

"I see something odd, as well," Jamana added. "Perhaps it is not just you."

Curasir flipped his hand in a dismissive gesture. "You see only what all humans see," he told Jamana. "We are hard to perceive with your eyes."

"Why? What causes it?"

"I will put this as simply as I can." Curasir steepled his long fingers together. "We Eldanim exist in two worlds simultaneously. This world, and an… Otherworld, if you will. That is why most people always feel something is strange when they look at us, but you, Seri-Belit, see much more."

"I'm seeing your form in the Otherworld?"

Curasir pointed to his own right eye. "With this eye, I constantly see the Otherworld." He pointed to his left. "With this one, I see this world. You are only seeing my form in both worlds because your power has barely begun to grow, and because I exist in both worlds."

"You see both worlds all the time?" Jamana exclaimed. Curasir nodded. "I think that would drive me insane!"

"Some are unable to bear it," Curasir said. "They wear a patch over one eye, or take more extreme measures."

"I think I caught a glimpse of your Otherworld," Seri recalled. "When we were outside, on the wall," she told Jamana. "It didn't look like a very nice place."

"It is not. Nevertheless, the Otherworld is the source of the magic within this world," Curasir said. "The two are linked in many, many ways."

"But why is this happening to me? I'm not Eldanim!"

"Maybe one of your ancestors was?" Jamana suggested.

"Don't be ridiculous, if you can help it," Curasir snapped. "Our two races are in no wise compatible."

"Then what is it?"

"As near as I can tell, this is an offshoot of wild magic," Curasir said.

"But there's never been wild magic like this!"

"I know of one other case, but that was many, many years ago. Suffice it to say that this is extremely rare. So rare, in fact, that I came to be of assistance to you."

"You came here… for me?"

"I did. It is not what I told your Master and the other mages, of course. And it is true that I wish to be involved in the Passing, at least as an observer. But my primary reason for coming was you."

Seri didn't know what to say.

Curasir leaned forward. "Listen to me, for I cannot instruct you openly or interfere with your education here. We must take advantage of brief times together, when we may. Do not speak of this to your Masters."

Seri furrowed her brow, but nodded.

"Your vision is going to continue to change. You will gain more and more glimpses into the Otherworld. I do not know if you will become able to see both at once, but at the very least, you should understand what is happening. Should the visions become harmful to you in any way, or if you cannot bear them, put a patch over the eye and come find me. I will do whatever I can to help you."

"Thank you," Seri whispered.

"It is I that should thank you. No human has been able to perceive the Otherworld in… well, in many years. I will be fascinated to hear your observations."

With that, Curasir got to his feet. Seri looked up at him and once again saw him in two forms. Now that she understood what she saw, it wasn't as unnerving. She tried to get a better look at Curasir's other form and squinted. He smiled.

"That will come in time," he assured her. He turned on his heel and strode from the room.

•••••

After the conversation with Curasir, Seri completely forgot about Jamana's secret. For the next few days, she kept to herself as she debated Curasir's offer of training. Come to think of it, he hadn't "offered" at all; he had simply announced he would be training her. He had not given her any choice in the matter.

She did not experience any more visions of the Otherworld and felt comforted by that. Perhaps her talent had already reached its zenith.

Her suspicions regarding Master Simmar's death continued to nag at her. Curasir's arrival seemed oddly timed. Had he been here sooner? Was he involved, somehow?

Jamana caught up with her as she came out of the copyist room. "You have been avoiding me!" he accused, but his grin remained as huge as ever.

"No, I haven't. I've just been… thinking."

"How can I tell you my secret if you're too busy thinking?"

Seri wrinkled an eyebrow. "I thought you didn't have permission to tell me."

"That was then. This is now. Come on!"

Seri hesitated. "I just… I…"

"I will not accept any answer from you, except 'Yes, Jamana. Show me this secret.'"

"Yes, Jamana. Show me this secret." She gave an exaggerated sigh.

"Wonderful!" He bowed and led the way.

Seri had to admit her curiosity grew the longer they walked. Jamana took her toward the Masters' quarters, but then rounded the corner which led to the Inner Sanctum stairs. Right before reaching the stairs, Jamana turned into a small hallway that appeared to go nowhere. More like an antechamber for visitors before they went downstairs, Seri assumed.

Jamana checked to make sure no one else was nearby, then knocked on the left wall of the antechamber. They waited for a few moments. Seri opened her mouth to say something, but Jamana raised his hand.

Right at Seri's eye-level, a portion of the wall slid inwards and off to the side, revealing a passageway barely wide enough to crawl through. Dravid grinned at her from inside.

"What are you doing here?" Seri's voice exploded with joy.

Dravid laughed and jumped down from the passage. Seri grabbed him in a tight hug, then released him just as quickly. She took a step back and composed herself. Jamana looked even happier than usual. Was he bouncing on his toes?

"Well?" Seri asked. "Are you going to explain?"

"I did not want to leave," Dravid said. "After they made me get on the boat, I waited until we were out of sight of the island. Then I paid the rower to bring me back. He didn't care, and I paid him very well." He gestured back at the passage. "Just before the incident, Jamana and I had discovered these passages. I've been hiding there since. Jamana brings me food."

"Which is easy, since I keep getting sent to work in the kitchen," Jamana said.

Seri shot him a look. That explained his frequent kitchen duty. He was deliberately getting himself punished. What a friend.

"It's not bad at all," Dravid said. He looked back into the passage. "I have a good place to sleep, and there's so much to learn back there."

Seri eyed the passage. "Where does it go? Why is it here?"

Dravid grabbed the edge and effortlessly pulled himself back up. "Come on. I'll show you!"

Jamana gestured. "You go ahead, Seri. I am too big for that little tunnel." He offered his hands for her to step on.

Seri stepped on his hands and accepted Dravid's help in climbing up. "It'll be tight here just for a moment, while I put the cover back up."

Seri pushed herself up against the wall and let Dravid get past her once he got the cover in place. It was a surprisingly intimate moment and she felt a surge of embarrassment. Once Dravid moved far enough ahead, she followed on hands and knees. She had expected the passageway to be totally dark, but small slits here and there let light stream in from somewhere. It had been bad enough learning her way around the citadels themselves. She became completely confused in these secret passageways once Dravid took a couple of turns.

"Don't worry about getting lost," he said. "There aren't that many passages and I've mapped them all now."

Seri found the passages clean, to her relief, and quite spacious. "Jamana could have fit in here," she said aloud.

"I know it. I think he doesn't like enclosed spaces. He came in just a little bit the first day we found these, but hasn't come back."

"How did you find them?"

Dravid chuckled. "Honestly? It was my big mouth. I said something stupid about Mandiatans, and Jamana did not approve. He tossed me into the wall. I hit the entrance and it came loose. After that, I just had to explore it all."

Seri frowned. She couldn't picture big, gentle Jamana throwing someone against a wall. Dravid must have said something truly insulting.

The passage opened up into a tiny room about a quarter of the size of Seri's bedroom. A mattress took up most of the room, leaving only a narrow gap beside it. Dravid dropped down onto the mattress and laughed. Seri crawled in and stood up beside him. Dravid pointed and Seri looked up. Above her head, a glass window let the sun shine in.

"We've tried to find that window outside," Dravid said. "We've walked all over as much of the top of the citadel as we can, and, well, we just can't find it."

"So this is where you've been the last couple of weeks?" It was a stupid question, but Seri felt somewhat uncomfortable. After all, she was standing inside a young man's bedchamber. Her mother would have been shocked at the impropriety.

"Most of the time," Dravid said. "I wander through the other tunnels and listen in on some things. Jamana brings me books to read, too."

"But... why? Why are you doing this?"

Dravid sat up, looking a bit grim. "My father was against my becoming a mage," he said. "If I were to return home to Kuktarma, he would never let me leave again. If I am to continue my education, I must stay. When the new master is chosen and arrives, I will reveal myself to him and plead my case. With any luck, he'll admire my dedication and let me stay on as his acolyte."

"Or he may punish you for your disobedience and send you home, anyway!"

"I'll take my chance." Dravid shrugged. He sat cross-legged. "Now that you know the secret, you can come any time," he offered. "There's a lot to see in here."

"Like what?"

He grinned and reached for the passage they had entered. "Let me show you something incredible."

He led the way back up the passage and took a different turn. At least, Seri assumed it to be a different turn. After a few minutes, Dravid paused, then turned himself around to face her.

"Look here." He pointed at the side wall of the passage. Seri saw a tight grid of metal that allowed airflow. Beyond it, she could see a room, but couldn't make out any details.

"It's one of the rooms the Lords stay in when they come for the Passing!" Dravid said, excitement lacing his voice. "The passage circles around and has one of these grids at each room."

Seri's head filled with the possibilities. "Were these passages designed to spy on them?"

"I don't know, but that's only half of it. Follow me!"

A few feet later, Dravid turned into a new passage that sloped up in a gentle curve. "We are now below the pillars that support the King's throne room," he explained. He touched a portion of the wall with a slight indentation. "This is one of them."

After a long crawl upward, the passage leveled out and they entered another tiny room. Like Dravid's bedchamber, a glass window let the sunlight in, but the floor demanded Seri's attention.

In the center of the circular room gaped a three-foot-wide opening. Dravid gestured for Seri to come closer. "But be careful."

She came to the opening and looked down. Her mouth dropped open. An enormous chamber waited below them. She instantly knew it must be the Inner Sanctum, where the Passing took place.

Like their vantage point, the Sanctum was circular. Six platforms, divided by round marble pillars, surrounded a high dais directly below them. Behind each platform hung a huge tapestry depicting the crest of each of the six lands. Seri's eyes instinctively sought out the golden sheaves of grain on a purple field, Arazu's symbol. After a glance at the other tapestries, her eyes wandered back to the central dais. The stone below them looked as if it had been scorched many times.

"The Heart of Fire," she breathed.

"The what?"

"That's where it manifests," she said. "Master Hain told me. When the King releases his power, it forms a heart of fire within the matrices of the other powers."

"Oh. I never knew that." Dravid nodded, eyeing the scorched platform.

Seri stared down at the dais, the platforms, the tapestries. And abruptly, everything changed. Instead of the Inner Sanctum, she stared down into a swirling vortex. At first, her brain refused to process what she saw. It was too bizarre. As her eyes gained focus, she began to comprehend. The vortex churned with a myriad of colors, swirls of light, light that seemed almost physical. The spinning of the vortex moved at a uniform rate, but everything else spoke of chaos. Curving beams of light shot out from it in every conceivable direction, dozens every second, sometimes more than she could count.

Dravid grabbed her by the back of her robe and yanked hard. She blinked and the vortex vanished. She stared down into the Inner Sanctum, empty once more.

"Are you all right?" he asked. "You almost tipped over!"

Seri took a deep breath and let it out. "Yes, I think so. Sorry. I... saw something."

"Does it have to do with the star-eye thing?"

She glanced at him. "I guess Jamana told you about that."

He shrugged. "He tells me lots of things."

Seri pulled back away from the opening and closed her eyes. This had been far worse than anything she had ever seen. And what did it mean? If the Otherworld was the source of magic, as Curasir had said, it made sense for this spot to be significant. But what she had seen did not look stable. In fact, it looked more than anything as if it were.... unraveling.

(((17)))

Despite his mother's warnings, Marshal made several more surreptitious attempts to control the strange power within him. He made sure not to bring his hands together again. He succeeded only once in channeling a vibration from one hand into a small tree. The resulting explosion sent a few shards of wood flying in all directions. One grazed his cheek, but the wound was almost indistinguishable from the scars left by the curse-stalker.

Two weeks of travel went by without event. Aelia pressed on doggedly, continuing to travel seven days each week, ignoring Rest Days. At first, Victor had balked at this, worried that they would get cursed for traveling on a Rest Day. Aelia calmly explained that curses only resulted from serious crimes, no matter what overzealous priests might claim.

They passed through five villages over the course of their journey. For the most part, people treated them kindly and without malice. Marshal's scarred face elicited a number of stares and comments, but no one attempted to interfere with them. Marshal began to doubt Volraag's threats had been serious.

The weather continued to warm as they descended out of the foothills. They saw their last snow only six days out. Afterwards, generally cloudy skies produced little precipitation.

The first rain of the season arrived on the day they reached the large town of Efesun. The size of it made Drusa's Crossing look quaint in comparison. Efesun sat on the Trebia River, which flowed down from the mountains, circled the outer edges of Varioch, and cut through Rasna before it reached the sea. Victor's mood brightened when Aelia announced they would be staying at an inn that night.

Marshal had never stayed at an inn. In fact, he had never slept anywhere but at home or out in the wilderness. He paid little attention to the innkeeper and Aelia's negotiations. Instead, his eyes wandered through the common room, fascinated by the variety of other travelers. Short, tall, skinny, fat, virtually every shade of skin from pasty white to nearly jet black.

"People come here from all over to trade stuff from the mountains," Victor said beside him. "You could probably find just about anything here."

"Just the one night?" the innkeeper's loud voice asked. Marshal turned back to see Aelia handing him some coins. He wondered where she had gotten them. Villagers almost never paid her in coin.

"Yes, and we'll be looking for passage across the river tomorrow," Aelia said. "If you have any suggestions, I would welcome them."

The innkeeper, a stout man dressed in immaculate clothing save for a filthy hand towel tossed over his shoulder, furrowed his brow. "Across the river?" he repeated. "Not down it? There's naught to find across the river, milady, exceptin' the Great Plains."

"Nevertheless, that is our course," she said. "Boys, let's find our room."

The small room contained only two unusually soft beds. Marshal tested one while Aelia took off her coat and stretched. "I am exhausted," she announced. "Victor, if you two want to get something to eat in the common room, just have them charge it to me. I'm going to bed early." She hesitated a moment, then added: "Just be careful."

Victor and Marshal returned to the common room and found seats at a table. The heat in the room felt almost oppressive, thanks to the crowd and an enormous fireplace. Both boys shed their coats.

Marshal again wondered at the diversity of the crowd, but something else soon drew his stares. The serving girl who brought them some drinks dressed nothing like the girls back in Drusa's Crossing. Her tight pants emphasized the shape of her hips, and her neckline plunged so low her ample bosom seemed on the verge of spilling out at any moment. Victor asked her for two plates and she moved away, swaying between the tables with careful grace.

Victor nudged him hard. "Stop staring!" He glanced around. "But to be honest, I'm right there with you. She'd keep me warm at night. I can tell you that much!"

Marshal looked at him, wondering about Careen, the girl Victor had left back home.

"It feels so good to be indoors again!" Victor said. "I am so sick of sleeping outside." He frowned a little. "Your mom mentioned going to the Great Plains. I sure wish she'd tell us where we're going. I don't suppose you know?"

Marshal shook his head.

"Yeah, I didn't think so. She likes her secrets, I guess."

Victor's attention was drawn to two men at the next table playing Mages and Lords. He elbowed Marshal and pointed. Marshal gave the game a cursory look. The deck appeared newer than Victor's old copy, but otherwise looked the same.

"Wait! What's that card?" Victor exclaimed. He got to his feet and looked down at the game.

One of the players looked up. "The High Master Mage, o' course. Haven't you played before?"

"I've played all my life!" Victor said. "But I've never seen that!"

"Then you haven't been playin' with all twenty-one cards," the other player said, chuckling.

"But… there's twenty cards…"

"Twenty-one. Devouring fire, boy. How do you even play the game without the High Master?"

Victor argued half-heartedly, but Marshal lost interest. His eyes wandered around the room again. Mentally, he tried to identify the lands each traveler hailed from. Those from Ch'olan were easy to spot with their brown skin and unique clothes. Those with even darker skin must come from Mandiata. Some of these men must be from Rasna, but he couldn't tell for sure.

Victor returned to his seat, fuming. "High Master Mage! Hmph. Looks like a woman on the card to me. Stupid card. Stupid rules." He scowled at the ongoing game. "Can't believe I've been playing wrong all this time," he said in a much quieter tone.

The serving girl returned with their food - pork and boiled vegetables. Despite Victor's warning, Marshal couldn't help staring some more, especially when she bent over to set the plates on the table. It gave him an unfamiliar feeling, a longing he couldn't explain.

The girl smiled without scorn, a look Marshal wasn't used to seeing from girls his age. "You have pretty eyes underneath those scars," she said. "Do you have a name?"

"Ah, he can't speak," Victor said. He leaned closer toward the girl. "Truth be told, my older sister and I have been caring for him for years. He was abandoned, left for dead, actually." He put his arm around Marshal's shoulder. "I like to think of him as the brother I never had. I feel responsible for the poor soul, you know?"

Marshal shook off Victor's arm and shoved him. The girl laughed, drawing attention to herself from nearby tables. She patted Victor's hand. "I think if the truth were really told, it wouldn't be quite like that," she said. She smiled at Marshal again, though this time it seemed tinged with pity.

Marshal scowled at Victor as she left them.

"What? You didn't like my story?" Victor leaned in close and whispered, "It's better than the truth. I mention the word 'curse' and everyone will want to throw you out!"

Marshal took a bite of the pork. The meat had more flavor than usual, and some herbs were unfamiliar, but he liked it. Beside him, Victor sighed. "I didn't even get her name."

After a few more bites, Marshal's mood soured. The pity in the girl's eyes consumed his thoughts. The food felt like iron in his stomach, weighing him down and poisoning his guts. He pushed the plate away and stood up.

"Where are you going?" Victor asked.

Marshal walked toward the door, ducking past other patrons who ignored him.

"Don't be too late," Victor called after him. "I don't want to explain to your mom that you ran off!"

"His mom, is it?" Marshal heard the serving girl ask. Despite his mood, he smiled.

Marshal stepped outside and experienced a drastic temperature drop. He shivered, realizing he had left his coat with Victor. Rather than return for it, he rubbed his arms and set out down the street, anyway.

The sun had set only a few minutes earlier, and a slight grayness still tinted the cloudy sky. The rain had stopped for the moment, but water dripped from everything. Muddy puddles dotted the ground, making his passage difficult. The twilight and dampness matched Marshal's mood. Even in a completely foreign place like this, he couldn't escape the pity. Victor certainly hadn't helped.

A child about half his size dashed past him, ignoring the puddles as if she were in a desperate hurry.

A second later, he realized why. Half a dozen other children of various sizes charged past him in pursuit of the first. A couple of them called after her. The word "curse" caught Marshal's attention.

The children turned down an alley only a block ahead. Marshal picked up his pace to follow them.

The pursued child stood with her back to a wall. Light spilled out of the windows around her, giving Marshal a clear view. She wore ragged clothes hardly substantial enough for the cold weather. Her right arm looked twisted, malformed like the bones of a bird's wing. She held it tightly to her chest as she looked around at her tormentors.

The other children mocked her, throwing out insult after insult. Marshal recognized the slurs; he had heard them often enough throughout his life. For a moment, he almost turned away and returned to the inn. But something inside him rose up in his chest. Maybe memories of Titus, or maybe the serving girl's pitying look had aroused his anger enough to act. He stepped into the circle of children.

They fell silent. In the dark, all they could tell was that an adult had entered their domain. Like all children, they immediately felt the dread of authority and perhaps a little shame.

"She's a cursed one," one of the boys offered.

"Look at 'er arm!" another said.

Marshal stepped into the light beside the girl and turned to face the other children. They reacted in shock.

"Look at his face!"

"He's cursed, too!"

"Stay back! He might curse you! Grown up curses can spread!"

"Can not!"

"Can too!"

Marshal took a step toward the children, hoping to intimidate them into abandoning this entertainment. While most of them fell back, one boy wasn't impressed. He waved a stick at Marshal.

"We should smack both of them!"

"Are you crazy? He's a grown up!"

"A cursed grown up! He deserves it, too!"

The other children seemed to be regaining their courage. Marshal saw one bend down and pick up a large rock. He needed to end this. Unable to think of anything else, he pulled out Volraag's dagger.

Several of the children gasped. As a group, they began to back away.

"We didn't mean anything," one girl whimpered. "She's just cursed, is all."

The children broke and ran. Marshal took one step after them and put the dagger away. In the shadows, he thought he spotted a taller figure, hooded and standing silent at the entrance to the alley. He remained motionless as the children rushed past him.

At that moment, a bright light erupted behind Marshal. He turned and blinked several times. It came from somewhere beyond the alley. Had a building caught fire? No, fire would flicker. This light held steady. Not quite sunlight, but something like it. He felt he should know it, but not like this.

Then he saw the shadow. At first, he saw only the usual outline of a man, elongated somewhat by the light. He couldn't see the figure of the man himself, somewhere within the light. The light blinded him if he looked at it too directly.

The shadow stretched. Where it had been long and thin, it grew longer and thinner, reaching from one end of the alley to the other. How tall was the man who could cast such a thing? More than that, the proportions were all wrong. Angled light could exaggerate shadows, but not like this. The source could not be human. Nor did it seem anything like the eidolon he had seen before.

As abruptly as it had come, the light vanished and with it, the shadow. Marshal shut his eyes to regain his night vision. Only then did he remember the hooded figure he had seen before the light. He turned back to the end of the alley, but the hooded man had disappeared too.

He felt a small hand reach out and take his. He looked down and saw the girl with the twisted arm. With the light and shadow, he had completely forgotten she was still there.

"Thank you," she whispered.

Marshal knelt in the mud beside her and gingerly touched her arm. He gave a rueful smile, trying to indicate that he understood. She reached up with her good arm and brushed his scars.

"Until all curses are lifted," she said. She broke away and ran down the alley and out into the street.

Marshal looked around, from one end of the alley to the other. What had happened? In the growing darkness, none of it seemed real any more. He made his way back onto the street and looked for the inn.

<h1 style="text-align:center">(((18)))</h1>

The current helped propel the rowboat into the shoreline with enough force to ground it. "Watch your step gettin' out," the boatman offered. "The Trebia's like pure ice right now. Get your foot in that and you'll be wantin' to cut it off."

"Thank you, sir," Aelia said. She got to her feet, leaned on Marshal, and stepped across to dry land.

Marshal saw how many coins Aelia had been forced to pay the man. It seemed an exorbitant sum just to cross a river, but the crossing had not been without difficulty. Due to the high banks and cliffs on this side of the river, they had actually started the crossing half a mile upstream from Efesun. The boatman insisted this was the nearest spot with a low bank suitable for landing. The skies remained cloudy as ever, but it had not rained again.

"How far are the Great Plains?" Victor asked. He clambered after Aelia.

"Not far," the boatman answered. He pointed downstream and up. "You can see them from up there. Great views all around."

Marshal looked. The bank rose rapidly into a high cliff. At its peak, a large rock platform jutted out over the river before it turned the bend and passed Efesun.

"Come on, Marshal. Let's go check it out!" Without waiting, Victor started to climb.

Marshal jumped out of the boat and landed awkwardly. Aelia caught his arm and steadied him. The boatman immediately pulled on his oars to get back into the main current. "Theon's wings shelter you!" he called.

Aelia glanced up at the cliffs. "You go ahead," she said. "I'll wait down here with our baggage." Marshal nodded and dropped his pack. He scrambled up after Victor, ignoring the usual numbness and tingling in his hands and feet.

In short order, the two young men reached the top and stood on the rocky outcropping. Below them, the Trebia River churned as it began to swing around to Efesun. They could see the entire town from their vantage point.

Marshal thought he recognized the inn they had slept in. He couldn't see the alley where he had the strange encounter. He wondered what had happened to the little girl. For that matter, how did such a small girl get cursed? How could she have done something so wrong? Or was she, like him, the child of one of the Lords?

"I still think it's stupid," Victor said. "Why a High Master Mage? There's no such thing in real life. Everyone knows there are only six Master Mages on Zes Sivas."

It took Marshal a moment to realize Victor was talking about the card game again.

"My father gave me that deck." Victor turned to look at Marshal. His face had an odd look around his eyes. "Your mom said it would fade… but it hasn't. Not much." He looked away, past Efesun, perhaps toward Drusa's Crossing.

The Bindings toward home. Marshal wondered what that felt like. He reached his hand toward Victor's shoulder, but stopped when it shook. Stupid gesture, anyway.

"Tell me your curse."

Marshal and Victor spun around. A man stood a few feet behind them, hooded and clothed from head to toe in shades of gray.

"Who are you?" Victor asked, his hand instinctively straying to his flail.

The man reached up and pulled his hood back. Marshal and Victor took a step back simultaneously. The hood uncovered a hairless head covered in dead-looking skin a horrid shade of grayish-green. Large strips of it flaked off, revealing even more unhealthy looking skin below. His parched lips looked as if they had not tasted water in a week.

"I am not here for you," he told Victor, his eyes on Marshal. "I am only here for the cursed one."

Victor stepped between Marshal and the stranger. "You know, I didn't think anyone could be uglier than Marshal, but you proved me wrong. What happened to you?"

The stranger's eyes flicked to Victor. "Step aside, and I will not harm you."

Victor let his flail hang down. "Can't do that. I'm bound to him."

"That is… unfortunate."

The stranger leaped forward, hidden blades emerging from both wrists. Victor swung his flail in an uppercut. The stranger easily dodged under it and slashed with one of his blades. Victor fell back, dropped his flail and clutched at his chest. Redness seeped through his fingers, and he dropped to a knee.

Before Marshal could even think about reacting, the stranger lunged beside him. One blade rested against his neck while the other pointed at his heart. Both of Marshal's hands, held out helplessly, began to vibrate.

"Tell me your curse."

Marshal stared into the eyes of the assassin. Unlike the diseased flesh that surrounded them, the eyes shone clear and bright. The light brown irises appeared as sparks of life itself surrounded by death and decay.

"Tell me your curse!" The assassin seemed almost desperate for the answer.

"He can't!" Victor growled between clenched teeth. He kept one arm held tight against his chest while he tried to find his fallen flail. "He has no voice!"

The assassin looked taken aback. Uncertainty filled his eyes. Marshal could feel a seizure building up within and tried to focus it. If he could channel the power through his hands, maybe he could blow this killer off the rock. He gritted his teeth, concentrating.

The assassin glanced back at Victor. "Then you must speak for him," he decided. "Tell me his curse, or I will kill you once I am done with him."

Victor breathed hard, his face red and furious. "I'm not telling you anything!" He found the flail's handle and lifted it.

Out of the corner of his eye, Marshal watched Victor stagger to his feet and swing the flail once more. The stranger threw Marshal to the ground, shoving both of them under the flail's trajectory. Victor screamed in pain and collapsed. He rolled away from them, holding his chest.

"My curse is a death that never ends," the assassin whispered to Marshal. "It is proof that there is no justice in this world, no meaning, just as there will be no justice or meaning for your death." He paused.

"Are you... shaking?" His eyes widened slightly. "This is not the trembling of a coward, but..."

Marshal gritted his teeth, closed his eyes and opened his mouth in a silent scream. Concentrating this hard brought physical pain to his head, but the results were spectacular.

Rather than channeling the power upwards toward the enemy, his body channeled it down into the rock below them. A loud crack echoed across the river, followed by a sound almost like the shattering of glass. The entire rock platform exploded into countless shards that plunged downward along with Marshal and his attacker.

The shock of the frigid water drove the air from Marshal's lungs. He struggled desperately to get back to the surface. His head erupted from the water and he gasped, sucking in what air he could before the river dragged him under a second time. The current swept him around the bend in the river. Searing pain pierced his body all over, especially where his exposed skin contacted the water. He flailed about, but his arms didn't seem to be responding as he wanted.

He managed to get to the surface again, pulling in air once more. Even so, he knew some of the icy water had found its way into his lungs. He felt a deep cold permeating his body. He thrashed, trying to get some momentum toward the shore, but continued to be swept along against his will. He caught a glimpse of docks and several small boats as he rushed past Efesun. Did no one see him?

What had happened to the assassin? Marshal flailed in a circle, but saw no sign of his attacker. Only a supreme effort kept his head above the water, and he knew he couldn't keep it up for long. He plunged under, only to rise again and again. The cliffs gave way to more trees along the bank.

A hand with a grip like iron took hold of his left arm, and he jerked to a stop mid-rapid. His shoulder felt like something had broken. The water continued to pour over him, trying to pull him down and away, but the hand held firm. Someone dragged Marshal out of the water and onto a sandy bank.

His body immediately began to convulse in chills, like his usual seizures, only wet and cold. He had a vague sense of a large figure standing over him.

Heat flooded him as an impressive fire erupted only a foot away. Strong hands removed his clothing, holding him through the convulsions. His body began to calm.

He looked up at his rescuer through bleary eyes. He saw a tall figure with extremely angular features and eyes that didn't seem to match somehow.

"Fear not, Marshal, son of Varion and Aelia," said a commanding voice. "I am Talinir of the Eldanim and I am here to help you."

•••••

Stripped of his clothes and wrapped in blankets beside a roaring fire, Marshal felt warmth begin to return to his body. Talinir left him briefly and returned carrying Victor, with Aelia close behind.

Marshal couldn't stop staring at his rescuer, though he tried a few times. A glance at Victor showed that he wasn't the only one. Victor, his expression just shy of open-mouthed wonder, never took his eyes off the stranger who claimed to be Eldanim. Only Aelia seemed unfazed. After greeting Talinir with a respectful bow and bandaging Victor's chest, she focused her attention on Marshal. Despite her fussing, she could do little. Talinir had taken care of everything.

After checking on something in his pack, Talinir stood and hung an unusual pot of water over the fire. Marshal's eyes followed his frame all the way to his face. Talinir was tall, remarkably so, but seemed taller still. Marshal couldn't figure it out. Something about his height seemed impossible. When they had been standing a few minutes ago, he towered over Victor, at perhaps six and a half feet. But he seemed even taller, somehow. It was as if Marshal's eyes couldn't fully grasp him.

He wasn't exceptionally skinny, either. His muscles matched his frame. Marshal's arm still ached from the strength that had pulled him out of the water. He had never felt a grip that powerful, even when Balaes the blacksmith had been demonstrating how to hold a hammer.

"The tea will be ready soon," Talinir said. He added some leaves to the pot, and a pleasant aroma spread out from the fire.

The Eldanim's sharp and angular face breathed in the steam. His chin, cheekbones, nose - their distinct edges appeared almost carved from dark tan rock. His dark hair, not quite black, hung past his shoulders.

But his eyes kept drawing Marshal's attention, even more than the odd height. Talinir's eyes did not match. The left eye, blue and quite ordinary, glanced at Marshal over the fire. The right eye, though, was solid black, sprinkled with shining white spots of various sizes, like a tiny globe full of stars.

The more Marshal watched, the more he noticed something unusual. Talinir seemed inordinately distracted every so often. He appeared smiling and pleasant most of the time, but every few minutes he would tilt his head (always to the right, Marshal noted) and frown. He seemed to be seeing or hearing something the rest of them could not detect. Marshal suspected it had something to do with the strange eye. He wondered what Talinir could see. With a start, he remembered the assassin. He looked around, peering into the brush.

"I saw no sign of your attacker," Talinir said, as if reading his thoughts. "He must have been swept further downriver."

"Who was he?" Aelia asked, looking at Victor.

The other young man tore his eyes from the stranger. "He was a cursed freak! His skin was peeling off and he--"

"Was he after Marshal or both of you?" Aelia interrupted.

"He was after Marshal. I tried to stop him. I really did."

"I know you did, Victor." Aelia adjusted the blanket around Marshal's shoulders. "Volraag must have sent him."

With a sigh, she got to her feet and faced Talinir. She bowed for the second time. "Most noble warden of the Eldanim," she began, "I cannot thank you enough for saving my son's life."

Talinir inclined his head and stirred the tea.

"In fact, I am exceedingly pleased to see you, regardless of the circumstances. We were searching for you."

Talinir arched his eyebrows. With the angularity of his face, they formed shapes more like arrowheads than arches. "You were looking for me?"

"Not you specifically," Aelia admitted. "I regret that, until now, I did not know you by name. But we were searching for the Eldanim. Had we failed to meet one of you, my plan was to enter the Great Plains in search of Intal Eldanir."

Talinir spread his hands, one holding the wooden spoon. "You have found me. What can I do for you, Aelia, daughter of Evander? I know you have been seeking my people. We heard your call weeks ago. I was unaware that any humans held a Ranir Stone."

A strange expression crossed Aelia's face, Marshal noted. He had never heard his grandfather's name from anyone's lips but his mother's. How had Talinir known it? And what did he mean by her call? Was it the time Marshal had seen her chanting in the dark? Maybe the Ranir Stone was the glowing thing he had seen.

Aelia put her hands on Marshal's shoulders. "If you remember my father, you will know why this is important. My son is cursed, through no fault of his own. I wish to petition the Eldanim to lift his curse."

Marshal's eyes widened, and he heard Victor's intake of breath. So that was what Aelia had been planning all this time. It made some sense. The Eldanim were said to be creatures of magic. Curses were caused by magic. If anyone could undo a curse, surely it would be them. He felt a strange feeling amid the chills. Hope. But even as the feeling rose, he pushed it back down. Curses lasted until death. This was the way of the world.

Talinir seemed unaffected by Aelia's statement. With careful skill, he removed the pot from the fire and poured the steaming liquid into four cups. "I find that adding sugar dulls the sharpness of the leaves and allows one to enjoy the flavor even more," he said.

"What's sugar?" Victor wondered.

Talinir stopped in mid-pour. "You don't know about sugar?" He looked to Marshal, who also shook his head. "Amazing. Well, then I shall add extra, so that you will really enjoy this." He took out a sealed pouch, opened it, and began measuring quantities of a brown grainy substance into the cups. "I am lying to you, I must admit. I always add extra."

Throughout all this, Aelia stood stiff, a confused expression growing on her face.

"It's ready," Talinir announced. He handed one cup to Victor, and another to Marshal. He offered the third to Aelia, who stared at him.

Talinir met her gaze for a moment, then sighed. He set the cup down on the ground near her. He returned to the other side of the fire and sat cross-legged on a large rock. He took a sip of his tea and smiled. He took another sip and set the cup beside him.

"I do not believe you will find receptive ears to your petition," he said. "Humans created the curses. They must deal with the consequences." Seeing the look on her face, he hastened to add, "That is the prevailing opinion, I should say. I do not say that I agree with it. But the majority of the High Council are strongly opposed to any involvement with humans."

"Then why are you out here?" Victor asked.

Talinir smiled. "I am a warden. A select number of us roam the country around Intal Eldanir, guarding it from harm."

"What harm?"

"Ah, that would require a lengthy explanation. Perhaps another time."

Marshal finally took a sip of the tea. The sweetness surprised him so much that he almost didn't notice the flavor. On rare occasions, his mother had obtained honey and sweetened some tea with it, but this was different. It lacked the thickness and distinct flavor of honey, but included even more sweetness. His second sip gave him more of an idea of the tea's flavor itself, dark and spicy, though muted by the sugar. What a wonderful combination. He drank deeper, letting the warmth of it flood through his body.

"Ah, you see? Sugar in tea. One of this world's greatest accomplishments."

(((19)))

Everything made sense now.

Kishin retrieved the pack he had hidden before his confrontation with Marshal and checked it for tampering. It had taken him hours to make his way back after being swept down river. An inconvenience, but not discouraging.

No wonder Volraag wanted this young man dead. He had to be Lord Varion's first-born son. Nothing else could explain enough k'uh to shatter rock.

Kishin glanced up at the cliff bank. He could see the spot where the rock platform had been. What rock remained looked scarred and unnatural.

Once Kishin killed the target, the power would pass to Volraag. And he had offered "usual rates." Kishin snorted. He would demand much greater payment, once he had accomplished this one.

That in itself had become much harder now. Discovering the target had power created new factors to consider, as well as the unusual nature of his curse.

More disturbing was the help the target had obtained. Kishin had not encountered one in many years, but he recognized an Eldani warden. If the target stayed with him, it would make things far more difficult. The Eldanim were imposing warriors, and the wardens were the best of the best. They trained to literally fight opponents in two different worlds at the same time.

He smiled grimly. What he had considered an easy job had turned into a significant challenge. Since the coming of his curse, Kishin had found few pleasures remaining in his life. But a challenge of this magnitude could be immensely gratifying. When he succeeded in taking Marshal's life, it would be the most pleasure he had enjoyed in many years.

<h1 align="center">(((20)))</h1>

Marshal woke the next morning with a start. In his dreams, the leper assassin had started growing until he became the shadow man from Efesun. In the aftermath of the fight, he had almost forgotten that strange encounter the night before.

As so often happened, he would have to move on with his questions unanswered. Somehow, he suspected the warden had a good idea about the nature of the shadow man, if anyone did.

Talinir sat awake, watching the fire. When he saw Marshal sit up, he prepared a cup of tea and offered it to him. "This will help wake you up, while warming you," he said.

Marshal accepted it gratefully. The tea tasted just as sweet as the night before, but this time he was used to it. He smiled and inhaled the steam coming off the cup.

Talinir chuckled and sat back with his own cup. "Whenever I can, I start the day with this. Not only does it taste wonderful, it spurs the mind into wakefulness." He took a sip. "Some of the other wardens prefer a drink made with crushed beans. Can you imagine? It actually smells quite wonderful, but I prefer tea. I've worked for years to concoct the perfect recipe. You can come up with so many different varieties, you know."

While he enjoyed the warden's conversation, Marshal couldn't help wondering about more serious topics, like the assassin. Talinir seemed happy to babble on about his tea, but said very little when asked about other things the night before.

Talinir noticed the expression on his face and leaned forward. He spoke in a low tone, even though Victor and Aelia still slept. "I know that you are concerned over many things. I pledge to you now. As long as I am with you, no harm will come to you or your mother. You have the word of Talinir, Eldani warden." He made a curious gesture with three fingers laid against his face, one across his eye and the other two pointing toward his ear.

Aelia yawned and sat up. Talinir fetched another cup and poured it. "Another cup of tea to start your day, madam?" Aelia accepted the cup with a few blinks and a nod.

Marshal took another sip, then realized he felt a strong need. He got to his feet and sought privacy. When he returned, Victor had awakened, grumbling as usual. After a short breakfast, all four of them set out together with Talinir in the lead. From what Marshal could gather, he had agreed to lead them to Intal Eldanir, his city.

What would that be like? As fascinating as he found Talinir, Marshal had a hard time imagining an entire city of Eldanim. Talinir doubted they would be willing to lift Marshal's curse. So what was the point of going? Did Aelia think she could change their minds?

All his life, Marshal had trusted his mother. He never had cause not to. But the past few weeks had changed all of that. She had secrets, so many secrets, things she had never told him. Now, out of nowhere, she wanted to get his curse lifted and had brought them to petition the Eldanim, of all people.

Marshal felt again the weight of Volraag's dagger. It was always there, beckoning him. He still didn't think he had the strength to use it on himself. He berated himself for his cowardice.

Everyone Marshal knew had aspirations, goals in life. Many in Drusa's Crossing only aspired to continuing the family business, whether fisherman, blacksmith, or farmer. Others, such as Victor, aspired to leave the village and find purpose elsewhere.

Marshal had no aspirations. He was cursed, and that's all there was to it. He had never dared dream that things could be any different. Now, the possibility had been dangled in front of him, however remote, and it terrified him, if he was honest with himself. For if he began to believe it, then so much would change. He could have aspirations, hopes, dreams.

But dreams died. Hopes failed. And aspirations, unless carefully controlled, only led to misery. This much he had seen in his short life, and he knew it to be true.

The cursed had no future.

•••••

Talinir showed himself a swift trailblazer. Despite there being no real road beyond the Trebia, Talinir led them by open paths, mostly easy to traverse. It wasn't long before they emerged from the woods and the Great Plains stretched before them.

Marshal stared in awe. The line of trees from which they had emerged curved off in either direction until it faded from view. The ground in front of them was flat. Just... flat.

"Edin Na Zu." Victor had heard the expression once from a visitor from Arazu. Marshal suspected Victor had no idea what it meant, but he liked it for some reason.

Growing up at the feet of the mountains, Marshal had assumed the whole world to be the same. The earth beneath his feet curved up and down, forming hills and valleys, crevices and peaks. Towns grew on flat areas, such as could be found. Never in his life had he imagined a flat area this massive, this vast.

"There's no end to it," Victor said. Indeed, at the furthest distance they could see, the sky seemed to come down to meet the grass.

"Hailstones and coals of fire!" Talinir murmured. Marshal glanced at him. The Eldani warden was not awestruck over the plains - why would he be? He stared straight ahead at something Marshal couldn't see.

"I need the three of you to remain right here," Talinir said. His tone of voice had become commanding again. "Whatever you see... or think you see, do not interfere."

"What?" Victor's question went unanswered as Talinir strode forward into the open. He dropped his pack and unsheathed the sword from his belt.

All three of them stared at the sword. It gleamed in the weak sunlight, flawless and smooth. The blade stretched around two and a half feet long with a slight curve. Marshal couldn't tell whether it held a double or single edge. But as Talinir took a few practice swings, Marshal's eyes couldn't stop following it. The air behind the blade shimmered as it swept through.

Talinir took a dramatic stance about ten feet away, facing away from them. He held his sword in front of him, both hands grasping the lengthy hilt. A long moment passed. Abruptly, he took a step backward and swung up, releasing the sword with his left hand. Then he dodged to the left. His blade swept down and back.

Fascinated, Marshal watched as Talinir continued what seemed to be an elaborate dance of some kind. He stepped forward, back, right and left, dodged rapidly, walked slowly. His movements constantly changed, but he wielded the sword through it all - thrusting, slashing, blocking.

"I've heard about this," Victor said. "It's a kind of practice, where you go through a series of moves in a row. You do it over and over to learn them by instinct."

"Perhaps," Aelia said. She did not sound convinced.

In fact, the more Marshal watched, the more he became sure Talinir battled in deadly earnest. The few times he caught a glimpse of the warden's face, it appeared grim and determined. He did not have the look of someone practicing. And why would he have warned them not to interfere?

Talinir's movements became quicker, more urgent. His long hair whipped through the air and around his face. At times, his strikes and dodges became a blur, too fast to understand. Sweat dripped from his head.

Marshal thought he saw something and waited for another opportunity. When Talinir fell back and rolled to his left, he got a full look at the warden's face and confirmed it. Talinir kept his "normal" eye closed. Whatever he fought could only be seen with his starry eye.

In the next moment, Talinir soared six feet through the air and landed hard, rolling uncontrollably. Marshal took an instinctive step forward. He wasn't alone.

"He is wounded!" Aelia exclaimed.

"Is he fighting an invisible monster?" Victor grabbed his flail and took another step. He stopped when Marshal grabbed his arm. "What are you doing? He needs help!"

Marshal shook his head. If he understood, Victor could do nothing to harm the enemy, and he might succeed only in getting himself or Talinir injured further.

Talinir leaped to his feet, the front of his tunic torn to shreds. Marshal thought he saw blood.

"*i hatel indalanim!*" Talinir cried. He lifted his sword in the air, and Marshal swore the air around it warped, curving around the blade. As if in response, his hands began to shake. He let go of Victor. The power flowed through him. He felt it leaving his feet and entering the ground, which trembled in response. Victor shot him a look.

Talinir took three steps and leaped into the air. He landed, or seemed to land, in mid-air, at a height of about eight feet. He stabbed his sword down with both hands, screaming something Marshal couldn't make out.

Again, Talinir tumbled through the air, clearly not in control of himself. He landed hard and lay still. Victor rushed forward, his flail at the ready. Aelia followed, cautious but determined. Marshal stood alone, unsure and trembling.

Victor rushed past Talinir and stopped, looking around. What could he possibly do now?

Aelia knelt beside Talinir. The Eldani waved her back and climbed to one knee. Marshal approached them. His power faded again, back to the familiar tingling that almost never left.

"It's all right," Talinir called to Victor. "It's dying now. It won't trouble us."

Victor turned back, a perplexed expression on his face. "What was it?" he demanded.

Talinir's chest rose and fell in deep breaths. "Tunaldi," he said. "The enemy I spoke of."

Marshal stepped close enough to see Talinir's chest. Aelia pulled away the torn tunic with gentle concern. "The wounds don't look too deep," she said. "But…" She pursed her lips and wrinkled her brow. Marshal looked closer. Talinir's chest, which shared the sharp angles of his face, bore three large scratches, equally spaced. Marshal had seen wounds of this size before, but not like this. Something appeared extremely wrong about them, but he couldn't identify it. He looked to his mother.

Talinir closed his eyes. "The wounds go beyond your ability to heal, though I do appreciate the help," he said. "They require starlight to fully close."

Victor glanced at the sky. "It's still early morning, and it's been cloudy for days."

Talinir gestured back to the edge of the plains. "Bring me my pack."

Marshal ran back and retrieved the warden's pack. When he returned, he found Talinir stretched out on the ground while Aelia worked to clean his wounds. "In the side pocket there." Talinir pointed. Marshal pulled out something that resembled a leather water pouch.

Talinir took the pouch and unscrewed the lid. He turned it upside down and squeezed over his palm. Three drops of a thick, viscous liquid oozed out. He handed the pouch and its lid back to Marshal.

With a sigh of relief, Talinir laid his head back on the ground. He held his hand above his head, the palm facing him. The three drops began to glow. Marshal knelt down to get a better look. The glow of the drops formed into beams that played across Talinir's face. Marshal had never seen starlight during the day, of course, but he assumed he saw it now.

"Liquid stars?" Victor asked. "What's next? Moon bread?"

"It is called starshine," Aelia said. "It is not true starlight, but is close enough for his needs." She frowned at Talinir as she wrapped a bandage around his chest. "I do hope you are using it in moderation, sir warden."

"Of course," Talinir murmured. His normal eye grew distant and unfocused. He seemed to have fallen into a kind of trance. Once Aelia finished with the bandage, she looked down at his face, shaking her head.

"He'll be like that for an hour or so," she said. "I guess we're not getting very far today."

Marshal sat on the grass and looked out across the plains. So many questions raised in the space of a few minutes. What was a tunaldi? Why was it invisible? Were there more of them about? And then there was Talinir's sword. He looked down at his hands again. Why had his power reacted to it so strongly?

"Tell me your curse." The words startled Marshal out of his reverie. He stood and turned, knowing what he would see.

(((21)))

The assassin stood at the tree line, blades in both hands. He looked exactly as he had at the river; the fall had not affected him.

"You again?" Victor got to his feet, still holding his flail, but he winced in the process.

Aelia's eyes narrowed and grew dark. "This is the assassin?" she asked. When Victor nodded, she reached out and slapped Talinir.

The killer took two steps forward. "The warden took three starshine drops. He will not be able to help you now." The assassin's hood hung down again, revealing his decaying face. "I am here for the mute one. You others may go free, providing you tell me your curse."

"I'm starting to think you're my curse," Victor said. He stepped over Talinir and stood beside Marshal.

"No," the assassin said. "You have already told me your curse. You are bound to this one, and when I kill him, the Binding will torment you."

Marshal heard a "sssh" sound and glanced back. Aelia had drawn Talinir's sword. She stood and stepped over the entranced warden. Victor made to follow her, but she put out a hand and stopped him. She walked out alone to face the assassin.

The wind had picked up and whipped Aelia's dirty blonde hair in a flurry to the side of her head. She stopped, unconcerned, the strange sword held at an angle to her side. The assassin cocked his head with what seemed a curious expression.

"You wish to know my curse, assassin?" Aelia's words fell like heavy stones in the open air. "I am Aelia, daughter of Evander. I watched my father betrayed by his best friend, exiled, chased across hundreds of miles, and murdered for protecting me. I have been destitute, hunted, harassed, oppressed, mocked, and raped. You might call any of these things curses. I do not. They shaped me into the woman and mother I am today.

"Behind me stands a young man who is the greatest treasure and blessing of my life. You seek to take that from me. I tell you that you will have to kill me first." She lifted the sword and pointed it toward Kishin. "Do your worst."

Silence ruled the plains. Victor leaned toward Marshal and whispered, "I don't know about him, but your mother scares me!"

Marshal gave a slight nod. He had seen Aelia stand up for herself many times, but never with this intensity.

"So be it," the assassin said. He inclined his head in a bow, then charged forward, his thin blades held out to either side.

Aelia dropped back into a defensive stance, one leg back, the sword held parallel to the ground and across her body.

Right before he reached her, Aelia's opponent swept both blades across himself, then scissored them back, aiming for her outstretched front leg. Unmoved, she deflected them both with a downward swing of Talinir's sword. The clash of metal resounded across the plains, beginning their duel. The assassin attacked, Aelia deflected or dodged, over and over. They danced back and forth, neither showing any clear emotion. As before, Talinir's sword left shimmering air in its wake with each of Aelia's swings.

The assassin drew back a few steps. Aelia did not follow, seeming content to continue her defensive posture.

"Your skill is impressive and unexpected," he acknowledged. "Unless I am mistaken, you appear to have trained with Sakura, though I fail to see how that is possible. You are not one of the Holcan."

"I told you my father's best friend betrayed him," Aelia said. "Before that, he trained me well."

The assassin's hairless eyebrows arched, clearly impressed. He launched another attack. Using his twin blades to his advantage, he slipped past Aelia's defenses and scored a shallow gash across her left thigh. He paused again.

"The problem with Sakura's techniques is that they're almost all defensive," he said. "You may hold me off for a while, but you only delay the inevitable. You cannot stop me."

Marshal was tired, tired of being helpless, tired of letting others fight for him. He started forward, only to have Victor grab his shoulder.

"Are you crazy?" Victor's face showed what he thought the answer to that question might be. "I tried to stop him last time and couldn't. You don't even have a weapon!"

Marshal showed him Aelia's short sword.

"Do you even know how to use that? Come on, Marshal. He's a warrior and we're not!"

Marshal scowled at Victor. For years, Aelia had given him some basic instructions with the sword, though of course he had never shown anyone until now.

Victor let him go. "All right. Let's come at him from either side, then. Might give him something else to think about, at least."

While Victor started moving around to Aelia's right, Marshal ran around to her left. Victor began swinging his flail in a wide loop, limiting the assassin's movement in that direction. Marshal couldn't do the same with his sword, but he moved closer, staying in one of Aelia's defensive stances. He clenched his other fist, trying to focus some of the vibratory power into it. Maybe he could get a hand on the assassin and release the magic directly against him.

Aelia noticed their actions. "I appreciate the thought, boys," she called, "but--"

"But this was the most foolish choice you could make," the assassin interrupted. He feinted at Aelia, forcing her to throw up a defense, then whirled toward Victor.

Marshal took another step forward with the enemy's back toward him. The leper stabbed out toward Victor, who dodged back instinctively. The assassin flipped backwards, rolled, spun, and stabbed. The blade in his left hand pierced Marshal's chest.

"You brought my target toward me."

Aelia screamed and lunged forward. Victor's face paled and he almost dropped the flail.

Marshal looked down at the long, thin blade that had penetrated his sternum. So that's what it felt like. Not much different from getting punched. Then the assassin ripped the blade out and dodged back from Aelia's furious assault. As the blood spurted out, the pain erupted in Marshal's chest.

He dropped the sword and grabbed at his chest with both hands. He wasn't conscious of falling to his knees, or anything else that happened around him. Aelia had always told him the most important thing to do was stop the bleeding, but the blood forced its way around his hands and fingers, running down his chest, dripping to the ground.

Was this dying? Victor screamed something, and part of his brain considered what would happen to the other boy when the Binding broke, unfulfilled. At least Aelia would be spared any more pain and suffering. Volraag would get what he wanted. A lot of good this power would do him; it couldn't even… even…

Marshal slumped to the ground, rolling on to his back. Above him, the sun peeked out through the clouds. It must be nearly noon.

The ground rumbled beneath him. His power? No. Something else. The pain overwhelmed his mind and he faded into darkness.

(((22)))

Seri had just entered Master Hain's office when the earth began to shake again. It started with a mild tremor. The stones of the citadel shook. Master Hain's desk vibrated and a pile of papers slid off.

"Again? Well, that wasn't too--"

A second tremor struck, much stronger than the first, cutting his words off. Both of them struggled to keep their feet as everything around them shook. In the distance, Seri could hear the crash of items small and large falling in different rooms.

"Out!" Master Hain barked. "Get out of the citadel!"

Seri wasted no time in reacting. She threw open the door and raced down the hallway. Familiar now, she turned several corners and descended one wide staircase before finding the way out into the courtyard. Dozens of people poured out from the citadel's doors, with no regard to rank or propriety, from the Masters themselves down to the lowest servants.

Another tremble, stronger than ever, knocked most of them off their feet. Most stayed down, some crying out to Theon, others curling up and closing their eyes. The shaking lasted at least a full minute, though it seemed much longer. A few rocks fell from the exterior wall.

Then it stopped. The cries faded.

Seri cautiously got to her feet. She noticed Curasir first. The Eldani stood unmoved a few feet away from everyone else. His gaze focused toward the center of the island. What did he see in the Otherworld? Did it shake, too?

The fourth tremor erupted, dwarfing the previous tremors with its power, dwarfing even the quake from the day of Seri's arrival at Zes Sivas. She fell again, landing on the stone walkway and tearing her robe around one knee.

The earth split. A narrow crack started a few feet away, next to a kitchen worker who rolled away in terror. The crack widened and lengthened rapidly, running across the courtyard and reaching from the citadel itself to the outer wall.

More screams filled the air. Seri scrambled back away from the crack, as did everyone else. But the crack divided, sending a spur that seemed almost to pursue her. Despite her best efforts, she found herself looking down into the earth. She braced herself, sure that it would continue to widen and she would fall, swallowed up by dirt and rocks. The thought horrified her beyond any fear she had ever imagined.

The trembling ended with a jerk. The crack stopped. A final minor tremor shook everything for a few seconds. And then it was over.

Seri stared down the crack and breathed a sigh of relief. She closed her eyes and breathed slowly in and out, calming herself. She opened her eyes.

The crack no longer descended into the ground. Instead, it contained flat earth like everything around it, but not the same at all. The bright sunlight of midday didn't touch the earth within the crack. Instead, it looked dark and dim, lit by another type of light she couldn't identify.

She looked up. The air above the cracks appeared the same. "It's a crack in the world itself," she whispered to herself. She had no doubt she could see Curasir's Otherworld bleeding through. Was everyone else seeing the same thing? Her eyes darted from person to person.

People began to recover, helping one another up, and gathering in small groups to discuss the experience. Some stared at the cracks, or down inside them, but no one looked up. They could not see the Otherworld like she did.

Jamana spied her and rushed to her side. "Are you hurt?" he cried.

Seri shook her head and started to get up. Jamana took hold of her arm, letting her lean on him. She looked back at the cracks in the world. What did it mean? Would they stay like that? And what if--

Something moved in the Otherworld.

With only the narrow crack showing, she couldn't identify the thing, but it looked much larger than a human. Jamana said something, but she couldn't hear him. She kept her focus on the moving thing. It was like looking at an oddly-shaped slice of a moving animal. She caught a glimpse of the skin, covered in large hexagonal scales with occasional rough protuberances. As it moved by, she also noticed deep creases and a heavy fold in the skin itself. The creature looked enormous, far larger than the largest cattle she had ever seen.

Were any of the other cracks near enough to show more of the creature? Seri turned, but in that instant, the vision ended. Her view of the Otherworld vanished, leaving the cracks as nothing more than cracks in the earth. And walls.

She looked around again. Curasir still stood in the same place, but instead of looking toward the center, he now gazed directly at her. Wait. It wasn't at her. Seri tilted her head and tried to trace Curasir's stare. Was he? Of course. He was staring at the creature. It lived in the Otherworld and the Eldani could see it with his left eye.

"We have to find him!" Jamana's voice broke in.

Seri shook herself. "What?"

"Dravid!"

• • • • •

Jamana led the way, running as fast as his robes would allow. Seri followed. They hurried around the same course they had taken on the day they found Master Simmar, rounding between the citadels and to the interior door.

The door hung off its hinges, and Jamana pulled it out of their way. He and Seri stepped over a few chunks of debris and entered the hallway. The oil lamps that usually lit the way had all fallen from their stands. Most had shattered on impact. A few flames remained on the ground, lapping up the spilled oil.

Heedless of the threat to the hem of his robe, Jamana raced down the hall and turned into the antechamber with the secret entrance. The passageway's door had fallen. Rubble covered the floor, but the tunnel looked clear.

"Dravid!" Jamana yelled down the tunnel.

Seri reached for the tunnel. "Boost me!" she told Jamana. He complied and she started down the tunnel. Despite the damage at the opening, it appeared clear.

"Wait."

Seri looked back. Jamana took a deep breath and climbed into the passage himself. She nodded and turned back. The passageways seemed darker than before. Some of the slits that let the light in must have been blocked.

Working from the memory of her one previous visit, Seri tried to lead the way. She called Dravid's name several times, but received no answer. She hesitated at one intersection. Was it right here or at the next turn?

"I can't… I can't…" Jamana's low muttering made her turn back to look. He clutched his head, eyes closed. "I can't do it."

"Wait here," Seri said. "I'll go on ahead and check."

She scrambled through the tunnel as fast as she could. Was that a voice? She stopped and waited. Sure enough. A muted voice called out, but she couldn't make out any words.

"I think I hear him!" she called back to Jamana.

Without waiting for a response, she rushed forward. This must be the right turn. She turned right and stopped. The passage had caved in. Rocky debris of all sizes filled the entire way ahead. A tiny spark of light came through the top, shining through the dust that hung in the air.

"Help." She had no doubt of it this time. Dravid's voice came from somewhere beyond this barrier.

"Jamana! I need you!" She looked back down the passage where he still lay, holding his head. "The way is blocked and Dravid is calling for help!"

He lifted his head and opened his eyes. With a pained look, he began moving forward, slowly but surely.

Seri turned back to the blockage and began pulling chunks of rock out of the way. Dust rained down around, making her cough. In a few minutes, Jamana came up behind her. She handed him the rocks so that he could shove them down the other passage. As they worked, the opening at the top grew larger, letting more sunlight in. Jamana muttered in a low voice. Seri couldn't tell if he was complaining or motivating himself.

After several minutes of work, the opening had grown large enough that Seri thought she could get through. She coughed again and grabbed on to the edge of the broken tunnel above. It was an awkward position, but she managed to pull herself up high enough that her head extended out into the open air.

She looked out over the extension of the Citadel of Mages. All around her, the massive pillars rose up, holding the extension from the Citadel of Kings, the throne room itself. To her horror, Seri saw that one of the actual pillars had toppled and shattered a large section of the roof here, caving in a lengthy portion of the tunnels.

"Seri, can you get out? You're blocking the light!" Jamana's voice seemed to come from far away, muffled as it was by the stone.

She awkwardly pulled one arm and then the other out of the tunnel. With an effort, she scrambled out completely. She stood with care, testing the stability and brushing dust from her robe. Jamana's face appeared below, smeared with dirt and grime.

"One of the pillars has fallen," she told him. "I'll see if I can find Dravid." He had to be here somewhere. She had heard him!

She followed the ruins of the tunnel, stepping carefully and watching for places where the roof might still cave in. Only a few feet away, a large section of the roof had caved in near the edge. It looked like the pillar had fallen there, shattered the roof, and then rolled to the side.

"Over here." Dravid's weak voice came from the caved-in section.

Seri made her way to a solid spot that allowed her to look down into the ruins. Dravid lay in what was left of his hidden bedroom, surrounded by fallen rubble and shattered glass. A large chunk of stone covered much of the left side of his body, pinning him in place. Seri couldn't see his leg at all.

"Good to see you," Dravid said, trying to smile. His face looked wrong, as if it had been bled of some of its rich color. It had only been a few minutes since the quake. Whatever damage the stone had done to him must have been significant for him to look that bad already.

"Hold on!" Seri said. "Let me help Jamana get here!"

She picked her way back to the tunnel opening. Jamana had already made it much larger, but he still couldn't quite squeeze out. Seri took hold of a larger rock and pulled as Jamana pushed from below. With that piece out of the way, they shoved enough of the remaining debris to either side, allowing Jamana to force his way out. Both his sleeves were torn in multiple places. He ripped them off at the seams as he got to his feet and looked around.

"Over here." Seri led him toward Dravid, but Jamana pushed on ahead. When he saw his friend, he impulsively jumped down into the rubble. It shifted under his weight and came to a stop.

"Are you crazy?" Seri shouted. "You could have brought more down on top of him!"

"I'm okay," Dravid said.

"You are not," Jamana said. "Stop trying to talk." He threw a head-sized chunk of rock out of the way and stepped up next to the large piece that pinned Dravid. He took hold of it, braced his legs, and heaved. His muscles strained. Sweat erupted across his shaved head.

The stone shifted imperceptibly.

"Seri-Belit!" he called. "I need you!"

"As if I can do more than those muscles," she whispered to herself. She found an edge that looked solid enough, sat, and swung her legs over the side. She slid over and landed awkwardly next to Jamana. She looked down and chuckled. She had landed between two larger rocks and stood on Dravid's mattress.

"You're in my bed," he said. Then his eyes closed and his head slid down.

"No, no, no!" Seri grabbed Dravid's head and shook it gently. "Don't go to sleep!"

"We have to move this rock!" Jamana insisted. "We need to get him out!"

Seri reluctantly let Dravid go and moved next to Jamana. She positioned herself to lift. "Now!" Jamana said. They both strained. Nothing happened. Seri let go.

"I'm not doing anything!"

"We cannot let him die here!" Jamana cried. He heaved again. Through gritted teeth, he screamed with the effort. The stone moved about an inch. Dravid groaned.

At Seri's arrival, Master Hain had moved a rope to her with magic. Could this rock be moved in the same way? Without any clue of what she could do, Seri placed her hands on the rock. She closed her eyes and tried to concentrate. But she didn't know what to concentrate on? The stone itself? The star in her eye? "Please, please," she whispered. To her shock, she felt a tiny vibration run through the stone. She looked up and saw Jamana staring at her. He had felt it too!

Another figure landed next to them with a rustle of robes and a cloud of dust. "Stand aside."

Seri looked up into Master Hain's face. The mage stepped past her and laid his hands on the stone pinning Dravid. He closed his eyes and concentrated. A low hum filled the air.

Jamana wiped sweat from his head and watched, his face a picture of anxiety. At first nothing happened. Seri glanced at Master Hain's face again. He still had his eyes closed, but didn't seem to be experiencing any difficulty.

The stone began to vibrate. With a louder hum and a clatter, it split apart into hundreds of small shards which collapsed and slid across Dravid and his surroundings. Jamana hurried to dig out his friend.

"Well, young acolytes," Master Hain observed. "I suppose it is high time that we actually taught you some magic."

(((23)))

Marshal had never thought much about the afterlife. Enduring his current life seemed enough to think about. When he woke up after the assassin's attack, he didn't know what to expect.

His brain struggled to understand the light that struck his eyes. It wasn't sunlight, firelight, or lamplight. It seemed steady like sunlight, but not as bright and yellow. As his vision adjusted, he realized he was staring up at a sky full of stars.

But such stars! On cold nights in Drusa's Crossing, on the mountain foothills, the stars sometimes appeared close enough to touch, filling the sky from horizon to horizon.

But this… he had never seen anything like it. Stars filled the sky, but they were HUGE. Marshal had never seen a single star like this, let alone a sky full of them. Some of them approached the size of the full moon in size, and exceeded it in brightness. Even more astounding, they varied as much in color as in size. Marshal saw white, blue, yellow, even red, and a myriad of shades between.

In some parts of the sky, he saw even more: swirls of color behind the stars, twists of dimmer light that stretched wide bands across the blueish-black blanket of the heavens. The beauty of it all overwhelmed him. He realized he was holding his breath. He let it out and took several rapid breaths, as a tear ran down his cheek and lodged in his ear.

"Shift in ten."

The voice came out of nowhere. It sounded young and feminine, but unlike any woman he knew. She had the same commanding tone as Talinir, but with a stronger resonance. It couldn't be Theon, could it? Would Theon have a girl's voice?

Marshal lifted his head and pulled his view from the sky. The blaze of starlight illuminated everything around him almost like daylight. He lay in a bed of some kind, far softer than he was accustomed to. But beyond that, he couldn't seem to see anything. He blinked, trying to understand his surroundings.

"Shift in eight."

Walls rose up around him. Or did they? His eyes couldn't seem to focus on them, but neither could they perceive anything beyond. He lifted up further and looked over the side of the bed. He could make out some kind of stone floor, but again, he couldn't quite focus.

A motion caught his eye. He thought he caught a glimpse of an extremely tall figure standing a few feet away. It made him think of the giant shadow he had seen in Efesun. But like the walls, he couldn't focus on it.

"Shift in five."

Marshal let his head settle back down and returned his gaze upwards. Thinking hurt too much. Far better to watch that glorious sky. It was soothing, in a way, like comfort itself wrapped up in light. He relaxed and breathed easier. So beautiful.

"Shift in two… one… now."

The walls Marshal had tried to focus on snapped into view in his peripheral vision. White stone with faint marble swirls appeared out of nowhere. For a moment, his bed sat in a room without a ceiling, looking up at those incredible stars. And then a ceiling made of the same white marbleized stone faded into view, cutting off the starlight. A heaviness settled over his chest, an anguish for what he could no longer see.

"Shift completed." The owner of the voice stepped into view. An Eldani woman reached out her long-fingered hand and touched his forehead. Somehow, she must have pulled him back from the afterlife. What a horrible thing to do.

"The effects of the starlight will fade shortly," she said. "How does your chest feel?" Marshal stared at her, not knowing how to react. She resembled Talinir somewhat, with the same angular features, though hers appeared more delicate. She also seemed much younger. Longer, lighter hair framed a face that contained the same strange eyes, but boasted longer eye lids and eyebrows that actually curved. The overall effect made her appear closer to human, though, like Talinir, she seemed somehow taller than she appeared. Despite that, Marshal believed her to be the most beautiful woman he had ever seen.

"Oh, of course. The curse." She placed two of her fingers fully on his forehead, cool against his skin. She closed her eyes, and a look of concentration passed over her face, followed by perplexity. "That's strange."

She opened her eyes and stepped back, looking at him curiously. "I should be able to perceive your thoughts, but..." She frowned. "Fascinating. The curse must be more extensive than just the vocal blockage. Tell me, if you can, has your mother ever tried to teach you some form of hand communication?"

Nod is yes. Marshal nodded. Aelia had tried many times in his childhood. It never worked. He could never remember what she showed him, even after a few minutes. The meanings of the gestures always disappeared from his mind. He was so stupid.

"And it never worked, did it?"

Shake is no. Marshal shook his head.

The Eldani woman sighed and looked away. "What have they wrought?" she whispered. Turning back to Marshal, she gave a half-smile. "You poor boy. Locked inside your head, with no way to ever communicate beyond the most basic. The curse will not allow it." She closed her eyes and took a deep breath before opening them again.

"Enough of that. My name is Eniri. I have been tending to your pains. How is your chest? Does it hurt?" Her fingers gestured lightly over Marshal's chest.

With a rush, Marshal's memories returned. The assassin had stabbed him in the chest! Why wasn't he dead? He grabbed at his chest and realized two things immediately: he had no tunic, and he had no wound. He sat up, staring and feeling all over his chest. Not even a scratch.

"Warden Talinir brought you here. After treating your wound, we shifted your room into the Starlit Realm," Eniri said. "The starlight accelerated your healing. While it doesn't have the usual effect on humans, the restorative powers are impressive."

She moved to a doorway Marshal hadn't noticed. "Your clothes are on the end of the bed," she said. "I will let you get dressed. After Lady Siratel does a final examination, you may rejoin your mother and friend."

●●●●●

Marshal found his clothes, cleaner and neater than he had ever seen them, on the end of the bed. He dressed quickly. In the process, he discovered other injuries had vanished, as well. He had sustained a number of cuts and bruises in the fall into the river, but could find no trace of them. He felt his face, but the scars remained. That hadn't changed.

Getting through the door proved more confusing than he had anticipated. He could see the frame, molded around the shape of a door, but could find no handle or means of opening it. The frame and even the door itself appeared to be the same marble-white stone as the walls.

He reached out a tentative hand and pushed on the door. To his surprise, it swung open with little effort. A long hallway stretched before him. Unlike the room he had left, wood panels lined these walls - oak, he thought. A narrow band of white stone bisected the wall at waist height, except where it crossed the four doors that lined either side. Cool light filled the hallway, but Marshal couldn't discern the source.

Eniri waited two doors down. She gave him an appraising look. Marshal looked down at his clothes. Had he done something improper? Eniri smiled at his reaction, which only made him more nervous. Her clothes, unlike his, appeared tailor-made with care to fit her precise measurements. Marshal had rarely seen a blouse and pants so elegant.

"This way," she said. She walked to the third door on the right and pushed it open. Marshal followed and looked into a dark room. He glanced back at Eniri.

"Come in, my child." The voice from the room sounded like Eniri's but had a stronger sense of command and age to it. Marshal didn't dare disobey. The door rotated shut behind him.

He closed and opened his eyes to adjust them to the darkness. The room was not entirely without light. Tiny pinpricks dotted the ceiling and walls, in an apparent imitation of a star field. What made them glow?

"Forgive the darkness," the voice said. "When you are as old as I am, it is difficult to endure the harsh light on this side."

Marshal could now make out a figure sitting in a large stuffed chair against the wall. He couldn't tell much about her in the darkness, but even here, his eyes wrestled with the strange sense of tallness. He took a step closer.

"Come, come," she said. "I am Lady Siratel. Judging by your age as a human, you would consider me to be ancient, I am sure. How could one such as I possibly harm you?"

Marshal moved next to the chair. Lady Siratel reached out a wizened hand and grasped his upper arm.

"I know of your curse, child. Fear not. You are only here so that I may examine you. Humans are not used to exposure to the Otherworld as you have just experienced. I must determine if there are any lasting effects."

None of this made any sense. How would she determine that? What was this Otherworld or Starlit Realm, if not the afterlife? Marshal wished someone would speak plainly.

Lady Siratel stood. It seemed to cause her pain. She grimaced and put both hands on either side of Marshal's head. "This will be difficult with the curse in the way," she murmured.

Marshal had no idea what she was doing. Unable to see her clearly, he stood and waited. Nothing happened. Her hands stayed in position. She remained silent for a long time.

"Difficult indeed, but not impossible," she said at last. "My, you had difficulties on the way here. That assassin is particularly fascinating."

Marshal jerked. Was she reading his mind? Seeing what had happened to him? Surely not. Aelia must have told the story already.

"Too far back. I want to see your most recent memories… ahh. There we are." She paused. "Yes, the starlight is overwhelming for those unused, but I do not think you suffered any ill effects."

Marshal's head filled with the brilliant stars he had seen in the other room. The ache of loss filled him again.

"Perhaps I spoke too soon. Your affinity for the stars' beauty is surprising. I fear the longing may never leave you fully. Still, perhaps in time… Shall I? Yes, I suppose I should. The curse makes it exceedingly difficult, but not without reward, I believe."

Lady Siritel's hands tightened. "I am sorry, child. I said I would not harm you, but this may be slightly painful."

The tiny star lights around the room exploded in brightness, shooting beams of light across the room. Marshal shut his own eyes instinctively. It was too much. Yet even with his eyes closed, he could feel something striking him all over his body. Tiny spots of pressure, very light but distinctive. Could he actually feel the beams of light?

"Oh. Oh, my. That…" Lady Siritel's voice trailed off and she gripped his head even tighter. Marshal felt a painful pressure beginning to build behind his eyes.

"The stars… they… No. No, it cannot be. That…" Her breathing rate increased. Marshal could sense her chest rising and falling rapidly in front of him. The pressure continued to build.

"The stars… the stars in your future…"

Marshal gritted his teeth as the pressure became almost unbearable. He reached for Lady Siritel's hands, but her grip grew stronger by the second. He felt both hands begin to shake.

Lady Siritel's shriek pierced his ears. She released Marshal and collapsed back into her chair. He stumbled backwards and opened his eyes. The stars had dimmed again. The pressure in his head vanished. Eniri burst through the door.

"Lady Siritel!" she cried. "What happened?"

The elder woman pointed toward Marshal, her hand shaking. "The stars…" she whispered.

Eniri knelt beside Lady Siritel and placed her fingers against her forehead as she had done with Marshal earlier. "What is it, my lady? What about the stars?"

"In his head, in the time to come… I saw the stars…"

Lady Siritel sat bolt upright, pushing Eniri's hand away.

"They fell!"

(((24)))

"This is nothing less than the breakdown of the fabric of reality!" Master Plecu's voice rang out through the Conclave of Mages, followed by a low murmur.

The Conclave had gathered, but unlike the last time Seri had been in this room, a large audience waited for them. It seemed every resident of Zes Sivas wanted to observe the Masters as they debated the earth's shaking from the day prior. Apprentices, acolytes, and servants alike crowded into the seating tier, barely able to contain their numbers. A dozen or more people had been injured, though none as bad as Dravid. Rumors claimed numerous new Bindings between residents who had helped each other.

Seri noticed Curasir seated in a separate chair of his own, not within the Masters' half circle, but off to the side. He seemed content to observe, at least for now. Looking toward the stage, Seri's eyes couldn't stop wandering to the empty seat within the half-circle. Kuktarma had not yet sent a replacement for Master Simmar. Only five Masters debated.

"Nonsense," said Master Korda. "It is troubling, but there are numerous possible explanations." Jamana's Master looked like a larger and broader version of Seri's friend. He spoke with a heavy accent and such a deep timbre that Seri had difficulty parsing his words at times.

"We have discussed each alternate explanation and rejected them all," Master Hain said, a note of irritation in his voice.

"You have rejected them, perhaps," Korda said. "I have not."

Seri spared a glance at Jamana, who sat beside her. His face betrayed no emotion, yet she knew he was still troubled over Dravid's condition. The healers had taken charge of their friend, but he had not

129

yet regained consciousness.

"Will you at least agree that this is no natural phenomenon?" Master Alpin of Varioch asked.

"It seems highly unlikely," Korda said.

"Then what is left?" Plecu said. "Wild magic has never been this powerful. In Theon's name, what could--"

"There are other gods besides Theon," Master Tzoyet broke in. His quiet voice, distinct enough to interrupt Plecu, made it difficult to make out his words.

"What did you say?" Alpin asked.

"There are other gods. Perhaps we have angered one of them."

"Blasphemy!" Plecu shrieked. "How dare you speak thus in the heart of Antises!"

Masters Alpin, Plecu, and Hain all touched index fingers to their palms. Around her, Seri noted many others throughout the crowd do so, as well. Jamana did not.

"The Book of the Law states that there should be no gods above Theon," Tzoyet said. "He is Almighty. But there are gods below him."

"Semantical blasphemy," Alpin said.

"Does the Book of the Law not say that Theon is greater than all other gods? Did he not bring judgment on the gods that our nations served before the Great Cataclysm? How can he be greater, how can he bring judgment on something that does not exist? Perhaps they have returned, seeking vengeance."

Murmurs swept through the crowd. Seri frowned. She knew rumors circulated that some of the people of Ch'olan and Mandiata had taken to serving other gods in addition to Theon. But she had no idea the practice had spread this far. Then she stifled a chuckle, remembering how she had been too nervous to mention religion in her appearance before the Conclave. Clearly, they had no qualms over debating it amongst themselves.

"It seems more likely that this would be Theon's judgment for those who abandon him and serve other gods!" Master Plecu cried.

"Oh?" Korda said placidly. "How many of you have done so? The quaking is centered here, so if it is judgment, it must be judgment on those present."

"You twist my words!"

"Masters, please," Hain said, tapping a thick staff on the floor. "Let us not engage in personal accusations. We all seek wisdom and knowledge here, not blame."

Curasir stood. "If I may?" he asked.

Hain nodded. "Let us hear from the ambassador from the Eldanim."

Master Plecu looked about to say something, but apparently thought better of it and sat down.

Curasir strode to the middle of the half-circle, facing the Masters. In doing so, he put his back to the crowd. Seri breathed a sigh of relief. Every time his gaze had come near her, she had tensed up.

"Master Tzoyet is not altogether incorrect in his statements," the Eldani said. "There are other powerful beings in this world. Whether you call them 'gods' or not, they exist. Ignoring them is perilous."

"But do you think one of them is responsible for this... this devastation?" Alpin wanted to know.

"I do not." Curasir bowed his head for a moment. The room grew quiet. He lifted his face and spoke again. "As you all well know, the Eldanim were strongly opposed to this body's actions in the past. By binding most of this land's magic into specific human bloodlines, you endangered all that is. In time, you acknowledged this error and attempted to mollify it with the ceremony you call the Passing. It was never a permanent solution."

"You told me you were here to offer help and advice, not condemnation," Hain said, his face a stone.

"Indeed. While the Passing may accomplish its purposes normally, you have been missing a key portion of the power since you lost your King. This is hardly news to any of you, but indulge me for a moment.

"The power to rule was broken into seven portions. However, the portion given to the King was equal to at least three of the Lords. What that means for our world is that when you conduct your yearly Passing now, you are not just missing a small part: you are missing a full third of the power, the power necessary for maintaining this world's very structure. Is it any wonder that it has begun to react?"

"What would you have us do, then?" Korda asked. "We do not possess the skill of the ancient Conclave. We can not restore what has been taken, even if the Lords were to agree to it."

"Your only hope - indeed, this land's only hope - is to find your high King," Curasir said. "Until his power is included in the Passing, the trouble we experienced yesterday will only increase."

Something seemed off. Seri leaned forward and stared at the back of Curasir's head. Why wasn't he even mentioning the Otherworld? He knew it was bleeding through the cracks. He had surely seen it far more than she had.

"Do you think we haven't tried?" Alpin said bitterly. "Everyone searches for the King's descendants. Any of the Lords would seize at the opportunity to be the one who restores a King to Antises!"

"Perhaps there are… other ways," Curasir said. "I will discuss them with you at a later time. For now, I would make one other suggestion: you should move up the time of the Passing."

"Impossible!" Tzoyet exclaimed. "The necessary preparations, the travel arrangements for all six Lords and their retainers: it would be a logistical nightmare to change all of that!"

"What would you rather have?" Curasir asked. "A logistical nightmare? Or a supernatural one?"

A long silence followed.

"Your words have wisdom," Hain said at last. "But what you ask is difficult to achieve. We could, perhaps, move the Passing two weeks sooner? That would still give us six weeks to prepare."

Tzoyet and Plecu grumbled under their breaths, but said nothing in opposition. Hain looked at each of the other Masters in turn. No one responded.

"Very well. We shall accelerate our schedules and send messages to each of the Lords. Given the nature of the crisis, I hope that they will not delay in their responses." He banged the staff against the floor. "This gathering is dismissed."

(((25)))

Eniri hastened Marshal back out into the hallway. She went back in and tried to calm Lady Siratel for a few minutes, kneeling beside her chair. Marshal waited in the hall. If the old woman had seen stars falling in his future, what did it mean? She was so upset, as if she blamed him for the falling stars. It made no sense.

Besides, stars fell all the time. Marshal had seen them on many clear nights in the mountains. What could be horrible about... oh. Maybe it wasn't the stars he saw every night. Maybe she was talking about the stars in that other place, where he had woken up. If those stars fell... that would truly be a great loss. The simple absence of them right now created a pull inside him. If only he could get back there somehow.

Eniri re-emerged. "I think the lady will be all right," she said. "I've never seen her that agitated." She looked at Marshal with a raised eyebrow.

How was he supposed to react to that?

Eniri blinked and looked away. "I am not used to being around someone who I couldn't read," she said. "You are a very confusing young man."

Not much he could do about that.

"Come this way. Your mother is waiting in the lobby."

Eniri led him to the end of the hall and turned the corner to the right. This hall only traveled a few feet before again turning left. After passing three more doors, it opened up into a large room lined with windows. A couple dozen chairs and benches filled the room. Aelia and Victor waited on one of the benches.

On seeing her son, Aelia leaped to her feet and rushed across the room to meet him. Eniri stepped to the side and waited while Aelia

133

embraced, kissed, and fussed over Marshal. It was only moderately embarrassing. Victor stood nearby, looking awkward.

Someone was missing. Marshal looked around the room.

"Talinir is all right," Aelia said, recognizing his question. "He is reporting to his masters."

Victor approached. "So… you're all right now?" he asked.

Marshal pulled his tunic open to reveal smooth skin. Aelia touched his chest and put her hand to her mouth.

Victor stared. "That's… not possible. You were almost dead!" He looked at Eniri. "What did you do to him?"

Eniri cocked her head. "Our healing methods are radically effective," she answered. "Thanks to the light of the stars, the Eldanim rarely suffer for very long."

"Huh." Victor snorted. "When I lay out under the stars, all I get is cold."

"Not quite the same thing," Eniri said.

Marshal moved past the others and stared out the window. He looked out onto a street paved with white stone, lined by buildings of stone and polished wood. It was nothing like Drusa's Crossing or Efesun. Unlike the towns he knew, these buildings seemed designed more for their appearance than their functionality. He could see no discernible purpose for many of the curves, turrets, railings, and other design elements. Some of those balconies couldn't even be accessed, from what he could see.

"Isn't it insane?" Victor asked from behind him. "Did you ever dream we'd end up in an Eldanim city?"

"It has been many years since any human set foot in Intal Eldanir," Eniri said. "You are all greatly honored."

Marshal continued to stare until Aelia put her hand on his shoulder. "Come, we'll show you where we're staying." She looked to Eniri. "Unless there is further need for us to stay here?"

Eniri shook her head. "Marshal should be fine," she said. "He may feel some fatigue shortly. Otherwise, I do not think there will be lasting effects."

Marshal glanced at her, wondering why she didn't mention Lady Siratel's vision. Eniri smiled at him in response. Perplexing.

"Yeah, wait'll you see our rooms!" Victor said.

Aelia led the way out into the street. Marshal followed, but paused at the door and looked back. He smiled at Eniri. He couldn't think of anything else to do. He wished she had been able to read his thoughts.

That would have been… interesting.

Outside, he noted the cloudy sky, much as it had been yesterday when they fought the assassin. Was it yesterday? He had no idea how much time had passed.

As they walked down the street, several Eldanim passed by, walking alone or in couples. All of them inclined their heads in respect toward Aelia and mostly ignored the boys. In every case, Marshal found himself straining to focus. Like Talinir and Eniri, they all appeared taller than their actual height. Even when he walked past a young woman clearly shorter than he, it still seemed wrong. He could look down on the top of her head, but she still seemed taller.

They all appeared similar with the sharp angles and starry right eyes, but each possessed distinctions of their own. Skin tone and hair color varied widely throughout, including some he had never seen before. They wore clothing mostly similar to what he was used to - tunics and pants - but equally as varied, and always decorative in ways he had never considered. They appeared to favor dark colors, setting a stark contrast to the white stone of the street. Some wore strange strips of colored cloth wrapped around their necks and hanging down either in the front or back. He could see no discernible purpose for the strips, except to keep the neck warm, which hardly seemed necessary. Two younger Eldanim walked by wearing patches over their right eyes. Marshal tried not to stare.

No one mocked him. No one stared at his scars. No one called him "Curse Boy."

After walking a couple of blocks, Aelia opened the door at a two-story building that resembled an inn. That is, it resembled an inn far more decorative, clean, and impressive than any Marshal had seen. The interior, however, resembled more of a manor house than an inn. No one greeted them at the door. Aelia led them upstairs to a set of rooms that had been set aside for the three humans.

"Look over here!" Victor moved around the rooms, pointing out everything. At first, Marshal found himself fascinated by the enormous fireplace, the soft beds in the two sleeping rooms, and the striking beauty of the furniture. But as the tour advanced, he realized Victor's attitude fascinated him even more.

He watched his guide out of the corner of his eye. Victor seemed to be genuinely excited to be sharing these things with someone. If he didn't know better, Marshal would have thought Victor enjoyed his company. Anyone else watching might have thought they were friends.

That couldn't be true, of course. Victor was only relieved Marshal hadn't died, thus ruining his chance to escape their Bond. Everyone knew that once Bonded, if the one you were supposed to protect died before you could save them, your own life was ruined.

Victor didn't actually like him. He had made that clear many times. Even as he reminded himself of this, Marshal felt an ache inside. What would it be like to have a real friend? For some reason, his thoughts danced to the stars he had seen in that other place, and the ache of loss grew.

"Are you hungry?" Aelia's question broke into his thoughts.

Marshal shook his head. He gestured, not knowing how to communicate what he wanted to know.

"You want to know what happened? How we got here?"

Nod is yes.

"Hope you don't mind if I eat while she talks," Victor said. He strode across the room to a solid wood table that held a variety of fruits. After looking them over, he took what looked like a green apple and took a large bite.

"Talinir saved you," Aelia said. "When you were stabbed, he woke up. I don't know why or how. He should have been out much longer. Instead, he just… jumped up, took his sword from me, and ran it through the assassin's belly."

"He's amazing," Victor said around a mouthful. "I want to learn how to do what he does."

"Talinir picked you up and then--"

"He just screamed at the sky!" Victor broke in, waving his apple. "Like it was some Eldanim password or something, and then! This entire city! Just appeared out of nowhere! And it was floating!"

"Which one of us is telling this story?" Aelia asked, smiling.

"You can finish," Victor said.

"There's not much else to tell," Aelia said. "Talinir rushed into the city with you, and we followed. He took you to the healers, and we were forced to leave you there. The Eldanim gave us these rooms and left us alone so far. This morning, they summoned us to meet you. That's all there is, really."

Marshal's eyes glanced out the window at the street. Was it also floating above the Great Plains? How was that possible? For that matter, how could an entire city appear out of nowhere?

He sat on the windowsill and looked out without seeing any more.

The Eldanim could make a city float and vanish. They could heal someone at the very point of death. They could fight invisible monsters. If they could do all that, was it not reasonable to think they might be able to lift his curse?

Until now, he had pushed such hopes down. They weren't even worth considering. But after all that had happened in the past couple of days, could he accept the possibility? Should he? Dare he?

His face twisted in concern and he looked up at Aelia. She had always been good at reading his moods and this was no exception. She laid her hand on his shoulder.

"Talinir believes the High Council will reject my request," she said softly. "I do not know if he is right. Regardless, I will make my plea directly to them when they agree to hear it."

She bent down and looked him in the eyes. "Either they will lift your curse, or we will find another way," she said. "I have put this off too long, and I am sorry for that." She wrapped her arms around him.

"You are loved. You are valuable. You have a purpose in this world." Somehow, her whispered words, though he had heard them countless times before, contained the comfort he needed for now. He relaxed and returned her hug. Nothing else mattered, for now.

(((26)))

Talinir came to see them in the early afternoon. When he entered the room, he greeted Aelia, then went straight to Marshal. The warden knelt in front of him.

"I made a promise that no harm would come to you or your mother," he said. "I failed to keep that promise. I am sorry that I did not anticipate the assassin's attack so soon after my fight with the tunaldi."

Marshal felt awkward. He didn't blame Talinir, and didn't know how to respond.

"How did you manage to wake up right when he needed you?" Victor asked.

Talinir looked at him, but remained kneeling. "When Marshal was stabbed, my promise was broken. That is what woke me."

"A broken promise woke you up?"

"Among your people, words are not as effectual, I am told," Talinir said. "Among the Eldanim, a spoken promise is as powerful as the Bond that connects the two of you."

"You mean it's magic?"

Talinir hesitated. "You would call it that."

"Well, it is or it isn't, right?" Victor cocked his head and wrinkled his brow.

"I am not sure how to explain that."

Talinir turned back to Marshal. "Regardless, I must atone for this. Whenever you do leave Intal Eldanir, I will accompany you and protect you again, as long as you need me." He placed a hand over his heart and the other on Marshal's shoulder. "I make this my oath."

Victor's eyebrows went up. "And an oath is stronger than a

promise?"

Talinir looked irritated. "Yes."

Victor rolled his eyes. "We're just one big bundle of Bindings here," he said. "But at the rate Marshal keeps getting in trouble, I'm thinking we'll have plenty of opportunities to rescue him."

In the past, when Victor made statements like that, they were grumbling, resentful. Now he sounded practically cheerful about it.

Aelia sat in one of the ornate wooden chairs near the table. She looked thoughtful. "Talinir, there is one thing I would request of you," she said.

The warden stood and faced her. "What is it, my lady?"

"Victor has already expressed an interest in learning from you. I think it would be wise if you were to train both of the boys in the use of the sword. I've given Marshal some basic training, but he needs much more."

Marshal looked up.

"Considering what happened with the assassin, I believe you are correct," Talinir replied. "We will start tomorrow."

Aelia visibly relaxed a bit. "Have you conveyed my request to address the High Council?"

"I have. They will be meeting the day after tomorrow, and will make time for you then. Is there anything else you require today?"

"Not that I'm aware of," Aelia said. "Harunir and Indala are excellent hosts."

"I am not surprised," Talinir said. "In that case, I will leave you all to relax and enjoy the rest of your day. I'll be back for the two of you men tomorrow morning at first light."

Before they could even respond, Talinir strode out of the door.

"Devouring fire! He's going to teach us!" Victor said. "That's... that's..." Unable to think of the right words, he stopped, then seemed to remember something. "Oh, uh, thank you, Aelia."

"You're welcome," she said. "You were right. You both need to learn how to defend yourselves better. We don't need to repeat what happened with the assassin."

"Uh... yeah."

Marshal wasn't sure what to think. On the one hand, learning more swordplay would be a good skill to have. On the other, why should he bother? If his curse was lifted, he would soon have access to real power, magical power. Even if it wasn't lifted, if he managed to stay hidden here in the Eldanim city, all he had to do was wait until Lord

Varion died and he would still inherit the power. What good were swords against that?

• • • • •

In the early evening, the home owners returned. From what Marshal could grasp, the Eldani couple lived on the first floor of the house and reserved the second floor for visitors. That seemed odd. How many visitors could there be to an invisible city?

When their hosts' daughter returned soon thereafter, Marshal experienced a pleasant surprise. It was Eniri.

After some greetings and small talk, all six of them settled down for dinner around a table that could have handled ten or twelve people with room to spare. Marshal surveyed the food apprehensively. He was used to certain tastes and had never been comfortable trying new things. He recognized a few items, but others left him perplexed. He had never seen a more bountiful table.

Harunir reached out his hands to his wife and daughter. "Please join us," he said. "We begin each meal this way."

The humans joined hands with each other and the Eldanim. Marshal had only a brief moment of panic between the realization and the action of holding hands with Eniri. He had never held a girl's hand before, even for something this simple. He hoped his hand didn't start shaking.

All three Eldanim looked up. Marshal glanced to either side and did likewise. For the first time, he noticed the ceiling had an engraved pattern that looked much like a star field. It wasn't black, and the stars were difficult to make out, but there was no mistaking the design.

"We who wait for the ransoming of all worlds, we thank you for your provision." Harunir's declaration sounded heartfelt.

Were they talking to the stars? Or Theon? Marshal quickly forgot his temporary curiosity when he realized everyone had lowered their heads, and he still held Eniri's hand. She smiled and gently pulled loose.

Platters and bowls began moving around the table, and Marshal felt pressured to put many things on his plate. He took small portions of a number of different fruits, only some of which he could identify. Corn was literally the only vegetable he recognized, but he was surprised to discover it tasted sweet, unlike the generally tasteless stuff he knew from back home. He liked the sliced ham, but not the thick gravy that had been poured on it.

Eniri made a few comments as the meal progressed, pointing out things for him. He tried to respond in the only ways he could, but felt inadequate. Even as he tried a few of the unfamiliar foods, he found himself wondering what it would be like to spend more time alone with the Eldani girl.

"These are fantastic!" Victor said loudly. He held up a breaded piece of meat Marshal didn't recognize. "Is this chicken?"

Indala smiled. "Yes, breaded and fried in vegetable oil. You like it?"

"I could eat these every day! Why aren't there any bones?"

Beside him, Eniri laughed. Marshal frowned. Victor's enthusiasm could always make girls smile. Marshal couldn't even express whether he liked the fried chicken pieces. Girls would always be attracted to Victor, not him. Who could blame them? Victor was far more handsome, with his blonde hair, scruffy beard and thick muscles. What girl would ever prefer Marshal? Even if by some miracle the Eldanim removed his curse, his face would still be horribly scarred. His life felt more pointless than ever.

His appetite vanished. Indala was trying to explain the process she used to prepare the chicken. Ignoring her, he got to his feet and left the table.

Aelia stood and took a step after him. "Are you all right?"

Nod is yes. Marshal left the room.

When Victor returned to their bedroom a short time later, Marshal sat alone, staring out the window.

"Theon's pillars! I don't know if I've ever eaten that much in my entire life!" Victor collapsed onto the bed and rubbed his stomach. "Whatever else the Eldanim may be, they know how to cook!"

Marshal rolled his eyes, though he knew Victor wasn't watching him.

"I just can't get used to their appearance," Victor went on. "No matter how much I try, there's something strange about them."

He sat up. "I mean, their women are beautiful, right? At least the ones we've seen. Like that Eniri downstairs - incredibly beautiful, isn't she?"

Marshal turned to look at him, but found Victor staring at the ceiling.

"But she's still so... strange. I can't imagine myself being with one of them, you know? I mean, it's like she's beautiful, but not attractive, if that makes any sense?"

Marshal cocked his head. This was interesting talk coming from Victor.

"I wonder if they see us the same way? Maybe Eniri is down there with her mother right now saying something like, 'Those human boys look nice, but they're so strange looking! So much hair and everything is curved!'" Victor affected an attempt at a high-pitched voice, which made Marshal smile.

Victor jumped back up. "Ha! Usually it's me that's talking about a girl's curves!" He joined Marshal at the window and looked out toward the setting sun.

A long moment of silence followed.

Victor slapped Marshal on the back. "Well, we get to start training tomorrow! Best get some sleep!"

(((27)))

Kishin knelt alone amid the long grass, face down and eyes closed. Never before had a target escaped him at the point of death itself. By all rights, Marshal should be dead. The healing powers of the Eldanim created an unfair advantage.

No, not unfair. Simply challenging. Yet another challenge in this most unusual pursuit.

Kishin scratched more skin off his arm. As pleasurable as a challenge might be, this one had turned a corner. Even he could not defy the full protection of the Eldanim.

For twenty years, Kishin had been in the business of killing. Lords and nobles from four of the six realms had hired him to do the one job they could not perform themselves. He had killed and killed and killed again. His targets had ranged from common peasants to children of the Lords themselves. In all that time, he had never failed in an assignment.

And he would not fail now.

After his first murder, the curse had struck him. The despair had followed, driving him nearly to the point of ending his own life. And then it occurred to him. How much worse could it be? Inspired to find out, he sought out a neighbor who had mocked him as a child. Slitting his throat had been extremely satisfying. And no further curse had followed. In that moment, he knew he was free, free to do whatever he liked, because no curse could be greater than the one he already bore.

Killing did not become his obsession. Curses did. In time, he realized everyone was cursed, whether they admitted it or not. Convincing them to admit it started as a game, but soon became his primary goal. The killings were secondary. They must be made to see.

His curse, though horrible, was no different from everyone else.

Once others understood and embraced their curses, they could be free, too.

Marshal's curse troubled him. Muteness was unusual, but not unheard of. But it seemed like something someone might earn for small violations of the Law. Somehow, Kishin suspected that Lord Varioch had committed a more serious crime. In which case, he was missing something. Something significant. Why wasn't the curse more substantial?

The more he pondered it, the more troubled he grew. The mental exercise provided a welcome respite from his current pain.

He opened his eyes.

The sword still waited. His own starshine should have done enough by now, though. Enough to let him survive what needed to be done next.

He took the sword's grip in both hands, hesitated, then pulled swiftly. It slid out of his stomach in a smooth motion. Blood spurted for only a few seconds before the wound sealed.

He gasped and closed his eyes again, waiting for the pain to subside. It did not take long. He opened his eyes and lifted his head. He was fortunate that the others had been so focused on saving Marshal, rather than finishing him off.

Even if he never saw his target again, he had already profited from this assignment in a greater way than he could have imagined. An Eldani warpsteel blade. He wiped his own blood in the grass and lifted the sword into the light. This was worth more than everything he owned, and they had left it behind for him. In seeking to save Marshal, they had made him more deadly than he had ever been.

He lifted his face higher and glared at the gleaming city that floated in the air before him. Marshal would emerge again, one day. And when he did, it no longer mattered who protected him.

He would die.

(((28)))

"The magic of Antises is all about vibration," Master Hain announced.

Seri looked around the room they entered. She had never been in this part of the citadel. The room looked somewhat like a smaller version of the dining room, with numerous tables arranged in order. Someone had arranged a multitude of various small items on top of the tables.

"Vibration is everywhere in the universe," Master Hain said. "It is one of the fundamental forces of all creation."

Seri cocked her head. "I've never heard that before. In the university, they taught us about fundamental forces. There were three of--"

"We do not share our insights with the universities," he interrupted. "But you must accept what I am telling you, or nothing else will make any sense."

"Sorry, Master."

"Very well. Now, vibration itself may or may not be classified as magic. After all, anyone can cause vibrations of some kinds - pounding a drum, ripples in the water, and so on. But considering how magic itself is so intricately tied into vibration, we might almost consider those to be examples of what you might call ordinary magic. That is, magic that can be performed by anyone at any time."

Seri tried not to frown. It seemed a strange way of beginning her training. She wasn't sure she agreed with Master Hain's description. She kept her mother's admonishment in her head and kept her mouth shut.

"Though we cannot perceive it with our ordinary senses, everything vibrates," Master Hain went on. "Our bodies, this table, the citadel itself. Everything vibrates at its own speed, in its own way. The great

Masters of the ancient age were said to be powerful enough to sense those vibrations. Sensing led to understand. And understanding led to... control.

"No one has that kind of power today. The Lords, of course, possess immense power, but most of them don't seek its mastery. And here, at Zes Sivas, enough magic remains that we can sense it, understand it, and control it for our own purposes."

"So you vibrated that stone apart to save Dravid!" Seri exclaimed. She gritted her teeth at the stupidity of stating such an obvious thing.

Master Hain nodded. "And when I rescued you from the water?"

She frowned. "You used vibrations to send the rope to me? How does that work?"

"It will take time to explain. Now. Zes Sivas is full of magic, as I said, and you have now been here long enough that your body should be attuned to it. Now we can begin your training."

"You mean all this time I was waiting, it was just about getting attuned? Why couldn't you have told me that from the beginning?"

"It was never just about getting attuned, acolyte. I had to see if you were truly worthy of the training. If you could follow simple instructions. If you were willing to work."

"Oh."

"Since you should be attuned to the magic of Zes Sivas, it will respond to you, once you learn how." He gestured to the nearest table. "First, you must learn how to sense the magic."

Seri stepped up to the table. Two wooden blocks sat on it. They appeared identical.

"Hold your hand over each one in turn," Master Hain instructed. Seri did so.

"Do you feel anything?" She shook her head.

"Now, close your eyes and concentrate. One of these blocks has been infused with magic. The other has not. See if you can tell the difference."

"Should I touch them?"

"No, but hold your hand close."

Seri did as instructed. She held her hand over one block, closed her eyes and concentrated, just as she had with the stone pinning Dravid. She felt nothing at all. She repeated the process with the second block. Again, she felt nothing. "I can't tell."

"Keep trying," Hain said. "Your journey to become a mage begins here, but you must take this first step."

She tried again. And again. She switched to her left hand. Then back to her right.

When she was almost ready to give up, she finally felt something. At first, she thought she had imagined it. She switched her hand from one block to the other, then back again. No, it was there. A tiny hum, the slightest movement, could be felt above the block on the left. She lifted her hand slightly, then lowered it again. It felt like a tiny muscle spasm in the palm of her hand.

She opened her eyes and pointed to it. "That one."

Master Hain nodded in approval. "Well done." He pointed at the other tables. "You will find a variety of items on each of the remaining tables. One or more items on each table have been infused. Take your time, and find them all. When you have collected all of the infused items, bring them to me in my office." He made to leave.

Seri looked around. Some tables had three or four items. Others had more like a dozen. Her heart sank.

"This will take all day!"

"Would you rather return to copying the names of the dead?"

She sighed and straightened her back. "No, Master. I will do it."

"Good. I didn't believe I had chosen inaccurately this time." He left the room.

"This time?" What did he mean by that?

Hours later, she brought Master Hain a collection of fourteen items, including seven blocks, four buttons, two coins, and one serving spoon. The buttons had been the hardest.

"You found all but three. Well done."

Three? She was certain she had found all of them. Frustrating.

"Don't feel bad. Most acolytes miss five or six the first time."

Somehow that didn't make her feel much better. She wanted perfection.

"Now go get some sleep," he instructed. "You have strained your senses for hours. After a night's rest, you will be amazed at what happens."

"What do you mean?"

He smiled. "Just go to bed. I prefer to let you experience some things for yourself."

(((29)))

Talinir held up his sword. "All worlds know battle," he announced. "As a warden, I fight here and in the Otherworld. And when I die, I will fight for all that is good and holy in the third world."

"There's fighting in the afterlife?" Victor asked. "I've never heard that."

After a surprisingly restful night's sleep in the too-soft beds, the two young men had eaten breakfast and gotten ready early. Eniri had walked them to the training grounds. She stood nearby, a slight smile on her face as she watched. Marshal found her presence distracting, but he tried to focus on Talinir's words.

The warden hesitated after Victor's question. "There is battle ongoing even now in the third world," he said at last. "We cannot see it or perceive it in any way, but battle continues between powers that are as far beyond us as we are above the insects. When I die, I believe I will join that battle."

"Huh." Victor looked thoughtful.

Marshal surveyed the training ground, trying to avoid looking at Eniri. Talinir had brought them to a private, small arena of sorts. A simple wooden wall surrounded the circle of sand they stood upon. Marshal knelt down and ran his hand through the sand, a new experience for him. He frowned at the coarseness and brushed it off his fingers.

Talinir walked to a stand of weapons and selected two swords. He turned and offered them out, hilts first. "Take these," he said. "You will not be fighting with them today, but I want you to get a feel for the weight and balance of the blades."

Victor took one. "These aren't the same as the sword you were using before," he pointed out.

"No, they are not, although they are still superior to most human-forged swords. The magical fires we use to forge our steel are far hotter than yours, making the steel itself purer. These are perfect for your use," Talinir said. "Warpsteel swords are… well, they're even more special, like the sword we made for Akhenadom. I'll explain another time."

"Warp… steel?"

"Another time."

Marshal took the sword that Talinir offered to him. His hand had been tingling all morning, as was often the case, but the minute he grasped the sword's hilt, the tingling stopped. Strange.

This sword looked like a traditional broadsword, though not quite as wide as ones he'd seen before. The two-foot long blade looked pristine, far longer than Aelia's short sword. Marshal could fit both hands on the hilt, but it seemed to be intended for only one hand most of the time.

Victor moved away from the others and took a few practice swings. Marshal moved slower. He tilted the sword and felt the balance shift. He tilted it back and felt it again. He lifted it up and down, observing the changes in the way it felt. On instinct, he slid his left foot back and turned half-sideways, holding the sword so that its weight balanced perfectly.

Talinir raised one of his odd-shaped eyebrows. "That's a basic defensive stance," he said. "Aelia taught you that?"

Marshal nodded. The stance and the sword felt right. It felt natural. It felt good. The balance of the blade felt so easy, so smooth. He wanted to toss it in the air and catch it. Somehow, he managed to restrain that impulse.

"Victor, I want you to stand the way Marshal is standing," Talinir said. As he helped both boys adjust their stances, he went on speaking. "Everything has a balance to it. Just as you felt the balance of the sword, how its weight shifted as you moved it, you must also recognize the balance of your own body. In this stance, your center is lower than normal. That helps you maintain your balance."

"We stand sort of like this when we're pulling fish in from the river," Victor said. He demonstrated, holding his sword as if it were a fishing net he was pulling. "My father said it was to keep the fish from pulling you in."

"It's the same concept," Talinir said, nodding. "If you were to block a blow from another sword, or deflect a beast's attack, while standing fully upright, it would knock you backwards, because of the weight shift. By shifting your own weight down lower, like this, you can prevent that."

"Now, if someone charges you…" He lunged forward at Victor, who stumbled back.

"Wrong. You lost your stance and left yourself open. If I had a weapon just then, I could have easily finished you off." Talinir looked to where Marshal watched. "Marshal, take a step backward."

Marshal hesitated, then slid his right foot back toward his left foot, before stepping back with it. He maintained the low stance throughout.

"Good. That was well done. Your other option would be to rotate your forward leg back, while your back leg stays put."

Talinir helped Victor adjust his stance, guiding him into position.

"Today is going to be all about stances and endurance. You're not going to be actually fighting with these swords. We'll switch to wooden practice swords for that. But I wanted you to be familiar with the weight and feel of the real thing."

For the next two hours, Talinir took them through several basic stances. Some Marshal knew. Some he didn't. Talinir made them move back and forth across the arena while staying in a low defensive stance. Through it all, he insisted they keep their swords held up. It didn't take long before they both tired of the swords' weight. Despite the cool temperatures, sweat soon drenched their bodies. At some point early in the first hour, Eniri left.

"Can we practice without the swords?" Victor asked.

Talinir smiled without humor. "I told you part of this was about endurance. If you were in a battle and the enemies kept coming, would you lower your sword because you got tired?"

"How many enemies?" Victor muttered.

Marshal didn't mind at all. As long as he held the sword, his hands neither tingled nor shook. Aelia's sword didn't have this effect on him. He couldn't remember the last time he had gone this long without those feelings. Maybe never.

It was curious, though. If the shaking and tingling came from the magic power of his birthright, did the sword actually block the magic? He carefully set the sword down on the sand.

"Marshal! I said to keep your sword up!" Talinir said.

Marshal ignored him and stared at his palms. A few moments went by. Talinir strode to him, irritated. In that instant, the familiar tingling spread across his hand, like thousands of tiny needles.

"Are you hearing me?" Talinir demanded.

Marshal picked the sword back up. The tingling stopped. Fascinating.

"Don't take another rest unless I tell you to," Talinir warned.

Was the sword completely blocking the power, though? He had only one way to be sure. He stared at the hand holding the sword and concentrated. For a long time, nothing happened. Slowly, so slowly it took him a while to notice, the power began to build up. After a few more moments, his hand began to shake.

"What are you--" Talinir's eye bulged. "Marshal! Drop the sword! Now!"

Marshal could no longer hold the sword, anyway. It tumbled out of his hands. He grabbed at it and missed. After two hours of working leg muscles unused to being worked, he lost his balance. He stumbled and went down to one knee. His palm struck the surface of the sand.

The power exploded from his hand. Sheets of sand erupted upwards. Stinging particles struck every inch of their bodies.

"AHHHH!" Victor dropped his own sword and covered his face with both hands. Talinir stood upright, unmoving, with both eyes clenched shut.

The sand rained down around them in a coarse shower. It took at least half a minute for it to finally stop falling.

Victor and Talinir shook sand from their bodies, brushing off what didn't fall off. Marshal remained on his knee, annoyed and embarrassed.

"Devouring fire, Marshal!" Victor ran fingers through his hair. "Watch what you're doing!"

"He nearly channeled it through the sword," Talinir said. "That would have been far worse."

Victor shook his head again, raining more sand. "How could that have been worse?"

Talinir knelt in front of Marshal and reached out to place a hand on his shoulder.

"I am sorry, Marshal."

Marshal looked up, curious. What did Talinir have to be sorry about? He wasn't the one who had blown up the arena.

"I should have anticipated this," the warden said. "Eldani steel, even in these basic blades, is designed to be a channel for magic. I did not consider that your powers would also find an affinity there."

Talinir pulled Marshal's sword out of the sand and held it as if it were a fragile thing. "Yes, I can feel it. You had already channeled a great deal of power into this." He glanced at Victor. "Too much power, and the sword itself might have exploded. Would you call that worse?"

Victor nodded with a frown. "I'm never going to get all of this sand out of my hair."

Talinir stood. "I think that's enough for today," he said. "Tomorrow morning, we'll meet again. Aelia won't be meeting with the High Council until the afternoon. I'll bring out the wooden practice swords. They'll be safer." He smiled at Marshal. "For multiple reasons."

<h1 style="text-align:center">(((30)))</h1>

When Seri woke up the next morning, she immediately felt the change. At first, the disorientation overwhelmed her, and she almost fell out of the bed. What had happened? Everything seemed so… so… real. The bed, the walls, the blankets: they all seemed more distinct and solid than they ever had before.

And more than that: she could feel Zes Sivas. Exactly as she had felt the magic in the items during her testing, she now felt the magic of the island. But the scale went far beyond that. The magic in the items had felt like tiny vibrations in her palm. This, this felt like a massive resonance pulsing down below. She could sense it, feel it calling to her. She longed to reach out and tap into it somehow, to feel it course up through the ground into her body.

She clambered out of the bed and put her hands onto the floor. Even though she knew multiple levels of the citadel stood between here and the island itself, she still felt stronger being a little bit closer to the power. Her hands trembled when they touched the floor.

"Magnificent."

Startled, Seri looked up to see Curasir standing in her doorway. She scrambled to her feet, grabbed the neckline of her nightgown and held it close. Had it been gaping open while she crawled on the floor? She fought embarrassment and a bit of fear.

"This… this is not proper," she stammered.

Curasir's expression did not change. "Oh, have I violated a human social custom? I apologize." He sounded so cold, like his apology didn't mean anything. "I only wanted to tell you that I wished to speak with you again, regarding the Otherworld. But…" He smiled. "I am pleased to discover that you have found your connection to the island's power."

"Yes." Seri didn't know what else to say. How tightly did the nightgown cling to her body? Conscious of her bare feet, she thanked Theon that at least the gown reached to her ankles and didn't show more. At the same time, her senses felt the power of Zes Sivas pulsing below, calling to her.

"I will look forward to seeing how you adapt to this," Curasir said. His non-starry eye seemed to be examining every inch of her. "I expect great things from you." He turned away and disappeared.

Seri breathed a sigh of relief. She hurried to the door and shut it. Only then did she let go of her neckline and relax. Her whole body trembled. Had she been shaking the entire time?

What was it about the Eldani that had unnerved her so? It wasn't just his presence in her bedroom and her state of undress. Embarrassment made sense, but not fear. She would not be frightened like this if a human had been at her door, like Dravid, for instance. For a moment, she lost her train of thought as she imagined the previous scene with Dravid standing there… How would she feel if…

She closed her eyes and shook her head. Focus. Curasir admitted unfamiliarity with human societal conventions. Or so he said. If true, his presence should not be taken in the same way as any other man's. But it wasn't just that. Nor was it the bizarre effect he had on everyone's vision, unable to focus on his true form.

There was something more, something that had made her shake with… was it fear? Anxiety? Maybe the magic of Zes Sivas reacted to the different magic of the Eldanim and confused her. Maybe.

She got to her feet again. Before anything else, she needed to speak with Master Hain. Actually, before anything else, she needed to get dressed.

•••••

"You have taken your first big step into understanding the magic of this world," Master Hain said.

"It's almost overwhelming!" Seri said. She had hurried to his office as soon as possible. "Is it always like this?"

"The feeling will fade somewhat, but now that your senses have awakened, you will always be able to feel the power of Zes Sivas below you." He held up a finger. "Be warned, however. When the Lords start arriving for the Passing in a few weeks, the power that is present will increase exponentially. By then, you should be used to the normal levels of power and able to handle the changes."

Seri frowned. "And if I ever leave the island?"

"Your connection to Zes Sivas will grow weaker the further you travel from it. This is why most of our order are rarely able to do any kind of magic away from the island," Master Hain explained. "Within the six lands, we are valued, not as much for our magical prowess, but for the wisdom and knowledge that we attain during our studies."

While he spoke, Seri realized she could feel the magic in Master Hain himself. It was much like the magic she felt below, but smaller and contained. As he walked about the room, she could sense the vibrations of his presence, like tiny pulses against her skin.

A thought occurred to Seri. "You said I'll be able to feel the Lords' power when they arrive. Would I be able to feel it off the island?"

Master Hain nodded in approval. "Yes, once one is attuned, it is easy to sense those who have power. This is why wild magic practitioners try to avoid all members of the Conclave of Mages. We can recognize them wherever we meet."

"So… why is it that no one has been able to find the King? Wouldn't he be the easiest of all to detect, with all of his power?"

"You are making very logical connections. That is good. The problem of the high King is indeed perplexing. As was said in the council yesterday, everyone has been looking for him for hundreds of years." He paused and cocked his head. "I say 'him,' but in reality what we are searching for is the King's family. Whoever now carries the power of the high King has never actually been King, of course. We are at least two to four generations removed from the last true King who sat here at Zes Sivas."

"Could it be a woman?"

"That is… plausible, but unlikely. As has been established for hundreds of years, the powers given to the Lords and King pass down to their eldest male child."

"But what if they didn't have one?" Seri pressed.

"Yes, as I said, it is plausible. But throughout the generations, Lords and Kings have made every effort to be sure they sired a son and heir, taking multiple wives when necessary, regardless of societal conventions."

"Lord Enuru has no son," Seri said. "And he is not a young man."

Master Hain nodded gravely. "The situation is considered the gravest among all the Lords," he said. "However, Lord Enuru seems dedicated to Lady Lilitu, despite efforts to persuade him to take another wife or mistress."

"Because he actually loves her." Seri had only met Lady Lilitu the one time, just prior to her journey to Zes Sivas, but she had been immensely impressed by the great lady.

"From what I have observed, that is probably true," Hain acknowledged. "But he still bears the responsibility to pass on his power at his death."

"They don't even have a daughter. What would happen to his power if he were to die?"

"No one knows for sure." Master Hain paused. "I presume that it would pass on to Lady Lilitu, as his closest family member, but that is questionable. It is not a blood relation, after all."

"And if they were to both die without an heir?"

"It has never happened. We simply don't know. Would the power itself seek out a new Lord? Would it simply return to the ground of Antises, as it was before? This was not foreseen by our ancestors."

"Could that have happened to the King? Could he have died without an heir? And his power went back to the land?" Seri's head swam with the speculation. But even as she said it, she knew. The earthquakes would not be happening if the King's power had returned to the land.

"No." Master Hain shook his head firmly. "We would know. The power here at Zes Sivas would grow, not with all of the King's power, to be sure, but enough of it that we would know. No, somewhere out there, Antises has a King. He just doesn't know who he is, or he doesn't want to come forward."

"Or she," Seri added.

Master Hain rolled his eyes. "Or she."

(((31)))

When Marshal woke up the next morning, all the muscles in his legs seemed to be screaming. An odd sensation since he himself had never screamed. Across the room, he heard Victor roll over and groan. His companion stood up and promptly sat back down on the bed.

"I don't know if I can stand!" he said. "We walk for miles to get here without a bit of soreness, but a few hours of stance training does this?"

It did seem strange. Maybe the leg muscles used in the stances weren't the same as those used in walking. Marshal tried stretching a little before getting to his feet. It helped but still hurt. His arms also felt sore from holding the sword, but they ached less than his legs.

Aelia opened their door, letting light flow in. "Time to get up, boys," she called. "Talinir will be expecting you shortly."

"Tell him we've decided to go ahead and die in bed, instead," Victor said.

"I'll give you five minutes, and then I'll come drag you out," Aelia said. She closed the door.

"Ugh. Whose idea was this, anyway?"

Marshal endured more of Victor's complaining as they got dressed. Marshal assumed he needed to express his feelings out loud, even if no one could respond to him. What would that be like? Once dressed, they grabbed a quick breakfast and walked back to the training grounds. They knew the way now. Eniri was nowhere to be seen this morning.

Talinir greeted them when they arrived and offered them a pair of wooden practice swords. Marshal took one and examined it. The weapon was carved, expertly but not decoratively, in the shape of the sword he had held the day before. The balance felt similar, but it didn't weigh quite as much. It also didn't stop the tingling in his hand. He tapped the blade against his palm. There would be no cutting with these, but a solid blow with one would probably leave a serious bruise.

"As you've already figured out, these practice swords are not harmless," Talinir said. He held one himself, making it look practically weightless with the way he moved it around. "You will get hurt. I advise you to get used to it now."

"After teaching myself how to use a flail, I'm used to bruises," Victor said.

"I can imagine." Talinir chuckled. "But that does bring up a good point. A sword is not a flail, Victor. The two weapons are used in completely different ways. You'll have to resist the urge to try your flail attacks."

"Someday, I'd like to be good at both."

"There's no reason why you can't, as long as you're willing to work hard. Speaking of which, let's get to it."

The warden dropped into a defensive stance, sword poised in front of him. "Come at me, both of you," he said.

Marshal and Victor looked at each other. Without further consultation, they moved in toward Talinir, both trying to keep their stances straight. Before either of them could even swing a blade, Talinir stepped in toward them. He swung a quick uppercut that smacked Victor's sword hand hard enough to make him drop it, then cut across to knock Marshal's sword into the ground.

Victor shook his hand and grimaced. "Okay, so what was the point of that?"

"Just establishing how large the gap is between us," Talinir said. "After learning a few moves, I don't want you thinking you're ready to take on all comers. This is an art form, and there are artists in this world that are more talented than I am." He paused. "Not many, mind you, but there are a few." Another pause. "I think."

"Ha!" Victor picked up his sword and resumed his stance.

"Keep in mind that your goal is not to strike your opponent's blade. In fact, you should try to avoid it as much as possible. It will only damage the blade. Most humans I know would prefer using a shield for that purpose. I prefer dodging, parrying only when necessary. Let's get started."

Talinir showed them some basic strokes and had them repeat the exercises over and over, again making them work the stances back and forth across the arena. If their legs had been hurting when they woke up, they were in agony by the time the warden finally called a halt.

Although he had difficulty keeping his grip on the wooden sword, Marshal found everything else about the exercises totally natural. When Victor struggled to get a particular stroke correct, Marshal executed it almost perfectly on the first try. Talinir appeared to be going out of his way to compliment and encourage Victor without praising Marshal's skill too much. Marshal understood. The last thing he wanted was to give Victor another reason to resent him.

After retrieving the practice swords, Talinir sent Victor to fetch some water for all three of them. Then he turned to Marshal with a critical eye.

"Aelia taught you well," he said. "You're adapting to this even faster than I anticipated. Have you practiced against anyone else?"

Marshal shook his head.

Talinir nodded. "Then you may be one of the most naturally talented swordsman I've ever encountered. I'd want a second opinion from one of the other wardens, of course. But... given enough work and practice, you could become a master at an early age." He grew pensive, looking away. "But what good..." He trailed off.

Marshal knew what he was thinking. What good would be a sword master who couldn't communicate? He could never pass on his skills to anyone, never teach anyone. Unless his curse was lifted.

Victor reentered the arena, carrying the water.

"Get a drink and then head home," Talinir said. "You should have enough time to get cleaned up and grab something to eat before it's time for Aelia to meet the High Council."

• • • • •

The High Council chamber brought Marshal to a stand-still. He stared until Victor gave him a gentle shove toward his seat. He managed to sit down, but continued to gaze around him in awe.

A domed roof towered over the circular chamber. At its base, it could easily hold four or five houses. Several hundred chairs filled the floor, all facing the same direction. An angled floor allowed those in back a clear view of the front. All the chairs faced a dais lined with stairs. Eight feet up from the ground, it clung to the rounded wall. Twelve fully enclosed podiums lined the wall, spaced evenly apart. A thirteenth podium stood on a much smaller dais right in the middle of the observation area. Whoever spoke to the high counselors would be standing in the midst of all the watching crowd. It would be quite the audience; Marshal didn't see any empty seats.

But the dome itself kept drawing Marshal's attention. It loomed above him in an unbelievable combination of glass and metal. He had never seen so much glass in one place. And to have it curved! He could see the cloudy sky without hindrance. While fascinating, he couldn't help but think of the sky full of giant stars he had seen before. This dome must have been designed with that place in mind.

The high counselors took their places behind their podiums. Marshal and Victor sat with Talinir not far from the thirteenth podium, where Aelia waited. She caught his eye and smiled. He smiled back, but didn't feel it. Something felt strange here, though he couldn't place it. He glanced at his hands. His tingles themselves seemed to be tingling.

One of the high counselors in the center, a male even taller than Talinir, stepped out from behind his podium. He made no sound, but merely stood in the open. The crowd quieted. The counselor spun on his heel and returned to his spot.

Another of the counselors, a woman with a resonant voice, spoke. "This session of the High Council of Intal Eldanir is called to order. Let those with ears to hear, hear. Let those with minds to reason, reason. Let those with hearts to understand, understand. Let those with wisdom to speak…" She paused. "Speak."

After another longer pause, she spoke again. "The High Council will now hear from Aelia, daughter of Evander, a human of the primary world."

A murmur swept through the crowd.

"Guess they don't hear from us humans too often," Victor muttered.

Aelia waited for the murmur to die down, then stepped up to the podium. Marshal thought she had never looked prettier, standing there with a firm set to her mouth, her long blonde hair loose and hanging down her back.

"Most noble counselors," Aelia began, "I am keenly aware of the great honor bestowed on me by allowing my voice to be heard in these chambers. As most of you know, this is my second trip to Intal Eldanir, having been here years ago with my father. We sought sanctuary with you for a brief time then." She paused.

"We do not do so this time. Regardless of other decisions, we will not be staying long. Events are even now transpiring that will force us to depart this glorious city before many days have passed."

Marshal blinked. What events was she talking about? And how had she gotten any news from the rest of the world?

"And yet, here you are," said the female counselor. "You came here for a reason."

"Yes," Aelia said. "I did. I came for the simplest of reasons, and yet the most difficult. I come to you as a mother, as one who would give her very life for her child. I come pleading, begging, for that most elusive of goals - hope."

"Speak plainly," another counselor called.

"I speak for my son, who has no voice of his own!" Aelia said. Her voice rose. "He is cursed! Cursed through no fault of his own, but because of the actions of the evil man who sired him. And so I come to you, the Eldanim, mightiest of all in the ways of magic. I petition you here and now: remove my son's curse!"

Marshal caught his breath. He knew it was the reason for their journey, for their visit here. But hearing it said like this… It changed everything. It made it… real.

For almost half a minute, no one spoke.

"Why should we do this?" asked a counselor on the far left of the dais. "Humans created the system of curses that binds Antises. Why should the Eldanim interfere in it?"

"Because it is the right thing to do!" Aelia said. "What has been done to Marshal is wrong in every sense. The original system of curses was warped by those in power, and one of the descendants of those powerful men took advantage of it, leaving me with a cursed child."

"Regardless, humans created this. Humans should deal with it."

"We have not the power to do so!" Aelia cried. "We are weak, powerless before that which has been done to us! This is not how Theon intended things!"

"It is not our place." The counselors spoke one at a time to Aelia. Marshal no longer cared which ones did the talking. His eyes remained fixed on his mother. She had tears in her eyes, but her voice remained firm and strong.

"You spoke of what a mother would do for her child," said another counselor. "You have another option."

Marshal's throat caught. Another option?

"If you will not do it for, for the rightness of the action," Aelia said, "then you should do it because it is in your own self interest."

"Explain."

"You knew my father. You know that Marshal is both my son and the son of one of the six Lords. If ever there were an opportunity to change all of Antises, this is it!"

"Why would we wish to change Antises?"

"You have wished to change it since Akhenadom and his Lords first bound the magic of Antises to themselves!" Aelia said. "You hated what humans did to the magic of the land. This is your chance."

"When the humans bound the magic of Antises, we swore to leave them to their own destruction," a counselor said. "As much as we might wish to change things, our word binds us. We cannot interfere."

Aelia stood silent for a long moment. Marshal had never seen her looking so resolute, so strong. She bowed her head and her hair fell around it.

When she didn't say anything else, a counselor turned to look at the others around him. "If there is nothing else," he began.

"You should save my son," Aelia interrupted. "Because he is the best chance you have to save yourselves."

"What do you mean?"

Aelia brushed her hair back, wiping away a tear at the same time. "You have tried to keep it a secret," she said. "You have tried to pretend. But your secret is open to me. You are at war."

This time, the murmur that ran through the crowd grew louder than ever. The counselors looked stricken or horrified.

The first counselor stepped out from behind his podium again. The crowd quieted.

"Clearly, the warden who brought you here has spoken out of turn," the first counselor said. "We will deal with him."

"Talinir is not to blame," Aelia said quickly. "He did his best to keep the secret, even going so far as to do battle with one of the tunaldi in front of us."

The first counselor visibly relaxed. "It is true. We are at war with those beasts. They roam--"

"They are not your enemy!" Aelia said. "You cannot convince me that you fear creatures such as those, however fearsome they may be." She stared directly at the first counselor. "No. You are at war with the Durunim."

The chamber erupted, not with a murmur, but with shouts and cries of consternation.

"Who are the Durunim?" Victor asked.

Talinir's face had gone white. "How did she find out?" he whispered. "How?"

"Where did you hear that name?" the first counselor shouted over the crowd.

Aelia waited until the sound died down again.

"What does it matter where I heard it?" she asked. "Your secret is known. And more than that." She paused again. "You blame us for the damage done to Antises, for the unnatural use of its magic. You are right to do so. But how do you respond? You withdraw! You hide!

"The Curses and Bindings do not affect you! You are free to live your lives as you wish, and this is how you do it? By hiding from the rest of the world? You transport your entire city to the Otherworld for weeks and months at a time, spending more time there than in this world.

"And all the while, you fight an enemy that you created!" The crowd erupted again, but Aelia kept going, speaking louder. "An enemy that you yourself risk becoming, by your own actions! How can you win a war, when you work so hard to become that which you fight?"

The first counselor took a step forward and raised his arms until the crowd quieted. Another counselor spoke up again. "Counselors, before we discuss this further, there is one other speaker from which we must hear."

After a quick consultation between three of the counselors, they asked Aelia to step down temporarily while someone else spoke. As Aelia stepped down, Eniri took the podium.

"What wisdom do you offer, Eniri, daughter of Harunir?" the first counselor asked. He had re-taken his position behind the podium.

"I speak not for myself," Eniri answered, "but for Lady Siratel, the seer."

The counselors nodded. They were expecting this.

"Honored counselors, Lady Siratel can not be here today, because she remains in a state of near catatonia," Eniri said. She waited for a quick murmur to end. "She entered this state after reading the life of Marshal, son of Aelia."

"Has she said anything about what she saw there?"

Eniri nodded. "Yes," she said, perhaps realizing not everyone could see her. "She spoke over and over about falling stars."

No murmur followed this statement. Instead, a silence fell over the entire chamber, an oppressive silence that could almost be felt. For a brief and insane moment, Marshal wondered if his own curse had fallen on everyone else.

"Was there anything else?" a counselor asked at last.

"No," Eniri said.

"You may step down, daughter," said another. Only then did Marshal recognize Eniri's mother, Indala. Perhaps they had a friend on the council after all.

Aelia re-took the stand and waited.

"The humans cannot be allowed to leave," one of the counselors said. "They have learned our darkest shame."

"Who would listen to them?" another shot back. "Many humans do not even believe we exist!"

"And what of the vision? Can we risk letting this boy out of our sight to fulfill it?"

"Counselors! We must first decide on Aelia's original request," said the first.

"Is Lady Siratel's vision more or less likely to come true if we lift the curse?"

"Is such a thing even possible?"

The debate continued on for several minutes before the first counselor asked for a vote. "Are there any who believe we should grant Aelia's request?" he asked. "Stand forth."

Three counselors stepped outside of their podiums, then a fourth, Indala, joined them. Marshal felt relieved. He had wondered if they would even be welcomed back to the house.

But no other joined them. Eight counselors remained opposed.

"The request is denied."

Aelia slumped forward, her head down. Marshal pushed aside Talinir's hand that reached for him and jumped to his feet. He rushed to his mother's side and embraced her. She returned his hug with warmth and strength. "You are loved," she whispered. "You are valuable. And you have a purpose in this world!" The words, so familiar to him, had never sounded fiercer.

"Are there any who believe that Aelia should not be allowed to leave Intal Eldanir?" the first counselor asked. Only two counselors indicated their support of that idea.

"Very well." The first counselor stepped out from behind his own podium and walked to the edge of the dais. He looked directly at Aelia, who lifted her face from Marshal.

"Aelia, daughter of Evander. You and your son and his bondsman have been our guests here, and you are welcome, in honor of your father and yourself. However, we do request that the three of you will leave this city within three days' time. After that, it is our intention that Intal Eldanir will once again be concealed from the primary world."

"It will be done," Aelia said, her voice no longer strong. She buried her head in Marshal's shoulder again.

A long silence followed. One by one, the high counselors left the room. The gathering was over. Marshal's feeble hope had been dashed.

<h1 style="text-align:center">(((32)))</h1>

Seri placed two wooden blocks on a tray and held it in front of Dravid. "Go on," she urged.

"I don't get it."

Though he was conscious again, Dravid remained bed-ridden and clearly in pain. His skin tone looked much healthier than it had when they had found him under the stones. His left leg had been crushed, and the healers held little hope he would ever walk normally again.

"Just hold your hand over each one," Seri said. "One has magic in it. The other doesn't."

Dravid raised his eyebrows, but put his hand over one of the blocks and then the other. He went back and forth a couple of times. "I don't feel anything," he complained.

"I know, it took me a while, too. Try closing your eyes and concentrating."

"I don't see what the point of this is supposed to be."

"Do you want to be a mage or not?" Seri demanded. "This is what Master Hain did with me yesterday, and-- and you won't believe what it's done to me today."

"What it's done today?"

"Yes, now shut your mouth and eyes and concentrate."

Dravid chuckled and obeyed. "I'm still not--"

"Keep trying."

For the next hour, Seri repeated the exercise with Dravid. She had asked Master Hain for permission and he had granted it without hesitation. Apparently, he was sympathetic to Dravid's plight of not having a Master to instruct him. When she mentioned this, Dravid wasn't surprised.

"I'm bound to him now," he pointed out.

"What?"

"He saved my life. I'm bound to him. He won't be able to get rid of me, until I return the favor."

"Huh. I hadn't even thought of that." Seri had known people who were bound to each other, of course. But she had never seen it actually happen.

Dravid caught on to the magic quicker than she had expected. By the end of the hour, he could pick the correct item within a few seconds. Seri felt somewhat annoying that he caught on faster than she had, even with the pain that continued to distract him. He tried to hide it, but it washed over his face every few minutes. Twice, he fell back against the pillow and had to rest. When that happened for the third time, Seri returned the items to the cloth bag she had brought them in.

"Are we done?" Dravid asked.

"For now," Seri said. "I don't know if that was enough. I spent a lot longer on it, but you've caught on faster. Maybe that'll work for you."

"Enough for what?"

"You'll find out in the morning. If it worked."

"Uh… all right."

"I have to go. I have other chores to do today." That wasn't entirely true. But as much as she liked Dravid, she disliked the whole situation more. Dravid still might die, and she couldn't handle that. Seeing Master Simmar's death had been enough.

"Oh. Well, uh, thank you for, um, coming to see me." Dravid seemed to be stumbling over his words a lot more than usual. The usual lilt to his voice even sounded flat.

"We're in this together," Seri said. "You, me, and Jamana. We're all going to be Master mages someday."

Dravid's eyes darted away. "Maybe."

Seri punched the side of the bed, and Dravid jerked in response. "Don't give me that. You got caught in an accident. You're still a part of this."

"I-- I wasn't supposed to be there, Seri," he said. "I was hiding, refusing a direct order. If I had gone home when I was told, I wouldn't be here now, with… this." He pointed toward his leg. His face grew more pained. "I didn't tell you when you came in, but… but they're saying they might have to cut my leg off. They don't know that I overheard them, but I did."

"Dravid, I…" She grabbed his hand. "Listen, we'll get through this.

We're on Zes Sivas! Magical, miraculous things happen here all the time! Who knows what-- what could happen?"

He responded with a forced smile that didn't look right at all. This was not the Dravid she knew, the Dravid who had welcomed her here and embraced her as a friend. His true smile always spread to others. It could not be contained.

"I don't have many friends," Seri said fiercely. "So I'm not about to lose one! Don't you give up!"

"I'm... I..." Dravid trailed off, unable to answer.

"All right. I'll be back tomorrow. We'll see if anything changes then."

●●●●●

Seri hurried out of the infirmary. Once in the hallway, she leaned against a wall and took a few deep breaths. Dravid's situation depressed her, but it could be much worse. Even Dravid himself didn't realize that just yet.

Regaining her composure, she straightened up and started down the hall. She still felt unsure about this section of the citadel. She had avoided it as much as possible. When she came to an intersection in the hallways, she paused to get her bearings.

She felt a tiny vibration down her neck at the same time she caught a glimpse of him. Curasir strolled in her direction from the left. That made her decision. She turned right and picked up her pace. She did not want to talk to him right now.

The hallway curved to the left and a handful of windows opened to the right. It followed the outer curve of the citadel's West side, if she remembered correctly. There should be a stairway down at the far end. Or was it up?

As she neared the end of the curving hallway, Seri glanced back. To her surprise, she saw Curasir, barely beyond casual notice. He appeared to have stopped to look out one of the windows. She groaned and sped up. The stairs went up, not down. That meant she would enter the top level, with the library. A good place to get herself lost and avoid unwelcome company.

After twisting and turning her way through several rows of bookshelves, Seri paused to catch her breath. She sat down on a nearby stool and listened.

She heard nothing. No footsteps, no rustling of books. Perhaps

Curasir had not been following her, after all. She let her shoulders slump and relaxed.

What a day it had been. She woke up feeling the power of Zes Sivas, only to have Curasir invade her bedroom. She learned from Master Hain, spent time with Dravid, and now this. Her emotions traveled up and down.

She felt a prickle at the back of her neck, similar to the feeling of power she felt below the island. But whereas Zes Sivas was a massive, pulsing fount of power waiting to burst forth, this was something else entirely: a swirling miniature maelstrom of power that seemed to be moving toward her, somewhere nearby. The vibrations felt totally different, more chaotic and strange.

She got to her feet and stepped on top of the stool. On her tiptoes, she managed to peek over the top of the nearest bookshelf.

At first, she saw nothing. She closed her eyes and felt for the maelstrom. Once she had its direction fixed in her mind, she turned her head that way and opened her eyes.

Curasir's mis-matched eyes stared back at her.

He stood two rows away. She could make out the top of his head over the shelves, though he seemed much taller, as always. And those strange eyes looked right at her.

Seri ran.

She no longer merely hurried, trying to avoid an annoying encounter. She ran in fear. Curasir held power within him that dwarfed that within Master Hain, who had spent most of his life absorbing magic from Zes Sivas. What did that mean? How did he keep finding her? Why did he keep finding her?

The rational side of her brain told her he only wanted to talk, as he had said earlier. He had spotted her in the hallway and was trying to catch up with her. Nothing malevolent in that.

But her emotions and her newly awakened magic senses screamed the opposite. Something felt very wrong.

Which way to the exit? She turned several corners. Why was this library so unorganized? What else did all those Master mages have to do, anyway? They couldn't straighten out their own books?

She spotted the exit at the end of another row and ran that way. She expected to see Curasir turn the corner in front of her, a smile on his face, looking as casual as ever. But it didn't happen. In fact, when she focused, she could sense him behind her somewhere.

She exited the bookshelves and rushed down the stairs. Only one place she could think of might be safe from the Eldani's pursuit. She descended two more sets of stairs and worked her way across the citadel to the other side. It didn't take long to find the entrance to Dravid's tunnels.

Jamana wasn't around to boost her, but enough debris still cluttered the hallway that she was able to push some in place and climb up by herself. She crawled through the tunnels as quick as she dared.

After passing several intersections, she paused and tried to determine Curasir's whereabouts. She could still feel him, somewhere behind her, but not far enough away for her liking.

If she could sense him so easily, could he sense her, as well? Of course. It made perfect sense. How then, could she ever elude him? If he wanted, he could climb into these tunnels as well. Then she'd be trapped. The thought of the Eldani coming through the narrow tunnel toward her while she couldn't get away terrified her.

Maybe… maybe she could disguise herself. Not in the traditional sense, obviously. But maybe she could hide her own magical… essence? What was it called? Another question for Master Hain.

She focused her memories and sought the right tunnel. It took a few tries, but eventually, she found her way back to the passage that climbed upward. She scrambled up until she reached the small room with the hole in the floor. The Inner Sanctum waited below.

She collapsed and caught her breath yet again. Here, above the heart of the magic of Zes Sivas, she could be hidden, couldn't she? She tried to reach out and detect Curasir again, but the power below drew her senses in until she could feel nothing else. It dominated her. She felt goosebumps erupt over every inch of her flesh as the power vibrated over her. She had been overwhelmed by the feeling when she woke up, but now it threatened to strip away everything about her. Hidden above such incredible power, her own tiny essence surely could not be felt by her pursuer, but the power itself scared her just as much.

She waited. The power would not harm her, she told herself. Be patient.

As her tension eased and her fear subsided, Seri's rational side began making some good points. If Curasir's essence felt so wrong to her, why did it not bother Master Hain? Or any of the other Masters? They all seemed to interact with him without any anxiety or trouble. Maybe she had a problem because her senses had only awakened. She wasn't used to him. That's all. Maybe.

Five or six minutes went by. Seri felt no sign of Curasir. She could still feel the power of Zes Sivas pulsing out toward her, almost begging her to take it, somehow, and use it. But she felt nothing more. Unable to contain her curiosity any longer, she crawled to the hole in the tiny room's floor and looked down into the chamber below.

Curasir stood below.

She gasped and jerked back, but soon realized he hadn't been looking up. Cautiously, she peered over the edge again.

Curasir stood on one of the six platforms, holding a hand outward toward the central dais. He stood completely still, and his face gave away nothing. But somehow, Seri got the feeling that he was fascinated. He rotated his hand in slow motion, as if feeling something.

Then he took a step forward, off the platform, and vanished.

Seri stopped herself from gasping again. Where had he gone? Immediately, the answer came to her. The Otherworld. Could he step between worlds that easily?

There was only one way to be sure. Seri covered her right eye with one hand and stared with her left. Somehow, there had to be a way to force her star-eye to work. She blinked a few times, but nothing happened. She closed both eyes and concentrated. She imagined focusing everything inside at her left eye. Then she opened it.

Once again, she saw the swirling vortex in the Otherworld, the physical form of the power that had been pulling at her all day, the heart of Zes Sivas. She stared transfixed at the endless colors, the myriad beams of light constantly erupting. It took almost a full minute of staring before she realized something had changed.

Some of the beams behaved differently. They shot out from the vortex, then curved back inward instead of continuing on their way.

Only then did she see the figure in the midst of the vortex. She knew it had to be Curasir, but it didn't look like him. This figure towered almost ten feet tall. Was this the form that her eyes could sense but not actually see when she saw him in the regular world? Despite his height, his proportions still seemed off, as if he had been stretched too far.

And his skin had become pitch black. Amid a thousand thousand colors, the Eldani's skin had changed, not just to a darker shade, but to something else. It seemed more than black, more like the entire absence of color.

The beams of light that curved out and then plunged back came back to him. Each one arced its way to his outstretched hand and open palm. Whatever color the beam might be, it no longer mattered once it struck Curasir's palm. It vanished into his nothingness. He absorbed the light and color and did not change. The act unnerved her in ways she couldn't comprehend.

Seri blinked and it all vanished again. She stared down into the empty chamber. But she had seen the other side, and it shook her beyond her comprehension.

(((33)))

"Bondsman," Victor grumbled. "I'm a bondsman."

Marshal ignored him. Dark thoughts roiled through his mind. What hope had there ever been? Lifting his curse? Why had he even considered it? He knew it wouldn't happen. Why hope? Things never worked out for him. That was the real curse, not his voice. Everything always went wrong.

"Isn't a bondsman a slave?" Victor said. "I'm not a slave."

The two young men walked back to the house by themselves. Aelia had stayed behind to make one final appeal to some of the counselors individually. She had little hope of success, but felt she had to make the effort. At least, that's what she told Marshal. Who knew what she actually thought any more?

This whole trip had been her idea. But for eighteen years of his life, she had kept secret the fact that his curse, the torment of his life, could be ended. Then, only after danger came to their village, she revealed the existence of a chance for healing. And now, she had even admitted the existence of another option, another chance. How many ways were there to lift a curse, anyway? And how many other secrets had she hidden?

"You are loved," she always said. And then kept secrets that could help him. Was this how you showed love?

"And if I were a slave, I wouldn't be yours, that's for certain," Victor said.

Enough.

Marshal turned and punched Victor in the stomach as hard as he could. Victor staggered back a couple of steps and stared at him in shock.

"What was that for?"

Marshal swung again, but this time Victor was ready and dodged out of the way.

"Have you lost your senses? What is wrong with--"

Victor couldn't complete his question because Marshal charged into him, fists swinging as fast as he could. A few blows connected, but with little force. At first, Victor tried to ward off the blows, but then Marshal's fist connected with his chin, and his head snapped back.

"Hailstones! That's it!"

Victor shoved Marshal away and punched hard, catching him on the left cheek. He staggered, but dropped back into the defensive stance Talinir had taught them. When Victor stepped forward to punch again, Marshal was ready. He deflected Victor's fist and swung with his left, nailing him in the side. His knuckles connected with ribs.

Victor grunted and took a step back again. This time, Marshal made the mistake and stepped forward. Victor unloaded with three direct punches in a row. Marshal deflected the first two, but couldn't stop the third. The punch connected with his face and sent him sprawling.

"That's enough!' Victor said. "Seriously, man. What did I do?"

Marshal sat up, his jaw throbbing. He scooted up against the nearest wall and didn't get back to his feet. Tears trickled down through his scars, though not from the physical pain.

Victor noticed. "Aw, Marshal. What... I just..." He sighed, then winced. He felt his ribs. "You really got me there. That's going to be sore for a couple of days."

He looked up and down the street. Surprisingly, no one had seen their tussle. Or maybe the Eldanim had completely ignored them. At any rate, he couldn't see anyone. Victor slid down the wall and sat next to Marshal.

"I don't, I mean, I can't possibly understand what you're going through," he said. "These Eldanim. They're too full of themselves, if you ask me. I mean, they could help you, but they won't. Bunch of dung haulers."

Victor felt his chin and chuckled. "I guess... I guess if you need to hit something, better that it's me than one of them. They might get really annoyed then." He glanced back up. "But you know something? Your scars look really freaky when you get angry. Some people, their faces turn red. With you, it's just the scars."

They sat in silence. Marshal noticed Victor hadn't even considered that his anger might be directed at Aelia. He only focused on the obvious. It was so like him.

The pain from his face and knuckles actually helped him focus. Being angry at Aelia wasn't going to change anything. He couldn't lash out at her, or the Eldanim, for that matter. Victor's self-centered grumbling had pushed him over the edge, but it did no good being mad at him, either.

Still, he doubted he would ever take Aelia's word for anything again. That was a difficult thought. When you've depended on only one person for your entire life and you lose confidence in that person, where do you turn? Marshal had no answer. Even more disturbing? He found that he didn't care.

•••••

Back at the house, Marshal sought the solitude of the bedroom. Victor left him alone. He looked around the chaos of the room. Neither he nor Victor excelled at keeping things organized. Clothes and other items littered the floor and beds.

All of this would have to be packed back up now. They would be leaving the city. Who knew where Aelia would be dragging them this time? Regardless, he would likely never see Intal Eldanir again. He would never see that place with the stars again. He would never see Eniri again. And once outside the city, the assassin would be after him.

He reached under his pillow and pulled out Volraag's dagger. Once again, he wondered if his half-brother had the right idea. Maybe things would be better for everyone if he just killed himself. It would be better for Aelia, Victor, Volraag…

But if he tried it here, the Eldanim would save him, like they had done a few days ago. Even so, he contemplated the dagger a bit longer before sliding it back under the pillow. That choice, if he took it, would have to wait until they traveled well away from the city.

His jaw ached. He touched it and winced. No doubt he'd have quite a bruise from Victor's punch, not that anyone would notice. To do that, they'd have to actually look him in the face. No one did that except Aelia.

And Eniri, come to think of it. Ever since she had walked up beside his bed after the stars, she had always looked him directly in the eyes. The scars didn't seem to bother her.

Victor opened the door and stuck his head in. "Indala wants to see you," he said. Marshal raised his eyebrows. Victor only shrugged.

He emerged from the bedroom to find Indala and Eniri both waiting. Victor stood nearby, clearly not sure of his place in this meeting.

Indala stepped forward. "I wanted to apologize to you directly, young Marshal," she said. "The high council erred today."

Marshal nodded. This seemed somewhat pointless.

Indala hesitated. She glanced at her daughter, then seemed to make a decision. She reached into a pouch on her belt and withdrew something.

"I cannot lift your curse on my own," she said. "Indeed, if it could happen, it would require a concerted effort by many of our most powerful. However, I can help protect you on your journey, as you seek another way." She lifted up her hand and displayed a small four-pointed star made of some kind of metal.

"Mother," Eniri said in a harsh whisper. "It is not yours to give!"

"Is it not? My ancestors forged it and those like it centuries ago. If anyone can lay claim to it, I can."

"What is it?" asked Victor, moving closer to get a better look.

"It is a Star of Indalanim," Indala said. "This will protect you, Marshal. As long as it lasts, no blade can harm you."

Marshal's thoughts immediately went to the dagger. But how could he refuse such a gift? He could always set it aside, if he wanted to.

"Remove your tunic," Indala instructed. Marshal blinked. He glanced at Eniri and then slowly obeyed.

Indala stepped up to him and pressed the star against his chest, right above his heart. It felt cold, like iron, but seemed to hum as it touched him.

"*i hatel indalanim!*" she whispered. The star hummed and vibrated. A glow surrounded it. Marshal cocked his head, trying to see. He felt almost nothing, but the star sank into his skin. The skin didn't open up; the star passed right through it. He no longer felt it at all. Where it had been, a faint gray imprint of the star remained.

"Whoa." Victor almost reached out to touch it, but stopped himself.

Indala nodded in satisfaction. "That should last you until you reach Reman, and well beyond, if I were to guess."

"And it'll really protect him?" Victor asked.

"Only from blades," Indala said. "They will not be able to pierce his skin. That is, no ordinary blade. I do not know if it would protect him from warpsteel or some other enchanted weapon."

"Huh."

Eniri shook her head, her mouth slightly agape. "That was an astounding gift. Marshal, you have no idea of the immense value of that star."

Marshal half-smiled. He pulled his tunic back on. Aelia always said he was valuable. Now maybe that much was true, in a way.

Victor wanted to test Marshal's new invulnerability, but Aelia and Talinir arrived at that moment.

"We will depart tomorrow," Aelia announced. "We have no reason to wait the full three days."

"Are we going to Reman?" Victor asked.

Aelia seemed surprised to hear the question. "Yes," she said. "That is our destination." She looked to Marshal. "Our only hope now is to attempt to lift the curse at the temple of Theon." Marshal looked away from her.

All three of the Eldanim looked troubled, he noted. They knew something he didn't. Again, Aelia kept secrets. Had he ever been able to trust her?

"I will be ready," Talinir said. "I gave you my oath, Marshal. We will continue our travels together, as long as you need me. I will protect you."

Indala had not told Talinir of the Star, either. Wouldn't that make his job easier? Maybe she didn't want him to let down his guard, thinking Marshal already had protection. So many secrets.

"We'll leave you, and prepare the evening meal," Indala said. "Come, Eniri." The two Eldani women headed downstairs, leaving Talinir alone with the three humans.

Aelia collapsed in a chair as soon as they left. She put her head in her hands and took a deep, shuddering breath. Victor shot a concerned look at Marshal. He ignored it, and walked to the window. The city looked so clean, yet so empty.

Talinir knelt beside Aelia. "If I could lift the curse myself, I would do it in an instant," he said. "As would Harunir and Indala, those of us who know you, those who understand humanity and not--"

"Not the evil corruption they imagine us to be," Aelia said bitterly. "My grandfather believed that the Eldanim were the only hope to change things in Antises. My father thought it was possible, but discovered the truth later in life. I thought they would at least help with this one thing."

"Too many of us are stuck in our ways," Talinir said. "We have no Bindings and Cursings to control us, as you do, but that does not make our chains any less restrictive, though we forged them ourselves."

"And now you create the enemy that will one day destroy you all."

Talinir sat back. "How did you find out about the Durunim, may I ask?"

"I know how to listen and observe," Aelia said. "It's nothing more complicated than that."

Marshal examined the window, pretending not to listen. The glass had a metal frame, and could be rotated in the middle to allow air to flow in. It was an ingenious design. He had never seen anything like it in a human-built window.

"What are the Durunim, anyway?" Victor asked. "I'm getting really tired of not knowing what's being talked about around me."

"They are the true enemy we face in the Otherworld," Talinir said. "I will speak no more of that subject."

Marshal could picture Victor scowling and trying to think of a good retort. He smiled in spite of himself.

He heard Talinir's voice again. "You don't have to go to Reman," he said.

"What else can I do?" Aelia asked. "That assassin is still out there. The young Lord will keep sending others after Marshal until one of them succeeds. We cannot hide forever."

"But if you were able to hide until Lord Varion dies, then Marshal would have the power to defend himself."

"Would he? Would the curse even allow that? You've heard what your healers have said. He cannot communicate at all, except basic ideas. Would it allow him to use power such as a Lord wields? No, the curse must be removed if he is to live."

Aelia's voice sounded so broken Marshal turned to look. She got to her feet and pushed away Talinir's offer of assistance.

"No matter the cost?" Talinir asked.

"No matter the cost."

<h1 style="text-align:center">(((34)))</h1>

Somehow, Seri made it back to her room. Her door did not have a lock, so she pushed her writing table in front of it. It wouldn't actually hold someone back, but it would at least give her more warning. The table itself gave her a twinge of guilt for not writing to her parents in the last few days.

She woke up the next morning with the magic of Zes Sivas calling to her, trembling at the edge of her consciousness, precisely like the previous day. Today was a Rest Day, so Master Hain would not be expecting her. She wished she could get training, because the call felt so strong. She longed to tap into the magic and use it. But the Masters held firm on Rest Days. No work.

When she ventured out of her room, she took her time, pausing at each hallway intersection, using both her vision and her magic sense to be on the alert for Curasir. She found no sign of him anywhere. Relieved, she hurried on. It didn't take long to track down Jamana. She dragged him to the infirmary.

"Why didn't you tell me?" Dravid demanded when they arrived. "I can feel everything!"

In her paranoia over Curasir, Seri had almost forgotten about attuning Dravid's senses. Together, she and Jamana, who had a similar experience to share, celebrated with Dravid and encouraged him. After the murder, the earthquake, and Curasir, it felt good to stop and enjoy the moment. Dravid even claimed the magical sense dulled the pain of his leg.

"What else have you learned?" Dravid asked after a while. "After you left me yesterday, did Master Hain teach you any more?"

"Um, not exactly." Seri took a deep breath and began the story, starting with Curasir's visit to her bedroom and ending with the scene in the Inner Sanctum.

"He turned black?" Jamana said. "You mean his skin? Was he darker than me?"

"It wasn't even black," Seri said. "I mean, it kind of was."

"Kind of?"

"I don't know. Everything looks different in the, the Otherworld. Curasir was black, but not what we call black. It's just the only word I can think of to describe it. It was almost like he had no color to him at all."

"Then he'd be white," Dravid said. "Black is a combination of colors. White is the absence of color."

Seri wrinkled her brow in consternation. "I don't know. That's all I can think of. He looked black to me, a black that was, um… a black that absorbed other colors. He was drawing in the colors and they vanished inside of him."

Jamana scratched his head. "This color thing… it confuses me. The Eldani told you that the Otherworld is the true source of our magic, is that not correct?"

Seri nodded. Out of the corner of her eye, she noticed Dravid wincing and gritting his teeth. He was trying to hide his pain again.

"Then why are you seeing colors there? Master Korda says that our magic is all about vibration. What does color have to do with it?"

"Maybe you should ask the Masters," Dravid said.

"I can't. I mean, I can't tell Master Hain about the visions," Seri said. "I'm afraid to even talk to him about Curasir. He's the one who brought him here."

"Did not Curasir say not to talk to the Masters about your vision?" Jamana asked. "Perhaps I am wrong, but that makes me want to talk to them. I do not trust that man. Or whatever he is."

"He did say that. I don't know. Master Hain is so set in his ways. I feel like admitting that I have a wild magic ability will only make him kick me out."

"There are ways to ask questions without telling everything," Dravid said. "You two are just not thinking right."

"Enlighten us, then, oh wellspring of wisdom!" Jamana exclaimed. He reached over and shoved Dravid's shoulder.

Dravid made a weak attempt at shoving back, but couldn't reach Jamana from his bed.

"Fine, I'll show you." He mocked a bow of his head at Jamana.

"Great Master Jamana, I have a question."

"You are beginning well, I am thinking."

Seri stifled a giggle.

"You have told me that all things have their own vibration. I know that the vibration will be different based on the substance of a thing, whether it is stone or wood, for example. Does that vibration differ between two items of the same substance, but different color?"

"Oh, acolyte, your question shows much stupidity," Jamana answered. "Go spend the next two weeks scrubbing pots in the kitchen while you reflect on your inferior intelligence."

Everyone laughed, but Seri had to admit that Dravid had it right. "I could ask about Curasir in a general way, too, I suppose," she said. "I could ask about why he feels so different to my senses. That wouldn't give anything away."

Dravid nodded. "You see? There are always answers, if you can come up with the correct questions." His smile returned.

"Such as, how hard will a certain acolyte have to work to walk again?"

The smile vanished. "That's not fair." A look of pain washed over his face again.

"Why is it not?" Jamana asked. "It is a question. But the answer is up to you."

Before Dravid could respond, Seri stood and grabbed Jamana's arm. "And we'll leave you to think about it," she said. "You're looking tired, and we should let you rest."

"But--"

"See you soon, Dravid."

Seri all but dragged Jamana out as he called a quick farewell. In the hall, he turned to her. "What was that? Why did we leave?"

"I'm sorry. I'm sorry. I just-- I needed to get out of there."

"Is there something wrong?"

"No, I, I can't say. But I need to get back to my room. I have to write my parents."

Seri hurried down the hall, leaving Jamana looking perplexed. He would have to live with it. Some things did not need to be discussed. She thought the Binding toward home had faded completely, but Dravid's situation had somehow woken it back up. She fought down the lump in her throat and kept moving.

(((35)))

The streets seemed all but empty the next day. Talinir and the three humans walked toward the outskirts of Intal Eldanir without passing more than four or five Eldanim. The still air unnerved Marshal.

"Why is it so quiet?" Victor asked.

"The city is preparing to shift worlds," Talinir said. "It is an involved process." He paused. "It's actually much easier to shift back into this world than into the other."

"Huh."

Ahead, Marshal could see the end of the road and the Great Plains coming to an end in the distance. A distant green line marked the trees that lined the Trebia River. As they drew near the city's border, he remembered what Victor had said about the city floating. How far up did it float? How would they get down? He had been unconscious when they entered and hadn't been near the edge since.

"How long will it take to get to Reman?" Victor said.

"It depends on how much we use the roads," Talinir said. "This won't be an easy walk. With me, you'll often be taking paths no one else knows, and they're not simple. We'll be avoiding civilization as much as possible. But… I would guess a month and a half will get us there."

"A month and a half?" When Talinir did not respond again, Victor muttered under his breath, but didn't ask any more questions.

It didn't take long to reach the edge of the city. The street came to an abrupt end. Marshal stepped close and looked down. The city floated about seven feet off the ground. It wouldn't be too hard to jump down, but with the high grass below, he couldn't tell if any rocks awaited them.

Victor nudged him. "Watch this," he said, and pointed at Talinir.

The Eldani warden bent down and placed his palm against the final bricks that made up the road's surface. He murmured a few quiet words in his own language.

Marshal felt a jolt, strong enough to make him reach a hand out in balance, but not enough to make him fall. He glanced around and saw the city rising higher. No, that wasn't right. The city wasn't rising. He and the others were sinking. A large segment of the road itself had detached and sank down to the ground while they rode it.

Victor had a huge grin. "Isn't it the greatest?"

When the platform neared the ground, Talinir stepped lightly off. The others followed. Almost at once, the platform began rising again. Marshal watched until it reached its starting point and seamlessly rejoined the road above.

"We need to get far enough away," Talinir said, setting out toward the Trebia.

The other three followed him, though with frequent glances back at the floating Eldanim city.

"Why does it float?" Victor asked. "The city, I mean."

"It's a necessary arrangement for shifting from one world to the other," Talinir answered without turning around. "The ground may shift and change over time, but when the city comes back, it won't interfere with anything else."

"What if a tree grows up in that spot?" Victor accelerated his pace to catch up to Talinir and walk beside him.

"It's also the reason we are situated over the plains. The chances of colliding with anything are very small. Even so, the wardens keep an eye out for things like that."

"I suppose it's the same on the other side? In the other world?"

Talinir nodded. "There are… plains on the other side, too."

"What do they look like?"

"That is hard to describe. It is the same, but different. The sky is full of giant stars, instead of sun or moon. The landscape is similar to this world, but not always the same."

Marshal thought back to his waking in the Otherworld. He had been so transfixed with the stars that he never looked anywhere else. He couldn't remember a single detail about the landscape. Not that it mattered. The stars were enough.

"This is far enough," Talinir announced. He stopped, turned, and looked back at the city. Victor glanced at Marshal and did likewise.

Aelia, strangely silent thus far, also looked back.

For a brief moment, Marshal wanted to keep going and ignore the city. The Eldanim had rejected him, after all. Why should he care what they did? But his curiosity proved stronger. He looked back just in time to see the process begin.

The city seemed to tremble momentarily. The air warped around it, as it had done with Talinir's sword in his battle with the mystery beast. And just like then, Marshal's hands began to shake. He clenched them into fists and held it in.

Intal Eldanir shimmered, faded, became solid again, shimmered some more, and then vanished away entirely. The Great Plains stretched out before them, empty as ever. Marshal unclenched his fists and felt the power fade, though his palms continued to tingle.

"Edin Na Zu," Victor breathed.

Talinir lifted his sword into the air -- a warpsteel blade again, Marshal noted -- and cried aloud: "Farewell, fairest city of two worlds. May your journey between them be safe. Return again to this realm, whole and protected. Until then, this world will be the poorer." He bowed his head for a moment, then sheathed his sword.

"Now!" he announced. "Let's make some adjustments. I'm carrying extra weight here." He lowered his overlarge backpack to the ground and opened it.

"What? I thought I was carrying enough already!" Victor complained.

"I don't think you'll object to this." Talinir took out a sheathed sword and handed it to Victor. He withdrew a second one and gave it to Marshal.

As soon as Marshal grasped the hilt, his palm stopped tingling. He sighed with relief. Talinir put one hand on top of his. Marshal looked up, confused.

"I'm going to trust you with this," the Eldani said quietly. "But do not try channeling magic into the sword. I will need to check it at the end of each day, just to be sure."

Marshal frowned, but nodded.

"Should this go on my belt or my back?" Victor asked.

"On your belt, of course," Talinir said. "You wouldn't be able to draw it very easily from your back. You are right handed, yes? Put it on the left side of your belt. Yes, like that. It will take some getting used to, and you may trip on it a few times."

"You don't expect them to fight the assassin, do you?" Aelia spoke up for the first time.

"He will be back," Talinir said. "I will try to keep our paths as secret as possible, but he strikes me as one who will find us, regardless." He hefted his pack and slung it back over his shoulders. "When he does, I may need help to defeat him. I will continue Marshal and Victor's training every day."

"Why would you need our help?" Victor wondered. "Last time, you stabbed him good. How do we even know he's alive?"

"Did you see his body when we left the city? No? Then he is alive, and more dangerous than ever. In order to save Marshal's life, I had to leave a warpsteel blade behind. In that assassin's hands, it will be especially deadly."

"Even so--"

"I caught him by surprise," Talinir interrupted. "I will not be able to do so again. I do not know his skill level, but I suspect it to be very high."

"I could not contain him for long," Aelia added. "He was highly skilled. He knew the masters and their techniques."

"The point is that I cannot be sure of defeating him alone," Talinir said. "We must be prepared for any eventuality. That is why they have the swords. Let's move on."

They started walking again.

"How do you plan to cross the Trebia?" Aelia asked.

"I do not think it wise to cross near Efesun again. It's too obvious. We will follow the river south until we find a safer place to cross."

The mention of Efesun reminded Marshal of his last night there. The shadow man. Was he friend or foe? Perhaps the assassin wasn't the biggest threat to their journey.

•••••

Talinir had not been joking. The differences between his leadership and Aelia's were enormous. They spent most of the day walking through the tall grass on the edge of the Great Plains, but at a strenuous pace. Aelia had never pushed them this hard on the road.

The air felt cool, but no longer cold. Only a scattering of clouds traveled the sky while they walked. Winter had moved on now. Marshal grew sweaty by mid-afternoon. He noticed the same of Victor and Aelia, but Talinir showed no signs of perspiration. Did Eldanim sweat?

Marshal put his hand to the sword's hilt at his side every few minutes. The relief it granted from his trembles was too much of a temptation to avoid.

They pushed southeast all day, eventually meeting back up with the trees near the Trebia River. They skirted the trees until twilight. When Talinir selected a spot for their camp, Marshal assumed that meant rest. But Talinir had other ideas. The warden insisted both he and Victor spend the remaining sunlight practicing their stances and movements with the swords.

"I really should have stopped sooner and given you more time," he said. "I'll do better tomorrow."

"Maybe right after we've been walking so long isn't the best time," Victor suggested between labored breaths.

"It's a great time," Talinir said. "As is first thing in the morning, which we'll start tomorrow."

Victor groaned.

Aelia had been gathering firewood while they trained. When it finally grew too dark to see, she lit the fire, and the three men joined her. Before he sat, Talinir looked up at the sky. "Still within the plains and few clouds. It will be a good star night." His voice communicated satisfaction.

Aelia passed out some dried meat. "We will eat better tomorrow," she said. "I'm too tired to cook anything tonight."

"Let me examine your sword, Marshal," Talinir said. He held out his hand, and Marshal obeyed. Talinir held the sword up and looked at it for a few moments.

"Yes, you've channeled a bit of magic into it throughout the day and our training time, but not very much. This is good. It should easily dissipate by the morning." He handed the sword back. "But continue to resist the urge to deliberately channel magic into the blade. Too much and, well, we'd have to find you a new sword."

"Aren't the swords designed to channel magic?" Aelia asked.

"Yes, that's the potential problem."

"Then can't you train him how to use that?"

Talinir looked flummoxed. "I-- I suppose that's possible. I've just never... I've never tried it before. I'm not sure how to communicate to-- that is, I..."

Aelia held up her hand. "Enough, warden. I understand. Teach him how to use the sword for now. Maybe later, you can work on the rest."

Marshal frowned. She kept making decisions about his life, and he had no control over it whatsoever. He got to his feet and moved off into the darkness. The others would assume he was going to relieve himself.

He wandered far enough away until he could no longer hear their conversations. The cool night air felt good after the day's workout. He closed his eyes and inhaled deeply. For a brief moment, he wondered what would happen if he began running, leaving the others behind, running and running…

Stupid thought. Talinir would find him in no time. Besides, he was too tired to run away. He sat down in the tall grass and looked up at the stars still emerging for the night. The moon, almost full and glorious, outshone them all. Beauty filled the sky, but nothing like the stars he had seen in the Otherworld. He felt an ache in his heart at the thought. Someday, he had to see those stars again. The ache intensified.

He closed his eyes and bowed his head. So many thoughts wrestled for his attention, thoughts he could never, ever share with anyone else. Eniri had confirmed that. No wonder he had so much trouble just remembering what nods and shakes of the head meant. The curse went deeper than even he had understood.

The thought of Eniri changed the projection of his reflections. He had little hope of ever seeing her again. He felt sad about that. She had easily been the most beautiful girl he had ever known. His thoughts wandered down trails he had never seriously contemplated before.

And yet… Aelia had not given up hope. She had another plan to remove his curse. If it worked, then maybe he could return to Intal Eldanir and visit Eniri again. Best of all, maybe he could get back to the Otherworld, the Starlit Realm.

He felt a tiny sting on his arm. He opened his eyes and saw a glow. It was a thrummer. He waved his arm, and it took off into the air, its abdomen glowing with a faint green light. Its wings made a soft humming sound.

Marshal had not seen one of the magic-seeking insects in over a year. They were rare up in the foothills. A memory filled his head of the first time he had seen one glow. He was around five years old, and Aelia had prevented him from swatting the tiny creature when it stung him. She held him in her lap and they watched the glowing insect circle around and around them until its glow faded.

The thrummers would bite anyone, but were especially drawn to those with some kind of magic within. Aelia had blamed it on his curse. The thrummers couldn't tell the difference between curse-magic and other kinds. They just liked magic. It made them glow. Most people never saw it happen and regarded the insects as only slightly less annoying than mosquitoes.

Marshal felt another tiny sting on the back of his hand. It didn't hurt much. He lifted his hand slowly and watched in fascination as the insect began to glow. Its color began as a shade of red, then shifted into other shades, the longer he left it alone. The brighter it glowed, the faster it beat its wings and the more it hummed.

He stood and held his arms out from his sides. Another thrummer landed near his elbow, and he felt another sting on the back of his neck. He waited, feeling another sting and another. If they had been mosquitoes, this wouldn't be worth it, but thrummer bites never left welts.

He closed his eyes and waited. When he could feel over a dozen insects biting him at once, he shook himself and opened his eyes.

A spectacular sight awaited. A cloud of colorful, humming insects swarmed all around him. Swirling, twirling, humming and glowing, the thrummers tried repeatedly to settle on his skin again, but he shook them off. He sank back down into the grass, watching the insects circle him. Red, green, blue, yellow, orange, violet - every color was represented and glowed with varying levels of brightness.

Marshal sprang to his feet and ran, trailing swirls of glowing thrummers. Inwardly, he laughed in delight. He looked over his shoulder, watching the insects chase him. He lost his balance and tumbled through the tall grass. He rolled to a stop on his back and looked up. The thrummers circled his fallen form, swirling just outside his reach. Behind them, a vast array of stars had emerged in the night sky. It wasn't the Otherworld, but the combination of the moon, stars and thrummers created beauty enough. It filled his aching heart with a feeling he had rarely experienced. It took a moment for him to find the right word to describe it.

Joy.

(((36)))

Kishin crept another inch closer. In order to defeat the Eldani warden's watchfulness, he dared not move any faster. If he moved again for another quarter hour, it would be too soon. Patience was a skill requisite in an assassin. To kill the daughter of the Lord of Ch'olan, Kishin had once waited for three hours concealed in a snowbank, unable to move until his target had ventured exactly three feet away from her bodyguard. She had not confessed her curse before dying. Neither had the bodyguard.

Here, he had only the tall grass to conceal himself, but he made it work. The moon had set, leaving the night illuminated only by the campfire he approached.

Only two figures sat there now. His target and the young man bound to him both slept. The mother and the Eldani warden remained awake, talking and occasionally feeding the fire.

Kishin had left his new sword behind, along with his other gear, for tonight. He did not intend to kill his target just yet, but to see what had changed in the city of the Eldanim. It would not do to rush in without full knowledge of the situation.

He felt the ground immediately in front of him and found nothing that would proclaim his presence. He moved another inch. If he leaned forward, he could hear their conversation. Aelia and the Eldani spoke in low voices.

"…the cost. Is it worth it?" The warden's voice was strong in spite of his attempts to keep it quiet. His words were easy to make out.

"How… say that?" Aelia said. "… my child. How can … … sacrifice for him?" Her softer voice was harder to hear, but the longer he listened, the more words he could distinguish.

"All parents sacrifice for their children. That doesn't mean you must go this far."

"But it's … only way left! If there's any hope…" She trailed off.

Kishin scowled and broke his rule. He moved another inch forward earlier than planned. This conversation sounded significant.

"If there's any hope of lifting Marshal's curse," the Eldani said. "I know, I know."

Only Kishin's years of controlled responses kept him from losing his balance in shock. Lifting a curse? Impossible. Ridiculous.

"Then why do you question me?"

"Because you are still young. You have many years ahead of you. Regardless of this hope, that is true. There is a limit to the sacrifice a parent is called to make."

"And … do we draw that line?" Aelia pleaded. "If my child were sick with the plague, would I not risk myself every day to care for him? Would I not stay by his side to save his life, at the risk of my own?"

"Of course, but--"

"There is no difference! Marshal's very life is threatened. The only way for him to survive is for his curse to be removed. We went to the Eldanim, and they turned us down. All that remains is the temple."

The temple. In Reman? Did the priests have a way to remove curses? How had he never heard this before? How was it possible?

"I can guide you back across the plains," the Eldani insisted. "We can go to the other side. Beyond it--"

"There is nothing beyond it! Outside of Antises, the world is barren and ruled by barbarians, and…"

"You do not know that. If we go far enough, we may find something. And if we go far enough, we can leave these problems behind."

Aelia did not speak for a long moment. Kishin resisted the urge to move closer again.

"Do you truly believe that Volraag will give up? That his assassin will give up?"

Not likely.

"No," the Eldani admitted.

"Then our path is clear. Please do not speak of this any more on our road to Reman. Let me enjoy what time I have with my son." She stood. "Goodnight, Talinir."

"Goodnight, my lady. I will honor your request."

As Aelia readied her bedroll, Kishin moved an inch back. He had heard enough, and it had shaken him.

Curses could not be lifted. The laws of the universe would not permit it. This was the way of things. Nothing could change that. But the conversation had implied not just one, but two ways to lift a curse.

Kishin supposed it made sense that the Eldanim might be able to do the impossible. They were creatures of magic, after all. Simply because he had never heard of them lifting a curse didn't mean it wasn't possible. But they had rejected Marshal, despite taking him in and healing him. That meant either they couldn't actually do it, or they didn't want to try because of the difficulty, or they simply did not want to interfere in the human world. Any possibility might be true.

But the temple? In Reman? Preposterous. Priests did not have that kind of power. Maybe the mages of Zes Sivas, but priests? Ridiculous.

He had never been to Reman's temple, but Kishin had once killed a priest in the temple of Tenjkidi in Mandiata. He couldn't recall taking on an easier job. The priest was fat and ignorant of anything outside his own tiny sphere of influence. Strangely, when Kishin had pressed him, he had admitted a true curse - impotency. Theon sometimes displayed a strange sense of humor.

Walking among the priests had given Kishin some insight into their world. They worked to remind people of Theon's justice and encourage them to keep the laws. Nothing more. They had no magic, no true k'uh. How could they possibly lift a curse?

Yet Aelia seemed convinced it could happen, and that it would cost her dearly. The Eldani wanted to talk her out of it. He seemed to believe it, too.

No. It was a fool's errand. The impossible was still impossible, no matter what someone might believe.

Kishin knew one thing. The closer Marshal came to the city of Reman, the easier Kishin's job would become. For now, he would follow and wait for opportunity.

Time was on his side.

He gathered himself to move further away when a movement by Talinir caught his attention. The Eldani had spread his own bedroll and lay on it, looking up at the stars. But he looked uncomfortable, shifting around. Curious.

Talinir glanced in the direction of Aelia's bedroll. Then he dug in his pack and removed a leather pouch. He squeezed one drop of liquid into his palm and laid back down. He held his hand above his face and the light from the starshine washed over it.

Interesting. Kishin looked to the sky. Thousands of stars shone down tonight, but apparently not enough for the warden. Kishin knew a weakness when he saw one, a weakness he could exploit.

(((37)))

"The easiest thing in the world is to destroy something," Master Hain said. "That which can be built can be destroyed. But to restore something already destroyed? That takes true power."

He placed several fist-sized chunks of hardened clay on the table in front of Seri. She opened her mouth to ask a question, but he warned her with a raised finger.

"This is why the priests teach that one day Theon will restore the world itself. For while we believe he created it all, it is now broken, damaged. And if he can restore it one day, then that is true power. For what greater power can there be than to restore a broken world?"

Seri nodded and looked at the clay. She wanted to ask the color question, but so far this morning, Master Hain had not allowed her to speak.

"Unfortunately, for our purposes, the easiest way for me to teach you to channel the magic of Zes Sivas involves destruction." Master Hain sighed and pointed at the clay. "We will start with clay, as it is one of the easiest substances to work with, and it won't cause a lot of damage should you lose control."

Lose control? Seri had not considered that side of things. A mage with no control over her powers would be insanely dangerous. What would the Conclave do if an acolyte couldn't gain control? Would she be banished from the island? Or worse?

"You've seen me destroy a stone, so there's no need for me to demonstrate. Instead, we must work on your channeling. Pick up one of these." He gestured.

Seri picked up a chunk of clay and waited expectantly.

"Now, this clay is solid enough to hold its shape, but if you squeezed hard enough, you might be able to break it," Hain went on. "Do not squeeze it. Instead, hold it loosely in your palm, like so." He demonstrated, and Seri imitated him.

"Close your eyes. There is no magic bound within the clay, so do not focus there yet. Instead, focus on the call of Zes Sivas. You have felt it for two days now. It should be very familiar."

Seri nodded, her eyes closed. The call was always there, vibrating, straining, begging her to use it.

"This is where you accept that call."

"How?" The question popped out of Seri's mouth before she could stop it.

"Hush. Concentrate. Open yourself up to the power."

Seri stood still and tried to follow his instructions. Nothing happened. After another minute, she admitted, "I'm not sure what I'm supposed to be doing."

"It is calling to you, yes?"

"Yes."

"If you were outside and a familiar voice called to you, the first thing you would do is turn toward the sound of their voice," Master Hain said. "Zes Sivas is calling. In your mind, turn yourself toward it." He waited a moment, then went on: "When you see the friend who is calling you, what do you do? You react in pleasure. Maybe you run toward him. In your mind, express your pleasure toward the magic, run toward it… and then embrace it."

Seri kept her eyes closed and tried to focus. She tried communicating pleasure toward the magic. Nothing seemed to be working. She could feel the vibrations, just beyond her reach. Master Hain continued to speak in calm, measured words, repeating his analogy and encouraging her to keep trying.

After fifteen minutes with no success, Master Hain backed off and let her continue to try on her own. Frustrated, Seri tried and tried again. Another half an hour passed by with no success. Master Hain did not act impatient or disappointed. He uttered a few encouraging words every so often and continued to wait for her.

Seri bowed her head and opened her left eye. She wasn't sure what she expected to see, but at first everything looked the same. Then a thick beam of green-tinted light shot through the floor near her feet and continued on through the ceiling. It vanished only a second or two after it appeared. As she kept watching, she saw more beams of varying colors appear. They must come from the vortex she had seen in the Inner Sanctum.

After a few moments, she surreptitiously adjusted the position of her left hand and intercepted one of the beams, a pale green one. She gasped as she realized the power she had felt calling her for two days had now entered her body. It felt like spasms throughout her chest. She quickly closed her eye.

"Do you feel it?" Master Hain asked.

"Yes. I-- Yes!"

"Now! Focus on the clay!"

Seri complied. She focused for only a split-second. The chunk of clay exploded in her hand, scattering a dozen or so pieces in every direction. Three or four pieces struck her, but weren't moving fast enough to hurt. She opened her eyes and stared open-mouthed.

"I did it!"

Master Hain clapped. "Very good! I knew you would find the connection."

Seri did not mention the beams of light. Had she stumbled across a completely different way of doing magic? Or was this the way the Eldanim did it? It's what Curasir had been doing, or something to the same effect. Maybe Master Hain and the others did the same thing, but couldn't see it the way she could.

Master Hain placed another chunk of clay in her hand. "Try again," he ordered.

Seri repeated the process, but this time managed to speed up her focus on her star-sight (as she called it in her mind). She saw another green beam and started to reach for it, then hesitated. Did the color make a difference?

Instead of the green, she intercepted a reddish beam. She felt the power enter her again, but the vibration wasn't the same. It felt... less. She focused on the clay again.

This time, the chunk of clay came apart, but the pieces did not shoot out of her hand. Some of them tumbled off, while the others remained.

"Interesting," Master Hain said. "Most students pull in more power the second time. You pulled in less. Did you stop drawing it in early?"

"I'm not sure," she answered. "I think so. Can I try again?"

"Yes, but the reverse is also true. Try not to draw in too much."

Seri took another chunk of clay and tried again. This time, she waited, watching the various colors. Green had been stronger than red. So many shades. Which one should she choose? She settled on blue, reached out and intercepted the nearest beam.

Instantly she stiffened. The power rushed through her body. She could feel the vibrations stronger than before. Even her throat vibrated. She felt saliva pooling rapidly within her mouth. Could this be too much? She focused on the clay, bracing herself at the same time.

The clay exploded outward in a thousand tiny fragments. They struck the walls, her robes, and Master Hain. Where they struck, they seemed to melt into liquid, leaving tiny stains.

Master Hain chuckled. "What did I just say?" he said good-naturedly. "This is why we use clay. If this had been a solid rock that you shattered, we could have been seriously hurt. Never use more power than is necessary." He pointed to the remaining chunks of clay. "Here are a few more. There's a bucket under the table with still more. Take your time. Experiment. Learn the correct amount of magic to absorb for this task. What you did the second time was good. Practice until you can do that each time. Then clean up."

"Yes, Master." She picked up another chunk. Master Hain walked to the door, but stopped when she said, "Master? I know that a rock would be different, require different vibrations, but is there anything else that matters?"

He paused. "What do you mean?"

She held up the clay. "Well, this clay is brown. If it were red, would that matter?"

Master Hain furrowed his brow. "Red clay does have a slightly different consistency," he said.

"Yes, but does the color matter?"

"Color? No, color makes no difference. Only the consistency, the density of the item. If you were to paint one of these pieces of clay red and the other blue, it would make no difference."

Seri nodded. She had only asked because Dravid and Jamana would expect her to. It wasn't the color of the item that mattered, but the colors of the light beams. Perhaps the colors corresponded to different levels of vibration, different amounts of power.

Master Hain turned to go again, but she had another question. "Master?"

"Yes?" His response was almost a sigh.

"I, that is, you talked about how we could feel the Lords when they arrived. What about the Eldanim? I could sense him yesterday."

"Ah, yes. I neglected to mention that. The Eldanim are creatures of magic, of course."

"Yes, but it… it frightened me. He felt… wrong."

"You are one day into this profession and already you know what is wrong?"

Seri blushed. "I don't mean to question you, Master. It was just--"

He raised a hand to stop her. "No, no. You are an intelligent young woman and asking questions is one of the ways you get there. I apologize." He reflected for a moment. "The Eldanim are a different kind of magic than that which is of the land. It will feel different. Different is not necessarily wrong. Let your senses grow and develop. Your discomfort should work itself out. Now. Resume your practice."

Once Master Hain had left, she put aside the questions and tried again. She found another red beam and duplicated her previous success. With that taken care of, she set out to experiment. She soon figured out that shades of red, orange and yellow were ideal for this exercise, whereas the darker colors - green, blue, purple - were too powerful. In fact, one bluish-purple beam felt so strong that she held the clay up in the air above her before releasing it. At least one piece of the clay smashed a hole in the window, while the others impacted the walls at high speeds. On the other end of the spectrum, a reddish-purple beam had so little power that the clay didn't explode. It liquified in her hand and ran down between her fingers.

In the end, she made quite a mess of the room. She looked around and laughed. Splatters of mud and pieces of clay coated the walls, floor, ceiling, table and door. Time to find a broom and a few other supplies.

"Too bad I can't clean up with magic," she said, and laughed again. Ordinarily, she'd be annoyed at being tasked with this kind of job, but for now, it didn't matter. She could do magic!

Seri was a mage.

(((38)))

The Trebia River had not slowed its flow in the week since they had crossed it. If anything, it ran higher and faster than before. Marshal looked at the swift moving river and shuddered. He did not relish another dip in that frigid water.

"How are we going to cross?" Victor asked.

"We'll walk," Talinir said. "We just have to find the right spot. If we can't find one this morning, we'll have to wait until evening. Afternoons are more dangerous."

"Why is that?"

Talinir pointed at the water. "The river rises as the snow melts in the mountains, but snow melts slowly. In the afternoons, however, there's a greater chance of thunderstorms along the route. That can increase the flow quickly and dramatically."

Aelia frowned. "Surely you don't expect us to wade through this?"

"Oh, no. As I said, we just have to find the right spot."

Aelia looked dubious, but she followed as Talinir set out along the river bank, continuing their southeasterly trek. The bank here was a gentle slope, not at all like the high cliffs near Efesun.

"Are we looking for the narrowest spot?" Victor asked.

"Not necessarily. The narrow spots may be the deepest and fastest. However, if I remember correctly, the river widens ahead and grows shallower. That may be our spot."

Marshal admired the foliage as they walked. Many of the trees along the bank exploded with new leaves. Spring had advanced so much more than when they left Drusa's Crossing weeks ago. It gave him a warm feeling that didn't come from the sun, especially when he thought about the thrummers from the night before. The world wasn't

198

all despair and pain. Sometimes it held beauty too.

"Ah, up there, see?" Talinir pointed, but Marshal couldn't see what he saw. The Eldani warden ran ahead of the others, around a gentle curve in the river.

The humans caught up with him and saw the river had widened out around ten feet. But at its widest, it also became much shallower. The river bed was clearly visible. At its deepest, it couldn't be more than two feet.

"Even at knee deep, we'll be freezing after only a couple of steps," Aelia said.

"We'll make a fire on the other side, but it shouldn't be that bad," Talinir answered. He hurried on ahead and took a step out onto a rock the others hadn't noticed.

"You see? There are plenty of rocks through here. There's only a couple of places where we'll even have to jump a little. Come on!"

Victor gave Marshal a skeptical look, then followed Talinir's lead. Aelia gestured for Marshal to go next and she came last. Despite Talinir's assurances, all of them slipped at various points and got both feet thoroughly wet and cold. With the warden's guiding hands, however, no one fell in.

As soon as they reached the other side, all of them set to work getting a fire started while they shivered. It didn't take long before they had their bare feet stretched out to the roaring blaze. With their chilled toes thawed out, they all relaxed.

Marshal couldn't help noticing that Talinir's toes appeared just as angular as the rest of him. His smallest toes were almost pointed. Yet another reminder of the Eldanim's strangeness.

"Ohhhh." Victor lay back on the grass. "I think my feet could catch on fire and I wouldn't even notice. It'll be fine."

Aelia looked around and up at the sky. "Reman must be almost due east of here," she said.

Talinir nodded. "Yes. Perhaps a little bit to the southeast."

"So we have a straight path from here?" Victor asked.

"Oh, no. There are no straight paths, at least not lengthy ones. We'll weave in and out of the hills, villages, farmlands, forests and so much more between here and there. We'll cross a few streams, but nothing as big as the Trebia, at least until we get to Reman."

With his feet warmed, Marshal discovered an annoying itch on the instep of his left foot. He tried scratching it. When that didn't work, he took out the dagger and scraped at it. He could feel the pressure of the blade's tip, but it didn't cut his skin. For the first time, he had tested the spell, somewhat. At least he satisfied the itch.

"Careful. Don't cut yourself," Aelia warned.

Victor and Marshal's eyes met. Marshal narrowed his. Now was not the time to tell her. But he knew Victor would bring it up again soon. Somehow, he waited until the evening. While Aelia and Talinir held a lengthy discussion about politics in the six lands, Victor got up and beckoned Marshal to join him some distance from the fire.

"Have you even tested it yet?" he asked.

Marshal frowned.

"The magic thing," Victor said. "You know, the protection spell or whatever that the Eldanim put on you." He pointed toward the spot on Marshal's chest.

Shake is no.

"Aren't you curious?"

Marshal glanced back at his mother. She seemed completely preoccupied with the conversation. He took out Volraag's dagger. Victor looked as if Marshal had brought out a plate of Indala's fried chicken. It made him smile in spite of it all.

Marshal aimed the point of the dagger at his left palm, hesitated, then moved it down to the palm heel. He pressed gently. He could feel the pressure, but the point did not pierce his skin. He pressed harder. Still nothing.

"You sure that thing is sharp?"

Marshal offered the dagger to Victor. He tested the tip on his own forearm and drew blood almost immediately. "Yeah, I'd say it's sharp. This is the dagger the Lord's son gave you? Your half-brother?"

Nod is yes. It still felt odd to think of Volraag as his half-brother, though.

Victor moved the dagger through the air a few times. "Nice." He eyed Marshal. "Want me to really test it?" He slammed the dagger down into the ground. The blade disappeared all the way into the dirt. Victor pulled it back out and brushed it off. "Should I try to do that to your hand or something?"

Marshal grimaced. He shook his head and reached for the dagger. Victor handed it back with clear reluctance.

"Maybe I'll really try to stab you with my sword when Talinir isn't watching."

Marshal rolled his eyes. He stabbed the dagger down onto his thigh, not full force, but hard enough that it would have ordinarily pierced him. Instead, it bounced off. It didn't stop him from feeling the impact, though. He rubbed that spot on his leg. If someone did try to stab him, it would probably give him a significant bruise.

But the spell protected him from cutting. He drew the blade along his arm, from wrist to elbow. Nothing.

"Edin Na Zu," Victor said. "First you get these crazy magic powers because you're the son of a Lord. Now you've got a magic shield in your skin. Some guys just get everything, I guess."

Marshal looked at him in disbelief. He pointed at his own face. Everything? He pointed at his mouth, his throat.

Victor grimaced with a weak frown. "Yeah, yeah. Sorry. I wasn't thinking. You got the sorry end of the magic, too."

Marshal traced his facial scars from the curse-stalker.

"Yes, I know! I was there! And you're not the only one to get hurt, you know."

Marshal scowled at him.

Victor unlatched his own tunic with jerky movements. He pulled it open. A lengthy scar gashed across his chest, still red, still not fully healed.

"The Eldanim cured you completely," he said. "But they did nothing for me besides a little ointment and bandages. Or did you forget about that assassin cutting me?"

Actually, Marshal had forgotten it. That had been way back when the assassin attacked them the first time beside the Trebia. The ensuing fall into the river, meeting Talinir and so on, had driven it completely out of his memory. He closed his eyes and bowed his head. He reminded himself that Victor had no desire to be on this trip in the first place. He wouldn't be here at all if not for the Binding.

Victor sighed and latched his tunic back up. "I'm sorry, Marshal. I know it's still nothing compared to your troubles. I just… don't feel like you're the only one, all right?"

Nod is yes. Definitely yes.

(((39)))

Jamana's experience with Master Korda's training was far different from Seri's.

"I don't understand what you are saying," he said. "I saw no beams of light."

"I know you didn't," Seri said. "You wouldn't be able to. I'm trying to tell you that I'm different."

"But I can feel the magic," Jamana objected. "I can channel it, too. I destroyed seventeen balls of dirt." He gestured at a few intact balls on the table beside him.

"Clay," Seri corrected automatically.

"So I do not understand. Why do you need the light beams?"

"I don't need them. I mean… I don't know. I'm just different. That's all." She closed her eyes, concentrated a moment, then opened. "I can see them now. All the colors. They're shooting out from underneath. They're--" She stopped and cocked her head. Had that beam curved? "What are you doing?"

"Me?" Jamana held out his hands in confusion. "I am doing nothing."

"That's strange." An orange beam of light emerged from the ground near Jamana's feet and curved as it passed by him. It curved inward, towards Jamana's body, but then turned back outward and shot away.

"What is strange?"

"I-- It's not important. Never mind."

Jamana picked up a chunk of clay and tossed it in the air. "Shall we go tell Dravid of our new abilities?"

"Maybe tomorrow," Seri said. "It's already getting late." She eyed the clay, wondering if she could break it apart without touching it.

"I don't know if I will be able to sleep tonight," Jamana said. He focused on the clay and it crumbled apart. "Eighteen!"

"And now you have to clean up again." Seri laughed.

Jamana shrugged. "It is worth it, I am thinking."

Seri walked to the window and looked out. She had hidden in her room for most of Rest Day, then spent this day with Master Hain until now. Through it all, she had managed to avoid any sight or sense of Curasir. But she couldn't avoid him forever, could she?

"Curasir said I was the main reason he was here," she said aloud. "He's not going to stop looking for me."

"That does make it awkward."

"But would confronting him actually do any good?"

"I am still of the opinion that you should talk to the Masters."

"I tried. Master Hain wasn't concerned. He said I needed more time before I could understand these things."

"You do not become a Master Mage without much wisdom," Jamana said. He paused. "Though there are times I think that Master Korda has lost some of his with age." He chuckled.

"Yes, I know, I know. They're wise. I accept that." Seri paced in a circle. "But it's all so wrong. He came to my bedroom. He followed me around. His power is, is… I don't know. It's strange and weird and scary. And what was he doing in the Inner Sanctum?"

Jamana looked down. Seri stopped pacing and looked at him. "What? What are you thinking?"

Jamana spread his arms out and looked at her. "I believe you, Seri. And I will support you. But look at this from another perspective. Go through your list. Everything there could be explained away. There may not be a problem at all."

He was right and she knew it. Everything could be explained by cultural differences and her inexperience with magic. She had no substantive proof making Curasir sinister in any way. It was all based on feelings.

"Devouring *fire*."

It was so rare for Seri to curse, and she said it with such vehemence that Jamana erupted in laughter. He lost his balance and sat down on the floor.

"I'm glad I amuse you," Seri growled.

It took several moments before Jamana could control himself enough to answer. "Oh, Seri-Belit. I have not laughed that hard since coming to this island."

"It's true, though. I am a… an *akkanu*!"

Jamana laughed some more. "I don't even know what that is, but to hear it from your mouth is funny!"

"It's true! I worked so hard to get here, studied so much, and look at me! I'm throwing out all logic and reasoning over a bad feeling!"

"I wouldn't say that," Jamana said. "He did do some strange things. But--"

"But they might make sense from his point of view. I know, I know. Argh!"

Seri grabbed one of Jamana's clay balls and threw it at the wall. At the same time, she blinked and activated her star-sight. Before the ball hit, she snatched a violet beam of light and launched it in the same direction. One inch from the wall, the clay exploded with far more force than she had anticipated. One piece struck her left shoulder and spun her around.

Jamana's joviality vanished. He jumped to his feet and hurried to her side. "Are you all right?"

Seri winced and felt her shoulder. She could already tell she would have a bad bruise. "I'll be fine," she said.

Jamana looked at the wall. "You are lucky you were so far from it," he said. He moved closer and stared. Curious, Seri stepped up next to him. At the spot where the clay ball had exploded, the wall was smeared with dirt. But that wasn't what drew Jamana's stare. He reached up and inserted his finger into a hole. "How does dirt make a hole in stone?" he asked.

"Maybe it was already there?"

Jamana shook his head and looked at her. "What did you do?"

(((40)))

"I received an interesting report from Master Korda this morning," Master Hain said without a greeting. He sat waiting at his desk when Seri reported to him the morning after her first day of magic.

Seri's heart sank. Jamana had promised to clean up the mess, but Master Korda had certainly noticed the hole in the wall. And, of course, Jamana was not the best at keeping a secret.

"Magic is not a plaything, nor is it for showing off," Master Hain said, a dark expression clouding his face. "I had hoped that you would understand that, acolyte."

"Yes, Master. I'm sorry, Master."

"Unless I have given you explicit leave, or you have graduated from my training, you are never to use your power around others. Do you understand me?"

"Yes, Master."

"You or the other acolyte could have been seriously injured. This is a very serious matter."

"Yes, Master."

Master Hain seemed to relax a little. From her experiences thus far, Seri could tell he did not enjoy discipline and would rather avoid it altogether. Not like Master Korda. Jamana would be cleaning the kitchen again this evening.

"Excellent. I'm glad you understand." Master Hain stood. "Now, follow me."

He led the way down the hall and through the side door that led outside. From there, he crossed the courtyard toward the outer walls of the island. Seri could not help looking at what remained of the cracks in the earth and walls. Workers had filled them in as much as possible, but they could still be seen.

Master Hain took the stairs and led Seri up onto the outer wall. A warm breeze rustled their robes, not at all like the chill air that had been blowing the last time she came out here. It seemed like ages since Jamana had brought her here on that fateful day when they found Master Simmar. Strange. She hadn't thought of that in days.

Rather than drawing her attention to the citadels, Master Hain gestured out at the sea. "This is a much safer location, don't you think?"

"Safer?"

From a pocket of his robe, Master Hain withdrew a clay ball, like the ones she had practiced with yesterday. He tossed it to her. "Show me what you did last night." He pointed outside the wall. "But do it over there."

Seri concentrated. She was finding it easier and easier to activate her star-sight when she wanted. Then again, it wasn't full sight into the Otherworld, like she sometimes experienced. It was only the ability to see the colored beams of light. Sort of a half-sight?

This far from the center of the island, the beams appeared less frequently. It took her around twenty seconds to find a beam near the same shade of violet. Even then, she wasn't sure how she had re-directed the beam last night. She had acted entirely on impulse, through anger. She threw the chunk of clay out over the water, grabbed at the beam of light, focused on altering its course… and missed completely. The clay fell into the water.

"I, I'm sorry, Master. I guess I missed."

He offered another ball. "Try again."

It took a third attempt before Seri could focus and re-direct the beam properly. The clay shattered above the water, pelting it and the outer wall with dozens of small pieces moving at high speeds.

Seri looked to Master Hain. He stood unmoving, a flat expression on his face. Had she done something wrong? "Again," he said. How many balls of clay did he have in that robe, anyway?

Seri managed to duplicate the feat, though it took over half a minute to find the right color beam this time. Though it was still early in the morning, she felt tired, drained even. She looked back at Master Hain, waiting for his reaction. For a long moment, he did not speak.

"This should not be happening," he said finally.

"Sir?"

He turned his head to look at her. "You should not be able to do this.

I have not trained you, and there is virtually no way you could have figured it out on your own this quickly. Who has trained you?"

"No one, Master. I discovered it quite by accident last night."

"You would not lie to me?"

"No, sir."

"Hmph."

Master Hain stood silent again, looking intently at Seri. She wanted to wither under his gaze, but took a deep breath and stood firm. Whatever he was thinking, she could deal with it. Unless he sent her home. That would be horrible.

"Tell me how you discovered this. Quite by accident."

How to tell him without revealing her star-sight? "Well, sir, I was angry."

"Go on."

"I was angry at myself, really. Jamana had just pointed out something that made me realize I'd been very stupid about something. I grabbed the clay and threw it at the wall. Then I just, sort of, grabbed some magic and threw it, too."

"Hmph."

Master Hain sat on the wall's battlement and adjusted his robe. "I have trained five acolytes myself and observed the training of a few dozen others. In all that time, I have never seen this happen." He seemed remarkably calm for making such a revelation. "The power to project magic without making physical contact with the target is… well, it's a very advanced technique. Some mages never master it at all." He cocked his head. "And you have done it just three days after your atunement. Remarkable."

"Are you… angry with me?"

"Angry?" He barked a laugh. "Don't be ridiculous. I am fascinated. Thrilled. Intrigued. And slightly frightened, to be honest. We must advance with great care from this point. But angry? No, no, my dear. Not a bit."

Seri swayed a little and caught hold of the battlement to keep from losing her balance.

"Ah, I wondered about that. Tired, are you?"

Seri nodded.

"Channeling as much power as you have just done has that effect, especially if you're not used to it." He stood and gestured for her to lead the way down the stairs. "My recommendation for you now is to return to your quarters and rest for an hour. Do not practice any more magic until we agree on a course of action. I will think on this. Come see me after the noon meal."

Seri nodded, her heart racing with excitement and relief. Master Hain was going to help her. Now if she could understand Curasir, maybe things could settle down around here.

• • • • •

After her rest, Seri met Jamana in the dining room. Curasir usually came through around this time of day. She hoped to speak with him before going back to Master Hain.

Seri drew a deep breath. Her hand shook and she clenched it into a fist.

"You can do this," Jamana said.

"I know. But I'm glad you're here, anyway."

"I am sorry for telling Master Korda."

"You already said that."

"I am still sorry for telling Master Korda."

Seri smiled. "It's all right. It worked out for the best, I think. Master Hain is really impressed. I just hope I can keep things that way."

"You didn't tell him about the star in your eye?"

"No, that's-- there he is."

Curasir strode into the room, his presence commanding attention. He paused, spotted Seri, and walked to their table. Seri and Jamana both stood as he approached. As usual, she fought the inability to focus on his full appearance.

"Ah, there you are," he said. "You have been remarkably difficult to find the past couple of days."

"I know," Seri responded. "I wanted to talk with you about that."

The Eldani's odd-shaped eyebrows went up. "What about?"

"I've been avoiding you," Seri said. "I was really shaken up when you came to my bedroom, and my senses have been confused by your power, and I'm sorry. I was somewhat frightened and confused." Even now, she could sense the maelstrom of power that revolved around Curasir. She wondered if Jamana could sense it, too.

"There's no need to apologize," Curasir said. "You are young and just learning. Please, sit." He gestured.

All three of them sat again. Curasir faced Seri. "The power of the Eldanim is quite different from that of Antises itself," he explained. "As a wielder of that power, my essence will feel very strange to you.

Since your senses have only just awakened, it is only natural that you would be unnerved."

"Are you like a mage among your people, or are all the Eldanim like this?" Jamana asked. That was a good question. Seri reproached herself for not asking it first.

Curasir cocked his head, as if noticing the other acolyte for the first time. "Magic is a part of who we are as Eldanim," he said. "It flows through us no less than our own blood. We cannot be separated from it. So any of us that you meet will feel different from human magic users.

"That being said, I am… more practiced in the magical arts than most of my race. I suppose that, in a sense, I am the equivalent of an Eldani mage."

He turned back to Seri. "So. Tell me. How has the star in your eye affected your training thus far?"

Seri hesitated. How much should she tell him? Putting aside her fear was not the same as fully trusting him. But she needed instruction Master Hain could not provide. At the very least, she would not tell him about seeing him in the Inner Sanctum.

"It's… it's the beams of light," she said. "I can see them, absorb them, and even, um, re-direct them."

Curasir sat back. "I am impressed," he said. "I had not expected you to advance that rapidly."

"Yes, you're not the only one to say that."

"For now, I advise listening to your instructor and doing as he requests," Curasir said. "When you have questions or difficulties, come to me and I will help you, while keeping things within his training regimen as much as possible." He leaned forward. "You could have immense potential. Whereas most human mages must concentrate carefully and take their time to perform the most basic of tasks, you will soon be able to do the same within seconds. I would suggest that you not do things as fast as you possibly can. There is no need to show the Masters your full potential just yet."

Seri nodded, then frowned. "To what end?" she asked. "What harm would it be to show great potential?"

"Your goal is to keep your second sight, the wild magic, a secret as long as possible. Advance too quickly and they will grow suspicious. For now, the star in your eye is but a gleam. Most people will not notice it at all, and those who do will dismiss it as a trick of the light. There is a chance it will grow, however, or that other stars will appear.

Eventually, you will not be able to hide it. By that time, though, you should be powerful enough that they will want to keep you around, regardless of their opinions about other sources of magic."

"You could be a Master sooner than any of us!" Jamana said.

"The first woman Master, I believe," Curasir said.

"That… is why I came here," Seri said. "I just didn't think it would happen like this."

"Take your time, but study and practice hard. By this time next year, you should rival the power and skill level of anyone on this island."

"Except you, of course."

Curasir chuckled. "Yes, of course. But I do not plan to be here a year from now. Then again, who can see the future?"

(((41)))

Seri hurried from the dining hall to Master Hain's quarters. Although she had rested as instructed, her limbs still felt tired and sluggish. She hoped that as she got used to magic, this wouldn't be a regular thing. Imagine going through life constantly exhausted!

Master Hain was waiting for her, though he did not look impatient. He directed her to take a seat beside his desk. His eyes examined every detail of her appearance.

"Did you get some rest?"

"Yes, sir. As you instructed."

He nodded as if he could already tell. He walked to the desk, hesitated, then paced a few feet away. He still seemed to be debating something with himself.

"Ordinarily, as an acolyte progresses at this stage, I would move him slowly from clay to pumice to solid rock. The principles for breaking them apart are identical, as it is for even more solid forms, such as iron or even steel. However, given your… astounding aptitude, I wish to test your abilities at a higher level. We will move on to this."

He held out his fist. Seri extended her palm hesitantly, and he dropped something into it. It was a twig, no longer than three inches. Was he serious?

"I don't understand."

"Why not?"

"The progression you described is one of hardness, isn't it? Wouldn't a stick be less hard than rock?"

"Think about it. What is the difference between this stick and a piece of rock?"

She thought for a moment. "Is it because the stick came from a living thing?"

"Exactly." He smiled broadly. "Life is the difference. Living things are immeasurably different from non-living. If you can do anything with this twig, it will give us a much better idea of your potential."

Seri stared at the twig and had a horrible thought. "Can, can this power be used against a living person?"

"Can a powerful mage simply point at another human being and blow them apart? Have you ever heard of such a thing?"

"I've heard… stories of the past, but I dismissed them as fanciful, no more real than the night spirits or even the Eldanim. But I was wrong about that. So is it true with this too?"

"It is true that no matter where you go within the six lands, you will hear stories about powerful Lords blasting people apart with their powers. However, there are several reasons why I doubt these tales. Can you think of any?"

Seri thought it over. She had not failed to notice how Master Hain often turned her questions back to her. It was one of his teaching styles. She had to admit she enjoyed the challenge.

"I suppose that if they were doing that on a regular basis, there would be a lot of curses happening, but…"

"Yes?"

"But the Lords are not struck by curses themselves, because of the Betrayal. Instead, the curses fall on their children."

"That is correct. But what happens if a Lord makes multiple curses fall on his own child?"

"He wouldn't have a son, at least not one that could follow in his footsteps."

"Exactly. That is why, despite their reputation, most Lords do not abuse their power without considering the consequences. The most brutal throughout history have arranged for multiple children, ones to absorb the curses and one chosen to rule when the others are removed through… various means."

"That's despicable!"

Master Hain nodded. "But we are straying from the question," he pointed out. "You have thought of one reason why Lords would not be killing people with magic - curses on their offspring. Can you think of any others?"

"I imagine it would take quite a bit of power?"

"This is true, as well." He sighed. "Those reasons will do for now. As you learn more of magic, perhaps you will understand further. I will just say two things: I have never seen or heard confirmed reports of anyone being killed in this way. However, that does not mean that magic cannot be used against a living human. There are ways to use it that do not involve destruction."

"Wouldn't that--"

"You are stalling," he interrupted. He pointed to her hand. "See what you can do with that."

Seri looked at the twig. Master Hain hadn't told her how to handle it differently than the clay, so her only option was experimentation. Mindful of Curasir's warning, she took her time in activating her star-sight and finding a light beam that wasn't too powerful. She chose an orange one that shot up from the floor about a foot to her left. She waved her left hand and absorbed it.

"Why do you wave your hand?" Master Hain asked.

She froze. She hadn't even thought of how it looked to someone watching her. "I-- I was just trying to focus. That helps, somehow."

"Interesting. Proceed."

She felt the power she had absorbed vibrating within her and tried to focus it into the twig, as she had done with the clay. She released the power. The twig shook in her hand, but nothing else happened. Master Hain chuckled.

Frustrated, she grabbed a dark blue beam and tried again. The twig shook violently and fell from her hand, but remained completely intact.

"I don't understand."

Master Hain picked up the twig and held it up next to a rock in his other hand. "When I channel magic into this stone, it is absorbed into the stone itself, because the stone has nothing else within it. When I channel enough power, it breaks apart." The stone crumbled into tiny pieces that clattered to the floor. "But when I do the same to the stick, the magic is not absorbed. The stick has life, albeit very little since it has been removed from its tree. Instead, the magic merely works on it from an outward level, shaking it."

"So life and magic cannot co-exist within the same thing?"

"That is a partial truth."

"But not the whole truth, is it? Because otherwise, we couldn't absorb magic into ourselves. And the Eldanim could not exist, since they're full of magic, too."

"Set aside the Eldanim for the moment, as their magic is different. How do you and I absorb the magic?"

"We just do. We concentrate and pull it in, right?"

"Yes. Can a stick do that?"

"You're saying it's an act of will."

"Correct. A plant, though it is alive, has no will of its own and cannot choose to absorb magic into itself. But…" Master Hain held the twig up. It shook a little, then split into multiple pieces and fell out of his hand.

"How did you do that?"

"I waited until I could feel the life of the stick. Then I channeled the magic in between it, slowly and carefully."

Seri furrowed her brow. "I don't know what that means. How do you 'feel' the life of something?"

"Ah, just as you learned to feel the magic stored within items last week. You have awakened a new set of senses. Now you must stretch them and learn how to use them more thoroughly."

"But… how?"

"This is not something I can show you. You must experience it for yourself. And it will take time, even with your potential." He pointed to the door. "Take a walk outside the citadel walls. Spend some time with the trees. Break off a few sticks. Learn to feel the life within a thing. And then you will be on your way to understanding it."

• • • • •

Before following Master Hain's instructions, Seri stopped by the infirmary. To her surprise, Dravid wasn't in his bed. She searched until she found the nurse and asked about her friend.

"I'm sorry," she said. "I can't talk right now. I have to assist the doctor. Your friend is-- We have to cut the leg off. It's the only way to save his life." She hurried away.

Seri's heart sank. Poor Dravid. She wandered out of the citadel and made her way to the gates that led outside the wall. The long walk gave her time to think over Master Hain's words, but Dravid's plight filled her thoughts instead

She instinctively turned to the east, toward Arazu. A haphazard grove of cypress trees grew on this side of the island. Seri hadn't seen them since the first day she arrived. She walked with care, forced to watch her step among dozens of cypress knees protruding from the ground. She didn't recall seeing this curious method of growth on any other kind of tree.

Growth. Life. Master Hain wanted her to learn to sense it. But how could she focus on the life of plants while one of her only friends was having his life radically altered? In fact, he might be losing it entirely. There was no guarantee he would live through this. She had known others to die from less.

She put her back to one of the cypress trunks and leaned against it. She looked up through the emerging greenery at the sky and sighed. Everything had happened so fast in the past few days. The earthquake had been less than a week ago. Since then, everything had changed. Dravid. Curasir. Magic.

She closed her eyes and let her head rest against the rough bark. Maybe she would feel the life of the tree through her back. What difference did it make?

Dravid would need her support more than ever. Seri tried to imagine what it would be like to have one leg. The nurse said it was the only way to save his life. He wouldn't be in this situation if Master Simmar had not been killed. Too many mysteries! The deaths. The earthquakes. Even the missing King.

She pushed away from the tree. Her eyes flew open and everything changed.

She saw two worlds at once. They overlapped each other, coinciding in some ways, vastly different in others. It was jarring, bizarre, and somewhat nauseating. Curasir saw this all the time? She closed her eyes and steadied herself. She put one hand over her left eye and opened her right.

Everything returned to normal. The fresh green cypress leaves swayed in a light breeze. The sea lapped against the shore and numerous cypress knees. The wall of the citadel stood strong not far away. She closed her eyes again and covered the right this time. She took a deep breath and opened the left eye.

The Otherworld appeared so much darker, lit by the giant stars that dotted the sky. No sun. No moon. And no water.

That was perhaps the most bizarre thing of all. Instead of the sea that surrounded Zes Sivas, here in the Otherworld, a vast wasteland stretched in all directions. She could see dim shapes moving around in the distance.

The cypress trees were gone. The wall of the citadel and the citadels themselves were in ruins, as she had seen in her previous vision. Smoke still rose from somewhere within it, toward the north side of the island.

No beams of light erupted from the ground. She had a full view of the Otherworld, not the half-sight she had discovered that showed her magic. Did that make it impossible to do magic in the Otherworld? But she wasn't actually in the Otherworld herself; she was merely seeing into it. Without even realizing it, she uncovered her right eye. Her vision didn't change.

A clatter of rocks drew her attention back toward the citadel wall. Its ruins reached only about six feet tall here. As she watched, an enormous three-clawed hand or foot rose over the wall and grasped the top. It tore away a huge chunk, pulling brick and stone apart as easily as she might tear down a sand castle's wall.

A hairless head rose up over the ruined wall. Roughly triangular with a curved snout, it sniffed the air and slowly turned cat-like eyes toward Seri. It acted as if it could see her! The creature growled, revealing a huge mouth lined with sharp teeth, including a pair of lengthy fangs overlapping its bottom lip.

The monster lunged over the remains of the wall, bringing more of it down. A creature of tightly-packed muscle and massive claws, it stood on all fours, eight feet tall at the shoulder. If it had a tail, Seri couldn't see it from this angle. Even as she pushed back against the tree in terror, Seri analyzed the creature, trying to classify it. Its body structure seemed somewhat similar to the giant ground sloth of Ch'olan, but this was no slow-moving herbivore. It was a predator and it was coming right toward her.

She blinked, hoping to shed the second sight. Nothing changed. Desperate, she blinked again and again. She moved around the tree, putting it between her and the monster, though that didn't make sense. The tree was in a different world. But so was she! If the tree didn't affect the monster, could it harm her? Or did her vision place her within both worlds? At this point, she had no desire to find out.

She closed her eyes and tore at the tree's stringy bark. She could hear the heavy tread of the creature's foot, hear the raspy sound of its heavy breathing, feel its hot breath upon her face. But none of it could be real, none of it could be here! The tree! The tree was real! The tree was here! She ripped a piece of bark loose and opened her eyes.

The vision was gone. The creature was gone. Everything of the Otherworld was gone. She breathed a sigh of relief and knelt next to the tree, holding on to its solidity.

And then she felt it. The tree was alive. She could sense it, feel it beneath her fingertips. Life flowed through it like blood, pulsing with its own beat. It wasn't a powerful thing. It felt fragile, like she might lose it at any moment, or like the tree itself might lose it. The feeling was somewhat like sensing the magic stored within an item, but... not. Magic stored in an item felt static, waiting. This life felt moving, pulsing... alive.

Seri reached up and broke off a small twig. Time for the true test. She held it up and concentrated. Yes, she could feel the life inside, though it no longer had room to flow. It was slowing, congealing, dying. But it was still there.

This wasn't the place to test magic, though. If she tried to activate her star-sight, she might see the Otherworld and that creature again. The courtyard wasn't safe, either. She had glimpsed the creature, or one like it, in the courtyard during the earthquake. Better to move inside the citadel where the risks seemed somewhat lessened.

Only when she made it inside and alone in one of the practice rooms did Seri risk activating her star-sight. She had no difficulty, and immediately saw beams of light everywhere. She selected a yellow one and absorbed it. Then she focused on the twig.

Master Hain said he channeled the magic "in between" the life of the stick. Seri concentrated on sensing the slow life of the twig. Sure enough, she could feel something there, like gaps between the flow of life. She focused on them, willing the magic into those gaps.

The twig burst apart in her hand. Seri let out a yelp as a splinter pierced her palm. That wasn't part of the plan. She winced and pulled it out. She held her thumb over the puncture mark to stop the bleeding.

Master Hain had called this a higher level in magic. She had learned it in one day, thanks to some help from an Otherworldly monster. As delighted as she felt by the progress, Seri couldn't help but feel a little worried. Was everything supposed to come to her this easily?

(((42)))

Despite his words, Talinir's paths from then on never seemed to follow a straight line. Everywhere they went, they climbed up and down, pushed branches aside, and cut through undergrowth. He seemed determined to make their path as difficult as possible for the follower they knew still stalked them.

Three times a day, he insisted Victor and Marshal practice their swordplay. Both of them advanced at a steady pace, but Marshal still led Victor in almost every way. It was more than Aelia's training. Marshal continued to show a natural affinity for the stances, moves and grips, while Victor had to work hard on each and every step. It was the first time in his life Marshal had been truly good at something.

Victor did not take this well, at first. For all his life, he had been the first, the best at virtually everything in their little town. Marshal, to whom he was reluctantly bound, had always been last. To have the roles reversed, even for a single thing, galled him. But it also motivated him. Whenever Talinir would end the training session, Victor kept going. Sometimes, he would get out his flail and work at spinning it with his left hand while practicing sword strokes with his right. Talinir watched and occasionally gave him a few pointers.

Marshal didn't know what to think of it. It felt exhilarating to find something he was good at, but it also felt pointless. He had no ambition or desire to be a warrior. Even if, by some miracle, Aelia removed his curse, he wouldn't be heading off to join the army or anything. And with his curse, what was the point? To defend himself against the assassin? Small chance of that. Besides, he had magic, both to protect him and, as he got better at it, to attack.

Still, he could not deny the enjoyment he found in performing a set of maneuvers Talinir gave them. The purity of the form and smoothness of the movements appealed to him on more than simply an aesthetic level. And he adored the palpable relief from tingling hands he found just by holding a sword.

He also couldn't deny the slight thrill he felt in testing his skills against Victor. As they circled each other, swords at ready, he already knew the outcome. He could win this duel. He could already tell from Victor's stance and movements that he had not caught up to Marshal's own level yet. It wouldn't be difficult.

Victor made a clumsy swing not intended to connect, merely to test Marshal's defenses. He pivoted his stance back and to the left to avoid it. He could have used it as an opening for his own attack, but he didn't. It wasn't a real test of his skill.

So what would be? How could he use this duel to test or improve his own abilities?

The next time Victor made an attack, Marshal blocked it and spun in for his own attack. Except instead of connecting, he deliberately kept his swing in too close to his own body and missed Victor.

"Close one!" Victor noted.

That was it. A true test would be letting Victor win without making it seem like he had done so. Marshal smiled.

"Aw, don't do that!" Victor said. "You look scary when you smile."

Marshal feinted high, then swung a crossing blow down low. Victor narrowly spun his sword down in time to block it.

"Faster, Victor," Talinir called from the side. "You got lucky that time. Dodge, don't block, if you can."

The two young men both moved faster, shifting stances, lunging, swinging, spinning. Marshal managed to elude or parry every one of Victor's attacks, but made a couple of them look sloppy. Talinir reproved him on both. For his own attacks, he worked hard at making it look like he fell barely short of success each time. It was far harder than he had expected, but he kept it going.

Eventually, he had to let Victor win so the match would end. He watched for the opportunity to do it in a dramatic fashion. A simple tag from Victor's sword wouldn't be enough.

His moment came when Victor switched to two-handed swings to power his way forward. Marshal pretended to be driven back, then spun to the outside of Victor's attack, extending his blade all the way as he approached Victor's back. In the process, he shifted his stance, putting himself off-balance.

As he had expected, Victor spun to his own left in a desperate attempt to block Marshal's swing. Their blades met with only a slight impact, but it was enough to throw Marshal's already feeble stance completely off. Seeing this, Victor stepped in with his left shoulder and Marshal went to the ground. Victor's blade came down and stopped an inch or two shy of Marshal's chest.

"Hold!" Talinir said. He clapped a few times and approached them. "Well done, both of you."

Victor's face split in an impressive grin. Marshal kept himself from smiling and rolled to his feet.

"Victor, you continue to improve overall," Talinir said. "Be careful of trying to go for too much power over form. Marshal could have taken advantage of you in that last exchange if he hadn't botched his own stance." He clapped him on the back. "Now go clean up at the brook, while I talk with Marshal."

Victor nodded, sheathed his sword, and took off at a trot. Talinir waited until he was out of earshot, then turned back to Marshal.

"Now, what do you call that?"

Marshal looked at his sword. It wasn't like he could answer.

"I know what you were doing. Victor couldn't tell, because of his own ego, but it was obvious from my point of view. You let him win, and you did so very creatively."

Marshal couldn't tell if Talinir was reproving him or praising him.

"That was a good test, and done very well. However, it's not something you should continue to do. As Victor's skill level grows, he will start to recognize what you are doing. And then he will hate you for it."

That would not be good.

"No one wants to be allowed to win," Talinir explained. "They want to win on their own merits, by their own skills and strengths. If Victor thinks, for just a moment, that you are allowing him to win, he will resent you far more than he will if you're just better than him."

That was something to think about.

"Now go get cleaned up. And next time, beat him, even if you can do it in the first few seconds. I need him to be improving, too. The assassin may not be the only difficulty we face on this journey."

Difficulties? That was one way to describe it. How much simpler life had been back in Drusa's Crossing! Even though everyone else ignored him or hated him, at least he had a mother he could trust, depend on, and love. Then Volraag had shown up, and now he had…

Actually, in a sense, he had something more now.

Talinir didn't ignore him or hate him. In fact, he seemed genuinely committed to helping him. Marshal still didn't understand why. It seemed to have something to do with Aelia and his grandfather, best he could tell. At any rate, it made Talinir a strong ally, if not outright friend.

And then there was Victor. Before they left home, Victor had made no secret of his disdain for Marshal. Then they had been forced to leave, and thanks to the Bonding, Victor had to come. Despite this, over time and travel, the two young men had become something more than bound by magic. They were actually becoming friends.

All of them would probably be better off if he weren't around, Marshal told himself. But even so, it felt… good to be a part of a group. To belong. Even if it was only for a little while. In a few weeks, they would reach Reman. Since Aelia would not reveal her plan, he had no idea what might happen next.

In the meantime, Marshal resolved to stop being so withdrawn and actually enjoy his time with these people. It probably wouldn't last, so why not enjoy it while he could?

(((43)))

Seri woke to an insistent knocking at her door. "One moment," she called. She sat up and blinked. Had she really slept in her mage robes?

"Who is it?" she asked, hoping not to hear Curasir's voice. If it was him, at least he had learned to knock.

"It is Jamana."

Seri tried to straighten her hair then gave up. If she looked horrible, she looked horrible. Jamana would understand.

She opened the door. "Sorry," she said. "I fell asleep in my robes."

Jamana barely glanced at her appearance. "Then you must get ready as quickly as you can," he said. "Things have happened."

"What about Dravid? Is he okay?"

"I have seen him, but he is not awake. But that is not all."

"Just tell me," Seri sighed. "I'm still not fully awake."

"There has been another murder."

"What? Who?"

"Another one of the Masters is dead. I haven't heard who yet. Everyone is to gather for the Conclave."

"Give me just a minute."

Seri rushed through changing her clothes and pulling a brush through her hair. That would have to do for now. She joined Jamana and they hurried to the gathering.

If anything, even more people crowded into the room than the day after the earthquake. Seri and Jamana found seats in the back and watched anxiously with everyone else.

The Master Mages entered one at a time. Plecu of Rasna came in first, followed by Tzoyet of Ch'olan. Master Korda came next, and finally, Master Hain brought up the rear. Seri found she had been holding her breath.

"Master Alpin, then," Jamana whispered.

Master Hain waited until the other three took their places behind the podiums, then he stepped to the center and banged his staff on the floor. "This Conclave of Mages is called to order," he announced. "Four Masters are in attendance."

"Because the other two are dead!" someone in the crowd called. A murmur followed.

Master Hain remained unmoved. "It is true that Master Alpin's body was discovered this morning in his chambers. A message has been dispatched to Varioch, informing them of his death."

"Tell them the rest of it!" Master Plecu said.

"Master Alpin's body was… in a similar state to that of Master Simmar," Master Hain said after a moment's hesitation. "It appears they both died from the same malady."

"They were murdered!" Plecu insisted.

"We have not yet determined the cause of death."

"Was this related to the earthquake?" an apprentice asked. All the rules of formality seemed to have been tossed out the window.

"We have no evidence that points us in that direction," Master Hain answered.

"Let us be clear," Master Korda spoke up. "We have no evidence of any kind. We do not know if these deaths are related to Zes Sivas itself, the decay of magic, experiments these Masters were undertaking, or… whether they were murdered."

"Which raises the obvious question," Master Plecu said. "Who would want to kill a Master? Or two?"

"There's only one person here who isn't usually here," the vocal apprentice pointed out.

All eyes shifted to Curasir, who sat in his usual spot. When Master Simmar had been killed, which seemed like ages ago, Seri had wondered if the Eldanim had done it. Now a second Master had died in similar fashion. She had no doubt Curasir had the capability to kill a Master. But… he claimed she was the reason he had come. What would killing masters have to do with her?

"Why would I want to kill your Masters?" Curasir asked. Exactly. Why indeed?

Master Tzoyet eyed him. "We do not know," he said. "The doings of the Eldanim are a mystery to us."

"And they likely always will be," Curasir said. "I am not here to try to explain them, nor am I here to explain myself. What I have often learned among humans, however, is that the most obvious answer is usually the truth."

Something seemed different about Curasir. Seri narrowed her eyes and concentrated. His magical power seemed larger than the last time she had seen him. Seri tried to remember whether his power level had fluctuated in the past, but couldn't recall. He had always seemed impressive.

"And what is the most obvious answer in this circumstance?" Tzoyet asked.

"You have already seen Zes Sivas itself breaking apart from the current crisis. Is it not possible that those who wield its magic would also suffer?"

"And yet none of us have felt any ill effects, and neither of the dead men reported the same," Master Korda said.

"Could it have come on suddenly without warning signs of any kind?" Master Plecu said.

"It does seem unlikely," Master Hain observed.

The Masters continued their debate, going in circles around the issue. Curasir said no more. Seri pondered the issues on her own. Master Simmar had come from the Inner Sanctum when he died. That lent credence to Curasir's theory. But Master Alpin had been in his own quarters. It did not seem logical.

"How will this affect the Passing?" someone asked.

"During the Passing, the Masters' purpose is one of guidance," Master Hain said. "As long as we have one mage of reasonable training to assist with each Lord, it should not be an issue. We have informed both Varioch and Kuktarma of this."

"But how do we protect the Masters?" another apprentice asked. "Can we bring in some guards?"

"The issue is a delicate one," Master Hain replied. "At one time, there was a military presence on the island, but they were in service to the King. Were we to start a new guard here, there would be endless debates over how many would come from each land, who would be in charge, and so on."

"Suppose we each had a bodyguard from our own land?" Tzoyet said.

The Masters discussed this suggestion with some animation, though Seri lost interest. If the deaths were caused by magic with no animus, guards would be useless, and if the deaths were murders, then guards would still be useless against someone with that kind of power. Still, the fact that the killer had taken his time implied he wasn't all powerful, or at least wasn't in a hurry.

In the end, all four Masters agreed that if they so desired, they could petition their Lords for individual bodyguards. Seri suspected that all four, though they seemed ambivalent about it here, would immediately take that action. Something strange was happening on Zes Sivas. Any extra security seemed wise.

•••••

"Let's go see if Dravid is awake," Jamana said as they left the Conclave.

Seri hesitated. Master Hain had not summoned her, and he would likely be doing more consultations with the other Masters, at least for a while.

"All right," she said. "At least for a few minutes. Then I need to get back to training."

"You are doing well, then? Master Korda had me practice with the clay balls again."

"Mine was a little more than-- I broke a twig."

"A twig?"

"Yes, I made a twig come apart. Apparently, that's a big deal."

Jamana chuckled. "Such powerful mages are we."

They made their way to the infirmary. This time, Dravid slept in his usual bed. Seri tried hard not to look at the flatness of the sheet covering his left leg.

Dravid drifted lethargically in and out of consciousness while they sat beside him. Seri and Jamana discussed their mage training, the eccentricities of the Masters, and the quality of the dining hall's food. They never mentioned the deaths or Dravid's own situation.

Eventually, seeing Dravid wasn't going to regain full coherency any time soon, Seri tugged on Jamana's sleeve and they left the room. In the hallway, Jamana pounded against the opposite wall with a clenched fist.

"Are you all right?" Seri glanced around to see if anyone else had seen or heard him.

"No, I am not. Nothing is right in this place." Jamana turned. "We have two dead Masters, Dravid's life is ruined, and reality itself may be coming apart." He spread his arms wide. "And we don't even have a priest to talk with!"

Zes Sivas did not have its own priest. That thought had never occurred to Seri. She had grown up in a family that had little time for religion. Sure, they acknowledged the existence of Theon as the source of the Law, but everyone did that. Rejecting it too strongly is what led to curses. You had no choice in the matter. But talk with a priest? It was not something she had ever sought out.

Jamana's upbringing was clearly different. "Why would Theon allow this kind of thing? Isn't this the most sacred place in all Antises? Aren't the Masters themselves his chosen servants, even more than the priests?"

"I don't know," Seri admitted. "I haven't really thought about things that way."

"None of this is right! I am going to say this to Master Korda to his face. He is a Master? Then he will know."

"And he might send you to work in the kitchen again."

"For asking questions? Then he is not worthy of my service!"

Jamana seemed genuinely worked up. Seri regretted her kitchen jab. "I'm sorry. I guess I just-- I'm not very good at this kind of thing."

"It is not your fault, little Seri-Belit." Jamana took an enormous breath and let it out. "I am sorry, as well. This is all so frustrating."

"And scary. Don't forget scary."

A smile touched Jamana's lips, but only for a moment. "I am scared," he admitted. "The ground shakes. People are hurt and dying around us. It is not a good place to be. You would think everyone was getting cursed."

"Don't say that!" Seri glanced around to make sure no one else could hear. "You know those who are cursed are not allowed on Zes Sivas! If anyone thought Dravid was cursed, he would be forced out immediately!"

"I know. He is not cursed. It just feels that way. For all of us."

"The Passing is five weeks away. The Lords will be coming before that, along with their soldiers and retainers and so on. If there is a murderer, then all of that combined with the Masters will certainly be able to find him."

"If we are not all dead by then."

"Nah." Seri acted nonchalant with a confidence she didn't have. "He's only killed two people in the last month. At that rate, he won't even be able to finish with the Masters before the Passing."

"Let us hope you are right," Jamana said. "I must go now. I will see you… later."

Left alone in the empty hall, Seri tried not to let her own fear crowd in. Her thoughts were jumbled enough as it was. What if the killer planned to kill all the Masters? Even before the Passing? What would that accomplish?

(((44)))

Over the course of the next week, Seri had little time to worry about a possible murderer or the shaking earth. Master Hain bore down hard, focusing her training through a strict regimen.

He made her repeat tasks over and over again. Seri knew the value of practice, as she had been taught throughout her school years, but Master Hain emphasized it even more.

"The more times you repeat an action, the more natural it becomes," he said. "All of these things you are learning now are basics. You should be able to do them at a moment's notice with barely a thought. And the more attuned to the magic you become, the easier it will be to do greater things."

When he didn't have her practicing, Master Hain made Seri study. He assigned a dozen books for her to read, ranging from the history of Zes Sivas (which she already knew quite well), to philosophy lectures on magical theory (which she knew nothing about). Master Sekou's *Vicissitudes of Wild Magic and its Practitioners* was not on the list, but she continued to read more of it when she could.

She had little time to see her friends. She exchanged a few words with Jamana once or twice a day, usually at meals. Master Hain had not forgotten Dravid, either. He instructed Seri, when she would finish a particular book, to take it to Dravid for him to read. In this way, she actually got to see him more than Jamana. He recovered slowly, but the nurses started to teach him to walk with a crutch. The sooner he was out of that bed for good, the better.

Seri's magical prowess moved on from destroying things, which was extremely welcome. Rather than break rocks apart, she learned to use vibrations to move them, push them from one place to another.

Rather than shattering sticks, she learned how to create a gentle tear in a tree trunk for the purpose of grafting. (This required a quick remedial botany review.)

Master Hain urged her, above all, to study the nature of things. "Understanding leads to control," he repeated. "That is the goal."

"To control everything?"

"Of course not. We are not power-hungry despots. We seek control for the good of all. The world is changing. We do not fully understand what is happening. We need new mages, eventually new Masters, who will be better than we are."

"You want me to be better than you?"

"That is a Master's ultimate goal," Hain said. "If my student surpasses me, grows to a better understanding of Antises, and thereby is able to help save it, then my life will have been well spent."

From there, he led her to working with water. This process often ended with Seri, in soaking wet robes, making her soggy way back to her quarters to change into dry clothes. Water, or any other liquid, was not at all like the solid items she had worked with before. It required a completely different way of thinking, one that strained Seri's mind.

Master Hain admitted that liquid was one of his personal difficulties in working with magic. For a couple of days, he sent Seri to work with Master Tzoyet. She found him to be far less pleasant than Master Hain, and an even more demanding teacher.

Curasir stopped by to see her from time to time. He appeared during her training sessions twice, where he held lengthy discussions with Master Hain over her skill progression and her potential. Seri found this distracting and usually ended up breaking something. She wasn't used to people talking about her in such ways, in her presence.

At other times, Curasir approached her alone, in the dining hall or as she walked from one session to another. He asked about her visions. Surprisingly, she hadn't had any more since the day outside the walls. She mentioned that one to him, but didn't speak of the monster. It didn't feel right at the time.

She did discuss the beams of light with him in more detail. Curasir helped her clarify the spectrum progression of power she had already noticed, ranging from red to purple.

"And it's really more of a circle," Curasir said. "The purple then fades into red and starts over again."

"So... is a reddish-purple beam the most powerful, or the most weak?"

"Yes."

Curasir tried to explain the power didn't always work the way she thought it did. As far as destroying things, her first magic, it was straightforward. But the further you got into more detailed magic, the less the distinctions of the amount of power seemed to matter. It seemed more like each major color worked with different elements. Curasir did not clarify, insisting she needed to learn some things on her own.

Seri was thrilled the day she finally figured out the best color range for working with water. She had expected it to be in the blue range, but her every attempt ended in failure. It was actually green. Once she understood that, a whole new realm of possibilities opened up. Soon she could levitate water, move it around, and more. Master Hain seemed almost as excited as she did. If only it didn't leave her so exhausted every evening.

Then the messages from the six lands began arriving, and everything changed again.

(((45)))

"The supplies from Intal Eldanir will last a few more days," Aelia noted. She looked at Talinir. "I assume, as a warden, that you're sufficiently talented in foraging for game?"

The Eldani smiled. "You won't lack for food as long as you're with me," he promised.

"Good to know."

"I can fish," Victor offered.

The three of them rested at twilight after another day's travel. Marshal dropped a bundle of sticks next to where Talinir prepared to build the fire. He sat down, as well.

"It would be good to catch a few fish when next we cross a large enough stream," Talinir said. "Thank you, Victor." He started assembling the sticks.

"How is everyone handling this trip?" Aelia asked. She looked around at each of them. "Besides sore muscles, any difficulty?"

"I'm all right," Victor said. "Marshal?"

He thought carefully and then shrugged, pretty sure that was the correct response.

"What about you, Talinir?"

The Eldani looked surprised. "Me? This is... how I live my life. I'm used to it."

"And yet, you used the starshine again last night."

Talinir froze and then set his sticks down with care. "That is my own concern," he said.

"Is it? You promised to keep my son safe. How will he be safe if you are passed out in euphoria?"

Marshal looked at his mother. She sounded so stern, like when she had caught him disobeying her instructions as a child. It was so odd to hear her talk that way to someone else.

"That will not happen," Talinir said shortly. "I have not used more than one drop at a time."

"Unless I am mistaken, the stars last night were clearly visible," Aelia said. "Like tonight, we camped where it was easy to see them. We always do. Is that not enough for you?"

"Why do you question me? You are not Eldanim. You do not know what it is like."

"I know enough. You are dependent on the light of the stars. But you see them right now!" She gestured toward the heavens. "And with your other vision, you see the stars of the Otherworld constantly. Why do you need more?"

Talinir's resumed his work with stiff movements. He seemed to be fighting anger or some other strong emotion. Marshal couldn't tell which.

"For those of us who have seen the light of the stars of the Otherworld - not with split vision, like I do now, but fully within that world - it will always pull at us. We long to go back, to see it again, to bask in its beauty for all time."

Marshal caught his breath. That described the way he felt, when he remembered that other place.

"And the starshine satisfies that desire?"

For a long moment, Talinir did not answer. He snapped a large branch in two. The crack made Marshal jump.

"It does not satisfy," the warden said at last. "But it is enough. It reminds me of what it is like and gives me the strength to carry on within this world."

"Can you go without it?"

"Of course."

"Then do so!"

"Why? I suffer no lasting harm from its occasional use, and it comforts me."

"Occasional?"

Talinir did not answer.

Aelia sighed. "I do not say these things lightly, warden. I have but one goal in my life: to get my son to Reman and try to lift his curse. I will do whatever I must. But he must get there safely, and for that, I place my trust in you. I only want to be sure that the trust is justified."

"I have given you my word. You need not fear."

"I hope you are right."

A long silence followed.

"I am really good at fishing," Victor said at last.

Aelia chuckled and Talinir smiled. Marshal did not react. A new thought had entered his mind, and he was having a hard time dismissing it.

•••••

Marshal waited. He considered acting that very night, but decided against it. The subject was too much on everyone's minds. Instead, he waited.

Finding the right moment proved difficult. Talinir needed less sleep than everyone else, so he took his sleep only when Aelia was awake and alert. Victor offered to be on guard at times, but Talinir turned him down. Aelia insisted she was fine. Marshal noted she could be just as stubborn as Talinir in this regard.

His moment came two nights later. Aelia and Victor both slept. Marshal feigned the same himself, but kept one eye cracked open, watching Talinir. The warden seemed to be making sure all three of them were asleep. Then he walked a perimeter around the camp. Finally, he stretched out, and, as expected, dosed himself with a drop of starshine.

Marshal waited until Talinir's hand slipped to the ground. He appeared lost in a trance, like the time the assassin had attacked them outside Intal Eldanir.

Marshal got up, taking care to be as quiet as possible. The leather pouch lay on the ground near Talinir's hand. He picked it up, keeping an eye on the Eldani warden the whole time. He backed away a few steps, then turned and made his way outside the light of the low fire.

It looked easy enough. Marshal unscrewed the lid and squeezed the pouch over his left hand. A large drop of the thick, viscous liquid plopped out into his palm. He re-attached the lid with one hand and set it aside. He took a deep breath, laid flat on the ground, and held his left hand up above his face.

At first nothing happened. Had he done it right? He was about to get up when the drop began to glow. It grew brighter rapidly and burst into a beam that shot into Marshal's eye. He blinked. The beam played across his face repeatedly, intersecting both eyes multiple times. As it continued, he began to see… something else.

Spots danced before his eyes. The colors resembled the stars from the Otherworld, but it wasn't the same at all. Talinir was obsessed with this? What did Aelia have to worry about? Disappointing, to say the least.

The beam crossed his eye again. In that instant, his senses exploded. The spots became bolder, more colorful, stronger. At the same time, he felt a rising sense of elation. For no reason he could understand, his mouth split into a huge grin. His hand dropped to his side, but he no longer needed the light. A bright glow filled his vision, not quite the same as the starlight of the Otherworld, but not sunlight, either.

His elation grew, moment by moment. His breath came in ragged gasps that came faster and faster. His hands began to shake, but it wasn't the familiar shaking of his magic. His legs began twitching too.

He felt liquid of some kind entering his throat. He couldn't tell whether it was drainage from sudden congestion or something else. His rapid breathing became harder and harder as the liquid built up within. Choking. Gagging. But at the same time, he felt pleasure, raw and powerful, shaking his whole body.

A tiny voice screaming inside his brain warned of the magnitude of his danger. If this didn't end or he didn't roll over soon, he would stop breathing entirely. No blade-spell would protect him from that. And yet he didn't want anything to change. It felt so good.

The one rational part of his mind pushed back. He gurgled and felt liquid running out of his open mouth and down the side of his face. But no air entered. With no control over his body, Marshal did the only thing he could think of: he tried to focus his magic into his right palm. He moved his mouth again and again, trying to get air and failing. His brain overloaded with conflicting feelings of pleasure and desperation.

His eyes started to go dark. The dancing spots of light had vanished. With no air, he fought for consciousness.

Power erupted from his right hand into the ground. The force of it flipped his body into the air, rolling over and over. He smacked into a small tree and flipped the other way, somehow ending up face down.

His entire torso convulsed. Hot, horrible-tasting liquid poured from his mouth. He sucked in a rush of damp air only to vomit again. The process repeated itself until he had nothing left inside. But at least he could breathe again. He was alive.

He had no idea how long he lay there, his nose and cheek lying in his own vomit. Eventually, he regained enough strength and control to roll over. He lay still, looking up at the real stars and the moon, taking comfort in the air that flowed in and out of his body.

What had gone wrong? Talinir didn't have that kind of trouble. Maybe the drug worked differently on humans than it did on Eldanim. Or maybe he had used the wrong amount. That had been a pretty big drop. Maybe if he used a smaller drop…

His rational side screamed at him. Was he insane? Try that again? Only a complete fool would do that!

And yet… he still felt a warm, soothing but fading pleasure. For a little while, it had felt so good. Nothing else had mattered. It was wonderful. Powerful. Exciting. Maybe he should try it again.

It wasn't the same. He slammed his fist against the ground. It wasn't what he wanted. It was pleasure, and it gave him a taste, yes, but it didn't even touch the ache in his chest that happened when he thought of the stars of the Otherworld. It was a poor, poor substitute for the real thing. Tears sprang into his eyes, but he couldn't tell if they were tears of disappointment, frustration, or anticipation of trying again.

Because he would try again. There was no getting around it. If he could recapture that feeling again, even for a moment, wasn't it worth it?

A soft footstep came beside him. Marshal blinked several times and looked up at the face of Talinir.

"Oh, Marshal. I am so, so sorry."

•••••

Talinir picked up the starshine pouch. Marshal felt a sudden, irrational desire to leap to his feet and wrestle it out of the warden's hands. Instead, he sighed and closed his eyes. His whole body felt painful and drained.

To his surprise, Talinir sat down on the grass beside him. He opened his eyes and looked up. Talinir's face radiated sadness.

"I wondered," he said. "I wondered what effect your healing would have on you. You saw the stars there, didn't you?"

Marshal nodded.

Talinir let out a long breath. "You will probably never forget that sight. You feel it here." He patted his own chest. "Like I told your mother, I can see it even now." He pointed at his right eye. "If I close my left eye, it is all I can see. But it is no real comfort. It's not the same as being there, experiencing it, feeling the light of the stars play across your skin."

He held up the pouch. "Neither is this the same. It doesn't give the same experience, not even close. As I'm sure you now realize."

Marshal pulled himself into a sitting position. He spat, trying to get some of the bad taste out of his mouth.

"I don't know what effect the starshine has on a human, let alone one of your unique situation." He glanced around at the mess. "I'm guessing it didn't end very well."

Nod is yes? No. Wait. That wasn't right.

"But I'm also guessing that it felt really good, at least for a while. And you probably want to try it again."

Marshal looked up at him, feeling a twinge of hope. Maybe Talinir could tell him how much to use.

Talinir looked at the pouch in his hand, then tucked into a pocket somewhere that Marshal couldn't see. "If I have any say in it, that will not happen."

Marshal scowled.

"Trust me. I think I know how you feel. I've been there. My first experience with starshine wasn't much different from this." Talinir looked back toward the fire where Victor and Aelia still slept. "I would never tell your mother this, but I wish I could quit. I don't want to keep using this stuff.

"And yet I keep doing it. I can't stop. I'm trapped."

Talinir's voice held a vulnerability Marshal had never heard before. Usually, the warden sounded commanding, even during casual conversation. Now, there was sadness, even pain, in his words.

"I keep doing it because it feels good, at least for a while. When I come down from it, it feels horrible and I hate myself. But I keep doing it, anyway."

Marshal looked at Talinir's face. He kept looking down, his regular eye unfocused.

"I say I keep it around because it helps with healing when I suffer an Otherworldly wound, and that's partially true. But it's not the real reason. I do it because I would do anything, anything to be there again. To feel the joy, the beauty of the stars. But I am a warden, sworn to defend both worlds, but doomed to stay in this one. It is an honor, a great responsibility, and a curse. And so I use starshine. And I hate myself for it."

Talinir finally looked at Marshal. His gaze from his regular eye was piercing, but it still held pain within.

"I don't want that for you, Marshal. I don't want you to feel this way too."

Marshal wanted to rage. What difference would it make? He already hated himself for so many reasons. Why not enjoy a little bit of pleasure where he could find it? His life was horrible.

"I'll do a better job at keeping this in a place where you can't find it. I know you'll try again, because I would. But you won't succeed."

Talinir got slowly to his feet.

"I won't tell the others. But I'll take it easy the next couple of days. I won't push us too hard. I know you won't be feeling well. The desire is going to be really strong. But you can get over it."

He paused.

"You'll get over it, because there won't be any other choice."

(((46)))

One by one, the Lords sent messages confirming the new date of the Passing and announcing the dates of their arrival. Some would be arriving over a week before the actual date, while others would wait until only a few days in advance. Master Hain confirmed this was normal.

"Many other things happen besides the Passing itself," he told Seri. "Zes Sivas is the only true neutral spot in Antises. While the Lords are here, they negotiate new trade agreements, resolve diplomatic disputes, and so on."

One afternoon, as Seri practiced some new tricks with water, Master Plecu entered the room. He glanced at her actions, but didn't seem to see her. His eyes darted about and a ring of sweat circled the back of his head. He approached Master Hain with shaky movements.

"I have received word from Lord Tyrr regarding the Passing," he said.

Hain frowned. "Is there a problem?"

"No, no." Plecu took a deep, shuddering breath. "The opposite, in fact. He will be arriving three to four days in advance, as we might expect. And he is bringing someone with him."

Seri stopped pretending to practice and listened.

Plecu's face erupted into a nervous smile. "Lord Tyrr has found the lost King!"

Master Hain stood unmoving for a moment. "I assume there is proof of this claim?" he asked at last.

"The young man in question is able to give satisfactory answers for the movements of his family over the past three generations," Plecu said, his excitement growing.

"Anyone can fabricate a story."

"Hain, he--" Plecu broke off and almost seemed to dance in place. "He was able to create the Heart of Fire!"

"On his own? Without assistance?"

"That is what the message says." Plecu gripped Master Hain's arms. "This is it! The solution to all of our problems! At last the King is returning!"

The two Masters exchanged more hurried and excited words. At least Plecu's were excited. Master Hain seemed more muted and cautious. Seri returned to her practice, her thoughts a jumble. Eventually, Master Plecu left. Master Hain found a chair and settled into it with a deep sigh.

"Master? Do you doubt the news?" Seri asked.

He glanced up, as if startled to see her still there. He chuckled and waved dismissively.

"I don't know, quite honestly. There have been other claims before. Men who lusted for the power, or Lords seeking an advantage over their neighbors. Or a combination of both."

"But... the Heart of Fire? Could anyone else do that?"

"I don't know. I do not think so, but there are many things in this world that surprise me."

"Wild magic, perhaps?"

Master Hain looked up. "There has never been an instance of wild magic powerful enough for that. If it is a fake of some kind, I think the answer lies somewhere else. Still, I would not rule anything out just yet."

Seri sat on another chair. "Rasna is an odd location. Somehow, I expected that if the King were ever found, he would be hiding in some exotic, hard-to-reach place, like beyond the desert of Mandiata or something."

"That is perhaps the one aspect of this that troubles me the most."

"Really? Why?"

"The most divisive argument between any of the Lords right now is between Rasna and Varioch," Master Hain said. He steepled his fingers. "They are close to outright war over a large stretch of land on the border between the two."

"What makes this land so important?"

"It is mostly farmland, though there is a river that runs through it. Some rumors say that gold or some other valuable was found in the river. I do not know if that is the truth, however. It seems more likely that the border is just an excuse. The two lands have never gotten along, and their current Lords are the most aggressive either has had in some time. If they do not reach an agreement here in a few weeks, I believe it will likely lead to war."

Seri sat back, stunned. War between two of the lands was practically unheard of. There had been a few small battles in the early days, soon after the lands' establishment, when the people were new to Antises. Barbarians from beyond the Great Plains had invaded twice, but that was hundreds and hundreds of years ago. Kuktarma and Arazu had once fought back and forth over a collection of mines on their border. While it had lasted for a few decades, it had never erupted into full-scale war.

"That is why this new King could easily be a play for power from Lord Tyrr, to give him an advantage of Varioch." Master Hain seemed to be speaking his thoughts now, rather than explaining to her. "Assuming he is not real, it could not be proved until the actual day of the Passing, most likely. And if he can form the Heart of Fire, maybe not even then. That would give Tyrr time to demand a negotiated settlement. Lord Varion would have difficulty putting him off. But..." He trailed off.

"If he truly is the King, the dispute between the two Lands will be nothing. He could resolve it with a word, once he's coronated. But that would also take time. Would Tyrr be willing to wait that long? So many questions. So many questions."

Master Hain looked up again and blinked. "Shouldn't you be practicing?"

(((47)))

The news of the coming King changed the entire atmosphere of Zes Sivas. Ever since the earthquake, a nervousness had hung over everyone. With the second Master's death, that nervousness had erupted into full blown paranoia and despair. But now? Now hope had sprung up again.

Master Hain immediately sent a letter to Lord Enuru, which he dictated to Seri. He delivered the news as he had received it, and outlined his own suspicions and concerns. For all of that, Seri couldn't help but hope he was wrong. If the King had returned, then all could be made right again. The Passing would restore all that the land needed. The petty schemes of the Lords would be set aside as they had a new authority to govern them.

At least, that was the hope. The Lords would probably not be so accommodating, outside of Lord Tyrr of Rasna. Over the next few days, Seri heard this topic endlessly debated. While she practiced, Master Hain entertained a series of visitors including Curasir, the other three Masters, and a concerned group of apprentices. Some worried Lord Tyrr would now be the true power in Antises and this new King, legitimate or not, would merely be his puppet. Others thought Lord Varion would immediately declare war when he heard.

Seri doubted that last one. After all, news spread fast once it was released on Zes Sivas. The messaging system, a secret held only by the Masters and a select group of trained apprentices, reached all six lands in a swift manner that defied logic. By now, Lord Varion would have already heard the news, and as far as anyone knew, war had not begun yet.

Dravid improved on a daily basis. He found the news to be thrilling.

Seri delighted in seeing him return to his old self, for the most part. Waves of pain and anguish still swept his face every so often when he thought she wasn't watching. But most of the time, his smile returned to his face. It was a huge relief. Whether the new King proved to be real or not, Seri was deeply grateful to him for that alone.

Jamana, oddly enough, behaved the most skeptical of them all. He refused to believe. "Even if this is the true King," he said, "it matters not. Our lives will not change. You should take note of my words."

"I will," Dravid retorted. "And when the day comes, you will confess to me how wrong you were."

Curasir's reaction was not quite what Seri anticipated. He seemed delighted at the news. He enthused to Master Hain, rejoicing that the rift of Zes Sivas would soon be healed. "With the power of all the Lords and the King, stability will return," he proclaimed. "Once this happens, perhaps we can heal the rift between men and Eldanim, as well."

"You have high hopes," Master Hain said.

"I am a positive thinker," Curasir said. "I have not the gift of prophecy, but I envision a new age of peace and prosperity for both our peoples."

"Of all of us, you were the last one I expected to be so excited."

"Why should I not? You know how much the failing magic has worried me. At last, it will be healed. This will be wonderful."

Seri listened to all of the conversations, but contributed little. For once in her life, she didn't feel like expressing her own opinion much. Her growing magical prowess had consumed so much of her focus and even her emotions. The more she used the power, the more she gained control of it, the more confident she felt. At times, though, her emotions seemed to take on the properties of the magic she used. When she used beams of light from higher on the color spectrum, she found her emotions getting stronger, more passionate. Colors on the lower end of the spectrum seemed to depress her.

With so much going on inside her head, both mentally and emotionally, she couldn't bring herself to argue anything. It required too much effort. Her letters to her parents grew more brief. Every night, she collapsed in her bed, exhausted but continuously thrilled.

(((48)))

Marshal was sick for three days. He hid the reason for it from Aelia, but not the symptoms. He couldn't hide his weakness and nausea. Fortunately, he had a built-in excuse. Throughout his life, he had always been susceptible to sickness of all kinds. All part of the curse, he assumed. One more sickness, more or less, was not all that surprising.

Still, this one baffled Aelia. It did not resemble any specific illnesses she recognized. In the end, she concluded it must have been caused by something Marshal ate. A piece of spoiled fruit, perhaps.

Marshal felt tortured. He wanted the starshine. His eyes drifted to Talinir's pack every few minutes. He knew the warden had hidden it somewhere, but that didn't stop him from concocting dozens of ridiculous ideas to separate Talinir from his pack long enough to search it. In some of the plans, he even enlisted Victor's help, though how he could communicate such a plan never occurred to him. Even as he thought it, he knew it was pointless. But that didn't stop the thoughts.

It wasn't even the same as wishing to be back in the Otherworld. That was a call on his heart, and always would be. This, however, called to his senses. It called to his mind. He wanted it. He wanted it more than he had ever wanted anything.

For three days, he hated Talinir. He ignored him when he spoke, deliberately disobeyed him a number of times, and generally avoided him whenever possible. Talinir endured all this with calm and gentleness, and that angered Marshal even more.

On the fourth day, the craving dissipated, and Marshal felt like a fool. When Talinir offered him breakfast, he accepted it with a smile.

Talinir never spoke of his starshine experiment again, but Marshal did not forget.

Starshine was not enough. He needed to get back to the Otherworld, no matter what it took. The desire to see the stars again overrode even his desire to lose his curse. But the former could not be accomplished without the latter. Whatever Aelia had planned, it had better work.

(((49)))

A few days later, Zes Sivas welcomed new arrivals. Kuktarma's Lord and existing mages had finally chosen a new Master to replace Master Simmar.

Master Ganak arrived in the late afternoon with a flair for the dramatic. When his boat neared the dock, he launched himself into the air. A magic-enhanced leap took him twenty feet up and around the same distance forward to the shore.

"I haven't learned that yet," Seri whispered.

"That is why he is a Master," Jamana said.

Dravid stood beside them, leaning on crutches. He had needed assistance to make it this far, but he gained strength and proficiency with the crutches daily. His smile returned as he watched the new Master descend.

Ganak landed with a burst of energy that sent dust flying. Unlike the rest of the Masters identical in their conservative purple robes, Ganak wore a garment made of a single strip of red-orange cloth trimmed in purple, wrapped expertly around his body.

Master Hain muttered under his breath, something about tradition. Seri tried not to smile.

Master Ganak was a tall, powerfully-built man. Compared to him, even Master Korda, the largest of the existing Masters, looked small. He surveyed the gathered Masters, assistants, and acolytes, and nodded, as if their presence was acceptable and proper.

Master Hain stepped forward. "Welcome to Zes Sivas, Master Ganak," he announced. "We are all relieved by your arrival. The more wisdom we accumulate together in these dark times--"

"Yes, yes," Ganak interrupted. "I'm pleased to be here, as well. Now, who will assist my acolyte in carrying my things? I'd like to get right to work, starting with a full Conclave meeting, if possible."

"His acolyte?" Dravid's smile vanished. "I can't carry anything."

"He doesn't mean you," Jamana said.

Their eyes went to the boat that had finally docked. A young man in light orange robes strained to lift bags out onto the shore.

"You brought a new acolyte?" Master Hain said.

"Of course," Master Ganak said. "As you said, the more wisdom we accumulate the better. We must train the next generation as soon as we can."

Master Hain stepped closer and lowered his voice. Seri was close enough to overhear him. "It is not customary to have more than one acolyte at a time," he said.

Ganak looked surprised. "I only have the one," he said. His eyes darted to the side and saw Dravid. "Oh, you mean the disobedient one? I could hardly be expected to take him on in his current condition. I saw fit to find a new learner. I'll send that one home as soon as may be."

"It is not that simple. He is now bound to me."

"Hm. Well, perhaps you can find him a job in the kitchen or some such. It is not my concern." Ganak turned away. "Ho! Master Korda! How delightful to see you again!"

Master Hain stood open-mouthed. He shook his head and turned back to the acolytes. "Go and help the new arrival," he instructed. "Dravid, do not take this to heart. We will take care of you."

Seri and Jamana shot concerned looks at Dravid, then hurried down the dock to help the new acolyte. The Masters all moved toward the citadel, followed by their assistants. Dravid remained alone on his crutches.

"Welcome to Zes Sivas!" Jamana called.

The acolyte looked up as they approached. He was skinnier than Dravid, but about the same height. He had not shaved his head, leaving jet-black curls falling around his thin face. He looked uncertain.

"Thank you," he said. "You are the other acolytes?" His soft voice had the same lilt to it as Dravid's.

"I am Jamana of Mandiata, and this is Seri of Arazu. We welcome you to our little club."

"I am Adhi. Of Kuktarma. But you know that already. I'm, ah, not sure where to take these things…"

Jamana hefted two of the bags. "We will show you."

Seri said nothing, but she kept a pleasant smile on her face. It wasn't Adhi's fault he came to replace Dravid. That didn't make it any easier to like him. She lifted another of the bags and let Jamana lead the way. Besides, she was still trying to figure out how Master Ganak performed that leap.

Dravid leaned where they had left him. He tried to smile as they approached.

Adhi's eyes widened. "Oh! Uh, I wasn't expecting to meet you. I'm, uh, I--"

"It's all right," Dravid said. "New Master, new acolyte. I'm fortunate to be here at all."

After introductions, Jamana and Seri picked up the bags again. "We will escort Adhi to his new home," Jamana said. "Will you need help getting back to the citadel, Dravid?"

"I think I can manage."

Despite knowing it might be seen the wrong way, Seri couldn't help looking back at Dravid as they left. He moved slowly, with his head down. It was one of the saddest things she had ever seen.

They took the bags to Master Ganak's chambers first, then showed Adhi his room, almost right across the hall from Seri's.

"It is not much, but what does one really need?" Jamana said.

"Thanks." Adhi looked around, then back at them. "So… what can I expect here?"

Seri and Jamana looked at each other.

"Ah, it would be improper to tell you too much," Seri said. "Your Master will be in charge of your training, and it may be different than you expect at first."

"But we can help you get around," Jamana added. "This place is very confusing at first."

"Oh. Thanks."

"I'm going to check on Dravid," Seri said. "I'll see you later."

She hurried away without waiting for a response.

●●●●●

She found Dravid still outside, leaning against the citadel's inner wall. His hand caressed the filled-in crack from the earthquake. The setting sun cast odd shadows from the outer wall.

"I don't believe Master Hain will exile you to the kitchen," she said without preamble.

Dravid looked up with a start, then relaxed. "If he does, what could I say? I have no voice in anything any more." His words were short and bitter, not his usual self at all.

"You are still an acolyte," Seri said. "Your senses have attuned to the magic. It's just a matter of learning how to use it now. Jamana is learning. I am learning. You will, too."

"For what purpose?"

"What do you mean?"

"The Master Mage of Kuktarma has disowned me. Even if Master Hain trains me to apprentice level, what then? I will not be welcome in Arazu, and Kuktarma will only want mages approved by their own Master. I would be a mage without a land."

"That's still years from now," Seri pointed out. "And who knows what could change by then? Look, the King may be coming back now. If that's true, then the island's population will grow. There will be more of a need for mages to live and work here again."

"If. Maybe. Perhaps."

"That's all we have in this life!" Seri narrowly kept herself from shouting. "You want a guarantee? There aren't any! Everything can change. Everything does change!"

"You have a guarantee," Dravid said. "Seri-Belit, next Master Mage of Arazu."

"Don't be ridiculous. There are several Arazuan mages and an equal number of apprentices all in line ahead of me."

Dravid tapped a finger near his eye. "But they don't have this. You'll be surpassing them all in no time."

"So you're not just bitter over your own circumstances, you're jealous of me? Would you feel better if I weren't here?"

"I… No, of course not. I just--"

"I came out here because I care about you! I told you I couldn't afford to lose any of my friends. I still don't want to lose you. But you have to want it, too. I can't care for both of us."

Dravid hung his head. "I'm having a hard time caring about anything right now." He looked back up. "Seri, I have nothing. I am nothing."

"You are not nothing! You're my friend!"

"I can't live my life as nothing more than Seri's friend."

They both remained silent. Despite the situation, Seri still found part of her mind trying to analyze Master Ganak's leap and how to replicate it. She hated herself for even thinking about it when her friend was hurting, but her brain couldn't leave a challenge alone. Besides, that part of her brain argued, if it were possible to expand that power, imagine what it would do for Dravid.

Dravid took a deep breath. "Look, I'm sorry," he said at last. "I am not good company to be around right now."

"Maybe that's when you most need the company," Seri said.

Another silence descended. Seri could barely make out Dravid's face in the gathering twilight.

"It's getting cool out here," she said. "Let's go inside."

Dravid pushed off from the wall. "I guess."

Impulsively, Seri grabbed Dravid's left crutch and yanked it out of his hand. Off-balance, he managed to fall against the wall and held on. "What was that for?"

"I am your friend and I am going to help you get inside."

"So you take my crutch? How does that help?"

She stepped up in place of the crutch. "So you can lean on me instead."

Dravid's brow wrinkled and it looked like he almost smiled. Still his expression was shot through with pain, pain of all kinds. He snorted and put his arm out. Seri slipped under it and put her arm around his shoulders. Together, they took one step, then another.

"This would be easier with the crutch," Dravid said.

"I don't care about what's easy. I care about you."

"That doesn't make much sense, you know."

"When have I ever made much sense?"

Dravid chuckled at that. His foot caught and he almost pitched over, dragging Seri with him. They both regained balance at the same time.

"You're going to be the death of me," Dravid said.

"No. I'm going to be the life of you."

(((50)))

Two weeks out from Intal Eldanir, Talinir gave them a rest day beside a small creek. Even Aelia appeared grateful. The past two days had been grueling. Talinir had been trying to make up for the time lost while taking it easy on Marshal. But he acknowledged he had maybe pushed too hard.

"How are we doing on our timing?" Victor asked.

Talinir looked up from a cup of tea. "We've done well. I'd say we have three to four weeks left to Reman."

Marshal, who was rinsing his feet off in the water, looked back at them. That was sooner than he had expected. He couldn't decide whether to be pleased or not.

"I have still seen no sign of any pursuit," Aelia said. She also held a cup of Talinir's sweetened tea. All four of them enjoyed it now. "What of you, warden?"

"I saw something a week ago," he said, "but I am not confident. He will stay far enough back that I can't locate him for certain."

Marshal cocked his head as he looked around. Something seemed odd, but he couldn't quite place it.

"Then how do you know he's there?"

"A man like that does not give up."

Talinir got up and joined Marshal next to the water. "You have the look of a man who has noticed something, but doesn't know what it is."

Marshal blinked. The warden's intuition was unfathomable. He pointed down the creek. Whatever had drawn his attention was down there. He just hadn't figured it out yet.

Talinir walked down stream a few yards and looked around.

250

Marshal scrambled to get his boots back on. Talinir moved further. Their movements attracted Victor's attention too.

"Ah, I see." Talinir waved. Marshal and Victor both hurried to his side.

Talinir pointed a few yards further downstream. "A large number of men crossed there yesterday, heading south, it seems." He pointed out broken branches and dislodged rocks. Though not visible from the campsite, they broke up the natural appearance. Marshal nodded, understanding what he hadn't been able to place.

"Who would be out here?" Victor asked.

"Let's go see." Talinir let Aelia know their intentions and then led the way across the creek and up the next hill. Victor and Marshal followed eagerly. Talinir's willingness to investigate surprised Marshal. Secrecy was their usual pattern, which meant avoiding other people at all costs.

Beyond the creek, the trail of the mystery men became easier to see. They clearly hadn't been interested in disguising their path. Talinir pointed to some footprints near the top of the hill.

"At least one horse," he said. "And maybe a dozen men on foot. Curious."

"Are we near any towns?" Victor said.

"No…" Talinir bent and examined the ground further. He frowned and moved on.

About half a mile beyond the hill, they pushed through into an open clearing. It took Talinir only a few seconds to determine which way the group had gone from here. They moved through a large grove and up another hill. As they neared the top, Talinir motioned for quiet. The three of them crouched low and then peered over the crest of the hill.

The trees ended here, opening up to a wide plain that raced down to a large river just visible in the distance. Marshal thought the creek beside their campsite probably connected with it somewhere nearby.

A large camp stretched out on the plain. Dozens of men moved back and forth between the tents and cooking fires. Far to their left, three squads of men practiced with spears. An armored man on horseback instructed them.

"It's a war camp!" Victor whispered.

"Hardly," Talinir said. "There can't be more than two hundred down there. Varioch's army numbers ten thousand or more. This can't be…"

"What? Can't be what?"

"We've moved further south than I anticipated. That river over there is the Amnis. It marks the northern border of the disputed land between Varioch and Rasna."

"So Lord Varion is planning war, after all!"

"These are not soldiers," Talinir murmured, his eyes fixed on the men below. "Aside from the leaders, these are nothing more than conscripts. They have little training and less equipment."

Marshal watched the spearmen and had to agree with Talinir. Most of them seemed unfamiliar with their weapons. Half weren't even in a proper stance.

"What does it mean?"

"If this were the only such camp, it would mean very little. But I suspect that is not the case. Varion probably has a dozen of these camps lining the border, preparing for the right moment. If Rasna has spies watching their army, they won't notice these camps. Varion is creating a new army, a conscripted army that he can throw across the border at a moment's notice. They'll engage the enemy and keep them busy while he marches in the real army. Most of these men will die, but they'll have served their purpose."

"That's horrible."

"Lord Varion is a man who cares nothing for human life, except in the sense of how it can benefit himself."

"Our next Lord will care more!" Victor shoved Marshal playfully.

Marshal scowled. It wasn't funny. He had no desire to be a Lord, or to march with armies. The army thing had always been Victor's dream. He wondered what he thought of it now.

The army's general purpose was to be on guard for foreign threats, though there hadn't been one of those in centuries. Men usually joined the army for only two reasons: gold or violence. It paid well, better than most common jobs. If you could prove yourself as a skilled fighter, you didn't have to go back to your own family's business, whatever that might be. That had been Victor's hope, the reason he spent so much time practicing with that flail of his. Then there was the other reason. If a Lord ever declared war officially, then the Laws of Bindings and Cursings no longer applied for soldiers, at least when it came to violent acts. Some men hoped for that.

But those were common men down there now, like the men of Drusa's Crossing. And if Talinir was right, Lord Varion planned on marching them to their deaths to serve his purposes. There was no glory, no honor in a fight like that. And for what gain? Marshal knew almost nothing about the disputed land, but surely it wasn't worth this many lives. He felt sick as they trudged back to their own camp.

●●●●●

That evening, Talinir kept the fire low. Even though the war camp was a mile away with a few hills in between, he took no chances. Marshal didn't blame him, but he suspected even the true soldiers in the camp would not have a chance against an Eldani warden.

Curiously, now that he thought about it, Marshal hadn't noticed Talinir being distracted by sights in the Otherworld much lately. Had they entered an area where the equivalent lands in the Otherworld were quieter? Or was Talinir simply doing a good job of guiding them while watching for dangers in both worlds?

"It's here somewhere," he heard Talinir say under his breath. Marshal looked up to see him rummaging through his own pack. That was unusual behavior for the exceptionally organized warden.

Talinir dropped the pack and looked around on the ground. His eyes traveled in ever-widening circles until he noticed Marshal watching. His eyes narrowed and he stalked up to him.

"Give it to me," he demanded.

Marshal looked back, confused. He had no idea what Talinir wanted.

"You're the only one who would take it," he said in a low voice. "Give it back."

Marshal spread his hands helplessly. He hadn't taken anything.

"What is the problem?" Aelia asked. Beside her, Victor set down the the cooking gear they had been washing.

"I have misplaced something," Talinir said. "I was hoping Marshal might have seen it."

Marshal shook his head. Shake is no.

"I guess he hasn't," Aelia said.

"What is it?" Victor asked. "We'll help you look for it."

Talinir hesitated.

"Well?"

"It's my starshine pouch," he said at last.

Aelia's eyebrows went up, but she said nothing.

"Oh, that stuff you use to heal, right?" Victor immediately began combing the ground around their camp. "It's pretty dark already. We might have to wait until morning to find it."

Talinir stared hard at Marshal, still accusing him. Marshal lifted his hands and shook his head again. He had no idea what had happened to the pouch. He didn't even know where Talinir kept it now.

All four of them searched as well as they could in the dim firelight, but without success.

"Maybe an eidolon stole it," Victor said. "I saw one yesterday. I think."

"They wouldn't do that," Talinir said without looking at him. He went back to searching through his pack.

"How do you know that?" Victor asked.

"Perhaps you dropped it down by the creek," Aelia suggested. "We can look in the morning."

Talinir's face didn't move. "As you say." He spread out his bedroll and turned away from the others. Marshal couldn't be sure, but it looked like the Eldani warden trembled a little. Already?

Remembering how bad he had felt after being deprived of the starshine after just one dose, Marshal worried. If Talinir had been using it as often as Aelia implied, then he would be in bad shape by the morning.

Who had taken the starshine, then? Aelia? Possible, but didn't seem likely. Victor had no motive. Marshal hadn't taken it. Could Talinir have merely misplaced it? That did not seem possible. That left only one conceivable answer.

Marshal kept his sword at hand throughout the night. He slept very little.

(((51)))

Marshal finally fell asleep not far from sunrise. When he woke up, he discovered Aelia back in command. Talinir would not be doing much of anything, it appeared. He lay on his bedroll, sweating and twitching.

"Guess we get another rest day," Victor said. He poured his cup out in disgust. Apparently, making Talinir's tea wasn't as easy as it looked.

"Victor, start searching all around the camp for Talinir's pouch," Aelia said. "Marshal, once you're up, go find us some more firewood for later in the day. Might as well be prepared."

Marshal nodded and got to his feet. He put on his sword belt, and walked down to the creek. After splashing some water on his face, he found a private spot to relieve himself. From there, he set out upstream to find Aelia's firewood. He had already cleared out everything close to the camp on the day before.

He heard Victor complaining in the distance, but soon moved out of earshot. He gathered a few sticks, but his concentration wasn't on it. Once far enough away from camp, he dropped the sticks and drew his sword. At least Aelia and Victor would stay safe now.

He stood at the edge of the stream and waited. This was a good place. The stream, barely more than a couple of inches deep in most places, flowed smoothly down a short incline here, trickling around rocks and tree roots. The early leaves of Spring shimmered in the morning sun, still damp with dew. One of the smaller trees beside the stream exploded in large white blossoms in various stages of opening.

He did not have to wait long.

"I would ask you to tell me your curse, but I already know it now." The assassin's familiar voice came from across the stream. Marshal turned to face him. The assassin stood there, clothed exactly as before. They stared at each other.

"You're more clever than I thought. You knew I had taken the starshine and came out to meet me away from the others. I respect that. As long as they do not interfere, I will not harm them."

Marshal nodded. The assassin idly swung his sword in an circular motion at his side. Talinir's old sword. Warpsteel. Indala had been unsure if the star would protect him from that. So be it. He took his stance and gripped his own sword with both hands.

The assassin's hairless brows went up. "I know the warden has been training you, but you cannot think that a couple of weeks has made you my equal."

Marshal did not move.

The assassin took a step into the stream. "You must know that what your mother seeks is impossible. Curses cannot be lifted. Not by any means."

Marshal scowled. Why did he keep talking?

He took another step. "You and I, we are condemned by Theon, whether justly or unjustly. It is what it is. It is who he is. There is no changing the will of God." He spat the last word in defiance.

Marshal grew tired of waiting. He took a step forward into the stream himself. The cool water trickled around his boot.

The assassin made a casual swing with his sword and Marshal dodged it.

"In a way, I envy you. In a few moments, you can ask Theon himself why we are all cursed. That is, if he'll let you talk even then. Do curses extend beyond this life, I wonder?"

That was a disconcerting thought. Surely curses did not last beyond death. Yet what little Marshal understood about Theon gave him no comfort. A god who allowed his misbegotten life could not be a god who cared much for humanity.

"Enough. You know your curse. Yet you won't embrace it. You cling to a bizarre hope of removing it. That will not happen."

The warpsteel blade swept through the air, creating that curious warping effect. Marshal blocked it, but staggered under the blow. The assassin was stronger than he appeared. He felt a vibration beginning in his hands, but he deliberately channeled it into the sword.

When Marshal blocked the next blow, the assassin held it there, pressing. Marshal looked across their locked blades into the clear and bright eyes. Again, the incongruity of the life-filled irises surrounded by dead flesh.

He felt a sudden impact against his stomach. He glanced down and saw that the assassin had attempted to stab him with an obsidian dagger in his left hand. The dagger had slammed against him, but refused to cut into his skin.

"Interesting. Some kind of light armor under your tunic?"

Marshal focused on the sword. How did he release the power once stored? Talinir had not explained that yet. He concentrated on imagining the sword as an extension of his hand.

Unfortunately, the assassin did not give him time to learn a new trick. He stepped back, pivoted, and swung again. The warpsteel sword battered aside Marshal's defensive attempt and the dagger swept at his leg. The blade did not cut him, but the impact knocked him off his feet. Marshal fell back into the stream.

No magical city nearby to heal him this time. This was it.

The blade of warpsteel stabbed down at his chest.

(((52)))

Finally! Kishin slammed the sword down at Marshal's chest. To his shock, the point of the blade stopped and did not penetrate. He almost lost his grip with the sudden jerk.

Even more shocking, Marshal's mouth burst open in a silent scream. His face contorted in agonizing pain. How was that possible? The sword hadn't pierced him.

What kind of armor could stop this sword? Kishin pushed harder. Marshal writhed, but the sword went no further.

Kishin dropped his dagger, reached down, and ripped Marshal's tunic apart. He took a step back and stared.

The youth had no armor. Beneath his tunic, Kishin saw nothing but bare skin. Where he had attempted to stab him, a massive bruise began to form, but the skin had not been pierced.

"How is this possible?" Kishin roared. Anger gave his next slash more force. The sword ripped through Marshal's tunic, but bounced off his skin.

Marshal rolled and came to his feet, still holding his sword. He held it shakily out toward Kishin. The young man looked barely able to stay on his feet, dripping wet but still fighting.

"The Eldanim did this to you, didn't they?" Kishin smashed at Marshal's sword with his own, sending him staggering back. He almost slipped and fell again.

"What is it? Some kind of blade warding magic? That's--" He smacked Marshal on the side of the head with his sword. "--Not--" He came back from the other direction and knocked Marshal's sword down again. "-Fair!" He slammed his sword against Marshal's hip.

The triple blow sent the target stumbling back. He fell into the water and rolled.

"There are other ways to kill," Kishin said. He stepped forward menacingly and Marshal scrambled back, trying to get to his feet. "I can strangle you, or beat you to death. I prefer to drain the k'uh from your body with your blood, but I will settle for less this time."

Kishin could not remember a greater rage than he felt now. This target had gone from something simple, to the biggest challenge of his career, to a denial of his preferred method of killing. And it dared suggest to him that curses could be lifted! That a man could live without a curse!

Marshal scrambled back some more, using one hand and both feet. He still held his sword in his right hand, in somewhat of a defensive pose. Kishin stalked in a circle around him. How to kill this one? Suffocation would probably be the easiest, if not the most satisfying.

Marshal pointed the sword at him again and closed his eyes. Kishin frowned. What was the boy thinking? Was he surrendering to the inevitable?

A wave of force slammed into him and threw him into the air. He crashed through several tree branches, then altered direction and fell into the stream. White flowers petals rained down around him. He sputtered and looked up.

Marshal looked as surprised as he felt, but he had regained his footing. He stood firm, taking hold of the sword with both hands again.

Madness. The target's magical power was unpredictable. That wave of force had hit him like a wall in motion. He felt bruises forming all over his body. However, one burst of power had been all that he had ever seen Marshal able to conjure. After that burst, the boy was now practically helpless.

"It was downright rude to start this without me," said another voice.

Kishin rotated. Victor stood nearby, sword in one hand, flail spinning slowly in the other.

"I told you before. I'm bound to him. You want to kill Marshal, you have to go through me." He pointed his sword at the assassin.

Kishin gritted his teeth. "With pleasure."

(((53)))

Marshal thought Victor had never looked more like a true warrior than he did in that moment. He stood tall and strong, both weapons at ready and a fierce look to his face.

"You all right, Mars?"

Marshal nodded and looked back at the assassin. In reality, he didn't know whether he was all right. Every time the assassin had stabbed or cut at him with the warpsteel sword, he felt as if it had worked. Except, of course, it hadn't. His skin looked battered and bruised, but remained unbroken. He hadn't felt pain like that with the dagger, so it must be something specific to the sword.

He took a step to his left. Seeing this, Victor took a step to the right. If they kept themselves far enough apart, they would have a better chance in fighting this enemy.

The assassin ignored him and focused on Victor. "You I can kill!" he snarled. He lunged forward. Somehow, Victor managed to block his swing with his flail and bring his sword around in a sweeping blow. The assassin dodged back, where he met Marshal's charge. He deflected Marshal's sword and punched him in the face.

Marshal stumbled, but kept his feet this time. At least, he did until the assassin shoved him. Both feet flew out from under him and he tumbled into the stream yet again. This time, his sword flew out of his hand and landed on the shore. His head bounced off a rock and he saw stars spinning around his eyes. He blinked several times and nearly lost consciousness.

When he finally focused his eyes, Victor was in trouble. He had lost his sword, but somehow managed to wrap the chain of his flail around the assassin's blade. The assassin, however, grabbed Victor's throat with an iron grip. Try as he might, Victor couldn't break it.

Unable to think of another option, Marshal grabbed a fist-sized stone from the stream and threw it at the back of the assassin's head. His throw struck true, but he only got a grunt of pain in response.

He grabbed another rock and held it for a moment. What if…? He concentrated and hurled the rock with all he had. In mid-air, it vibrated apart into about a dozen shards that slammed into the assassin's back. He screamed and stumbled forward, losing his grip on Victor's neck.

Victor staggered away and tried to yank the assassin's sword out of his hand with his flail. It didn't work, but he put some distance between himself and the killer.

But it wasn't far enough. The assassin slashed upward, cutting a gash across Victor's back from his left hip to his right shoulder. He screamed and went down, the flail tumbling out of his hand.

Marshal scrambled to the shore and grabbed his sword. He jumped to his feet and spun around. The assassin stood near the opposite shore, glaring at him as he tried to reach the stone shards still impaled into his back. He took a step forward, but nearly lost his balance.

"This is not over!" he snarled through gritted teeth. "The next time, I will not leave until one of us is dead."

He turned and reeled away into the trees.

Marshal hurried to Victor's side. He had managed to get his face out of the water, but not much more. He tried to push up with his hands, but cried out and let himself slump down again.

"Ahhh, Marshal, this is… bad one. Burns like fire. Might… want to… get your mom."

Marshal examined Victor's back, but couldn't tell much from all the blood. He stumbled back across the stream and moved down the shore as fast as he could. The impact point on his hip made running difficult. His head swam and he almost collapsed a couple of times. He couldn't remember hurting this bad.

Aelia met him halfway to the camp. She carried Talinir's sword and saw Marshal as soon as he saw her.

"I thought I heard someone screaming," she began, but stopped at the sight of him.

Marshal knew he must look horrible. He was dripping wet. His tunic hung in tatters. He knew he had huge bruises on his chest. His face probably didn't look much better. But only Victor mattered right now. He grabbed Aelia's arm and pulled. He pointed back the way he had come.

"Victor?"

Desperate nod means yes.

Aelia followed, but couldn't hide the look of concern on her face as she watched Marshal limp back. When she spotted Victor lying in the stream, she pushed past her son and hastened to his side.

"The assassin?" she asked. She knelt in the stream and pulled the ragged strips of Victor's tunic aside.

"Yeah, he got me good," Victor said.

"I can see that. Is he gone?" She glanced around. Marshal nodded.

"This wound was made with the warpsteel blade. It won't be easy for these muscles to heal." She frowned. "Marshal, give me your tunic. It's not doing you much good now."

Marshal stripped off the remains of his tunic. Aelia pressed it against Victor's wound. "Now you go--" She broke off and glanced up at his condition. "Never mind. You hold this in place. Hold it tight. Like that. Good. Don't let him try to get up." She got to her feet. "I'll need to fetch my kit from camp. Wait here."

Marshal did as he was told and waited. He shivered. Spring had arrived, but not so much that getting soaked in cold water wouldn't chill you. He hoped it wasn't too much for Victor.

"At least… you got him pretty good…" Victor managed. "Gotta tell you… never hurt like this… before."

Marshal reached down and put a finger on Victor's lips.

"Got it. I'll… stop."

It seemed like an hour before Aelia returned, though it couldn't have been more than a few minutes. "That fool Eldani tried to get up and come," she grumbled. "I had to make him lie back down. Why are all you men so stupid?"

Marshal didn't know how to react to that.

"All right." Aelia knelt next to Victor. "I'm going to have to clean this, which should be easy enough, and then stitch it up. Only then can we move him."

"That's… going to…"

"Yes, it's going to hurt. A lot. I'm sorry, Victor, but I must do this."

Without waiting for a response, she readied her needle and began. Marshal got to his feet and turned away. He never liked seeing this part. "Don't go far, Marshal," she said without looking up. "I'll need your help to get him back to the camp."

Victor tried to control his outbursts, but grunts and even a few sharp cries of pain escaped his lips in the process. Finally, Aelia finished. "All right, let's get you back to the camp and warm you up. I really need-- well, we'll see. Marshal? Help us here."

In the end, there wasn't much they could do to help Victor walk. They couldn't put arms around him without touching the gash across his back. They helped him roll up into a sitting position, then they each took one hand and pulled him up. The three of them walked together back to the camp where Victor collapsed.

(((54)))

Kishin staggered through the trees. Wrong, so wrong. All of this was wrong. When the Eldanim healed Marshal, it created a challenge. When they protected him from blades, it was just wrong. It wasn't fair.

Kishin prided himself on his uniqueness. No one else could kill like he did and get away with it. Antises had no greater assassin, perhaps no other assassin at all. In a world where harming another person could get you cursed, he stood alone. Lords and nobles of all kinds came to him, and only him, when they wanted someone dead.

Yet he kept failing. He had now faced this target three times and failed each time. Each time, he had been thwarted by something beyond the normal. First, he had discovered this target had power. Then the Eldanim had interfered. And now they had given him special protection.

He stumbled and grabbed a tree trunk for support. His strength bled out along with his blood. He needed to take care of himself, but also needed more distance between himself and the target. It seemed unlikely they would come after him, but he had learned long ago to always take precautions.

The failings were his own fault. He recognized that. In each case, if he had struck right away, without speaking, this job would almost certainly be over. At first, he had been driven by his own desire to force his target to acknowledge his curse. But that was impossible for a man who couldn't speak. Now... why say any more? He needed to return to a more simple assassination. No talking. Surprise. Kill. Nothing more.

This would have to be far enough. He tried to lie down gently, but collapsed once he got to his knees.

Lying on his stomach, he reached back and pulled as many shards of rock from his back as he could reach. Unable to get to at least two of them, he left them for now.

He fought against unconsciousness. He fumbled at his belt until he found his own starshine pouch. It wouldn't remove the shards, but would heal him enough until he could find other help.

Reman. He would kill Marshal in Reman. That was their goal, their hope for lifting his curse. When they were most preoccupied, that would be the moment to strike.

He would finally be free of this target.

(((55)))

Talinir stood by his bedroll when they returned. He looked weak and pale, far different than his usual appearance. Sweat trickled from his forehead.

"What did I tell you?" Aelia snapped at him.

"Are they well?" he asked in a hoarse voice.

"No. But I can't say much more than that yet." Aelia helped Victor move closer to the fire. "If you won't take care of yourself, Talinir, stoke the fire back up. These boys are soaked and probably half frozen by now. Get those pants off, Marshal."

She helped Victor remove his, also. Then she had to repair some of her earlier stitching work. The walk to the camp had pulled it loose.

Aelia then insisted on looking Marshal over. She clucked over the bruises on his face, hip and stomach, but her eyes narrowed as she looked at the massive bruise that had spread across most of his chest. "This is wrong," she murmured. She noticed the star marking above his heart. "What is this?"

Talinir looked from where he sat by the fire. "A Star of Indalanim," he whispered. "It's a protection spell of a sort."

"Well, it didn't protect him here." Aelia gently touched the bruise and Marshal winced. "I've never seen a bruise like this before."

"Warpsteel," Talinir said. "He was protected in this world, but not… It still caused damage."

Marshal didn't understand, but at least someone knew a reason for that incredible pain he had felt. He might try to get Talinir to explain more when he felt better.

"I think it'll be all right eventually," Aelia decided. "The best thing for you was probably that cold water. There's not much else I can do right now. I'll give you some willow bark to chew on. It should help with the pain."

Marshal chewed the bitter bark and shivered by the fire. Aelia gave some to Victor, also, then sat back looking troubled.

"He needs more than we have," she said at last. "The wound is too deep. I could make a salve to speed healing, but it might not be enough."

"Starshine," Talinir whispered.

"Yes, well, we've conveniently lost our supply of that, haven't we?" Aelia sighed. "Yes, I realize the assassin probably stole it to create this situation in the first place. But we don't have it now, and that's what matters."

She sat in silence for a while, watching as Victor's shivering slowed and stopped. Marshal helped add more fuel to the fire. Its warmth soon spread through him. After a while, he found some dry clothes and pulled them on. Talinir returned to his own bedroll. Marshal tried not to think about how he might feel right now.

"If I understand our location right, we are miles from any town large enough to have sufficient healing supplies, let alone something like starshine," Aelia said at last. Talinir looked up enough to nod.

"In that case, I can think of only one place where we might find what we need," she said, standing. "The war camp."

"You can't…"

"I can't let Victor die. That's what I can't do. Besides, I think I have a plan."

She looked over her own clothes. "I'll need to change. And Marshal, you'll need to dress as I tell you. We're going to fool some soldiers. Wait here." She took her pack and moved off into the woods for privacy.

Marshal looked anxiously at Victor. Once again, he was injured trying to help Marshal. And yet, because he hadn't actually saved him, the Bond still held. It had alerted Victor to Marshal's danger, but hadn't helped him much at all. What was the point? In their own way, Bindings caused almost as much trouble as curses.

Aelia returned and Marshal gaped at her. Her practical traveling clothes were gone. In its place, she wore an elegant dress like many he had seen in Intal Eldanir. It was a rich burgundy, lined with gold trim on the sleeves, waist and neckline. The top was tight and form-fitting. Aelia kept adjusting it as she approached. Marshal heard her mutter something about Eldani women and their chests.

"I'll have to wear my usual boots, but that only makes practical sense," she said. "Now, Marshal. You're to be my loyal bodyguard. Your face will actually serve us well here. We just need to gear you up a little."

Following Aelia's guidance, Marshal put on Talinir's vest, leaving his shoulders and arms bare. He strapped the warpsteel sword to his belt and put both his and Victor's swords on his back. Finally, Aelia showed him how to attach Volraag's dagger into a makeshift sheath on his left forearm. She stepped back to look him over.

"That should do it," she said. "Keep an angry expression on your face and you'll be intimidating enough." She took a deep breath. "I hope."

They set out and Aelia was silent for quite a while.

"If we are unable to find help, I am seriously worried about Victor's chances," she finally said as they walked up another hill toward the war camp. "Keeping a wound of that size from getting infected will be very difficult. And even if we prevent that, the depth of the cut will cause him severe problems for some time to come."

Marshal paused and looked around. He felt pretty sure this was the right direction. He hadn't been paying close attention when Talinir led them the day before. He remembered the clearing, and then... was it this hill?

When they reached the crest of the hill, he breathed a sigh of relief. It was the right one. The war camp stretched out below them, just as before.

"Follow my lead," Aelia said. "Just try to look intimidating."

With that, Aelia pushed through the final branches and strode confidently down the hill toward the camp. Marshal followed, doing his best not to limp. Look intimidating? He'd be lucky if he managed to keep the pain off his face. Even so, he tried to scowl as several armed men approached.

"You can't imagine how delighted I am to find you!" Aelia called before any of them could speak. "I need to speak with the officer in charge of this camp immediately!"

Talinir had described men like the four who came near as "conscripts." They certainly didn't look like professional soldiers. They carried spears, no swords, and only one had armor of any kind - a rough leather breastplate. Even so, one of them leered at Aelia. Marshal put his hand on the hilt of the warpsteel sword and stared at that one. The leer disappeared.

"Who, ah, who do I tell 'im wants to see 'im?" asked one of the conscripts, a red-haired, gangly sort.

"You may tell him that the Lady Aria of Reman is here," Aelia said coldly. "Go on. Run ahead and tell him that. My guard and I will follow with these other gentlemen." She made a shooing motion.

The conscript hesitated, glanced at Marshal, and then hurried back into the camp. Aelia resumed her leisurely but confident pace, escorted by Marshal and the other three.

Marshal's eyes darted about, observing everything he could. They passed a series of poorly erected tents in a semblance of a line. Only a handful of conscripts were sitting, lying, or otherwise occupied around them. Marshal assumed the rest were training or something. The ones they did see gaped open-mouthed at Aelia. A woman in the war camp, especially one in such fine clothing, had to be an oddity. If they spared a glance for Marshal, it was brief but curious.

They approached a larger tent that appeared much neater than all the others. The redhead conscript emerged from inside and held a flap open for his superior to exit. This man had a completely different demeanor and appearance from the others. He wore a gray uniform topped with a red cloak trimmed in gold. Marshal recalled the soldiers that had ridden into Drusa's Crossing with his half-brother weeks ago. Those soldiers and this man must belong to the same order of the military.

"What is all this?" he exclaimed, looking quickly at Marshal and Aelia. Unlike his untrained minions, his eyes immediately went to the sword at Marshal's side.

"What is your name, officer?" Aelia said.

"I am Decanus Scaevola. Who in the diabol's hells are you?"

Aelia was unperturbed. "I will overlook your language in light of the unusual situation," she said. "As I told your man here, I am Lady Aria of Reman. This is my elite guard."

"What are--"

"I am disappointed to find only a mere decanus here, but perhaps you can outshine your rank and assist me."

"Mere?"

"I assume you have a clinic here, of some kind. I am in great need of some medical supplies." Aelia went on rapidly, though maintaining her cold and aloof attitude. "My caravan was ambushed on the road back that way." She waved in the general direction they had come. "While my guard here was ultimately triumphant over the brigands,

I'm afraid my attendant was not so fortunate. He was gravely injured. We spotted the smoke from your fires and came here hoping to find what we needed to treat him."

"Brigands? In this region? And what would a lady--"

"Oh, you aren't going to be bothersome, are you?" Aelia rolled her eyes. "My husband has such a low opinion of the military as it is. Before we left Reman, he warned me to steer clear of any of your camps along the way. But Prince Volraag told him--"

"Prince Volraag?"

"Yes, a personal friend to our household, thank you. My guard here is quite close to him. They've sparred many a time." She looked to Marshal. "Do you still have that dagger the prince gave you?"

Marshal blinked, then pulled the dagger from its sheath on his forearm. He held it up with what he hoped was an intimidating glare.

Scaevola stared at the dagger, at Marshal's scarred face, the swords on his back and especially that one at his side. Then he looked back to Aelia.

"My pardons, Lady," he said, though Marshal could still hear some skepticism in his voice. "You were quite possibly the last thing I was expecting to encounter out here. May I ask where you were bound?"

"I was already on my way back to Reman, if you must know," Aelia said. "We had visited several towns along the border here. My family has been sellers of purple to this region for decades. I was trying to finish one final tour before any hostilities began." She sighed dramatically. "It looks like we were perhaps just a little too late. Those brigands were probably Rasnians, now that I think about it."

Scaevola nodded. "Of course, of course." He glanced at the men around him. "Valens, Rufus, Otho. You three escort the lady to the clinic and let her procure what she needs." He looked back at them. "And then escort her back to her caravan."

"I'm sure that won't be necessary--" Aelia began.

"I insist," Scaevola said, this time cutting her off.

"Very well. Gentlemen?"

Two of the men straightened up and gestured toward another tent not far away. Scaevola pulled a third aside and whispered something to him. Marshal eyed them, but couldn't overhear the conversation.

"Thank you, Decanus!" Aelia called as they moved away. "I will remember you to my husband. And the prince!"

Aelia searched the clinic as quickly as decorum allowed. Marshal could tell she was tense, but she managed to make it look like she did this kind of thing every day. She put her hands on her hips and gave a loud sigh.

"This is a meager assortment," she said. "You! Rufus, was it?" The redhead blinked and nodded. "Rufus, is this all the medical supplies you possess? I would have expected more for such a large band."

"No, ma'am, this is it."

"What I wouldn't give for a drop or two of starshine," Aelia said. "I don't suppose you even know what that is."

"I do," one of the other soldiers said. "Decanus Scaevola has some in his tent."

Aelia turned to him. "Which one are you?"

"Valens, your ladyship." Valens looked slightly more professional than the other two. His dark hair was trimmed neatly, unlike most of the conscripts they had seen so far, and he carried himself with an air of strength and competence. His stature and bulging muscles probably had a lot to do with that.

"Valens, I have two gold coins back at the caravan. If you bring that starshine along and let me have just one drop for my attendant, the coins are yours."

Marshal heard all three conscripts' sharp intakes of breath and almost smiled. He had no idea what Aelia planned to do once they got back to their camp, but just getting the starshine there would be an accomplishment.

"I'll see what I can do," Valens promised. He stepped out of the tent.

Aelia gathered up some cloth bandages and a jar of ointment. "This will do, if nothing else." She left the tent with her escort and walked resolutely back toward the Decanus' tent.

Valens met them, holding a tiny pouch. Scaevola stood nearby, arms crossed, his expression barely short of an outright glare. "Here we are," Valens said.

"Excellent. Let us proceed." She looked to Marshal. "If you will lead the way?" He nodded and started back the way they had come. He glanced back frequently to make sure none of them bothered Aelia. He observed Rufus bore a slight limp, not enough to slow him down but noticeable.

Along the way, Aelia did what she could to draw some more information from their three escorts. All of them came from small villages many miles to the north. Rufus had been a farmer, Valens a blacksmith. Neither had planned to join the military, but when the soldiers had come to their town, they hadn't been given much of a choice.

The third, Otho, was more close-mouthed. Throughout the walk, he said very little. Marshal gathered he had also been a farmer, but couldn't ascertain more than that. Otho was tall, almost like one of the Eldanim, though not as thin. His face held a bitter expression that never left him.

"How long have you been out here, training?" Aelia asked.

"Three weeks, is it?" Rufus said, looking to the other two. "Three weeks."

"How interesting. Are you eager for the fighting to start? To teach those Rasnians a thing or two?"

"We're just here because we have to be," Valens said before Rufus could answer. "We do as we're told."

Aelia nodded as if this was the answer she had expected.

The closer they got to their own camp, the more worried Marshal grew. He tried not to let it show, but he stole repeated glances at Aelia. She strode on, full of confidence.

When they arrived, the fire had burned itself out. Both Victor and Talinir were asleep. Aelia knelt next to Victor and checked his breathing.

"What is this?" Valens said. "This is not a caravan."

Rufus looked bewildered. Otho immediately dropped into a defensive posture, aiming his spear at Marshal.

"There's no need for conflict," Aelia said. Satisfied with Victor's condition, she stood again and looked at the conscripts.

"You lied to us!" Valens said. He also aimed his spear. "Decanus Scaevola said to bring you straight back if we discovered any deception!"

Otho took a step toward Marshal and glanced toward Valens. In that moment, Marshal stepped forward and grabbed the spear by its haft. He released just enough magic to make it vibrate. Otho swore and let go of the spear. Marshal swung it back around, drawing the warpsteel sword at the same time. He held both weapons at the ready.

Aelia held her hands up. "The deception was only necessary to save lives," she said. "As you can see, I have two injured men here, and--"

"This one's not a man!" Rufus exclaimed, looking down at Talinir.

"One injured man, and a sleeping Eldanim warden," Aelia clarified. "And I would be careful about disturbing him. If he wakes up angry, and knows what you carry there, Valens, I might not be able to hold him back."

Otho backed away from Marshal. "What about scar-face here? He just took my spear!"

"I don't know," Rufus said, stepping away. "Eldanim. My old gram said they could steal your soul."

"Stop it!" Valens said. "We have our orders."

"And you do as you're told, is that right?" Aelia asked.

"That's right. I'm a loyal soldier of Varioch, I am."

"Valens. All I'm asking of you is one drop from that pouch on your belt. One drop. Then you three can leave us, and we'll go our separate ways. We don't need any trouble." Aelia's voice had shifted from commanding to soothing.

Marshal positioned himself where he could see all three men. He scowled at Otho and lowered the spear a bit. Otho backed further.

"What's your play, then?" Valens demanded. "Are you Rasnians?"

"They don't look like Rasnians," Rufus said.

"Shut your lip, Rufus. Let me handle this." Valens aimed his spear at Aelia. "Well?"

"We are loyal citizens of Varioch," Aelia said. "We mean no harm to you or anyone else. We were attacked, and I just want to save this man's life. That's all."

"Why are you here?"

"We are on our way to Reman. We have business there, and this Eldani warden has offered to help us on the way."

"Eldani," Rufus murmured. He touched the palm of one hand with the index finger of the other, nearly dropping his spear in the process.

"Was the gold a lie, too?" Otho asked.

"No." Aelia moved to her pack and removed a pouch. She dumped three gold coins in her palm. "I have one for each of you. All I ask is that single drop."

Valens put a hand to the pouch hanging from his belt. Marshal felt a sudden surge of desire. That was starshine. These men posed no threat. He could take it, easily. He could spare a drop for Victor, but the rest could be his.

Talinir moaned and rolled over. Rufus nearly jumped out of his skin.

"What will it be, Valens?"

"Take the gold and let's get out of here!" Rufus urged.

Valens continued to hesitate. He looked from Aelia to Talinir to Marshal. Then he looked to Otho. "Are we in agreement?" he asked. "We tell the Decanus what he wants to hear. Agreed?"

"Agreed," Rufus said.

Otho looked long and hard at Marshal. Finally, he nodded. "Gold first." Marshal turned the spear around and offered it back. Otho grabbed it and stepped back again.

Aelia tossed the three gold coins onto the ground at Valens' feet.

Valens tore the pouch off his belt and threw it to her. "Take your drop, but no more. The Decanus will be wanting that back."

Aelia caught the pouch. She squeezed one drop onto her palm and threw it back. "Marshal, will you walk these gentlemen just far enough to find their own way back?"

Marshal looked at the pouch and gritted his teeth. The pull was strong, but he could resist. He had to. He started back toward the stream. After collecting their gold, the conscripts followed.

As they walked, Valens made sure Rufus and Otho would tell Scaevola the same story. They ignored Marshal as much as possible. Once they reached the clearing, Marshal stopped and pointed the direction back to the war camp. They gave him odd looks, but left without saying anything else.

He hurried back to the camp. By the time he arrived, Aelia had already finished with Victor.

"I have treated the cut on his back directly," she said. "He should heal almost completely within a day or so."

Marshal sat down and took a deep breath. He had been tense since they left for the war camp in the first place. In a way, that had helped mask his own pain. It now returned with a vengeance. He removed all his weaponry and stretched out on his bedroll.

"Get your rest now," Aelia said. "I'll watch over the three of you."

Marshal took a last look at Aelia sitting by the fire, the warpsteel blade across her knees. Her face, so confident with the conscripts, now looked worn and exhausted. He marveled at her strength, then fell asleep.

Victor's recovery was nothing short of amazing. Marshal wondered why he didn't suffer the negative effects from the starshine. At any rate, Victor was standing and walking around, though stiffly, the very next morning.

Aelia insisted they move their camp right away. Maybe the bribe of the conscripts would keep their mouths shut, and maybe it wouldn't. Either way, it was safest to get as far away as possible.

Talinir would not move easily. He moaned, vomited, and seemed barely able to stand. But somehow, with Marshal's help, he managed to walk a few feet at a time.

Moving that slow, they made little progress. Step by step, they left the stream behind. Aelia led them almost due east for now. With luck, they wouldn't run into any major trouble until Talinir could take over the lead again.

The slow pace gave Marshal some relief from his own aches and pains. He had tried to hide his injuries from the conscripts the day before, as much as possible. All that extra walking on his bruised hip, combined with a fitful night's sleep, made his own steps laborious today. Victor probably wasn't feeling too well, either, even with the starshine's help.

The only one of them in decent shape was Aelia, and she recognized that fact. She took care not to strain anyone more than he appeared able to accept. At the same time, she was determined to get them away. Her strength alone kept the party moving.

(((56)))

The shards of rock still lodged in Kishin's back burned. The pain, only just bearable, kept him going. If he didn't get them removed soon, infection could set in, and all the starshine in the world wouldn't be able to help.

Fortunately, the solution had presented itself. From his perch in a tree near his target's former camp, he watched the three amateur soldiers stumble around.

"I'm telling you, this is pointless. They're long gone! If Scaevola finds out we're gone--" said the redhead.

"Shut it, Rufus," the largest of the three growled. "Just see if they left anything behind."

As entertaining as this might be, Kishin had work to do. He dropped from the tree, sword in hand. All three conscripts took a step back and exclaimed in surprise. Tiring.

"Tell me your curse," he said.

"No curses here," the large one said. "Who are you?" He peered closer. "*What* are you?"

"Leper," whispered Rufus, the redhead. He stood to Kishin's right. Easiest target.

"Tell me your curse," Kishin repeated.

"You're the cursed one," the large one said. He stood the furthest away, directly in front. "But that sword you're holdin' is worth its weight in gold, if I'm not mistaken."

"Pretty," the third one said. He stood to Kishin's left.

"I will give you one last opportunity. All men are cursed. Tell me yours now, and I may let you live."

"I'll give you a curse!" The third man lunged forward with his spear.

Idiot. If he had used an atlatl like those Kishin had trained with as a boy, he would be more effective.

Kishin stepped back, easily dodging the spear. He pivoted on his left foot, spun completely around and slashed across the throat of his attacker. The conscript's eyes went wide. He dropped his spear and grabbed at his throat as the blood erupted.

"Otho!" screamed Rufus.

As Otho collapsed, Kishin turned and leaped off his right foot directly at the leader. He grunted and attempted to parry Kishin's strike with his spear. The warpsteel sword cut through the spear's shaft as if it were made of soft clay, but narrowly missed the conscript's chest.

He dropped the remains of his spear and snatched a dagger from his belt. Kishin nodded. This one had a little bit of training, at least. Not that it would help him.

Kishin stepped forward. The conscript stabbed at him. Kishin caught his wrist with his left hand and stabbed with his right. The sword cut through skin and rib cage as easily as it had the spear shaft. He yanked it back out and watched the conscript's eyes lose their focus before his body fell.

He turned to the last one.

Rufus dropped his sword and fell to his knees, cowering. "I am cursed, I am cursed, I am cursed!" he moaned.

Kishin stood over him. "Tell me."

Rufus pointed toward Otho's body, his hand shaking. "Four years back, I stole some corn from Otho's field," he said. "The next day, my foot twisted all on its own. Been that way ever since."

Kishin bent down and placed a hand on the red hair. "Embrace your curse," he said. "And you will be free."

Rufus looked up at him, clearly perplexed.

"I will let you live, but first, there is something you must do for me."

Rufus nodded, hope springing up in his eyes.

Kishin thumbed over his shoulder. "Look at my back and remove the shards you find there."

Rufus' expression alternated between amazement and disgust. Kishin turned his back on him.

"Go ahead."

(((57)))

Marshal woke up to see an eidolon standing over Talinir, sword drawn. He rolled out of bed, grabbing his sword. He barely managed to get his sword, still in its sheath, in between Talinir and the eidolon's descending blade. His wrist shook as the shadow sword smashed against his own.

The eidolon stepped back, perhaps surprised someone would resist him. Marshal got to his feet as fast as he could, drew his sword and aimed it at the shadowy form. Could he actually hurt one of these creatures? Until the two swords struck, he hadn't realized they could be touched physically. Or maybe they still couldn't. Maybe only the sword existed in the real world.

He had no more time to think about it. The eidolon stepped in and slashed at him. It was a good stroke, not unlike some of the moves Talinir had been teaching him. Whatever this creature might be, it knew how to wield a blade.

Fortunately, Marshal knew what he was doing, also. He dodged the slash and countered with his own stroke, aiming low. The eidolon jumped back to avoid it, but quickly struck back. Marshal deflected it, but was unable to strike back before the eidolon struck again. Marshal found himself stuck on defense, parrying, dodging, deflecting. For every three or four attacks the eidolon made, Marshal accomplished one. The creature clearly outmatched him, but he managed to hold his own for a few moments.

The two combatants moved around Talinir's sleeping body. Marshal worked to keep it there. If he allowed himself to be driven back, the eidolon might strike at Talinir again.

"This has to be the quietest duel in history," Victor said. He stepped up next to Marshal. Faced with two opponents, the eidolon backed off, but did not retreat.

Marshal glanced at Victor, who stood in a defensive stance with both sword and flail at the ready.

"What?" Victor said. "The stupid Bond woke me up, of course."

Now that the eidolon stood still only a few feet away, Marshal had time to examine it. The glimpses he had seen before had told him little of the shadowy creatures. This close-up view did not tell him much more. It looked exactly like people always described it: a man made out of shadow. But it wasn't an ethereal shadow; it looked more like a solidified shadow, if such a thing existed. It had hard edges, nothing wispy or vague, like one would expect from a shadow. The sword appeared to be made out of the same substance as the creature.

Victor inched forward. "We finally see it up close." He made a half-hearted strike with his sword. The eidolon dodged. "Seems a lot more solid than shadow, huh?"

Marshal stepped to his right. The tactic had worked, somewhat, against the assassin. Maybe it would work here, though he had his doubts. He had no clue what an eidolon was capable of. For all he knew, it might start flying at any minute.

As if to illustrate his thoughts, the shadow creature stepped to the left and vanished. It didn't disappear all at once, but looked more like it stepped behind something. Before Marshal could wrap his head around that, the eidolon re-appeared three feet to the left. Victor wasn't expecting that and barely managed to get his flail up in time. He clumsily blocked a sweeping assault that made him stagger back several steps. The eidolon darted back the other way and disappeared again.

"That's... hardly fair," Victor complained. He began swinging his flail, trying to keep it moving.

Marshal lunged forward and stabbed at the spot where the eidolon had disappeared the first time. He almost succeeded. The eidolon reappeared in almost the same spot. Marshal's sword slid along its waist, narrowly cutting it. If it had been human, Marshal wasn't sure whether he would have cut through clothing, or actually drawn blood.

With the eidolon off-balance, Victor attacked. His arms crossed as he slashed high with his sword and swept low with his flail. The eidolon could not block both. It leaped backward, going horizontal to avoid Victor's sword. It dropped its own sword in mid-leap so as to be able to land on both hands and somersault back to its feet. Marshal noticed the sword immediately vanished when it left the eidolon's hand. Curious.

"Now we have him!" Victor pressed forward, continuing his attacks. Before he could reach it, the eidolon again seemed to step sideways and vanished.

Victor spun around. Marshal rotated more slowly, watching every direction. The creature did not return.

"What are you boys doing?" Aelia sat up and looked at them from her bedroll.

"We were fighting an eidolon!" Victor said. "It just disappeared!"

"Oh, really?" Aelia's sleepy voice did not sound impressed.

"Marshal was fighting it, and that woke me up, and then we both were fighting it, and… now it's gone."

"Why were you asleep?" Aelia asked. "Weren't you supposed to be guarding?"

Victor stopped talking.

At that moment, Talinir groaned and rolled back and forth. Marshal sighed. All this to protect him, and the Eldani warden didn't even know anything had happened.

"It was really here," Victor grumbled. He took a last look around and sheathed his sword.

Marshal examined his sword to see if the eidolon had left any blood. He found nothing.

Victor probably thought the eidolon had been after Marshal, since the Bond had woken him up. Only Marshal knew it had been after Talinir. Why would a shadow creature want Talinir dead?

●●●●●

Talinir woke about an hour later with no knowledge of what had happened, nor any interest in it. Victor tried to tell him about the eidolon, but Talinir kept interrupting. He asked over and over if Victor had any starshine. Marshal somehow managed to keep from smiling as he waited for Victor to get tired of it.

Victor couldn't take it for long. "Why do you keep asking me? I've told you already! I've never had any of that stuff!"

"Are you sure?" Talinir asked. "Maybe someone let you have some and you forgot?"

"This is ridiculous!" Victor threw up his hands and stalked away.

"It's only been three days since he lost his supply," Aelia said. She continued her work of cleaning the cooking supplies. "Based on his addiction level, I expect he won't fully recover for another four to six days."

"Six more days of this?" Victor said. "If he keeps this up, I might want to just leave him behind."

Talinir frowned. "I can hear you, you know." His voice still sounded hoarse and strained, not at all like his usual tone.

"Once recovered, he will once again be the powerful warden that we need," Aelia said. "We must be patient."

Talinir stood shakily and leaned against a tree. "The best thing for me is to have something to do," he said. "We should probably keep moving."

Aelia shook her head. "Not today. This morning notwithstanding, you're not sleeping well yet. You need more rest. Victor and Marshal do, too. We can afford to wait one more day."

Talinir nodded and lowered himself back down. Marshal frowned. His bruises would be better off with another day's rest, but it seemed a risk. They still hadn't traveled far from that war camp. The assassin was still around somewhere. And now they had been attacked by an eidolon. Staying in the same spot did not sound like a good idea.

While Aelia busied herself with other tasks, Marshal kept an eye on Talinir. The warden kept his head downcast. He seemed restless, toying with various items, but never able to focus long enough to do much. His body shook with strange tremors every so often, and looks of pain would take over his face. The longer Marshal watched, the lower Talinir appeared to sink. Despite the strange facial structure, Marshal recognized the emotions Talinir was experiencing. They were all too familiar.

Aelia sat back. "And there's one more reason to wait," she said. "We are running out of some important supplies." She glanced at Marshal. "For one thing, you men seem determined to get all of your tunics ripped to shreds."

Marshal looked down at himself. The tears in his tunic hardly crossed his mind. The assassin's sword had not pierced his skin, but the tunic was another matter. Victor's clothing wasn't in much better shape.

"Victor! You're coming with me!" Aelia stood up.

"Where are we going?"

"If I'm right, we're only about two to three miles from a small town directly north of us. We can get there and back today without any trouble, I would think. I should have enough money left to get what we need." Aelia searched Marshal's face. "Can you keep an eye on Talinir?"

Marshal nodded. "Talinir can keep an eye on Talinir," the Eldani grumbled.

In short order, Aelia and Victor gathered only what they needed and set out. Marshal watched them go, then turned back to Talinir. He smiled and raised his eyebrows.

"I'll be all right," Talinir said. He leaned forward. "Now that they're gone, you can tell me. Did you find any more starshine?"

Marshal rolled his eyes and turned away. "I was just asking," Talinir muttered.

An hour went by. Marshal tried to find things to do. He straightened up their campsite, gathered more firewood, cleaned what he could. All the while, he kept watching Talinir. The warden spoke little out loud, but grumbled to himself from time to time. His other symptoms continued as before.

Marshal got up and started his own sword practice. His bruised muscles ached, but they needed stretching. More than that, he wanted to improve. Too many threats kept showing up. Besides, keeping his hand on the sword helped with his own shaking.

In a few moments, Marshal lost himself in the movements. He shifted from one stance to another, following a form Talinir had taught him. As always, he marveled at how comfortable he felt with a sword in his hand. It was so mesmerizing, he almost didn't see the dagger approaching Talinir's heart.

Marshal dropped his sword and lunged. He caught Talinir's wrist and held it tight. Talinir looked up at him in despair. "Let go," he whispered.

Shake is no. Marshal shook his head firmly.

"You don't understand." Talinir's voice trembled. "I need the starshine. Without it, I'll never be who I truly am."

Still holding Talinir's wrist, Marshal drew his own dagger. He showed it to Talinir and them aimed it at his own chest.

"Why would you do that? You can't hurt yourself that way, anyway."

Marshal shook Talinir's wrist and then his own. How else could he communicate? Talinir needed to know that he did understand.

Marshal dropped the dagger. He pointed emphatically to his own mouth and throat, then ran his fingers along the scars on his face. Then he picked up the dagger and pointed it at his own heart again.

"You… your curse. It makes you want to… kill yourself?"

Nod is yes. This was the most he had ever been able to communicate.

Talinir's eyes searched Marshal's face and peered into his eyes. Despair and desperation slowly faded, leaving only resignation and exhaustion. Talinir dropped the dagger. Marshal let go of his wrist. Talinir nodded, then stretched himself back out on his bedroll.

Marshal picked up the dagger and set it aside. He felt confused. When his own thoughts drove him near the same point Talinir had just faced, he didn't want anyone to talk him out of it. Yet he had now done that for someone else. Maybe he did want someone to stop him, after all. It occurred to him Talinir also led a solitary life, away from others. He wasn't cursed, but his job as a warden kept him from being around anyone else that might care for him.

For the rest of the day, he did not let Talinir out of his sight. When Aelia and Victor returned in the early evening, he welcomed them, but continued his vigil. Talinir had shown friendship to him and he would do the same.

•••••

Talinir seemed improved the next morning. He wasn't his old self yet, and acted exceptionally tired, but got to his feet first thing. He insisted on moving on, and Aelia agreed this time. They broke camp and headed east, guided by the warden.

Marshal felt extra tired himself. He had slept little. Someone had to keep an eye on Talinir, and he was the only one who understood the threat.

The day passed. They made steady but slow progress. Talinir seemed unsure of himself more often than not. Aelia helped him keep his focus on moving east.

Somewhere around midday, Marshal caught a glimpse of movement in the trees to his left. He stopped and let the other three keep moving. A shadow shifted behind a tree. He stared at the tree, but nothing else happened. Cautious, he moved on.

Around an hour later, Marshal again saw movement out of the corner of his eye. This time, he pretended not to notice and waited until he saw it again. He stopped and bent down as if he had discovered a problem with his boot. While adjusting it, he tilted his head until he got a clearer look.

An eidolon stood five feet away.

Marshal jumped back up and drew his sword. At his movement, the shadowy creature darted away and vanished among the trees again.

"Marshal! Are you coming?" Victor called.

He sheathed his sword and hurried to catch up. Victor waited for him. Marshal considered trying to explain, but decided against it. Too complicated. He would have to keep his own watch.

The rest of the day proceeded without incident. Marshal did not see any more of the eidolon.

When evening came, Talinir announced he would be taking the first watch while the others slept. Aelia looked at him skeptically, but agreed.

Marshal prepared as if he were going to sleep, but once Aelia and Victor were down, he sat back up. Talinir noticed right away.

"You don't have to watch me, Marshal," he said.

Marshal looked at him.

Talinir gave him a smile that spoke of pain and resignation. "I promise you. I will not try to harm myself."

Marshal raised an eyebrow.

"I have told you how important an Eldani promise is, haven't I? To break it would be like trying to break the Binding between you and Victor."

Marshal accepted that and returned to his bedroll. For now, he would trust the warden. Even so, he slept lightly, troubled by visions of shadowy figures.

(((58)))

Change seemed to come to Zes Sivas on a far too regular basis. Seri wondered if it had always been like this. Surely not. But things had been so crazy since she arrived. Historic, really. She arrived here hoping to make history by becoming the first female Master mage. Meanwhile, history had its own ideas. It hurried along with many other things that didn't even necessarily include her.

"That's so rude," she said aloud.

"What did I say?" Adhi asked, looking up anxiously.

"Not you." Seri sighed. The new acolyte could be so nervous, so afraid to offend.

"Seri speaks like that sometimes," Jamana said, gesturing with a broom. "She speaks to others not in the room, I am thinking."

Seri stuck out her tongue at him. Jamana chuckled. Adhi only looked confused. The three of them had been assigned to clean the special chambers set aside for the Lords who would be arriving soon for the Passing. Each of the suites had an antechamber for meetings, a second room that could be used for any purpose, and a large bedroom.

Adhi wiped down a large desk. "This is much better than the work I've had for the past few days," he said, glancing around to see if they heard him.

"Copying names of dead people? Been there!" Seri sang out. She fluffed a pillow and set it in place. "Whose room is this again?"

"Lord Varion of Varioch!" Jamana said. "You should pay more attention."

"Oh, right. He's the one who asked for special meals delivered privately," Seri recalled. "I guess he's too good to eat with the other Lords and Masters."

"Master Ganak says all of the Lords are selfish and obnoxious," Adhi said. He articulated everything slowly and carefully, as if he were afraid of using the wrong word.

"Let's see," Seri said. "They each have incredible magical power at their beck and call. They each rule over hundreds of thousands of people. And they're each completely free of the curses that threaten everyone else in Antises. How could they possibly be selfish and obnoxious?"

"You… are being sarcastic, yes?"

"Yes, Adhi. That was sarcasm." She shot a look at Jamana, who shrugged. Adhi was incredibly clueless at times. It made him so difficult to like.

Master Hain had tried approaching Ganak again regarding Dravid, but to no avail. The new Master insisted that Adhi was his one and only acolyte. He took no interest in Dravid or his fate. Angered by this attitude, Master Hain had taken over Dravid's training. They were working together right now, while Seri worked on this assignment.

Seri looked at the top of a bookcase. How did so much dust accumulate in only one year's time? "I wonder…" she mused. "If I infused the wood with just the right amount of magic, maybe all of the dirt would vibrate right off."

"And maybe you would blow it up!" Jamana said. "This is not the time to be experimenting, Seri-Belit!"

"Seri… Belit?" Adhi repeated.

Seri clenched her teeth. "Adhi. You are to forget you ever heard that name. Jamana. When you least expect it, you should be expecting your undergarments drawer to blow up in your face."

"I should expect it when I least expect it?"

"Exactly."

Jamana chuckled and continued to move the broom.

"I think we're pretty much done in here," Adhi said after a few minutes. He looked around. "Unless you can see anything else?"

Seri took a look around the room. Her eyes were drawn a small metal grid in the wall near the ceiling. She and Dravid had looked down into one of these rooms through one of those grids. The crawl tunnels circled over all of them. That might be interesting.

"No, let's move on to the next one."

Jamana led the way out and down the hall to the next suite of rooms. "This one is for Lord Enuru of Arazu," he said, throwing the door open.

"And Lady Lilitu," Seri added.

"He'll bring his wife with him?" Adhi asked. "Is that… normal?"

Seri bit her lip and let Jamana respond. "Is not unusual," he said. "Some Lords bring their whole families. Plus servants and so on. Master Korda called it poorly controlled chaos. I am looking forward to it."

"Because this place is so quiet, otherwise," Seri said. Pause. "That was sarcasm too, Adhi."

"Yes, I understood that one."

Seri grimaced and set to work. This room would be spotless when she was done. Nothing less would work for the Lady Lilitu. Seri still read her encouraging note almost every morning. The lady was an inspiration and always would be. She had single-handedly reformed Arazu's entire education system. If not for her changes, Seri would not have been able to graduate and seek her current position.

"Lilitu," Adhi said. "I have heard that name. Isn't she the one they say consults spirits?"

Seri bristled. "That's a slanderous lie!" she snapped. "People are just jealous of her success!"

Adhi backed away. "I'm sorry, I'm sorry," he said in a rush. "It was just something I heard. I'm so sorry!"

"You should be. You don't hear me repeating stories about Kuktarma's royal family. Theon knows I've heard enough of them."

"Actually, in Kuktarma, we take great delight in repeating stories of Lord Meluhha's family. His sons are famous for the number of women they, ah, have, um…" Adhi trailed off.

They worked in silence for a while. Seri was dusting again when she felt a sudden vibration gently push her feather duster. She looked in the direction from which it came. Jamana lowered his hand and tipped his head toward Adhi.

The new acolyte scrubbed at a desk as hard as he could, but he was hunched over, looking like a dog afraid of getting whipped. Seri sighed.

"Adhi, I'm sorry too," she said. "We have cultural and personal differences that we don't know about. They may seem strange, but it's part of what makes us different. We shouldn't assume things about others' intent. I'm sorry for being offended."

"Oh. Ah, thank you. I was just thinking about how hard it will be for the new King to deal with things like this. Do you suppose he'll have special advisors to help him understand all of the cultures?"

Seri blinked. She had assumed Adhi was cowering because of her anger, but he had already moved past it to contemplate deeper things. There was a mind hiding behind that narrow face.

•••••

As it turned out, Lord Rajwir of Ch'olan was the first to arrive. He reached Zes Sivas a full two and a half weeks before the Passing.

Seri regretted that she knew so little of Ch'olan society and customs. She found them fascinating. The most isolated of the six lands, Ch'olan had long kept to itself with little interaction with the others. Lord Rajwir was reportedly working to diminish that isolation. By arriving early, he no doubt intended to signal his receptivity to negotiation with the other Lords.

The Lord stepped off the boat clothed simply but regally. He wore an enormous red feather headdress, a simple robe open at the chest, a breechclout, and elaborate sandals. Myriads of precious gems decorated all of his clothing. Enormous jade earrings completed the ensemble.

Before greeting any of the Masters, Lord Rajwir stepped back and allowed his wife to debark. She stepped in front of him and glared at those assembled.

Seri caught her breath. In historical readings, she had sometimes come across a description of someone as a "warrior queen." Lady Ajaw of Ch'olan owned that title.

Like her husband, she wore a large feather headdress, though hers was primarily green. Her calf-length skirt was simple, but not restrictive. Her upper chest was wrapped firmly in place, leaving her stomach bare down to her hips. Seri swallowed hard at the scandal of it. She carried a large, round battle shield painted in swirls of green and orange. Her right hand rested on the pommel of a short sword tucked into her belt. She wore no shoes.

"If we didn't have a group of Master mages standing between us and her," Dravid whispered, "I'd be terrified right now."

"I am terrified even with them standing over there," Jamana said.

"Stop. She's magnificent," Seri said.

Six or seven attendants and scribes, all male, followed the Lord and Lady. But four females, armed similar to their Lady, stayed close, apparently as bodyguards. Seri wondered if one or more of them would be guarding Master Tzoyet. It had been weeks since the Masters had requested protection.

Master Tzoyet stepped forward to greet them and was treated with great deference. He introduced the other Masters, and the group made its way into the citadel. The acolytes stood aside and watched them.

"The power..." Dravid said.

Seri nodded. As Lord Rajwir passed by, she felt an immense magical power radiating from him. It wasn't quite as strong as the power of Zes Sivas itself, but felt very similar. Not at all like the maelstrom of Curasir. Come to think of it, she hadn't seen the Eldani for days.

"Imagine what it is like when he's at home," Jamana said. "Here, he is weakened."

Dravid gaped at him. "That was weak?"

Jamana nodded. "The Lords have strong Bindings toward their homes, stronger than the average person. That makes them weaker when they come here."

"I hadn't thought of that," Seri said. Her own Binding toward home had faded almost completely away weeks ago.

The warrior girls passed by the acolytes. Seri caught the eye of one of them, a black-haired young woman who fixed her gaze on Seri, then nodded as if in approval.

"If the rest of the arrivals are this dramatic, it will be an interesting time for sure," Jamana said.

"Just wait until Lord Tyrr arrives with the new King," Dravid said. "That will make this look like nothing."

Seri looked back out across the sea. For her part, she couldn't wait to see what happened next.

•••••

Seri examined the book on her stand. She had worked her way through most of*The Vicissitudes of Wild Magic and its Practitioners,* and wasn't much interested in anything else Master Sekou had to say. She had something else in mind now. Earlier, Master Hain had casually mentioned how the magic of Zes Sivas penetrated everything on the island, and thus everything absorbed some of that magic to one degree or another. In her earliest days of learning magic, she would not even be able to detect such a thing. But now, it might be different.

She blinked a few times and activated her star-sight. It seemed to be getting easier and easier to control. She leaned in close to the book and stared at it. For a long time, she saw nothing. A movement near the book's spine caught her attention. She squinted and looked closer. A pair of tiny beams of light radiated out from the book's spine. Barely an inch long, they faded in and out from view.

Seri reached out and twisted the nearest beam, bright yellow, onto her finger and pulled. It faded into her finger with a tremor. Immediately, she felt a strong sense of satisfaction and accomplishment. At the same time, an image of an elderly hand closing the book flashed into her mind. Was this Master Sekou completing the book? His satisfaction at accomplishing this task?

Thrilled, Seri grabbed for the second beam, dark blue. At once, a new image flashed across her mind, an image of an old man in mage's robes writing at a desk. He consulted some other open books, then continued his own writing.

Seri gasped and stepped back. It was Master Sekou! It had to be! The yellow beam had shown his happiness, his emotion, while the dark blue had shown the actual act. Amazing!

The applications of this magic could be enormous. Seri could find out the history of anything on the island, if it had absorbed enough magic. She could uncover mysteries that… She stopped as a thrilling but terrifying thought struck her.

Anything that had absorbed magic. Mysteries.

Seri wrapped her arms around herself to stop a tremble. Could it actually be that simple? There was only one way to find out, but the prospect frightened her more than she wanted to admit. She glanced out her bedroom window and saw the darkness of early evening. At this time, almost everyone in the citadel would be in their own rooms, studying or preparing for bed.

She took a deep breath and picked up a lantern. Leaving her room, she made her way down one hallway after another. The confusing tangle of the citadel's passages almost comforted her, teasing that she might never make it to her destination. Maybe that would be for the best.

As she passed near the Masters' quarters, she tried to keep her footsteps quiet. Disturbing one of them would unnerve her enough to abandon this idea. She wished she could have brought Jamana along for support, but he might try to talk her out of it.

Beyond the stairs to the Inner Sanctum, beyond the Lords' temporary quarters, she entered the Citadel of Kings. Even though nothing changed, she felt a shiver run through her body. Almost no one entered this building. No one needed to, after all. But the basement storage room she sought was here.

She lost her way, but returned back through two intersections and finally found her destination. Standing at the top of a tall, dark stairway, she tried to stifle more trembles. This must be the place. She took one step down and then another. Step by step, she descended. She couldn't be sure, but this seemed like the lowest basement in the entire complex.

That actually made sense, considering its current usage. At the bottom of the steps, Seri lifted her lantern high. The small basement was empty except for a single table, on which lay a long, tightly bound body.

Master Alpin had died almost three weeks ago, but no one from Varioch had come to take his body home yet. They were probably waiting until the Passing. According to Master Hain, this was common practice. In the meantime, the body rested here, preserved by some kind of "magical embalming." Master Hain had been reluctant to explain it, and Seri had little desire to know.

She stood still, not yet able to force herself forward. She took three deep breaths and slowly let each one out. She closed her eyes and whispered a quick prayer. She swallowed, opened her eyes, and stepped up to the table.

Master Alpin's body was thoroughly wrapped in thick cloths, for which Seri was grateful. She remembered the horror of Master Simmar's drained body.

She blinked. Star-sight activated. A quick perusal of the body revealed nothing. A waste of time. She knew it. No matter how much magic Master Alpin had absorbed in his many years here, surely it had all dissipated at his death, or in the days following.

Still... best to be thorough. She held her breath and leaned in close. She walked around the entire table, looking at the body from every possible angle, as close as she dared.

One dark blue beam of light, more feeble than a candle, wavered out from the Master's head. This one was even smaller than the one she had found on the book. She turned away and took another deep breath. She turned back, holding her breath once again, and grasped the beam between her thumb and forefinger.

Nothing happened. Seri frowned and pulled. The beam lengthened, then rushed with abrupt movement into her palm. She gasped as a face appeared in her mind, laughing with cruel abandon. Mocking. Evil.

Curasir.

<h1 style="text-align:center">(((59)))</h1>

Talinir grew more and more like his old self over the next several days. By the start of the next week, he appeared back to normal. But Marshal, who continued to keep a close watch, occasionally noticed a look of unsatisfied hunger in Talinir's eye. He might never be completely free of the drug.

Every day, Marshal worked hard on his sword training. The thought of both the assassin and a phantom of some kind stalking them motivated him. As much as he appreciated that Talinir was now able to fight, he did not want to depend solely on him. Day after day, morning and evening, he trained. His previous apathy had vanished. He had purpose now. He worked to make the stances second nature. He worked to make the sword feel as much a part of him as his arm. He worked to anticipate an opponent's movements. For many days after Intal Eldanir, he had gone to bed sore and exhausted. Now, he could push himself further than ever, and no longer feel the soreness. He went to bed tired, but it was a good tired.

As hard as Marshal worked, Victor worked even harder. Competition spurred both young men, but Victor felt it more. He knew Marshal had more natural skill than he did, and he didn't like it. When they dueled together, Marshal almost always came out on top. On the rare occasion that Victor won, he celebrated with abandon. Marshal didn't resent it; he wanted Victor to succeed. More than that, he marveled at Victor's ability to use both sword and flail. One of Victor's favorite activities now involved finding a large open area. He would move across it as fast as he could, spinning and striking with both sword and flail, whirling like a child's top. The first few times he tried this, he ended up tangling the flail's chain around his sword, or worse.

But the more he practiced, the smoother his actions became.

Talinir praised both of their progress. He expressed constant amazement at how easily Marshal adapted to the sword. He was likewise impressed with Victor's dual-wielding. As they improved, he instructed them on more advanced techniques. Sometimes he sparred with both of them at once. Despite their gains, they never once came close to defeating him.

Whenever he could slip off by himself, Marshal practiced with his magic. He never tried anything dramatic, or too powerful, but focused on controlling small bursts. Twice he tried to combine the bursts from each hand. Both times he fell into a seizure that left him shaking uncontrollably for several minutes. Fortunately, no one discovered him during those times. A few times, he tried to figure out how to channel the power through his sword as Talinir had mentioned. He could easily channel power into the sword, but couldn't figure out how to release it, as he thought he had during the last fight with the assassin. Talinir checked his sword periodically, to be sure the charge wasn't building up too much, but he never commented on it.

In the course of a week, Marshal spotted the eidolon at least three times, and thought he might have caught a glimpse several more. None of the others seemed to have noticed. At least, no one said anything. He caught Talinir staring off into the woods several times, but couldn't be sure which world he stared at.

On one occasion, Marshal saw a curse-stalker watching him. Apparently, it was scared off by the size or composition of their group, because it didn't come any closer and he never saw it again.

To his surprise, Marshal discovered that once he began trying to enjoy his relationships with the rest of the party, everything improved. Talinir's interactions during their training seemed more pleasant and encouraging. Aelia's concern over him seemed less like an annoying fussing and more like genuine care. And Victor's constant talking seemed less harsh and more playful, even constructive from time to time.

Marshal found himself enjoying the journey more and more, to the point that he began to dread the end of it. The lurking threats kept him wary, but not to the point of paranoia any more. His faith in his own abilities and those of his companions grew daily. But what would happen when they reached their destination?

(((60)))

Lord Sundinka of Mandiata was the next to arrive, three days later. He came simply, alone save for a handful of attendants and one scribe. Lord Enuru and Lady Lilitu arrived two days after that. Seri felt thrilled and terrified all at once. As with the previous arrivals, the acolytes waited while the Masters exchanged greetings.

"Lord Sundinka was pleased with my progress," Jamana said. "I'm sure Lord Enuru will be most impressed with yours."

"He's not the one I'm worried about," Seri said.

She took a deep breath. With three Lords now present, the amount of raw power that now surged around them was immense. And three more were yet to arrive, not to mention the king. It was difficult enough now. All of the power seemed to scream at her, demanding that she pull it in, use it. But that wasn't even possible, was it? Seri didn't dare make the attempt.

She had told no one yet about what she had discovered with Master Alpin's body. She tried to tell herself that the one image meant nothing. Could Curasir actually be the murderer? She had suspected him earlier, but he had alleviated those fears. Until now, anyway. Who could she tell? Would anyone even believe her? Master Hain respected Curasir and sought his advice often. Perhaps she could broach the subject with the Lord and Lady.

Curasir said he had come because of Seri. She was amazed at how much it hurt to know that was a lie. He clearly had other motives. Whether any of them actually included her at all remained to be seen.

Master Hain summoned Seri to the Lord's quarters only an hour after their arrival. She checked her hair, her robe, and most of all, whether the star in her eye was more or less visible today. It seemed to grow and shrink from time to time. Today, it looked smaller, thank Theon.

When she entered the suite, Master Hain stood chatting with Lord Enuru. They both turned to face her. Lord Enuru did not wear a shirt, like all of the male nobility in Arazu, though his long black hair and beard covered quite a bit of his chest. He wore multiple layered skirts of various colors. Gold jewelry embedded with elaborate gems hung from his neck, ears, and wrists. A thick silver crown circled his head.

"Here she is," Master Hain said. Seri immediately bowed.

"Come, come," Lord Enuru said in a pleasant tone. "No need for all that, my dear. Let us see you."

Seri stood upright and tried to smile. She looked directly into Lord Enuru's eyes and blinked. While she could sense the enormous magical power within him, his eyes reflected nothing but pain and… fear? What did a Lord have to fear?

"Seri has quickly become the most promising acolyte I have ever trained," Master Hain said. "Her progress is nothing short of astounding."

"Is that so?"

"If this continues, she will undoubtedly overtake our other mages and be eligible herself as my future replacement."

Lord Enuru's eyebrows went up. "Wouldn't that shake this place up?" He laughed. "A woman Master. My wife would certainly be pleased, though."

"My advancement is only to better serve you and Arazu, your Lordship," Seri said.

"Ah, well spoken also. It is good to meet you, young Seri. I have high hopes for your future. High hopes." He glanced at the door to the next room. "Now I believe my wife wishes to see you also. You may proceed."

Seri made a small curtsy and moved past the men. Master Hain was already speaking of the other Lords who hadn't arrived yet, but Lord Enuru's eyes followed her until she left the room. She felt pleased but also a bit unnerved.

Lady Lilitu sat beside a desk in the next chamber, and did not rise when Seri entered. She wore a long, luxurious yellow gown from neck to ankles that left only her right arm and shoulder bare. Long, dark tresses of her hair, braided with gold, stretched across her forehead above an oval frontlet of thin gold plate. A single white crystal twinkled in the center of the frontlet. Like her husband, she also wore gold earrings, bracelets and a necklace, decorated somewhat simpler yet elegant.

Seri could not help being astonished at the Lady's beauty. She was old enough to be Seri's mother, but appeared young enough to be one of her classmates. If not for the clothing, jewelry, and a deep wisdom that shone from Lady Lilitu's eyes, Seri might be bowing to a twin sister. She had already punched Dravid's shoulder for commenting on how lucky Lord Enuru must be.

"Welcome, welcome, my dear," the Lady said, extending a slim hand with carefully trimmed and decorated nails. "I am so pleased to see you."

Seri took the hand and bowed again, a little awkwardly. She had a catch in her throat. She had been looking forward to this moment for so long, and yet she didn't know what to say.

"Master Hain has informed me of your progress. I am delighted to hear of it. He says you're quite remarkable."

"Master Hain is an excellent teacher," Seri managed.

"I have no doubt of it," the Lady said. "But you and I, we both know that earning such praise from a man in such a place as this… it is a stunning achievement."

Seri beamed. "Praise from you makes it all worthwhile, my Lady."

"Oh, come now."

"It's true! You are my inspiration! Without you as an example, I might never have aspired this far. I read your note to me almost every morning!" Now that Seri's tongue was working again, she found it hard to stop it. "Your work with the education system in Arazu changed my life. I can't imagine that I would be here, if not for you."

"Ah, and here I thought it was from my consultations with the Lilim, the night spirits," she said with a twinkle in her eye.

Seri laughed with her, but almost choked when she realized: the twinkle in Lady Lilitu's eye did not come from the light. It stayed constant regardless of how she turned her head.

In the next room, Seri could sense Lord Enuru's well of power leaving. He and Master Hain must be going to see someone else. But as that power left, she became aware of two other things that shocked her even further.

First, she sensed the presence of Curasir. She turned left to see as he entered from the bedroom, a thoughtful smile on his face. She swallowed hard. Did he know? Did he suspect her? With him here, any thoughts of speaking to the Lady about him vanished.

Second, Lady Lilitu had her own power. It was nothing like her husband's, or even Curasir's. It was a third type of power. If the Lord's was a wellspring, Curasir's a maelstrom, then the Lady's was... a tightly-packed, smoldering ball of pure fire, vibrating within her. A third source of power. Seri's entire world seemed upended.

"I, I don't understand," Seri said.

The Lady stood and placed both hands on Seri's shoulders. She was a full head taller. "Fear not, my child. You and I share more than our sex. Let me see you more clearly."

Lady Lilitu put a hand under Seri's chin and tilted it up. They looked directly into each other's eyes. Seri could now see for certain that the Lady's left eye contained a star, not unlike her own. She took a deep breath and found herself shaking.

"I must admit that I did not tell you the exact truth on one occasion," Curasir said. "I told you that I knew of one other case like yours, but that it had been many, many years. It actually wasn't that long."

Lady Lilitu smiled and stepped back. "I am not as young as I appear, but no, it was not that long ago that the star first appeared in my eye. And now you have one as well."

"The odds are astounding," Curasir said. "Two of you, from the same region, both developing the same ability during the same time. This cannot be a coincidence."

"Your power," Seri managed. "It, it's different." She kept straining her senses toward Lady Lilitu, trying to understand it.

"Yes." The Lady held out her palm and a dancing flame appeared on it. Seri stared in fascination. This violated every rule she had learned so far. Vibration could not produce fire. Could it?

"There are more sources of power than you have been taught," Lady Lilitu said. She closed her hand and the flame vanished. "Once you have learned all you can from Master Hain, you must come to me. I will be your next teacher."

"Yes, my Lady."

"Do not speak of this to anyone else. In time, I or Curasir will tell you more. For now, be content with your current training, but never forget that there are greater things awaiting you."

Lady Lilitu took Seri's head in her hands and kissed her forehead. "I have spectacular plans for you, child. You will not simply be a Master on the Conclave of Mages. You will be something far greater."

She stepped back. "Return to your duties, acolyte. Work hard. You are destined for greatness."

•••••

Seri's head swam as she walked the citadel's halls. Everything seemed upside-down. The world had shifted. It was almost as if she had just been told that water was not, in fact, actually wet. How could this be? What did it all mean?

Curasir knew Lady Lilitu. The Lady also had a star in her eye. Curasir said this was not a coincidence. The Lady possessed a third source of power. Seri was destined to be something greater than a Master.

Greater than a Master? What was greater than a Master?

Dravid worked his way down the hall toward her. Over the past week, he had gotten skilled enough to only use one crutch now. "How was your meeting?" he called.

Seri looked up. "It was... enlightening," she said. "I, I was really, really... impressed by the Lady."

"What about the Lord?"

"He was there too." Seri moved past Dravid, her eyes distant.

"Um, all right..." Dravid pivoted awkwardly to follow her. "Are you all right? You seem a bit, ah, confused or something."

"I just have a lot to think about," Seri answered. "I really can't talk about it, but it was big. Really big."

"Now I'm going to have to go spy on them to figure this out."

Seri's head shot up. "That's not a good idea."

"Why not? We agreed it might be neat to look in on the Lords from the crawl tunnels, didn't we?"

"Yes, but not them. Trust me, Dravid." Seri glanced around. "I think they would detect you."

Dravid's face scrunched in perplexity. "I don't get it. I'm always quiet. Even quieter now that I have one less leg, right?" He tried to smile.

"They... their power is different. I seriously think it would be dangerous to try to spy on them."

"Well, now you absolutely have to tell me more."

"I can't!"

Dravid looked at her with a frown, then finally nodded. "All right, I'll take your word for it now. But you have to tell me more when you can."

"As soon as I can, Dravid, I promise."

"You'd better. You persuade me to keep going, and then keep secrets from me. Not entirely encouraging, you know." Dravid started down the hall again.

Seri caught up to him and took his arm. "I'm sorry. I would tell you, if I could." She glanced around. "I hear Lord Meluhha is arriving in two days. Will you be meeting with him about your status?"

"I doubt it. Master Hain has said he'll try speaking with him, but I don't expect anything. Lord Meluhha personally chose Master Ganak."

"You don't need either of them," Seri said. "You're going to be a Master without their help. Or something even better."

Dravid shot her a look. "What could be better than a Master of the Conclave?"

"I don't know. But everything's changing. Who knows what could happen next?"

(((61)))

As they approached more populated areas, Aelia and Talinir frequently discussed their path. At some point, they would have to join the main roads. Otherwise, they'd be cutting through farms and estates.

"Maybe Talinir should wear a hood," Victor suggested one evening. "I mean, he can't hide his face completely, but that might help a little."

"I could cover every inch of my body, and it wouldn't matter," Talinir said. "I would still stand out."

"He's right," Aelia said. "We've grown somewhat accustomed to it over the last few weeks, but no one can ignore one of the Eldanim."

Marshal looked at Talinir. It was true he'd gotten used to the warden's unusual appearance, not just his angular features, but the odd sense that he was taller. He could sense it, of course, but it no longer bothered him as much.

"We're going to stand out, anyway," Victor said. "It's not like we can hide Marshal's face forever." Marshal looked at him. Victor shrugged. "It's true."

"We'll have to make do, the best we can," Aelia said. "We're heading into Reman, which is Volraag's home."

"That makes it the last place he'd expect to find you," Talinir pointed out.

"True, but word might spread of one of the Eldanim escorting a scar-faced young man," Aelia said. "All we can do is try to minimize our interactions with other people as much as possible. If we need to get anything, Victor and I should be the ones to handle it. In fact, Talinir, it would be best if you didn't speak much, if at all. Let people wonder, if they must."

"They must," Victor said.

"Then we do what we can, and trust the rest to Theon," Aelia said firmly. "Get some sleep. Tomorrow, we take to the roads."

•••••

As expected, the party drew quite a few stares when they passed others on the road. The curiosity never seemed to make anyone bold enough to speak to them, though. Marshal wasn't surprised. The other travelers they saw rarely were armed in any way, yet their group had three swords in plain sight. Combined with his scars and Talinir's otherworldly appearance, it made them quite intimidating.

On their third day on the roads, another traveler joined them for lunch. They had stopped beside the road to eat. Marshal had taken a single bite when a dark-skinned man in a well-worn robe stopped in the same place.

"Greetings, friends. Mind if I join you?" Without waiting for an answer, he stepped off the road and found a place to sit next to Victor. He set his bag down and took a deep breath, smiling.

An awkward silence followed. Finally, Aelia spoke. "Welcome, priest. I regret that we have little to share, but what we have is yours."

"Oh, no need," he said. "I have my own." He rummaged through his bag and brought out a loaf of flat bread. He bowed his head over it and mouthed a few words. Then he broke it in half and began eating. Marshal glanced at Aelia. She shrugged and resumed her own meal.

The priest looked around at each of them while he chewed. Marshal noticed he did not react at all to Marshal's scarred face. "You're a fascinating group," he said. "I'm always thrilled to meet new people." He looked at Talinir. "And in all my travels, this is a first for me. I've never met a member of the Eldanim before. I am honored, sir." He lowered his head in a reverential bow.

Talinir nodded in return.

"Are you from Mandiata?" Victor asked.

The priest chuckled. "What gave it away? My accent?"

"No, it was--"

"I know what it was," the priest cut him off. "That was an attempt at humor. I don't always succeed in those attempts. Gives me something to strive for."

Marshal blinked. The priest's voice was low and soothing, but surprisingly rapid. Marshal had trouble keeping up with some of it.

"Mandiata is a long way," Aelia said. "You have traveled far."

The priest nodded, still smiling. "I have now enjoyed the privilege of visiting five of the six lands that make up Antises," he said. "Once I make it to Rasna, I will have seen them all."

"So you're on your way to Rasna?" Victor asked.

"Well, not yet. First, I am expected at the temple in Reman. That is my present course."

"We're on our way there too," Victor said. Aelia shot him a reproving look.

"Wonderful! We are traveling in the same direction, to the same destination. I hope you will not object to my following in your footsteps. I do so enjoy becoming acquainted with other travelers."

Everyone looked at each other, but no one seemed to know what to say.

"I take it by your silence that you're unsure if my presence will be detrimental to whatever pilgrimage drives you," the priest said.

"It's not that," Aelia said.

"If you stay with us, you will probably be putting yourself in danger," Talinir spoke for the first time. "We are likely to draw some… undesirable attention."

"All the more reason to have a priest along, then? I do not fear danger, though I admit I cannot foresee what sort of danger there might be on the road to Reman. This region isn't prone to flooding, is it?" He looked up at the sky, as if he expected a torrential downpour to begin suddenly.

"Not that kind of danger," Victor said. "People might try to kill us."

The priest raised both eyebrows. "Indeed? In spite of the curses? Interesting. I see you must have a fascinating story to tell." Before they could respond, he raised a hand and shook his head. "I won't pressure you for it. If you choose to tell me in your own time, that's wonderful. But if not, I will be content with what I have."

"If you value our privacy, and do not pressure us, as you say," Aelia said slowly, "then I have no objections." She looked at the other three. No one else said anything. Victor shrugged.

"Excellent! Now that that's out of the way, I suppose we should introduce ourselves, at the least. I am Nian, priest of the most high Theon, formerly of the great city of Tenjkidi, now itinerant. Mostly by choice." He looked to Marshal. "You've been quiet, my lad. What might your name be?"

"Oh, he--" Victor began.

"He doesn't talk much," Aelia said. "This is my son, Marshal. I am

Aelia. This is Victor. We are all traveling from our village in the northwest. This is Talinir, an Eldani warden. He joined us a few weeks ago."

"I am honored, honored indeed, to meet all of you. Chance meetings, such as this, often lead to great things, in my experience. Though, of course, I should not use such terminology. Chance is a myth. Theon arranged for our meeting, and its eventual ending is also of his arranging."

Aelia seemed to consider that. "Perhaps you're right," she said. "Time will tell."

<h1 style="text-align:center">(((62)))</h1>

The Lords of Kuktarma and Varioch both arrived three days later. Neither came with much ceremony. Lord Meluhha came only with attendants. Lord Varion also came with a small group of attendants and one other young man.

"Who is that?" Seri asked. He stood tall and strong-looking, with short blond hair and a neatly-trimmed beard. He straightened his cape, the most dramatic accent of his elegant but mostly practical clothes. His blue eyes swept the crowd, resting briefly on Seri before moving on.

"I think that's Lord Varion's heir," Jamana said. "They look similar."

Seri shot a look at Lord Varion. She had to admit that he appeared to be an older, fatter version of the young nobleman who continued to examine everyone and everything about him. He seemed to be analyzing any threats to his father, or to him.

His eyes again settled on Seri and he smiled. She felt her heart skip a beat. The nobles of Varioch had a much lighter skin tone than she was accustomed to, but she could not deny that the Lord's son was incredibly handsome.

"I don't like him," Dravid said. Seri shot a look at him. Dravid scowled. Had he been able to read her reaction? Embarrassing! Seri was thankful she didn't blush too easily.

"Did they bring a new Master?" Adhi asked. As often happened of late, Seri had forgotten he was even there.

"I do not see one," Jamana said. "Perhaps they have not had the time."

Once again, the acolytes stood by as the party moved toward the citadel. Lord Varion's voice carried over the crowd.

"I tell you, this fake King is nothing more than a play for power by that Rasnian!" he said. "It can't possibly be real!"

One of the Masters said something in response.

"He wants to have leverage against me for the land dispute, of course!" Varion said. "I will not be taken in!"

"Well, someone's convinced," Dravid said.

"Of course," Jamana said. "Varioch and Rasna are on the verge of war. Everyone knows this."

"Everyone knows it, but it doesn't actually happen," Seri said. "Master Hain wondered the same thing as Lord Varioch. Maybe the new King is a fake."

"We'll know in a few days' time," Dravid said. "Lord Tyrr is the only one not here yet. And there are only ten days left until the Passing."

(((63)))

Nian turned out to be a most interesting travel companion. His journeys had provided him with many fascinating stories, both of his own travels and those of the places he'd visited. Marshal found it all extremely interesting. After only a day together, he found himself captivated by Nian's every word. The only thing that bothered him was when Nian would divert off on a sudden monologue in praise of Theon. Marshal knew he was supposed to revere Theon. Everyone was. But in his mind, he couldn't separate the god from the curses.

"It's an enormous bull!" Nian exclaimed. "With a great hump on its back!"

Marshal blinked. Somehow he had missed the start of another conversation. Victor appeared to be baffled by something Nian had said.

"They use them in place of horses?"

"No, they have horses, as well. But they use these humped bulls for many of the jobs you might give to horses, or donkeys even. They don't have donkeys in Kuktarma."

"But we have bulls," Victor said.

"Not like these. They're much larger than anything you have here. And I did mention the humps, correct? Like a massive chunk of muscle just sitting there on top of their shoulders. And their eyes! I swear, when one of them is angry, their eyes turn red, like a gateway to the underworld. I know, let me tell you. I stared directly into them."

"You stared an angry bull in the eyes?" Aelia asked. She was smiling, an all-too-rare sight lately.

"It was in a small town on the northeast side of Kuktarma," Nian said. "This bull had gotten loose and was rampaging down the street. I helped a small child climb onto the roof of a nearby house. Their roofs are all flat, by the way. Very convenient. When the child left my hands, I turned and the bull was standing right before me, as close as I now stand to you!" The answer had seemed aimed at Aelia, but Nian looked at Marshal when he said it.

"What happened?" Victor asked.

"I stared into those red eyes, sure that I saw my death within them. I told Theon that I had hoped to see the pillars of Raeton before that, but if he wanted to take me, I was ready." Nian paused for effect. "And the bull turned. It lunged at the wall beside me, as if offended by it, then galloped off down the street."

Victor narrowed his eyes. "Did that really happen?"

Nian looked shocked. "I am a priest of Theon, good man! I would not lie to you!"

Victor continued to frown.

Nian glanced around, then leaned in closer to Victor as they walked. "I will tell you this," he said, pretending to whisper, "they taste delicious."

"You ate one, too?"

"The same bull. One of the villagers had to kill it, so we ate it. Now, you have to cook the meat an extra-long time, or it's too tough. But once you do, oh, it's delightfully savory. I can't believe how much of that bull I ate that night. I was full of it!"

Marshal did not know what to think of this priest. He behaved nothing like the traveling priest that visited Drusa's Crossing so regularly. That man was dour and serious all the time. Marshal couldn't recall ever seeing him smile. Nian's face almost never lost its smile.

"Why do you suppose there are no blessings?"

Marshal looked up in surprise. He had gotten lost in his thoughts again. Aelia and Talinir walked ahead of them, discussing something he couldn't hear. Victor had dropped further back, leaving Nian alone with Marshal.

"The Laws of Bindings and Cursings," Nian said. "Why isn't it the Laws of Blessings and Cursings, do you suppose? Wouldn't that make more sense? Blessings for what is right, cursings for what is wrong."

Marshal could only blink in response.

Nian seemed unfazed. "I don't expect you to answer," he said, his voice sounding far more serious than it usually did. "It's something I've often pondered over, and this present company makes it more profound than ever."

Had someone told him about Marshal's curse? Or the Binding with Victor? Marshal felt his hand start to vibrate. He grabbed at the hilt of his sword to calm it. If Nian noticed, he didn't comment on it.

"Would you like to know what I decided?" Nian went on. "The problem is not with Theon. It's with the men who claimed to serve him. The mages and Lords who created the Laws. Not the Laws as written, of course, but the magic that enforces them. In all of his writings, Theon gives his people a choice. He never compels. There are consequences to actions, of course, but I just... I don't see him being pleased with what men have done with his words."

Nian spread his arms and gestured at the farmlands they currently passing through. "I have traveled throughout Antises and it is the same everywhere. The law is observed. No one steals. No one kills. But... their hearts are not changed. Instead, they resent Theon and secretly curse him back. This cannot be what he intended."

Nian fell silent. His smile was gone. Marshal could not fathom why the priest had chosen him to hear this speech. He felt there was truth in what had been said, or at least that Nian felt it to be true. The problems of a god and what people thought of him seemed far beyond Marshal's life and the problems of the here and now.

(((64)))

Seri settled in to the new "normal" of Zes Sivas. She had little time for training any more, and Master Hain had even less. The Lords required numerous messages to be sent from one to another, prior to any face-to-face meetings. The citadel had several message-runners, but nowhere near enough, so the acolytes had been recruited for that purpose. They also ended up running other errands, from finding more bedding, to cleaning up messes, to delivering food and drink.

Lord Enuru also requested Seri specifically to take notes during his meetings with the other Lords. Though it sounded like an exciting prospect, it ended up quite boring. The Lords would inquire after each others' families, discuss the possibility of the new King, and then move on to their official business, which almost always involved some kind of trade deal. Seri dutifully wrote down everything that was said, but little of it made sense to her.

She did gain some insight into Lord Enuru's frame of mind, however. He held more face-to-face meetings than any of the other Lords. Arazu was the smallest of the six lands, and thus needed the most in trade. Unfortunately, it did not have much in the way of exports, which led to what Seri regarded as very unbalanced deals. Still, she could not fault Lord Enuru for his labor. He seemed to work harder than any of them.

Dravid had fewer assignments than the others, due to his condition. Seri wondered how he kept himself busy. At least he had stopped being so morose.

Lord Varion ended up being the most difficult, with his hand-delivered meals. They never satisfied him. Whoever delivered the meal had to make repeated runs back to the kitchen for different spices, drinks, or even completely different meals.

On the third night, Seri brought the tray of food. When she entered, Lord Varion was seated at his table, writing something. He glanced up as she entered.

"I'll eat in the bedroom," he said, looking back down. "Take the food there."

"Yes, your Lordship." Seri walked through the first two rooms. She hesitated once she reached the bedroom. Only one small table stood beside the bed here, and she would have to remove a pile of clothes to set the tray on it. She sighed. With no other option, she set the tray on the floor temporarily, then began to clear the table.

"That's good enough."

Seri jumped. How had Lord Varion followed her? She hadn't heard a sound. The presence of all the Lords on the island overwhelmed her magic senses almost all the time now, so she hadn't sensed him either. It seemed strange that a man so large could move that fast.

"Let me see you," Varion said, stepping into the room.

"Sir?"

"Your face is pleasant enough. Can't tell much about the rest of you through that ridiculous robe, but we'll get past that soon enough."

Seri swallowed hard. Was he implying…?

Lord Varion raised his hand. Seri felt a wave of vibratory power wash over her. Immediately, she felt calm and relaxed. At least, her body did. She felt disconnected from her own flesh, unable to control it. Her mind screamed in horror and protest, but the screams couldn't seem to make it to her mouth.

"Feel good?" Varion approached her. "I learned how to use the power that way very early. It makes things so much more… agreeable."

Seri blinked and her star sight activated. All she needed was one light beam strong enough, and she knew she could break out of this. Only… she couldn't move her hands. She couldn't reach out and grab a beam. She would have to wait for one to come to her.

But they weren't coming to her! All of the light beams coming through the floor in the room curved toward Lord Varion! His power drew all the other power toward him.

Never in her life had she felt so completely helpless. Seri desperately tried to channel something she just didn't have. No strength. No control over her own body. No magic.

Lord Varion touched her face, then ran his fingers down her neck.

"Lovely," he murmured. "Your skin tone is quite exotic."

Seri heard a movement above. Her eyes darted up and saw one of the air vents from the crawl tunnels. Noises came from within. Dravid! He must be up there right now!

"Sounds like a rodent problem," Lord Varion said, with a quick glance upward. "I'll have to speak to one of the Masters about that later. For now, let's get to know each other better."

His hands began to touch her through the robe. He removed her belt and dropped it. "I guess this just lifts off, then?" He grasped two handfuls of the robe and began to pull upward.

"Really, Father?"

Varion jumped and cursed. He let go of Seri's robe and turned around. Only then could Seri see his son standing in the doorway, arms folded.

"You unbelievable bastard," the son said. "The only available female on the island, and you're already after her."

Lord Varion spread his hands. "This is who I am, Volraag. You know this. Your mother certainly does."

"Let her go."

"Why should I? Are you jealous? It's not my fault you left your concubine at home."

"Not only is this girl an acolyte of Arazu, she's immensely favored by both the Lord and Lady."

Varion snorted. "Arazu! That pathetic strip of coastline? Why should I fear their retaliation? They have nothing." He glanced back at Seri. "Nothing except some attractive females, it seems."

Volraag rolled his eyes. "I'm serious, Father. I've been paying attention. All of the Masters here are impressed with her. Harm her and you'll have trouble with everyone." He unfolded his arms. "Even the Eldanim."

Lord Varion sighed. "Fine, whatever." He waved his hand and Seri felt the relaxed state evaporate from her. She could move again! She grabbed her belt off the floor and ran to the doorway. Volraag stood aside and let her pass.

"If you change your mind, my bedroom's always available!" Lord Varion called.

• • • • •

Seri rushed out to the hallway and leaned against the wall. In all her life, she had never been that close to… to being violated. Horrible, horrible thoughts fought for dominance in her racing mind. Part of her wanted to run as far away as possible. Part of her wanted to curl up and cry. And part of her wanted to turn around and use her power to collapse this entire wing of the citadel.

Volraag emerged from the room. Seri jumped and spun away, then stopped when she saw it was him. She noticed her hands were trembling and put them down to her sides.

"Are you all right?" Volraag asked. "Genuinely?"

"I, I will be." She had to be. This one incident would not ruin her life. Seri tried to remind herself of Lady Lilitu's words. Destiny. Greatness.

"I am sorry that happened," Volraag said. His voice was gentle and even seemed pained. "I will speak to those in the kitchen and make sure that you are not assigned this duty again."

Volraag glanced back at the door and sighed. "I will not tell you not to speak of this to your Master. That is up to you. I don't know what good it would do, though. As long as my father possesses his power, he's practically untouchable. Antises will be a better place when men like him have no power."

Seri put a hand to her chest and tried to control her breathing. Volraag noticed.

"Deep breaths," he urged. "You'll be all right. You're safe now." He started to reach a hand toward her, then stopped himself. Seri felt a surge of gratefulness for that. This was a man who could actually think through his actions. She tried to follow his instructions for breathing.

She realized she was still holding her belt. Putting it back on in front of the Lord's son would be highly improper, though leaving it off wasn't much better. At least, that's what the logical side of her mind said. The other side mocked her for even thinking such ridiculous thoughts at a time like this.

One thing troubled her most of all. "How… how…"

"How does he get away with that?" Volraag asked. Seri nodded. A man forcing himself on a woman was almost unheard of. The repercussions, the curses… oh. "He's a Lord. He's exempt from curses. Except, of course, the curses for his actions fall on his children."

Seri looked at Volraag in horror. She knew this to be true, of course. But to see it first-hand…

"So far, I've been lucky," Volraag said. "The curses haven't touched me. The consequences for his first crimes fell on his first-born, who, sadly, is now dead. Since then, he's fathered half a dozen offspring. As he continues his actions, curses have hit various ones of us. Just not me. Not yet, anyway."

At that point, Dravid lurched around the corner, moving as fast as he could with his crutch. "Seri! Seri! Are you all right?"

Seri held up her hand and Dravid came to a stop. "I'll be fine," she said. "Thank you. I heard you up there. I know you were watching."

"I, I tried to blast through, but I, I couldn't make it work," Dravid stuttered. "I came as fast as I could."

"It's not your fault," Seri said. "The Lord sucks in all the magic around him. I didn't know it worked that way. Otherwise, I could have broken free on my own."

Seri took a deep breath and turned back to Volraag. "Thank you," she said. His unusual blue eyes shone brilliant, even in the dim hallway light. "I cannot possibly repay you for your assistance, for… for… saving me."

Volraag closed his eyes and made a short bow. "As I said, sometimes power is in the wrong hands. It was my pleasure to help you. If you should ever need anything else, anything within my power, let me know."

He spun on a heel and hurried away. Seri watched him go. What a contrast between father and son.

Dravid touched her shoulder and she jerked away instinctively. He held up his hand. "Sorry, sorry. I just…"

"I know. I don't have to fear you. That was… Let's get out of here."

She let Dravid move ahead of her and surreptitiously put her belt back on. Little things. Little victories. Don't think about that man any more.

(((65)))

"What can we hope to find at Theon's temple?" Aelia asked Nian the next day as they walked. "Are the priests who work there honorable, like yourself?"

"Flattery is hardly necessary," Nian said, "and probably not accurate. The priests of Reman's temple are servants of Theon. What, specifically, are you asking?"

Marshal looked up. This was the first time Aelia had spoken of the temple in days. He still didn't know what hope she had in going there.

Aelia studied Nian for a moment before answering. "Can I trust you, Nian?"

Nian looked grave. "I never betray a confidence, my lady. Now, will you be asking me to trust you about your intentions at the temple? Or about your son's curse? Or about the reason you always keep someone on guard at night? Or the truth about your identity?"

"How did you know about his curse?" Victor demanded. Talinir's hand drifted to his sword hilt.

"It's not hard to deduce," Nian said. "He never speaks, never makes signs, never communicates in any way."

"That's--"

"And a thrummer landed on him last night and flew away glowing as bright as I've ever seen one."

"Fair enough," Aelia said. "You are observant. You also seem to genuinely care about other people. That is why I feel comfortable speaking with you."

"But should you betray her trust, you will have me to deal with," Talinir said. "And I am not bound by your curses."

Nian nodded. "I wondered about that, actually. It does answer a few questions that I hadn't worked up the courage to ask yet." He looked around at the others. "You've all known me for two days. I don't expect your trust. All that I know is through clever guesswork. If you ask it of me, I will never tell a soul that I even met you." He shrugged. "Besides, who would I tell? We're both going to the temple, and after that, I will be traveling on to the next land."

"I am seeking to have Marshal's curse removed," Aelia said with sudden bluntness.

Nian stopped walking. For the first time since he had met the priest, Marshal saw shock on his face.

Aelia stopped too, and faced him. "I see that I have finally rendered you speechless."

Nian found his voice. "I will admit that I did not anticipate that possibility. I am... surprised, to say the least, that you would be considering this course of action."

"Is it not possible?"

"Why would you even ask this?"

Aelia scowled. "Do not play games with me, priest. I am not some commoner who trusts the priests to explain the Law. I have read it myself. The provision is there."

"This is true, though some would dispute that. It's not in the Law itself, but in the Words of Aharu, which some see as an addendum..."

"Who's Aharu?" Victor asked

"The founder of the priesthood," Aelia said without turning. "A companion to Akhenadom. That makes his words a little hard to ignore, does it not?"

"Yes," Nian admitted. "Though Aharu is controversial to some, since he was both priest and mage. Even so, from the very beginning he wrote of this provision, but..."

Marshal perked up. From the very beginning? Then why had no one ever done it?

"But?"

"But most people have never read it or even heard about it. And no one has ever tried it. The cost is too high."

"Perhaps no one has ever loved a child the way I do," Aelia said, her voice soft and pained. "Or perhaps no one has seen the future of what he can do if I do this for him."

"You have seen the future?"

"In a manner of speaking."

"Now I'm significantly curious."

"There are some things I am not going to tell you." Aelia resumed walking. "But I do seek your expertise and knowledge. How do you think the priests at the temple will react to this?"

"If they do not laugh in your face, they will at the least try to dissuade you from this course of action." Nian repositioned his bag's shoulder strap and caught up to Aelia.

"I will not be dissuaded."

"They may even try to stop you by direct means."

Aelia cocked her head. "It had crossed my mind," she said. "But would they really go that far? What I ask is not against the laws of Varioch, Antises, or the Bindings and Cursings."

"They may be obstinate. But will Theon honor it, I wonder?" Nian mused. "Yes, it is within the law, I suppose, but it has never been tested, to my knowledge."

"Why wouldn't he? It is love, is it not? Is he not a god of love?"

"Yes, of course. I just... You raise many interesting issues. I am now exceptionally pleased that I met you. From an intellectual standpoint, that is."

"I wish someone would tell the rest of us what this all means," Victor complained.

"Of course. When--" Nian began.

"Not now," Aelia interrupted. "Marshal and Victor do not need to know the details yet."

Nian raised his eyebrows, but said nothing else.

●●●●●

At twilight, the travelers found an open space near the road for their camp. Both Talinir and Nian agreed that less than a week remained before they arrived at Reman, barring any further trouble. Thus far, none of the anticipated problems of road travel had occurred, much to Aelia's relief. Marshal wondered if Volraag even knew of their whereabouts. Probably not, unless the assassin had reported to him. There had been no sign of the mysterious killer for two weeks.

Victor and Marshal performed their usual end-of-the-day sword practice, which Nian found immensely fascinating. Everyone gathered for the evening meal, then prepared for bed. Marshal had the first watch for the night. He watched the others prepare their bedrolls and drop off, one by one. Even Talinir fell asleep. He seemed to do that more often since he lost the starshine. Only Nian stayed awake. He whispered to himself, gazing up into the sky.

Marshal sat silent as time passed. He kept his eyes away from the fire and watched the darkness. As he often did, he took out Volraag's dagger and toyed with it. What was his half-brother up to now? Was he waiting for them at the city they were nearing? Would he resort to more direct methods to kill Marshal? He snorted. That might be harder than expected, thanks to the Eldanim. He stabbed the dagger down at his thigh. No penetration. The protection spell did not seem to have diminished at all.

Keeping watch while camped beside the road was different than being in the wilderness. Out there, everything was dark. The only movement came from animals. Here, he could see lights in the distance on occasion: homes and inns along the road, or near it. Even late at night, travelers sometimes passed by, continuing on their way in a hurry, perhaps close to home, or perhaps they simply preferred walking at night.

One such traveler walked by their camp about two hours after nightfall. He stopped and stood on the road, facing Marshal, as if watching him. His dark shape was silhouetted against the full moon. Marshal sucked in a breath as he realized the watcher's dark shape did not come from the night. He was a creature of shadow, an eidolon. Again.

"Is that what I think it is?" Nian asked.

Marshal glanced his way. The priest sat up and stared at the shadowy figure. Marshal looked back. The eidolon still stood in the same place, unmoved. Marshal carefully slid his sword from its sheath.

"You call them eidolon here, don't you?" Nian said. "I'm guessing from your reaction that you've seen them before."

Marshal nodded without looking away. He got to his feet and took a step toward the road. The eidolon took a step backwards in response.

Marshal scowled. He was sick of these things following him everywhere he went. They had never seemed to mean harm to him, except for the attack on Talinir he had fought off. But they were annoying. Why did they always keep appearing? What were they? What did they want?

As if in response, the eidolon made an elaborate bow in his direction. It held its position for a moment, then turned and vanished into the night. Marshal dashed up onto the road, but the creature had disappeared completely. Marshal suspected that even if it were daylight, he would find no sign of it.

"Fascinating," Nian said. "I've never seen one behave that way before." He watched Marshal return to his place.

Marshal put his sword away and resumed his watch. Nian was silent for a minute or so before he resumed the one-sided conversation.

"Do you know these creatures are seen all over Antises? They're called by different names, of course. In Kuktarma, they call them bhoots. In Arazu, they call them Gidim. All of them whisper strange tales of these ghosts. Some people think they're the spirits of the dead. Others that they're some magical creatures like the Eldanim. The stories are endless." Nian paused. "And yet... they're never seen as friends of humans. But this one bowed to you. Was he being sarcastic or serious? Why...?" He trailed off.

Even if he could speak, Marshal had no answers. He glanced at Nian. Even through the darkness, he could tell the priest was watching him. After a moment of silence, he moved nearer to Marshal and sighed.

"I know you cannot communicate very well, but my conscience requires me to ask you something." He looked at Marshal, seeking a response. Marshal nodded, not knowing what else to do.

"Are you aware of what your mother intends to do in Reman?"

Marshal wrinkled his brow. He didn't know how to respond to that. Before he could figure out whether to nod or shake his head, Nian shook his.

"Never mind. I asked that wrong. Let me be clear. Do you understand the cost that Aelia would pay in this attempt to lift your curse?"

Marshal shook his head. He had suspicions, obviously, but Aelia had kept that part of the plan to herself.

"She plans to die, Marshal. To sacrifice herself for you."

That couldn't be right. No. Not Aelia. Not his mother. She couldn't die.

Nian studied him. "You didn't know," he said. "I thought not. Yet that is what is written in the Words of Aharu - that if a willing, uncursed person sacrifices herself for one with a curse, the curse will be lifted." He placed a hand on Marshal's shoulder. "Your mother wants my help at the temple. I cannot be a party to this if you are not in agreement. That is why I have told you. Do you want Aelia to do this?"

Marshal shook his head violently.

"I thought not. Then I will not allow her to go through with it." He patted Marshal's shoulder and withdrew his hand. "Besides, I cannot imagine that Theon would want her to do so. Perhaps… perhaps merely seeing her resolve will be enough. Maybe he will accept her intentions." He took a deep breath. "My conscience is settled, then. Rest easy, Marshal. I will not allow her to die."

Marshal made the same vow. Regardless of what she wanted, he would not permit his mother to die for him.

<h1 style="text-align:center">(((66)))</h1>

Seri spent a horrible night alone in her room. This was far more terrifying than her worries about Curasir. Lord Varioch might actually have the gall to come to her room. And how could she stop him? His power could not be matched, except by another Lord. As before, she pushed her writing table in front of the door, for all the good it might do.

If Lord Varioch's appetites were as strong as Volraag implied, then she was still in great danger. She had no weapons. Her magic was in flux, at best. She truly was the most unprotected woman on the island.

She barely slept. Every sound, every trick of the light had her scrambling to the corner of her bed, grasping for her magic, staring at the door.

In the morning, Seri felt her only recourse was to tell Master Hain what had happened. She needed protection, and her fellow acolytes would not be enough. As much as she loved them, they lacked the power she needed. She worked up her courage by the middle of the morning and then had to plead with Master Hain for a moment of privacy. He relented and excused himself from a discussion with two of the other Masters, meeting her out in a hall away from them.

"What is so important?" he asked, clearly impatient.

Seri lowered her head, unable to look him in the eye. "Lord Varioch tried to… to…"

"He tried to what?"

"Violate me." The small words fell into the empty hall like heavy weights.

Master Hain stood still for a moment. His face did not move. Then his jaw worked back and forth before he finally spoke. "But he did not succeed?"

Seri shook her head.

"Are you certain that was his intent?"

"Yes, sir."

"Tell me."

Haltingly, she told the entire scene, leaving out Dravid's part and the crawl tunnels. Master Hain's face grew harder than she had ever seen it. When she finished, he looked away.

"Come with me."

Master Hain led the way to the Lords' quarters. Seri was terrified he would confront Lord Varioch, but instead he walked to Lord Enuru's suite. He knocked and entered. She hurried to keep up with him.

Both the Lord and Lady greeted them. In swift words, Master Hain related what Seri had told him.

"Outrageous!" Lord Enuru slammed his fist on the desk. "Such a thing should not be!"

Lady Lilitu's responded in a different way. "Come, child." She gestured to Seri.

Seri approached her and started to bow. Before she could do so, Lady Lilitu grabbed hold of her and pulled her into a powerful embrace.

"Your mother is not here, so I must suffice," she whispered. "Have you cried yet?" Seri shook her head. "Then you must do so." The Lady looked up. "Could you two excuse us for a moment, please?"

Master Hain and Lord Enuru nodded and left the room.

"Let yourself go," the Lady instructed.

Seri found herself amazingly comforted by the Lady's embrace. Her muscles, so tense and trembling up until now, relaxed. A sob erupted suddenly from her throat. Her rational mind suggested this was unnecessary, but the rest of her immediately shouted it down. In a few seconds, tears poured from her eyes while her body shook. Lady Lilitu said nothing, but massaged her back and held her close.

At last, Seri's weeping subsided and she recognized the embarrassment of the moment. She pulled away. The Lady smiled and handed her a cloth to wipe her eyes and nose.

"Thank you, my Lady," she whispered.

"I have no children of my own, you know," Lady Lilitu said with a half smile. Seri was shocked to see evidence of tears in the Lady's eyes too. "But I like to think I would make a good mother."

"I think you would be a wonderful mother, my Lady."

"Then think of me that way while I am here. Come to me, should you need anything." She reached forward and wiped away another tear from Seri's cheek. Then she raised her head and called, "You men may return now."

When her husband and Master Hain came back, she wasted no time. "Master Hain, what steps will you be taking to protect our acolyte from this monster?"

"The Passing is one week from today," Master Hain said.. "All of the Lords will leave within a day or two after that. Seri-Belit needs only to be protected for seven or eight days.

"As I see it, your Ladyship, Lord Varioch is quite busy throughout most of the day. I believe Seri will be safe during that time, though I am going to insist that she never be alone. The evenings and nights are another issue."

Lady Lilitu tapped her fingers on the desk. "I am friends with Lady Ajaw," she said. "I am sure she would be more than happy to send one of her personal guards to be with you each evening. I believe even Lord Varioch would find it difficult to tangle with one of them."

Seri's eyes widened. The warrior women?

"An excellent idea!" Lord Enuru agreed.

Lady Lilitu turned back to Seri. "Is this acceptable, my dear?"

"Yes, my Lady, only…"

"Only what?"

Seri looked to Master Hain. "Is there any magic you can teach me that would help me break loose from the power he used on me? That was the worst thing of all. I had no control over my body!"

Master Hain frowned. "The power the Lords possess is almost insurmountable," he said slowly, with a glance at Lord Enuru. "I do not know if what you ask is possible."

"The other Lords are already afraid of Varioch," Enuru said. "He is the most ruthless of us all. It would be difficult to oppose him in his war against Rasna, let alone something like this. But… if the King has truly returned, then we might have a chance to force him down, in all things."

"One more hug, my dear," the Lady said, beckoning. Seri allowed herself to be embraced once more, and again, the lady whispered for only her ears. "What you ask is possible. I cannot teach it to you at this time, but I will send for you when I have the time."

She pulled back and looked Seri in the eyes. She nodded and smiled.

"Come, Seri," Master Hain said. "We will find your fellow acolytes and I will leave you with them."

Seri could not hide the enormous relief she felt, leaving the Lord's chambers. They had all believed her and wanted to help. She couldn't imagine what would have happened if they had thought she was lying.

• • • • •

Seri's new bodyguard met her at the evening meal. She arrived at the acolytes' table, looked them all over critically, then addressed herself to Seri.

"I am here as your guard, my lady."

Seri laughed nervously. "I'm not a great Lady. You don't have to call me that."

The guard inclined her head. Her rounded face had twin black stripes painted on either cheek, quite distinctive against her light brown skin. She appeared somewhat younger than Seri. She dressed in a similar fashion to the Lady Ajaw: calf-length skirt, bare stomach, tight wrapping around the chest, no shoes. Two green feathers hung from a tight braid on the left side of her head. Her round shield, painted orange with three green stripes, was somewhat smaller than her Lady's had been. A short sword hung at her side.

"I am assigned to guard you," she said. "That makes you a lady. We guard no others."

"Lady Seri!" Jamana mocked. "Who would have thought it?"

Seri scowled at him, then turned back to the guard. "Thank you for being here. What is your name?"

"I am Ixchel."

"Well, Ixchel, I am very pleased to meet you. Would you like to eat with us?"

"No, my lady. I am here to protect, not eat."

Seri wasn't sure how to respond to that. She introduced each of the three boys to Ixchel. All were suitably impressed, but Jamana couldn't keep from grinning.

They tried to include Ixchel in their conversations, but she had little to say. She stood near Seri, upright and alert, paying attention to everything that took place in the dining hall.

Seri caught Adhi's gaze fixed on Ixchel's bare midriff. She rolled her eyes. Men. At least Jamana and Dravid weren't... well, at least they tried to be subtle about it.

Seri finished eating and told the other acolytes good night. Ixchel walked side-by-side with her back to her room.

"Have you been guarding the Lady Ajaw very long?" Seri asked.

"I am the newest," Ixchel said. "Only six months."

Fascinated, Seri listened intently every time Ixchel spoke. Her voice had an unusual cadence to it. She spoke in short sentences, and her voice seemed to rise every so slightly through each word.

"That's probably why you're the one assigned to me," Seri said. "I hope it's not a boring duty for you. I'll do what I can to keep things interesting." She chuckled, but Ixchel did not smile.

"Duty is duty," she said. "Boredom matters not."

Seri raised and eyebrow. "We're going to be together for a week, you know. We might as well become friends."

"I am your guard. You are my Lady."

"All right, then."

Seri stopped trying. This was going to be interesting. At her bedroom door, she paused. "How will this work? Will you be coming in or..."

"I will stay out here."

"When will you sleep?"

"When I am not guarding you."

Seri nodded. She didn't know what else to say. "I... hope you have an uneventful night and are able to sleep well tomorrow."

Ixchel gave a curt nod. "As do I."

"Good night."

"Good night, Lady Seri."

Seri closed the door behind her and tried not to laugh. A Lady? Her? How ridiculous would that be? An image of the handsome Volraag popped into her head. Hmm. Maybe it wasn't so ridiculous.

She almost slapped herself for that thought.

(((67)))

Over the next few days, Seri slowly got used to the idea of having a bodyguard. To her surprise, Ixchel not only slept during the day, she did so in Seri's bedroom. She went to bed when Seri got up, and rose sometime in the afternoon. She met up with Seri in the early evening and followed her around until she went to bed herself. Seri appreciated it, and slept much better for it, but the arrangement felt strange.

As much as she appreciated it, Seri couldn't help wondering what good Ixchel's sword and shield would be against the power of a Lord. Perhaps the concept alone would be enough to discourage him?

In addition, Ixchel did not seem interested in any conversation topics. She spoke as she had the first evening: short sentences, and as little as possible. Seri grew frustrated. She wanted to know more about the girl, her training and upbringing, and Ch'olan in general.

Two days after promising it, Lady Lilitu sent for Seri. It was early evening, so Ixchel came along. She checked to be sure Seri and the Lady were alone in the suite, then left them to wait in the hallway.

"How is she working out?" the Lady asked.

"Well, I suppose," Seri said. She related her frustration.

Lady Lilitu chuckled. "Ch'olanites are notoriously close-mouthed with strangers," she said. "Give her time. Eventually, you may win her over."

"We don't have that much time," Seri grumbled.

"You may be surprised. Now, about the reason I summoned you."

"You're going to tell me about the other power?" Seri snapped her mouth closed. She was speaking too fast again. She should not be so familiar with the Lady.

"I'm afraid that I cannot tell you what you want to hear."

Seri opened her mouth, but stopped herself this time.

"You must be patient. I do not wish to interfere with your current training or disrupt that learning process."

Seri nodded her acceptance, though she wasn't sure what to think.

"What I can tell you is that there are other sources of power beyond Antises itself."

Sources? Seri's mind raced. More than those she already knew?

"I have not received permission to tell you of my source, but as your own skill and power grows, you will discover it on your own. Of that I have no doubt."

Seri wanted to ask so much more, but it seemed she wasn't going to get answers today. More than that, it seemed she wouldn't have a way to protect herself from Lord Varion's magic.

"I know you are disappointed, but I cannot help you further at this time. That is why I am pleased to hear how your new bodyguard is working."

Seri nodded again. As talented as Ixchel appeared, she doubted her efficiency against the magical power of a Lord.

"Keep her with you at all times, and I think you will have nothing to fear. The busier this island becomes, the less likely Lord Varion will even have an opportunity to bother you. I intend to take a hand in that, as well. I will send him messages every hour or two, asking for obscure details on trade agreements and such."

"Thank you, my lady."

Lady Lilitu smiled again. "I know this isn't what you wanted. But you must trust me, Seri. Someday, we will have a much longer talk about the sources of power in this world."

"Yes, my lady."

"We will speak again before I leave. I promise."

Seri nodded, bowed, and left the room. Ixchel joined her immediately. Seri smiled half heartedly. She didn't have what she wanted, but perhaps she didn't need it yet. Her curiosity about the Lady's words kept her up late that night. Someday, she would know all of these things. Someday.

• • • • •

The following day was another Rest Day. Seri was actually surprised to see the assembled Lords observe it without fail. They held no meetings or negotiations through the day and mostly kept to themselves in their rooms.

Seri spent much of the day with the other acolytes, who all appreciated a break from their work. Ixchel insisted on staying with her most of the day, as the situation differed on Rest Day. Lord Varion would not be busy. Seri was grateful, but felt guilty that Ixchel missed some sleep. At least they weren't running around everywhere, wearing her out. It was supposed to be a day of rest, after all.

In the mid-afternoon, the sleepy island woke up. A large ship approached, but anchored about two hundred yards from the island itself. Those in the know identified it as belonging to Lord Tyrr of Rasna.

"That means the new King is on board!" Dravid told them.

"The supposed King," Jamana said.

"They must be waiting until after Rest Day to come ashore," Seri said. She looked over the ship and wished she had studied more about them. This was certainly much larger than the boats in which the other Lords had arrived. Was it intended to impress, or was there another reason?

"Lord Tyrr wants to create the most dramatic entrance possible, no doubt," Dravid said.

"Anticipation is a clever tactic," Adhi said. Seri jumped. How did she keep missing that he was present?

They all stood silent for a moment, staring across the water. Even Ixchel looked interested.

"Nothing much we can do about it today," Dravid said finally. He hobbled back around and started toward the citadel. The others followed.

Seri paused. The cypress trees reminded her of her encounter in the Otherworld. She was about to say something, then remembered Adhi and Ixchel would not know what she was talking about. She didn't want to explain it, either. Enough people knew her secret already.

Early the next morning, virtually every resident and guest at Zes Sivas assembled on the shore, watching Lord Tyrr's ship. A longboat was lowered and began moving toward the dock.

"Master Korda says that arrivals always used to come on the other side of the island," Jamana said. "There was a large quay in front of the Citadel of Kings."

"What happened to it?" Adhi asked.

"It collapsed during the first earthquake. But almost no one had been using it, anyway. Not since the King left."

"Maybe they'll rebuild it now," Dravid said.

"There's a lot of people in that longboat," Seri said, straining to see. "I can't tell anything more yet."

"There are twelve," Ixchel said. Everyone turned to look at her, but her eyes remained fixed on the longboat. "Six of them are working the oars. Probably sailors. Of the others, I can only tell Lord Tyrr. He is the large man in the front."

"You can see that?" Dravid said.

Ixchel's eyes darted toward him, then away. "Yes."

A few moments later, they could all see. The longboat came nearer and nearer. On the dock, the five Masters waited. The five other Lords stood on the shore, along with the two Ladies that had come. Behind stood their retainers, assistants, bodyguards, and so on. The remaining population of Zes Sivas had to wait further back.

The sailors brought in their oars as the longboat reached the dock. One of them jumped out and quickly tied it off. He then knelt out of the way.

Lord Tyrr stepped onto the dock. A powerfully-built man, he was around the same size and appearance as Lord Varion, but not as corpulent. He gave a quick nod to the assembled Masters and Lords, then immediately turned and knelt as well, facing the longboat.

All eyes fixated on the young man who stepped somewhat awkwardly onto the dock. He regained his balance and stood tall and straight, looking over everyone. Like all the people of Rasna and Varioch, he had wheat-colored skin. His hair was reddish-blond and curly, with a light beard decorating his chin.

"He looks like a Rasnian," Jamana said. "Is that how the King is supposed to look?"

"I... don't remember," Seri said. "I'm not sure I've ever seen anything about the King's appearance."

Lord Tyrr and the sailor remained kneeling. Master Plecu joined them. Then, to everyone's surprise, Lord Rajwir, Lady Ajaw, and Master Tzoyet also knelt.

The King made a gesture of some kind. Lord Tyrr stood, as did the others. Tyrr stepped up beside the young man and turned to face everyone else.

"I present to you, at long last, the lost ruler of all Antises, King Tezan!" he proclaimed in a voice that carried to all the listeners. "Let all the lands rejoice! The King has returned!"

A significant number of people, especially among the workers, applauded. A few others made some polite clapping. Most remained still, waiting for confirmation of some kind.

Tezan put his hands together in front of him and appeared to concentrate. Everyone watched. Seri was surprised to realize she was holding her breath. Tezan pulled his hands slowly apart. A collective gasp erupted from dozens of mouths. Something glowed between Tezan's hands.

He spread his hands further apart. Between them, a bright yellow fire pulsed and moved. He lifted it high so everyone could see.

"The Heart of Fire!" Master Plecu exclaimed. Other voices picked it up, echoing and repeating. This time, loud applause erupted.

Tezan pulled his hands apart and the fire exploded into cinders that floated in the air before vanishing completely. Seri couldn't see his face, but his body language made him look pleased with himself.

Jamana's brow furrowed. "I thought the Heart of Fire manifested during the Passing," he said.

"That's what Master Hain told me," Seri said. "But he didn't say it wasn't possible outside that. I don't know."

"How else could he do that?" Dravid said. "From what I've learned so far, I don't see any way to create that kind of thing with any ordinary magic. None of the Masters have done anything like that."

Seri's eyes watched the longboat already on its way back to the Rasnian ship. Like all the others, it would soon pull away, leaving Zes Sivas and its occupants alone.

And then what? Was Tezan truly the King returned? If not, who was he and where did his power come from?

(((68)))

Tezan took Zes Sivas by storm. Over the next two days, he charmed and negotiated his way into virtually everyone's good graces. From what Seri heard, he was affable and friendly to everyone.

The biggest moment came on the second day, soon after noon. The Conclave of Mages met to consider Tezan's claim all together. All of the Lords and Ladies joined the usual crowd of mages and acolytes. Seri and the others found themselves pushed even further into the back for this gathering.

Tezan stood before the Masters with no podium of his own. As on the dock, he stood straight and tall. He seemed completely at his ease.

After perfunctory greetings, Master Hain got straight to the point. "Tezan of Rasna, are you the rightful heir of Akhenadom the Great, and thus claimant to the throne of Antises?"

"First of all, I am not Tezan of Rasna. I cannot claim to belong to any of the six lands in particular," he answered in smooth, articulate tones. "Because I do make the claim you say. I am Tezan of Antises, rightful King and heir of Akhenadom the Great."

A murmur went through the crowd. It was what they all expected, of course, but to hear it said so openly was still cause for discussion. The Masters waited for the sound to die down.

"Do you make this statement of your own will, and not by any coercion?" Master Hain asked.

"I do, and while I know you must ask such a question, it is somewhat painful for me to hear it. I recognize that you think Lord Tyrr might have some power over me, but the simple truth is that I came to him, not the other way around."

"Why did you come to him?"

Tezan let out a deep sigh. "Like my father and his father before him, I had resolved to remain in hiding. Our purpose in this was because my great-grandfather had decided that the system was wrong. The Laws of Bindings and Cursings themselves were flawed. We had hoped, by leaving Zes Sivas, to create an atmosphere where all could eventually be changed. Perhaps the mere absence of the King's power would cause the Laws to fall apart."

Seri could not see Tezan's face, but she took note of how he stood. He rotated now and then, to be sure he was addressing all of the Masters without focusing on any one or the other.

"As my father lay dying, just three months ago…" Tezan broke off, as if he needed a moment to regain control of his emotions. "Some of his final words to me were an admission that we, the royal family, had failed Antises. Despite our good intentions, the results were not what we had hoped. In fact, the opposite has occurred. Antises itself has suffered. The recent earthquakes are only the latest symptoms of the trouble caused by our absence.

"After I buried my father, and had mourned for an appropriate interval, I made my way to the nearest capital city, which happened to be Raeton. Once there, I sought an audience with Lord Tyrr, convinced him of my identity, and here we are." Tezan spread his hands to either side.

Master Hain asked a few more questions related to Tezan's heritage, his father, grandfather, and great-grandfather. In each case, Tezan answered without hesitation.

While he spoke, Seri looked over the crowd, trying to gauge their reactions. The majority seemed eager to believe, hanging on Tezan's every word. She couldn't blame them. She felt much the same way herself. But something nagged at her. Something about the magic.

Someone was missing. Her eyes searched every corner of the room and confirmed it, as best she could in this crowd. Curasir was not here. That seemed exceptionally odd. He had been one of the most excited about the coming King.

"And you have the power of the King within you?" Master Hain asked.

"I believe I demonstrated that yesterday," Tezan said. "But I will continue to prove it as often as needed. To be honest, I have not possessed the power for very long. As I said, my father died only three months ago. It was then that the power passed on to me. Initially, it was quite overwhelming. I have yet to gain full control, and I freely acknowledge that I have much to learn. I look forward to gleaning all the wisdom and training I will need from this body."

"Show us once more, if you please."

Tezan nodded. Seri could not see his front, but she assumed he was putting his hands together again and forming the Heart of Fire. The glow that burst from him confirmed that, as did the reflection in the eyes of all the Masters.

"I believe you call this the Heart of Fire," Tezan announced. "And it is the physical manifestation of the true King's power. No one else can do this, if I am correct."

Curious, Seri wanted to see Tezan's power. She blinked and her star-sight blurred her vision momentarily. She stared at Tezan and the room around him.

Beams of light, the magic of Zes Sivas, continued to erupt from the ground. But none of them seemed impacted by Tezan. They did not bend toward him, nor did he absorb any of them. His magic clearly did not come from here.

A sideways beam drew Seri's attention. She had never seen anything like it. A huge beam of multi-colored light flowed into Tezan, but it came from the side, not from below. Seri could only guess at its direction, which seemed to be somewhat southerly, if she were remembering her compass points accurately.

Tezan was not a massive ball of magical power, like the Lords who sat watching him. Seri could see each of their powers, all of them incredibly strong. Tezan radiated more power than any of them, but it did not come from within him.

Someone or something else was giving him power.

(((69)))

"Reman, city of hills," Aelia announced. She waved her arm, encompassing all they could see in front of them.

"Edin Na Zu!" Victor said. Marshal didn't blame him. He had never seen anything like it.

Nian chuckled. "Don't let anyone from Arazu hear you saying that," he said.

Marshal didn't know what he expected when seeing Reman. Perhaps something like Efesun, but on a larger scale. Or even something like Intal Eldanir, though he knew human designs would be different from the Eldanim's. Reman, capital of Varioch, did not resemble any of them.

The road they had been following crested a hill, allowing them to look down at most of the city. Spread over a number of hills, Reman created a widely varied look. Some areas contained densely-packed buildings, while others shared space between buildings, gardens, and open spaces. The central part of the city looked especially dense, but organized. Marshal thought he could make out a grid pattern to roads in that region. A tall, solid wall surrounded most of the city, though parts of it seemed to have sprawled outside.

"What is the round building there?" Talinir asked, pointing.

"It's an amphitheater," Aelia explained. "Used for big events, performances and such."

"And that tall, rectangular one?"

"That's the temple. Our destination."

"Why does it have a wall?" Victor asked.

"Historically, the only reason to have a wall is if you're anticipating an invasion," Nian said. "I'm not sure when this wall was built. Maybe at a time people still worried about barbarians?"

"I don't think it's that old," Aelia said.

"Kuktarma has many walled cities, but they have more reason, I think. They actually do a lot of trade with barbarians from outside Antises." Nian adjusted his backpack and started down the hill.

"So they're worried about an attack?" Victor hastened to keep up with him, followed by the others.

Nian shrugged. "Not so much. Their walls actually have another purpose - they help divert flood waters during the Spring. I don't think that's much of an issue here. Besides, barbarians haven't attacked in hundreds of years. They don't dare."

"Because of the curses," Talinir said.

"Exactly. In the early years of Antises, barbarians thought to plunder the six lands, but soon discovered there were severe consequences for their actions."

"Wait." Victor stepped in front of Nian and put out his hand. The priest stopped walking. "You mean people don't get cursed outside of Antises?"

"No. The Laws of Bindings and Cursings are bound up in the magic of Antises. They don't apply outside."

Marshal had never thought of that. Outside Antises, people were free to break the laws? Kill, steal, rape and so on? It sounded horrible... And yet...

After a long moment of silence, Victor said, "You'd think more people would leave, then."

"You should know why they don't, better than most," Aelia pointed out.

"Bindings."

Aelia nodded.

They resumed walking. Marshal found much to think about. Bindings kept people together. Curses punished them. That answered Nian's question from the other day. Why no blessings? Blessings wouldn't keep everyone in line. Everyone in Antises was trapped, in a way. It seemed so cynical.

• • • • •

It took another five hours of walking before they finally reached the city gates. The wall's construction fascinated Marshal. Most of the buildings he had seen thus far were made of brick. Not so the wall. It seemed almost like one giant piece of rock, towering far higher than any of the nearby buildings, but that was impossible. When Victor asked, Nian called it "concrete" and explained some process involving water and mortar, like the material used to hold bricks together. Marshal stared at it so much, he didn't notice the child sitting by the gate until he had almost passed him.

"Any coin, sir?" the boy called.

Marshal's stare shifted from the wall to the boy. Small and ill-fed, he sat beside the massive gate's opening with his legs outstretched. Marshal heard Aelia gasp. A moment later, he realized what she already saw: the boy's eyes stared past them. He was blind.

"Any coin?" the boy repeated, holding out a crude wooden bowl.

Aelia dug into her pack and found some coins that she dropped into the bowl. Nian knelt beside him. "I have no coins, lad, but perhaps I can help in other ways." He took out some bread and offered it.

Marshal and the others waited while Nian continued to speak with the boy. He gave him several other items from his pack, stood, and rejoined them, shaking his head. Marshal had expected him to look sad, but anger filled Nian's usually pleasant face.

"Was he... was he born blind or cursed?" Aelia asked.

"He's cursed," Nian said. He adjusted his pack and started walking down the street. Other travelers moved back and forth around them, gaping at Talinir and avoiding Marshal.

Victor caught up with the priest. "How could a child that small be cursed?" he demanded. "What could he possibly do?"

"He's an orphan," Nian said. "Somewhere in this city, an evil man -- or men -- is taking advantage of children like him. They send orphans to do their dirty work, letting them get cursed. If their curse is too debilitating, they send them out to beg, instead."

"That's horrible," Aelia said.

"We should do something!" Victor said. "We should find this man! Put a stop to it!"

"How would we do that?" Nian asked. "Would you hurt him? Kill him? Either way, you would bring a curse on yourself."

Victor gestured angrily. "Talinir isn't restrained by curses, right? He could solve it!"

"It would do no good," Talinir said. Marshal looked up at the warden and his face was pale. For a moment, Marshal wondered if he was suffering from the starshine withdrawal again.

"What do you mean? Why not?"

"If we remove one evil man, another will rise in his place. You have to change the system."

"If we lift Marshal's curse, it will be a start," Aelia said. "Let's focus on that for now."

While they conversed, Aelia guided them down multiple streets. She stopped once to ask for directions, then moved on without difficulty.

Marshal continued to be fascinated by the varied architecture throughout the city. While not as elaborate as Intal Eldanir, Reman's buildings did include a lot of decorative features. Most structures were made of brick, though he did notice a few that incorporated some of the concrete. Columns and arches seemed to be favored designs among builders.

After several turns, they spotted Theon's temple towering over the surrounding buildings. Unlike most other buildings, it appeared made of massive stones fit together seamlessly. The structure was simple, rectangular, and narrow.

In short order, they reached the gates to the temple courtyard. They stood open, revealing a huge open space within.

"Are we... are we going to lift the curse right now?" Victor asked.

"No," Aelia said. "But we need to make the proper arrangements."

• • • • •

"Welcome, children of Theon!" Two priests waited near the steps that led into the temple itself. The short one who had spoken was somewhat rotund and seemed short of breath. The other was of average build, but had a stern mien. Both displayed elaborate white robes trimmed in gold. Their eyes panned briefly over Marshal, Victor and Aelia, then focused on Talinir.

"Greetings, brothers," Nian called. He stepped out from behind Talinir and drew their attention. Marshal almost smiled at their startled reactions. Whatever they had been thinking about the Eldani warden, the appearance of one of their own undoubtedly threw off their thoughts.

Both priests made short bows. "You are welcome here, brother of the travels," the stern-looking priest said, his voice much pleasanter than his face suggested. "Tell us of your travels and your... most interesting companions."

Nian gestured broadly. "I am Nian of Mandiata. I have traveled much of Antises since leaving home," he said. "I met these good people on the road but eight days ago. While my visit is but the latest stop of a ceaseless wanderer, they have come for a much more serious purpose."

The priests looked over the others, though their eyes continued to be drawn to Talinir. "What might that be?" the rotund one asked. "We stand ready to serve in Theon's name."

Aelia stepped forward and knelt on the ground. Both priests' eyebrows went up. "I have come that my son's curse might be lifted," she said.

A long silence follows her words.

The stern-looking priest knelt and took Aelia's hand. "My daughter," he said. "Would that such a thing were possible. But it is beyond our power to…"

"It is not within your power, but it is within mine," Aelia said. "I know there is a way."

"It is within the Law," Nian pointed out.

"It is within the Words of Aharu," the portly priest corrected. "Not the Law."

His partner helped Aelia back to her feet. "Your dedication to your child is admirable," he said. "But this cannot be done."

"Why not?"

"Because no one has ever done it before!"

"That is not a reason."

Nian had taken out the well-worn Book of the Law Marshal had often seen him reading. He opened it and held it out. "The relevant passages are here," he said. "I looked them up and marked them, once I knew what this good woman was planning."

The rotund priest wiped sweat off his brow and took the book. He looked at the open page. "Yes, I am familiar with this, but… but it's just not done. Theon would not ask this of anyone."

"Is not the law from Theon himself?" Aelia demanded. "Did not Aharu found the priesthood? Who would know Theon better?"

"Yes, but--"

"Then he has asked it." Aelia pointed to Marshal. "My son stands cursed for the actions of his father, not for anything he has done. As his mother, I can take this burden from him. The law provides a way."

"The cost is… Have you thought this through?"

"I have. I am determined."

Marshal frowned. Not if he could help it.

"Only someone who is without a curse is even eligible," the other priest said, looking at the book again. "Are you…?"

"I am without curse," Aelia said. "I have not broken the curse laws."

The priests looked at each other. Clearly, they wanted to argue more, but didn't know what to say. Marshal wondered if anyone else had ever even tried to do this. And if they had tried, why had they not gone through with it?

"It would have to… take place within the holy chamber," the stern-faced priest said slowly.

"Unthinkable! No one is allowed within that room but priests, let alone a woman!"

"Is that part of the law or part of tradition?" Nian asked.

"There's no difference!" the short priest said.

"Well, yes. There is," his companion said. "The holy chamber's restrictions are not specifically spelled out in the law, but have been passed down for generations. To my knowledge, they have never been violated." He paused. "But neither has anyone seriously suggested lifting a curse, either." He searched Aelia's face. "Is this something you are absolutely certain about? Without hesitation or doubt?"

"It is."

"The other brothers will never accept this," the short priest argued. "I don't believe that I accept it. This cannot be done!"

"Do they need to know about it?" Victor asked. The priests looked at him in shock. He shrugged. "I mean, maybe we can come in at night or something, when no one's here."

"There are priests on duty at all hours! Theon does not rest in his work, so we must be ready to assist him at all hours!"

"Except…" Everyone looked at the stern-faced priest. "Except in two days' time. No one will be here then."

Silence followed again. Nian slapped his forehead. "Of course! The Passing! I lost track of the time!"

"What do you mean?" Aelia asked.

"On the day of the Passing," the stern priest said, "all of the priests will leave the temple and assemble on the beach, facing Zes Sivas. We will pray for a successful ceremony on this holy day."

"We will all be gone, so they may not enter!" the other priest insisted. "No one will be here to help them! Who would guard the holiest place?"

"I can do it," Nian said. "Perhaps that is the reason why Theon arranged our meeting."

"Preposterous! We don't even know if you are truly a priest!"

"Shall I quote the law for you? Would that help establish my credentials? Or shall I demonstrate the ceremonies of the Feast of Travels? Whatever you request, I will do."

"Perhaps..." The stern-faced priest raised a hand. "We will confer in private, where all of the details may be worked out. Is that acceptable?"

Nian looked to Aelia. "Will you allow me to arrange this for you?"

She hesitated for a moment, then nodded.

The shorter priest snorted. "I will still need to be convinced that anything needs arranging!"

"Then let us discuss that." The three priests moved away together.

"That was... crazy," Victor said.

"There is no telling how long they will argue," Talinir said. "We should find lodging. It seems we will be here at least two days."

"Two days," Aelia repeated. Marshal watched her as a pensive look came over her face. She was thinking of her death, the death that he would never allow.

(((70)))

Seri had a good guess as to where the power had come from, but she needed to be sure. She waited until evening, and then returned to the Conclave chamber. Ixchel followed, of course, but asked no questions.

Inside, she walked to the spot where Tezan had been standing. She rotated until she determined she was facing the same direction from which the power had originated.

"Ixchel, which direction am I facing?"

The warrior took a quick glance. "You're facing south-southwest."

"Good. Keep that in mind."

Seri led the way outside. The source of the power could be within the citadel, but she doubted it. Only a couple of rooms could be considered between the Conclave and the exterior wall. Neither of them seemed a likely spot for the source of a massive amount of power.

No, it had to be outside. And if it was outside, it had to be far enough away that the Masters and Lords would not detect it on their own. Seri walked until she stood on the shore outside the citadel's walls.

"Ixchel, am I facing south-southwest again?"

"Yes, my Lady."

Seri nodded in satisfaction. There it was. Unlike all the other ships, the Rasnian ship had not pulled out of sight. She could still see lights shining from on board. Somehow, Tezan's power came from that ship.

"Ixchel, I'm about to do something very dangerous, and you won't be able to protect me."

"Then I must ask that you not do this. Whatever it is." Ixchel stepped up beside her and grasped her sword hilt.

"You're not going to really stop me, are you? Aren't you just supposed to be protecting me from Lord Varion?"

"I am your guard. You are my Lady."

"You've said that. But are you going to force me not to do something dangerous?"

Ixchel sighed. "I cannot protect you from yourself," she admitted.

"Good. But keep an eye on me. I might get into more trouble than I can escape on my own."

"Where are you going?"

Seri pointed at the ship. "Out there."

Ixchel wrinkled her brow. "We have no rowboat available," she said. "I suppose I could make a raft. Given enough time." She eyed the cypress trees dubiously.

"No, I'm going to walk." Seri stepped up to the edge of the water and watched it lapping against the shore. She knelt and touched it with her palm.

"My lady, if you--"

"Quiet, please," Seri interrupted. "I need to concentrate."

She had only practiced this twice, and never to this scale. Still, before all the build-up to the Passing got insane, she had been working hard on her water magic. She understood the principles well enough.

Seri reached out and grasped multiple beams of light from Zes Sivas, focusing on the color green. The power vibrated within her, all the way up her throat. Again, she felt the saliva pool within her mouth. She fought the urge to spit it out. She wove the beams together and channeled it all into the surface of the water.

"Here we go." Seri took a deep breath and stepped forward. The surface of the water vibrated beneath her foot, but held firm. She took another step. It worked! She could walk on the surface of the water!

She continued forward a few more steps. It was difficult to stay on the narrow path she had created, but as long as she kept her eyes on the destination, she could handle it. She heard a grunt from Ixchel behind her and glanced back.

Ixchel had stepped out onto the water too.

"Ah, I don't know if that's a good idea," Seri said. "I can't promise this will last for both of us the whole way."

"Then at least I will be near you. For when you fall in," Ixchel said. "Can you even swim?"

"I can swim!" Seri's indignation was tempered by the memory of her last fall into these waters.

"In that robe?"

Seri didn't answer. She focused on keeping her path straight. She wasn't entirely sure how wide her magic path extended. There might be plenty of room for an occasional error, but she wasn't taking any chances. As she walked, she continued to pull in more magic and channel it downward.

Inwardly, she wanted to giggle and leap up and down. She was walking on water! This was easily the best thing she had done with her magic thus far, and she was still only an acolyte! While the Masters rarely displayed their power, what amazing things could they do, if she could already do this?

Ixchel, for her part, seemed amazingly adept at walking in a straight line. Across the water. Seri heard her murmur something.

"What was that?"

"A quick prayer, my Lady."

"Oh? What for?"

"Swiftness. In cutting your robe off when we fall."

"You know, you could be a little more encouraging."

"I am here to protect. Not encourage."

Seri rolled her eyes, which Ixchel couldn't see, of course. She determined not to say anything else. Who knows how far the sound of their voices could carry across the gentle waves? The early night was still and quiet. She felt only the tiniest of breezes now and then.

As they drew near the ship, Seri heard an occasional voice call out, followed by an answer. She couldn't see or hear a lot of activity, but at least two people were still up and working on the deck. It was called a deck, wasn't it? Seri hated to admit it, but she was quite ignorant when it came to ships. Or boats. Or whatever you called them.

They reached the ship itself. Seri was a little surprised to discover it in motion, then realized it was simply rocking on the waves. An anchor still held it in place. She moved along the side until she found a kind of netting made of rope. Perfect. She climbed onto it and motioned for Ixchel to do the same. There was no telling how long her water magic would last, anyway.

Now what? Climbing up onto the deck seemed a risky idea. Better to know where she should be looking first. Using her senses and star sight, she searched the ship for the source of magic.

To her surprise, she did not find one massive pulsing source of magical power on the ship. Instead, she found multiple sources, all of them extremely weak. None of them had anywhere near the power of one of the Lords, but she sensed dozens of them. And they all were inside the ship. In its… hold? Was that the right word?

Seri leaned in to Ixchel. "I need to get a look inside," she whispered. "Any ideas?"

Ixchel frowned. She whispered something too low for Seri to hear. Probably another prayer for her wayward mistress. Then she climbed past Seri to the ship's railing. Seri watched her go, amazed at her sleek and easy movements. How was she able to climb these ropes with bare feet, anyway? Didn't that hurt?

Ixchel paused at the top and appeared to wait for something. Then she launched herself in a smooth vault over the railing and disappeared from Seri's view. Seri waited. She heard nothing except the distant tones of a conversation taking place somewhere on board. Someone was talking, but she couldn't make out any of the words.

Then Ixchel's face appeared above. She gestured for Seri to come up. This turned out to be not as easy as it looked. Seri struggled repeatedly to get her feet in the right places. Her robe constantly got in the way. When she was close enough, Ixchel reached down and grabbed her. She let go as her bodyguard hauled her up over the railing and onto the deck. It didn't look dignified, but at least it worked.

Seri got to her feet and looked around. She and Ixchel were alone on this part of the deck. She saw two sailors on an elevated deck not far away, but they had their backs to the women. They appeared to be working on something. Ixchel gestured for Seri to follow.

She led the way to an opening with a set of steep steps that led down inside. Seri found it almost as difficult to keep her footing on the stairs as she had on the ladder. Robes made no sense for life on a ship.

They entered a small hallway. A door stood open to their right. Light and sound both flowed out. Seri heard the clank of pans. The kitchen? The hallway led to two closed doors to the left. Ixchel ignored them and led Seri to another narrow stairway leading further down.

This led directly into a large room full of hammocks. Sleeping men occupied some of them. A single oil lamp hung from the ceiling, its light very low. Ixchel put a finger to her lips and pointed to a door on the opposite end of the room. Seri grimaced, but followed. With every step, she expected one of the sailors to roll out of a hammock and raise the alarm.

Somehow, they made it across. Ixchel retrieved a key from its hanging place on the wall and used it to open the door. What was the point of keeping it locked if the key was hanging right there?

It was almost completely dark in the next room once Ixchel closed the door behind them. Seri wished she could manifest flames like Lady Lilitu. Then again, flames on board a ship might not be the best idea.

A spark flared in her vision and she blinked. Ixchel struck her flint again and this time was able to light a lantern Seri had not even been able to see. Her eyes adjusted and she saw they stood in a small room with no doors other than the one they had come in. A single porthole let air flow in and out.

Ixchel pointed down. Seri almost jumped. She stood right on the edge of a dark opening. She hastily stepped back.

Someone stirred down below. "What is it now?" asked a raspy voice.

Seri got down on her hands and knees. Ixchel held the lantern out over the opening. Seri looked down into the ship's hold. In the lantern's light, she saw several pale faces blinking and looking up at her in confusion. As Ixchel moved the lantern around, she saw more faces. The hold was full of people. Most were clearly of Rasna or Varioch by their skin tone, but she spotted a few others, as well. A horrid stench struck her nose. Too many people kept in too small a space for too long.

"Who are you?" one of them asked, a short, pale-skinned man with very little hair.

"I'm a mage from Zes Sivas," Seri said. "I was going to ask you people the same question. Who are you?"

Several people started to answer at once. Seri waved her hand. "Shhhh!" Ixchel drew her sword and stepped to the door to listen.

"One at a time, and quietly!" Seri hissed. She took the lantern from Ixchel and held it up herself so she could see them.

The pale man glanced around at the others, then took it on himself to speak. "We are Lord Tyrr's prisoners," he said. "We've been down here for days."

"Why would he bring--" Seri broke off as she realized the answer. "You're all wild magic users, aren't you?" A blink and she could see it. All of them had magic.

A murmur of confirmation rose up. Of course. Of course there wasn't another massive source of power Tezan was tapping into. Instead, he was using all of these people, their powers, all together. But how?

"Tezan. He's using your powers?"

"He's one of us," a woman said. "He and I used to work together before Lord Tyrr found him."

"Tezan is a wild magic user?"

"His power is to steal others' powers," the pale man said.

"It's more than that," the woman said. "He can borrow them temporarily, or steal them permanently. Even give power to someone else."

"We'll find a way to get you out of here and expose him," Seri said. "I--"

"No! You can't!" A number of voices broke out in consternation. Ixchel shot a fierce glare at Seri.

"Wh-why not?"

"Lord Tyrr has my son!" the woman said.

"And my wife!" added the pale man. "He has all of our family members locked up back in Rasna. If we don't cooperate, he will kill them all!"

Seri grew cold. Only a Lord could even suggest such a threat. No one else would be taken seriously. But after meeting Lord Varioch, she now understood.

Ixchel touched her arm and gestured. She didn't speak, but her face said it all. They needed to leave. Now.

"I'll find someone who can help you," Seri told the magic users. "I won't let this happen."

"Be careful," another one warned. "Lord Tyrr is dangerous."

"Everyone on Zes Sivas is dangerous," Seri said. She got to her feet and set the lantern aside.

Ixchel led the way back through the bunk room. One sailor started to lift himself up out of his hammock as they passed. Seri gasped, but Ixchel leaned over and did something. The sailor fell back again.

They made their way back up the stairs and onto the main deck without further incident. Ixchel made Seri wait for several minutes while she checked on the sailors on deck. Eventually, she returned and led her back to the railing. The sailors again seemed occupied with something in the other direction.

Climbing back down to the water proved even more difficult than climbing up. Near the bottom, Seri realized a serious problem with her plan. She needed to touch the water in order to re-create their passage back across. She ran through several different ideas in her head. None of them worked.

With no other options, she hooked both legs up to her knees into the rope netting. That meant she had to yank her robe up almost to her waist. She consoled herself that no one would see this other than Ixchel, who revealed more skin on a constant basis. Seri let herself hang down upside down, holding herself in place with her knees and one hand. She stretched the other down until she was able to touch the surface of the water. It took a little longer to find the right beams of light out here and finish the process.

Ixchel waited patiently while she struggled back upright, untangled her legs from the netting, and climbed the rest of the way down to the water. She gained her footing on the surface, feeling the slight vibration as before. Seri focused her attention on Zes Sivas and started to walk back. Ixchel followed close behind.

Seri pondered this discovery as she walked. Tezan was a wild magic user with the ability to channel power from others, even steal their powers, if he so chose. In her reading of Master Sekou's *The Vicissitudes of Wild Magic and its Practitioners*, she couldn't recall ever seeing a power like that. Was Tezan unique? Or was there something else at work here?

Come to think of it, if he could steal powers permanently, as the one woman had claimed, why hadn't he done that with all those on the ship? Why bring them along to channel their powers temporarily? That didn't make sense. Maybe Tezan hadn't told Lord Tyrr everything about his powers?

The world shifted.

Seri didn't even remember blinking, but suddenly, she could see the Otherworld. She stumbled and Ixchel caught her robe's collar to steady her.

The stars! Why hadn't she noticed them before? She had, of course, but the last time, she had been distracted by a monster. And her previous outside glimpse had only been for a couple of seconds. There hadn't been much time for stargazing.

Now… now she stood on the surface of the water and the stars surrounded her. Every direction she looked, gigantic stars illuminated everything around her. More stars than she had ever seen, ever imagined. And so many colors!

"My Lady?" Ixchel's voice seemed to come from far away. Seri ignored her.

Seri felt her heart expanding with every second she spent staring at the stars. The beauty, the sheer, unadulterated… beauty. Her mind couldn't think of another word to describe it, and yet "beauty" felt so small, so limited in scope. This was beyond beauty, beyond…

Her eyes settled on Zes Sivas. As she had seen before, the citadels lay in ruins and smoke drifted upward. Something was different, though. Beams of light erupted up out of the island, shooting up into the sky itself to merge with the light of the stars. Some of them curled back on themselves and fell down to the island. The vortex she had seen twice before loomed above the remains of the citadel walls. When she had seen the vortex before, it had been frightening, but small enough to fit within the Inner Sanctum, or so it had seemed. Now it appeared to have grown substantially. Seri couldn't help but feel that this was very, very bad.

Abruptly, her vision shifted again and she saw both worlds at once. In one, the ordinary stars shone in the dark night of her world. In the other, the giant stars shone in the bright night of the Otherworld. They overlapped each other, creating a cacophony of light, a confusing array of spots and beams.

The magic she had infused onto the water collapsed. The last thing she heard and felt before she plunged into the cold waters was the tearing of her robe. Ixchel's prayer for swiftness had been answered.

(((71)))

Aelia found an inn only a couple of blocks from the temple. While she arranged for their lodgings, she sent Victor back to let Nian know their whereabouts.

The inn was much nicer than the last one Marshal remembered, back in Efesun. It didn't match up to the standards of the Eldanim, of course, but was still far better than their usual lodgings.

Victor returned with Nian only an hour later, just in time for a late supper. To Marshal's surprise, the inn served baked chicken and potatoes, a rarity for him, but one of his favorite meals.

Although the innkeeper urged them to enjoy the city's night life, the entire party felt exhausted after the day's travels. They all went to bed early.

Marshal found great difficulty sleeping. He attributed part of it to the soft bed. Over the last few weeks, he had grown accustomed to sleeping on the ground. The bed felt completely wrong. He tossed and turned for hours.

In addition, his mind kept wandering. The day after tomorrow, Aelia would try to lift his curse by dying herself. He would not allow that. But Nian thought Theon might honor her intent. Would his curse be lifted, then? What would his life be like? To be able to speak when he wanted. To let people know what he was thinking.

Or what would his life be like if it failed, which seemed the more likely alternative? Where would they go from here? He re-visited all of their previous travels. Would he go back to any of them if the curse was lifted? Or if it wasn't?

What would it be like going back to Drusa's Crossing without his curse? Would he even want to? He had to admit he had little desire to make that journey. But going back to Intal Eldanir? That was different. He would love to return there. His mind thought again of the Starlit Realm, the Otherworld that the Eldanim could seemingly visit whenever they wanted. How glorious that would be. And he could see Eniri again. That took his thoughts in a whole other direction.

Soon after that, he finally succumbed to sleep, a dreamless sleep that took him far away from any of these questions and considerations.

•••••

The next morning at breakfast, Victor suggested walking around the city.

"That's a good idea," Aelia said. "You and Talinir should do that." Nian had already left to return to the temple.

Marshal frowned. Why not him?

"I need some time alone with my son, anyway," Aelia went on, "and it's safer if he stays out of sight as much as possible. Lord Varion is gone for the Passing, but we don't know the whereabouts of his son."

After a brief discussion, the others agreed. They finished up breakfast and left the inn. Aelia and Marshal returned to their rooms.

Marshal felt fidgety. Would he have to spend the whole day inside the inn, when this huge city waited outside? It seemed a terrible waste, and profoundly unfair. Maybe if he wrapped cloth around his lower face and wore a hood...

Aelia settled herself in a chair and looked at him. Marshal barely noticed as he continued thinking about ways to conceal his appearance.

"Tomorrow, everything will change for you, one way or another," Aelia said.

Marshal looked back at her. That was probably true. Here he was thinking about looking at a city, when tomorrow Aelia would try to lift his curse. Of course, she didn't know that he and Nian would not allow her to die.

Aelia sighed. "There is so much I want to tell you, but so little that you are ready to hear." She reached out her hand. Marshal hesitated, then stepped back and took it in his own. He knelt in front of her.

"I've told you about your grandfather many times."

Nod is yes.

"You have grown into a fine young man, Marshal, and you remind me so much of him." Her voice broke, and she looked down. "I've tried to raise you the way I think that he would have raised you, had your-- had Lord Varion not killed him." She looked back up and lifted her other hand to trace the scars on Marshal's face. Her touch barely brushed against his skin.

"He would have loved you so much," she whispered. She swallowed and grew silent for a while.

Marshal had no idea how to respond. He had been so focused on preventing her death that he hadn't really thought about what it meant - that she was willing to die, so that he might live without his curse. What kind of love was that?

She had kept so many secrets from him for so long. She still tried to keep this secret. She knew that if he knew, he would not allow it.

At that moment, his eyes caught movement in the shadows on the floor, cast by the sunlight streaming in through the window. Something had moved across the window and cast a new shadow across the floor. They were on the ground floor, so it was entirely possible for someone to walk by and block the sunlight. But the shadow didn't move. Watching them? Aelia didn't seem to notice. She appeared deep in thought.

Marshal jumped to his feet and turned to the window. The figure casting the shadow was a shadow himself. An eidolon looked back at him.

Even here, in the city, it watched him! What would it take to rid himself of these things? Even as his mind raced through these thoughts, the creature moved to its left and vanished.

Aelia stood up behind him. "Was someone there, Marshal? I thought I saw a shadow."

Shake is no, but he shouldn't do that. He shrugged instead. That seemed right this time. She hadn't believed Victor when he had told her about fighting the eidolon the last time. Even if he could tell her now, she might not accept it.

"Look at you, so broad-shouldered, so grown up." Aelia rested both her hands on Marshal's shoulders. "You're truly a man now, my son. I hope… no, I believe that you are ready to face whatever this world has to throw at you."

Marshal continued to look out the window. He wasn't sure if she expected a response, and if so, what it might be.

Aelia took in a deep breath and let it out. She took hold of Marshal's shoulder and gently turned him to face her. "Look at me," she said.

This again? He met her eyes. Their golden warmth was shinier than usual, enhanced by the teardrops that hadn't quite fallen yet.

"You are greatly loved, Marshal. Do you believe me?"

Nod is yes. How could he doubt that now?

"You are valuable, Marshal. Do you believe me?"

It was harder this time. She thought he was valuable. Talinir clearly thought he was valuable. The Eldanim who had blessed him had thought he was valuable. He had more proof of his value than he had ever possessed. He didn't understand why they thought he was valuable, but they did. He nodded.

"You have a purpose in this world, Marshal. Do you believe me?"

A purpose. Before all this had started, he thought that to be a ridiculous concept. Now? If his curse were truly lifted, and the power of Lord Varion came to him, he might have a purpose. Lord of Varioch? Conceivable, maybe, but still ludicrous. Was that why Aelia and the Eldanim thought him so valuable? Because he might become a Lord and have power? Did power make one valuable? Even so, power alone could not give someone a purpose. It was what you did with the power. Wasn't it?

Aelia took his silence for a response. "We all have a purpose in this world, my treasure. Perhaps my whole purpose was in preparing you for this world. If so, I hope I have succeeded. Your purpose… you may be getting ideas of it at last, but it is still so much more than you can imagine. I know this. I have seen it."

He furrowed his brow. What did she mean by that? Nian had asked if she had seen the future and she had been vague about it. Was it like that older Eldani woman who had seen the stars fall in his future? Thinking of her and the prophecy made him think of the Otherworld, the starlight realm. Again, he felt the pull on his heart, the desire to see it again, to bask in the light of the stars.

Aelia ran her fingers through his hair. "I wished for more time with you, but now I don't know what to do with the time that we have," she said, though she seemed to be talking to herself more than to him.

Marshal pointed outside. Aelia laughed. "Yes. We should go for a walk, too." She dabbed at her eyes with her sleeve. "Come, let your mother show you around Reman. I was younger than you the last time I was here, but I think I still remember most of it."

She took his hand and led him to the door. Marshal felt warmth surge inside him. Regardless of the secrets, she was still his mother, and she wanted to be with him today. Best to enjoy it while it lasted.

(((72)))

Seri tried not to think too much about how Ixchel got her back to her room. For the second time, she had experienced the waters of Zes Sivas first hand. It might not have been quite as cold this time, but she had been in it much longer. She had lost hold of the magic a couple hundred yards from the island. That was a long way to swim, even after Ixchel got her out of the robe. She had washed up on shore wearing only her undergarments, soaked to the skin. If anyone had seen her...

But they hadn't. At least, as far as she knew. Somehow, they had ended up back in her room, lost the soaking undergarments, and wrapped up in heavy blankets. Ixchel even managed to start a small fire in the fireplace Seri hadn't used once since her arrival. She wouldn't admit it was because she didn't know how.

After they sat there together for a long time, their shivering slowly subsiding, Ixchel looked Seri over. "You are more than I expected," she said at last.

"More what?"

"More everything."

"Um, thanks, I guess."

They sat in silence a while longer.

"What can I do about this?" Seri said at last. "I'm just an acolyte, and this... this is big. Enormous."

"The King is not real," Ixchel said. Seri nodded, then jerked. Ixchel's voice had been different. Instead of her usual cadence, her voice had actually grown lower with each word. It was practically the opposite of her usual tone.

Seri looked at her bodyguard and for the first time saw...

vulnerability. Sadness, even. Her face was downcast, and her eyes stared vacantly into the fire. The tiniest hint of a tear glistened in the corner of one eye. Ixchel was genuinely upset to discover the King was a fraud.

The weight of this truth settled on Seri. The King had not returned. All would not be made right. The vortex she had seen, the expanding magical vortex, would not be healed by the Passing. It might even tear Zes Sivas apart.

In that moment, Seri felt a resolve take its place within her. Regardless of what happened now, regardless of Tezan and Lord Tyrr's schemes, regardless of the Passing, only one thing mattered. The true King must be found. Even becoming a Master was secondary to that. Unless Zes Sivas, and by extension all of Antises, was saved, no one would care about Master mages, anyway.

"I'm going to find the true King," she said aloud.

Ixchel looked at her and raised her eyebrows. "You?"

"Someone has to. It's the only solution. And I probably have the best chance, with my vision, of anyone. Except Lady Lilitu, I suppose. And the Eldanim. But do they want him found? I wonder."

"Your… vision?"

"I'll explain later. It's a long story."

Seri fell silent for a moment. It was a nice resolve, a purpose, a quest. But it did nothing for the current predicament. Tezan needed to be exposed.

"Who can I tell?" she asked. "Can I go to Master Hain with this? He would demand to know how I got the idea to investigate. Not to mention his problems with wild magic in the first place. I don't know if he would believe me."

"Are you asking me?" Ixchel said hesitantly, again not at all like her usual cadence.

"No, I'm just speaking my thoughts," Seri said. "But feel free to jump in if you have any suggestions." She hesitated. "I could tell Jamana and Dravid, of course. But then we'd just have this same conversation. We're just acolytes. We need someone with power.

"I can't go to Curasir. He… I just can't. The most obvious choice would seem to be Lord Enuru and Lady Lilitu. But how do I tell them that one of their fellow Lords is this evil?"

"They might… find it hard to believe," Ixchel said.

Seri nodded. "They're still probably the best option, unless I can think of someone else, someone who would understand how evil the

Lords… can… be…"

Of course. Why hadn't she thought of him first? The obvious answer.

"Volraag."

"Lord Varion's son?"

"He saved me from his father," Seri explained. "He knows firsthand how evil they can be. Plus, Rasna and Varioch are almost at war. He would leap at the chance to expose Lord Tyrr!"

"Is that a good thing?"

"Of course! It's politics, Ixchel. And this one time, it works to our advantage."

Seri took a deep breath, closed her eyes, and let it out. She had a plan. That was all that mattered for tonight. She opened her eyes and smiled at Ixchel.

"Thanks for everything tonight, Ixchel. I don't know what I would have done without you."

"Drowned."

"That's probably true. I owe you my life." Seri gasped and put a hand to her mouth. "Does that mean…? Oh, my. It does, doesn't it? I'm bound to you now!"

Ixchel nodded. Her face made it clear she thought this was blatantly obvious.

"I never thought about that! Oh, Ixchel. How will we manage this? You'll be leaving in a few days. Will I have to come with you?"

Ixchel looked confused. "I will not be leaving."

"I meant when Lord Rajwir leaves."

"I will not be leaving."

"But… why not?"

"I have told you. I am your guard. You are my Lady."

"You mean… you mean your position with me is… permanent?"

"What else could it be?"

"I, I thought you would only be guarding me for a week." Seri felt incredibly stupid. "I had no idea…"

"This is our purpose," Ixchel said. "We are assigned to a Lady. We guard her. Until we no longer can."

"But, but weren't you already assigned to Lady Ajaw?"

"Yes. But she assigned me to you."

"She doesn't want you back?"

Ixchel's face looked pained. "She cannot take me back, once I have gone."

"I can't just, you know, assign you back to her?"

"It does not work that way."

"Oh, Ixchel. I'm so sorry. I've done this to you, and I didn't even know about it. I'm so, so sorry."

"You did not do it."

"But I did. If I hadn't told Lady Lilitu about my fears, she wouldn't have gone to Lady Ajaw, and you wouldn't be here. You must hate me."

Ixchel looked at her in shock. "I cannot hate you! I told you! You are my Lady."

"You need to explain what that means, exactly."

"I will guard and protect you until I die, or until you release me, or assign me to another Lady."

"I can release you?"

"Yes, but to do so would be the greatest dishonor I could face."

"Oh."

"Besides, as you said, you are now bound to me. Send me away, and you will suffer."

"But… did you have any choice in this? Were you forced to become a bodyguard?" To Seri, it almost sounded like slavery.

"It was my choice eight years ago. To become one of the Holcan is a dream in my land."

"You were just a child eight years ago!"

"And yet I chose. And here I am."

"I guess we're stuck with each other, then."

They both fell silent. Seri adjusted her blanket and let her toes peep out toward the fire. Now that she thought about it, she could feel Ixchel's presence beside her. It was almost like sensing those with a store of magic, only fainter and more familiar.

So this was what a Binding felt like. She would be able to sense Ixchel's presence, and according to her studies, she would instantly know when the other girl was in danger. She found it comforting, in a way. More comforting than having a bodyguard outside her door.

At that moment, she realized she could feel another Binding. It was weaker than what she felt toward Ixchel, but it was there. She could feel the presence of someone else, here on the island, to whom she owed a great debt. Not her life, but…

It was Volraag. He had saved her. It was a Minor Binding, since life itself had not been involved. How could she ever repay him? That might be problematic.

Still, it only confirmed her decision. She needed to find Volraag the next morning and tell him the truth about the King.

(((73)))

Despite being up so late, Seri rose with the dawn. Ixchel was surprised to see her emerge from her room so early.

"It's going to be a big day, Ixchel. I may need your help." She received a nod in return. Seri thought for a moment. "Let's find a messenger to send to Volraag. I don't think knocking on the Varioch suite's door would be a good idea."

After sending the messenger, Seri and Ixchel left the citadel. Seri led them in a quick detour through the dining hall to grab a pastry. Once outside, they sat on the stairs leading up the wall. Half an hour passed by, and Seri wondered if the messenger had even delivered her request.

At last, Volraag emerged from the citadel. He looked around, spotted them, and hurried over. How did he manage to look so good this early in the morning? It was downright disgusting. Everything about him from his hair to his impeccable clothing was immaculate.

Volraag's eyes took in Ixchel, but did not linger like most men. He focused on Seri. "I left a trade negotiation with Kuktarma," he said without greeting. "Your message made it sound urgent."

"It is," Seri said. "You told me that if I ever needed anything, to let you know. I need something."

"What is it?"

"Follow me." Seri got up and led the way up to the top of the wall. She pointed at the Rasnian ship.

Volraag looked at the ship, then back at her. "Yes?"

"Last night, my bodyguard and I snuck on board that ship."

"You... what? How did you do that?"

"That's not important. What you need to know is that Tezan is a fake."

Volraag's face hardened. "How do you know this?"

Seri pointed again to the ship. "That ship's hold is full of imprisoned wild magic users. That's all Tezan is: he uses wild magic," she explained. "But his power is to draw from their power. He has no power of his own."

Volraag took this in and looked back to the ship. "The entire hold?"

"Yes, there were a couple dozen people in there, if not more. That's why he can appear so powerful. Individually, they're not all that much, but put them all together…"

"And you can duplicate a King's magic," Volraag finished.

Seri nodded.

Volraag looked at Ixchel. "You saw this, as well?"

"My Lady does not lie."

"Of course, of course." Volraag appeared to be thinking. "Who else have you told about this?"

"No one yet. I considered several others, but you seemed like the one most likely to be in a position to do something about it."

"He must be exposed," Volraag said. "We cannot let Rasna have a puppet King over all Antises."

"Oh, but the most important thing is that the wild magic users are all prisoners!" Seri said. "Lord Tyrr will murder their families if they don't cooperate with him!"

Volraag nodded as if this did not come as a surprise at all.

"Let me be sure I have this right. Tezan draws his power from the other wild magic users, not from himself or Antises or anything else."

"Yes, he can transfer magic from one person to himself," Seri said. "Or another, I guess. That's what one of them told me."

"So if he lost his connection to them, he would have no power of his own."

"Yes, but how do we protect the families from Lord Tyrr?"

Volraag didn't answer. He stared out at the ship.

"Did you hear me?"

Volraag seemed to come to himself. He turned back. "Yes, I heard you. It's a complicated mess, but I believe I know what to do."

"You do? What?"

Volraag placed a hand on Seri's shoulder. Ixchel took a warning step closer. Volraag removed the hand and held it up with a smile. "I apologize, Holcan. Had I wished your Lady any harm, I would never have rescued her from my father."

Ixchel said nothing, but stared at him. Volraag chuckled.

"At any rate, thank you for telling me about this. I will take care of everything."

"You will?"

"Lord Tyrr and Tezan will be exposed. He will not become King."

"The Passing is tomorrow!" Seri said. "Will he--"

"He will not fool anyone at the Passing," Volraag said. "I will make sure of it."

"But what about the families?"

"The families will not be harmed, if I do this properly." Volraag glanced once more at the distant ship. "Thank you again, Seri. You have done a great service for the entire realm. All of Antises owes you a debt."

Volraag gave her a short bow and departed. Seri and Ixchel stood alone on the wall.

"Well. That went better than I had anticipated," she said. "What did you think?"

Ixchel looked surprised to be asked her opinion. "I am not sure. There is something about him I do not like."

"Really?" Seri watched the young Lord-to-be walking across the courtyard. "I think he's... pretty amazing."

(((74)))

Marshal and Aelia enjoyed their day together more than any day Marshal could remember over the past few years. They roamed the city and shopped the marketplace. They bought nothing, except a new deck of Mages and Lords for Victor. Marshal double-checked it to make sure it held all the cards. But the highlight for him was the moment they stood on a rooftop looking out over Lake Litanu. He had never seen that much water before.

"If we traveled south through Rasna, we would eventually reach the ocean," Aelia had said. "It's... well, this lake is really rather small in comparison."

Marshal couldn't see how that could be possible.

"Out there, in the center of the lake, is Zes Sivas, home to Kings and mages." Aelia had gotten a wistful look on her face. "I never got to see it. But you will. You will. I believe it." She was silent for a long time. When she whispered, Marshal could barely make it out. "I have to believe it."

That night, Marshal again had trouble sleeping. At one point, he rolled over and found Aelia awake and watching him. The look in her eyes was one he had never seen before, haunting and sad. He started to lift himself up.

Aelia's expression immediately changed. She put out her hand. "Hush. Go back to sleep," she whispered. "I was just checking on you."

Marshal put his head back down and closed his eyes, or at least pretended to. He kept one eye open enough to watch his mother. She took a deep breath and smiled at him, then moved away. He closed his eye fully and fell back asleep.

In the morning, her behavior mystified him. When she emerged from her room, Aelia was wearing the elegant burgundy dress she had worn to deceive the soldiers. Her hair shone with bright contrast to the darker ribbons woven through it. She looked more beautiful than he could remember.

"Wow," Victor said.

"You are stunning," Nian said in an odd tone. Marshal couldn't place it.

Aelia smiled and nodded to each of them, then glanced to Talinir. "Nothing to say, warden?"

"I have no words appropriate for this occasion," Talinir replied.

Aelia gave a slight tilt of her head to him and turned back to Marshal. "It is time, my treasure. Let us go to the temple."

The streets were quieter this morning, with fewer people going about their business. It wasn't a Rest Day, if Marshal remembered rightly. Today was the day of the Passing, though. Back in Drusa's Crossing, people knew the date, but that was all. It wasn't a big deal. He wondered if the people of Reman treated it like a Rest Day or if there were some kind of celebrations taking place in another part of the city.

The temple was deserted and the gates locked. Nian produced a key and let them in. The outer yard felt eerie in the silence. They started up the steps and Aelia paused.

"I must speak with Victor, alone," she said.

Marshal watched in curiosity as his mother took his friend aside and began speaking. He couldn't see Aelia's lips, but had no trouble seeing Victor's reactions. He appeared shocked and tried to say something only for Aelia to cut him off. Whatever she said then clearly upset him and he looked angry. Then his eyes widened even further and he shot a look at Marshal. She must be telling him her intentions. Marshal wished he could assure Victor that she wouldn't die. The conversation went on for almost ten minutes. How much was there to say? At one point, Aelia handed something to Victor. He looked at it curiously, then put it in his pack. From Marshal's point of view, it looked like a rock.

When they returned, Victor appeared subdued. He glanced repeatedly at Marshal, but didn't say anything.

"I believe we are ready now," Aelia said. "Shall we enter?"

"We are not alone," Talinir said. He stood at the base of the steps, facing the gates with his sword drawn. Marshal looked toward the gate and took a quick intake of breath.

Three eidola stood inside the gates, out in the open and facing them. Marshal looked around at the others. Clearly, everyone could see them this time.

"I will prevent their entrance into the temple," Talinir said. "You go on ahead."

"I'll stay with you," Victor said. He drew his own weapons and stepped down beside Talinir. The warden nodded.

"I don't understand," Aelia said. "Who are they? Why would they try to stop us?"

Talinir glanced back at them. "Now is the time, Aelia."

"This way." Nian gestured to them and they hastened up the stairs. Marshal glanced back and saw the shadow warriors moving slowly toward Talinir and Victor.

Nian pushed open the first set of doors leading into the temple. "You must leave your weapons here. This is the holy chamber," he announced with a broad gesture. "Normally, you would not be allowed in here. Beyond this is the holiest chamber. None of us may enter there, no matter what." Aelia placed her short sword on the final step. Marshal placed his sword beside it, but kept Volraag's dagger hidden within his tunic. Together, they entered the temple.

Marshal was surprised at the sparseness of the chamber. Based on the exterior, he had expected something massively elaborate. Four columns held up the rectangular roof that loomed far above them. To the left stood a long table, coated in gold, but bare. To the right, a basin of water was built into the wall itself. Water flowed from a hidden pipe into it, presumably draining out in a similar way, keeping the water constantly in motion.

In the center of the chamber stood an altar made of stone. The stains that ran down its sides spoke of innumerable sacrifices, though it stood empty now. An opening in the tall ceiling let the sunlight in directly above it.

On the opposite side of the chamber, a simple door stood closed in the shadows, apparently leading to the holiest chamber Nian had mentioned. Shading the door was a broad balcony that spanned the entire far wall and extended outward about ten feet. A simple staircase on the right wall led to the balcony. A bronze railing lined both stairs and the balcony itself.

Nian led them around the altar and stopped. He looked at Aelia searchingly. "This is it," he said. "Are you prepared?"

•••••

"We're not allowed to be there!" Jamana insisted.

"But we won't actually be there," Dravid said. "We'll be above it."

"How is this different?"

Seri chuckled. It was good to sit and talk again with just the three of them. Ixchel had gone to bed, and no one was quite sure where Adhi had gotten to this morning. Breakfast had come and gone, and the three friends had remained in the dining hall, talking for hours. She hadn't told her friends yet about Tezan, or the night's adventure. Volraag hadn't sent any word to her or anything since their talk, but she knew he would do something, and today was the day.

The Passing would take place today. The Lords even now prepared themselves, and would be entering the chamber right at noon. The Masters had already taken their places and awaited the proper time. All of this left the acolytes with nothing to do.

"I want to see it happen," Seri said.

"You too?" Jamana said. "I am surrounded by lawbreakers!"

"Oh, don't be ridiculous, Jamana. We're not allowed in the chamber. We won't be in the chamber."

"Hmp. Fine. You two can risk everything. I will stay out here, where I'm not in danger of being kicked out of the Conclave."

"You do that," Dravid said. "Let's go, Seri. It will take me a while to get there."

"And what do I tell your bodyguard when she comes looking for you?" Jamana asked.

"She won't," Seri said. "Ixchel will sleep through the whole thing. I'll see her again this evening."

Jamana shrugged. Dravid pulled himself up and hobbled toward the door. Seri patted Jamana on the shoulder and followed him.

Dravid had gotten much more adept with his crutch, but he still moved slower than most. Eventually, they reached the entrance to the crawl tunnels. During the clean-up after the earthquake, Jamana had fixed the door on the crawl tunnel. He had also set a small bench under it, to provide easier access.

Seri helped Dravid, though he insisted he didn't need it, and then climbed up after him. Together, they made their way through the now familiar tunnels.

Seri had not been in the tunnels since the time she hid from Curasir, not long after the earthquake had made a mess of them. Since then, someone, probably Dravid, had cleaned things out quite a bit. No dust, no rubble. It was as if nothing had ever happened.

"We'd better be quiet from here on," Dravid whispered, then began the ascent that led over the Inner Sanctum.

Eventually, they reached the observation space, as Seri called it in her mind. The sun filled the tiny round room with light through the ceiling's window. Dravid and Seri crawled to the floor's opening and looked down.

The chamber hadn't changed, though Seri noted it looked like someone had tried to scrub the floors. The burn marks on the central dais remained the same.

On five of the six platforms, the Masters knelt in solitude, waiting and meditating. On the sixth, Varioch's, two lesser mages knelt. Seri assumed they were the closest in line to be the next Master. She glanced upward at the sunlight. It should be noon at any moment now.

As if on cue, the Masters and the two other mages all stood. Master Korda stepped from his platform up onto the central dais. He spread his arms and looked up. Seri and Dravid ducked back.

"The hour has come!" Master Korda's magnificent voice boomed from below. "Beneath Theon's light, let the power of Antises return to its home and heal our land!"

A chorus of agreement rose from the others.

"Let the Lords of Antises come forward!" Master Korda cried.

• • • • •

"I need one last moment with my son," Aelia said. Nian nodded and took several steps away to give them some privacy.

Marshal looked at Aelia. She thought this was their last moment together, but it would not be

Aelia put her hands on his shoulders. "My treasure, remember all that I told you yesterday. I have little else to say to you today."

Marshal tried to reassure her with his eyes.

Aelia gazed back at him. "This is goodbye, Marshal. If we are successful, your curse will be lifted and your life... your life will change in so many ways."

He shook his head. No.

Aelia's eyes welled up with moisture. "Stay close to the friends that have joined us on this journey. Victor... he has changed since we began. I think he will be your truest friend, and not because of the

Binding. And Talinir will do all within his power to protect you." She glanced to the side. "Even this priest, though we have known him only a few days. He seems to be someone you can trust, perhaps someone you can… talk to."

Talk. Marshal had difficulty grasping the concept. That he might have an actual conversation with Nian? Or Victor or Talinir? Or… Aelia. To ask her all the questions he held inside, all that he desperately wanted to know from her.

"I wish I could be here, to hear you…"

She would be.

"…but this is the cost. To lift a curse, there is a price to be paid. I pay it willingly and without reservation. For you, my treasure."

Aelia pulled him to her in an embrace fiercer and tighter than any he could recall. His head swam. She genuinely wanted to sacrifice herself for him. But he would not allow it. He wanted to tell her that. But all he could do was return the hug in the same way it was offered.

At last, Aelia pulled away and kissed him on the forehead. She looked to Nian. "I'm ready now."

Nian stepped forward and gestured to Marshal. "This way." He walked to the stairs and began to climb them. Marshal followed, with constant looks back at his mother. She would be safe. She had to be.

Nian led him to the center of the balcony and pointed to a golden circle about two feet wide engraved in the floor. Marshal could make out a faint image of what looked like three circles connecting. He assumed it had something to do with Theon. "You must stand here," Nian told him. "If this is to work at all, if you have any hope of honoring your mother's resolve, you cannot leave this spot until it is done. Do you understand?"

Nod is yes. But…

Nian put a hand on his shoulder. "Whatever happens, do not leave this spot. Everything depends on it. If you love your mother, if you respect what she is doing for you, you must stay right here!" He leaned in closer and whispered, "She will not die. But do not leave this spot."

Marshal nodded again.

Satisfied, Nian left him there. Marshal looked around. The balcony was empty other than this gold circle. He stepped to the edge of the circle and put his hands on the railing. From here, he could see Aelia, but the sunlight streaming in from the open roof above kept getting in his eyes. He tried shading them with one hand.

Aelia stood beside the altar, looking up at him. Even when Nian returned and spoke with her, her eyes never left Marshal. His hands began to tremble.

Nian appeared to be doing something behind Aelia. He guided her to stand directly against the altar, still facing Marshal. Marshal couldn't tell, but it seemed that Nian passed something -- a rope? -- around Aelia's waist.

A shadow passed in front of the sun for a brief second. Marshal glanced up and immediately regretted it. He blinked to recover his vision. When he could see again, he looked back to Aelia.

An eidolon stood beside her, sword drawn. And then Marshal saw the blood.

(((75)))

Seri risked a quick peek and saw that Master Korda was no longer looking up. She and Dravid both resumed their observation. In the gap between platforms, the door to the Sanctum opened. Lord Tyrr stood in the opening, resplendent in his uniform of gold and bronze.

"From the land of Rasna, we welcome Lord Tyrr!" Master Korda said.

Lord Tyrr entered and strode confidently to Rasna's platform to his immediate left. Only then did Seri recognize the platforms and banners were arranged according to geography, rotating around the room from the southwest to the southeast. The doorway stood directly south, where the lake opened into the ocean.

"From the land of Varioch, we welcome Lord Varion!"

Seri repressed a shudder as Lord Varion entered the chamber. Over a week had passed since her encounter with him, but she didn't think she'd ever get over those hands touching her, pulling on her robe…

Dravid touched her shoulder. She realized she had closed her eyes and gripped the edge of the opening with white knuckles. She relaxed and smiled at Dravid. "I'll be all right," she mouthed.

"From the land of Ch'olan, we welcome Lord Rajwir!"

As ever, Lord Rajwir looked amazing in his feather headdress and jewels galore.

"From the land of Mandiata, we welcome Lord Sundinka!"

Lord Sundinka's adornments were almost as elaborate as Lord Rajwir's, though instead of feathers, he wore a tiger pelt across his shoulders.

"From the land of Arazu, we welcome Lord Enuru!"

Seri smiled as she looked down at the beloved Lord Enuru. From here, she could see the beginnings of a bald spot on the top of his head. For some reason, that struck her as hilarious.

"From the land of Kuktarma, we welcome Lord Meluhha!"

Lord Meluhha was clothed similar to Master Ganak, wrapped in a single wide piece of elaborate cloth trimmed in gold. On his head, he wore the largest crown of any of the Lords, a half-circle that flared outward.

"Finally, we welcome the claimant to the throne of all Antises, Tezan!"

Tezan entered and stood alone near the door. Compared to the Lords' finery, he appeared humble in his simple clothing. Seri gritted her teeth at the audacity. The nerve! False humility from a deceiver.

Master Korda took his place on Kuktarma's platform. Master Hain stepped to the center.

"As the most senior Master of the Conclave, it falls to me to oversee this illustrious moment. Let us begin. Lord Tyrr, if you will?"

Lord Tyrr stepped to the edge of his platform and raised his hands. He closed his eyes and appeared to concentrate. Seri heard Dravid's sharp intake of breath before she saw what happened. On the central dais, golden light pooled in the center. It spread outward, growing and changing shape, while remaining a flat surface. The growth was slow, but relentless. About five minutes passed. Lord Tyrr lowered his hands and almost lost his balance before Master Plecu caught him. The dais was now covered by a square-shaped floor of glowing, pulsing liquid light. Each side was easily twelve feet long.

Lord Varion took his place in turn. As he focused, the light grew straight up from one edge of the bottom square. When he was finished, a twelve-foot wall of light stood to one side of the floor.

One by one, the other Lords performed their parts. Each one looked absolutely exhausted by the process. Each one added a new side to the cube of light. Lord Meluhha, the last of them, crafted its roof.

Seri stared down at the cube of light. It seemed so alive, so pristine, so different from the chaos of the vortex she had seen in the Otherworld. As she watched, she imagined she could see stars moving about on the surface of the light. The sheer power radiating from below filled her body and mind. She almost felt like she was floating.

"Tezan?" Master Hain spoke, the sound of his voice breaking over half an hour of silence. "If you would, please? The Passing awaits the Heart of Fire."

Seri tensed. Here it came.

•••••

Kishin dropped onto the altar. A cloud of dust puffed outward at his landing. This was more like it. Solid stone construction. It reminded him of home.

The priest looked up in horror at him. "Who are you? What are--"

Kishin leaped down, kicking the priest in the face. He went down easily. A ceremonial knife clattered across the floor. For a moment, he thought he saw a shadowy figure standing near, but then it vanished.

The assassin turned and faced the mother. She was bleeding, but her eyes still held strongly to life. She stared at him in defiance.

"You're too late," she whispered.

"This is an abomination," he said. He looked to the balcony and then back to her. "And a waste. Your son will die whether you succeed or not."

Aelia lunged at him, but her movements were already weak and she was bound to the altar itself. Kishin eluded her without effort and started up the stairs.

"Marshal! Marshal!" Aelia called. "The assassin! He's… here."

Kishin tasted bile. This job had gone so far beyond his usual tasks, and now it threatened everything he believed. "We are all cursed!" he shouted. "There is no escape. Curses cannot be lifted."

He stepped onto the balcony. The boy stood there on top of a circle made of gold, engraved into the floor. He wore no sword, but Kishin knew that did not make him any less dangerous. Already, the boy's hands shook. His own sword would be useless against the Eldanim enchantment. In fact, he had taken too long in getting to the target. He would probably be unleashing his k'uh at any moment.

Marshal lifted his hands and Kishin moved. He leaped up and to his left as the balcony shook. When the ball of his left foot landed on the railing, he vaulted higher into the air. As he passed over Marshal, he backhanded the young man across the face.

Kishin landed lightly on his feet on the other side of the golden circle. Marshal staggered from his blow, but managed to keep his footing and turn toward the assassin. Interesting. He seemed concerned about staying within the circle.

Kishin jabbed Marshal in the stomach and followed up with a devastating punch to the right side of his face when he doubled over. Another blow to his back sent the boy to the floor. This was too easy, and exactly the situation he had needed all along. Marshal was weaponless and separated from his protectors with no chance of anyone coming to his aid.

"Marshal!" Aelia's voice called, sounding weaker. "You… are… loved."

Kishin froze. An irrational fury began to rise within his chest. He kicked viciously at Marshal, who had curled up to protect himself. Let the mother spout her platitudes. He would beat this target to death with nothing but his own hands.

•••••

Tezan stepped close to the central dais and took a deep breath. He lifted his hands, closed his eyes and focused. Within the cube of light, another light pulsed into being. Unlike the golden light of the walls, this light shone red, a sparkling, growing heart of red flame. It seemed to fold in on itself over and over, even as it grew, slowly filling the interior of the cube. A few gasps and murmurs came from the assembled Lords and Masters.

Seri frowned. Volraag had promised to take care of this. Why was Tezan succeeding? Why…?

Tezan stiffened and almost stumbled. He opened his eyes. From her position, Seri could see something was wrong with him. He seemed to be straining.

The Heart of Fire had nearly filled the cube of light, but it had stopped growing. As Tezan strained, it seemed to shrink a little. By now, the Lords and Masters had also noticed something was awry. Master Hain took a small step toward Tezan, but did not say anything.

The Heart of Fire shrank again, then again. Only a slight contraction each time, but clearly visible. Tezan gasped and reacted physically to each change.

Volraag had come through. Tezan must be losing his connection to the wild magic users. One by one, he was losing their power. One by one. A horrible thought struck Seri. It couldn't be true. But how could she know? How could…?

"Is there a problem?" Lord Varioch's odious voice echoed below.

"A moment, please, your Lordship," Master Hain said. He stepped off Arazu's platform and approached Tezan.

Seri pulled away from the opening. She had to know. It couldn't be. She turned to the southwest, as near as she could tell, closed her eyes and concentrated. "Come on, come on," she whispered.

She opened her eyes and two worlds filled her vision. She ignored the Heart of Fire overlaid onto the vortex below. Instead, she focused everything she had to the southwest, toward the ship. She couldn't see it in either world, of course, but maybe she could sense those on board? Seri focused her magic senses to the fullest she had ever tried. She grabbed multiple beams of light and channeled them within herself to boost her own power, not even realizing what she had done.

There. She could see the wild magic users, or at least sense them in her mind, like dozens of tiny little lights of power, all grouped together.

And then one went out. It vanished completely. Another one followed it. Then two more.

"No, no, no, no, no!" Seri whispered.

Dravid scooted up next to her. "What is it? What's happening?"

"He's killing them!" she sobbed. "He's killing all of them!"

"Killing who? What are you talking about? What--" Dravid gasped.

Seri broke away from her senses and looked down again. Tezan had fallen to his knees, but still held his hands out. The Heart was shrinking rapidly now.

The lights from the ship continued to go out, one by one. Seri looked at Dravid and felt a burden of horror that overwhelmed everything else. It was her fault. She had told Volraag, and now they were dying. And she could do nothing about it.

"Tezan? What is wrong?" Master Hain asked.

Tezan collapsed, dropping his hands. Seri could hear his words echoing her own thoughts. "No, no, no, no. They can't. I didn't want… I failed…"

• • • • •

A second kick slammed into Marshal's side. The pain shocked him into motion. He pulled Volraag's dagger out, rolled over, and plunged it into the assassin's thigh. He received barely a grunt in response.

"Marshal…" He could hear Aelia, but couldn't see her from the floor. How had this happened? Talinir and Victor were fighting the eidola. How had one gotten inside, and why would it hurt Aelia? He needed to get to her!

Still holding on to the dagger's hilt, he tried channeling some of his power through it. The assassin shouted in surprise and fell back, grabbing at his thigh.

"You… are… valuable…"

Marshal scrambled to the railing, pulled himself up and looked down. Aelia was looking up at him. Blood pooled on the floor around her. She looked so frail and weak. But her gaze radiated love and determination.

Marshal felt something welling up inside his chest. He opened his mouth.

A looped rope flipped over his head and down to his neck. Before he could react, he was yanked backward and felt the rope tighten rapidly. He tried to grab it, but it was too tight already. He struggled for air.

"Nice trick with the dagger," the assassin's voice whispered in his ear. "Let's see you magic your way out of this."

Marshal tried to force his fingers beneath the rope. Failing that, he flailed wildly at the killer behind him. His eyes darted down for a final look at Aelia, and then the killer dragged him back from the railing. The sun was in his eyes again, but even that began to dim.

"Marshal…" Her voice was barely audible now.

Something, something was building inside him. It wasn't only his power, though he felt that as well. Something else was happening. It began somewhere deep inside his chest and pushed its way up slowly beneath his ribcage, passing his heart whose pounding seemed louder than he had ever known.

"You… have…"

Bright spots competed with blackness dancing before his eyes. The pain and pressure around his neck competed with the lack of air for his focus. In desperation, he stretched his arms out in front of him, trying to ignore the pain. He pushed it away, along with whatever was growing inside him, focusing on one simple thought, one final act to free himself. He closed his hands into fists.

"A… pur…"

A purpose! He had a purpose! Those were her words, the words he had heard so many times from her wonderful voice, the voice that was even now failing.

"What? What is this?" The assassin's voice sounded bewildered all of a sudden. The rope loosened ever so slightly.

Marshal brought both arms back as hard as he could, elbows bent to slam into the assassin behind him. At the same time, he released his power, not through his closed fists, but through his elbows.

His power threw the assassin back across the balcony and slammed him into the stone wall. The rope fell away from Marshal's neck and he lunged forward to the balcony. The strange feeling had reached his neck and was pushing further up now.

From his tortured throat, from vocal cords that had never once vibrated in his life, from lips that had never uttered a sound since birth, from deep within his soul, the boy from Drusa's Crossing screamed his first word, a first word no different from that of most other children, cried out not in imitation or joy but in agony and terror yet no less full of love.

"Mama!"

(((76)))

The last of the tiny lights went out. The Heart of Fire faded away and vanished completely. Silence reigned over the Inner Sanctum, broken only by the sobbing of one man, a false King who had been revealed in the cruelest way possible.

"What has happened?" Lord Rajwir asked at last.

"The so-called King is a fake!" Lord Varion roared. "Exactly as we should have expected from Rasna!"

"Vetis take me! I know nothing more than you do!" Lord Tyrr shouted.

"My Lords!" Master Korda's voice boomed over them all. "Please. As always, we must let the matrices return to the land for two hours before they return to you. I urge you all to go to your rooms and rest. When the Passing is complete, we will discuss this--"

A strange wave of power washed over the entire room. Seri sat up and gasped. Unleashed magic had struck her, and apparently everyone else. Below, the Lords and Masters all exclaimed in consternation. Something unexpected had happened. Seri felt as if the power had communicated something, as if there were information in it. But she couldn't comprehend what it meant.

"I felt all my bones shake!" Dravid said. "What was that?"

Seri looked down into the Inner Sanctum again. The Lords stood looking around in confusion. The Masters, however, had all fallen to their knees. They seemed much more shaken by the wave of power than they had been by Tezan's exposure.

"It… can't be!" Master Tzoyet said.

"We all felt it," Master Hain said. "All of you."

"What was that? And why does it matter?" Lord Varion growled. He pointed at Tezan, who still lay weeping on the floor. "We should deal with that one!"

Master Korda climbed to his feet shakily. He stared at the cube of light. "A curse has been lifted," he said. Seri inhaled sharply. That's what the wave of power had been trying to communicate. Somehow, she knew Master Korda was right.

"That's preposterous," Lord Meluhha said, but his voice was filled with uncertainty.

"Our world has just changed," Master Hain said, still on his knees. "Everything has changed."

"What are you talking about?" Lord Varion said.

"Please. Please return to your rooms," Master Korda said. "We will discuss what to do when the Passing is complete."

"What about him?" Lord Tyrr pointed at Tezan. Seri wanted to snarl.

"I will have him locked in another room to await our discussions," Master Korda said. "We will take care of him."

More arguing ensued, but eventually the Lords all agreed to return to their rooms. They were all exhausted, after all. The Passing took away their power, and when that power departed, they were overwhelmed with the loss of it and their own Bindings toward home.

After the Lords left and a pair of apprentices escorted Tezan out, the Masters gathered together. Seri and Dravid couldn't hear all of their agitated discussion. Their attention focused not on the false King, but on what had happened next. "The end of all curses is near!" Master Ganak's voice rose loudly above the others. "It's the prophecy of Aharu!" "Don't be ridiculous!" snapped Master Tzoyet. Their words overlapped and grew difficult to hear again.

Seri, however, had only one thing on her mind. She turned to Dravid.

"Guide me to the vent overlooking Lord Varion's chambers!"

● ● ● ● ●

Marshal vaulted over the railing, heedless of the gold circle, the assassin, or the drop below him. He landed hard but somehow kept his footing. He stumbled forward and stopped in front of his mother.

Though blood still dripped onto the floor, she was motionless. Her head and arms hung lifeless. The only thing holding her up was a rope that bound her to the altar. Marshal fumbled with the knot until it finally came loose. He caught Aelia and lowered her gently to the floor.

"Mama." Sounds came from his lips again. It felt so strange. How many thousands of times had he opened his mouth wanting to speak to her and nothing came out? Yet now her name slipped easily off his tongue. The curse was lifted.

"Mama." It was the name she had always used to refer to herself throughout his childhood. The only name by which he had known her in his mind. When he grew old enough to understand, he realized her name was Aelia, but that was the name for other people. For him, her name was and always would be Mama.

As if it came from far away, he heard a yell and the sounds of swords clashing. But his mind failed to grasp what it meant.

He reached out a trembling hand to touch Aelia's face. He lifted a lock of hair and brushed it to the side.

Why? He wasn't worth this. Speaking. Not speaking. What difference did it make? How could she do this? For him? Even as his mind asked the questions, his heart screamed the answers. It was her love, her never-ending, unconditional love.

"You… are loved," he said with effort, his tongue stumbling over the "l" sound. Every syllable was familiar to his brain, but completely new to his lips.

All his previous thoughts and anger toward his mother seemed so foolish now. How could he have ever distrusted her? What was wrong with him that he would think that way? She had always, always been thinking of him.

Marshal had no concept of how much time passed while he sat beside his mother. Occasionally the sounds of conflict outside intruded on his thoughts, but he paid no attention. Assassin. Eidolon. Neither mattered. Only his mother.

•••••

Dravid led Seri through the passages, but he kept glancing back at her, clearly shaken by what had happened. "What was that?" he asked as he crawled. "What happened with Tezan? You know something, don't you? Why were you crying?"

"He's not the real King," Seri said. "I found out two nights ago. I told someone that I believed would help reveal him, but, but… he did something else. Something horrible."

"I don't understand."

"I'll tell you everything," Seri said, "but I need to see what is happening in Lord Varion's rooms."

"We're almost there."

Dravid crawled past one of the curious metal vents and stopped. He turned around and gestured. This was it. Seri moved up beside him and looked down.

Lord Varion rested heavily in a huge armchair, his hands covering his eyes. His chest raised and lowered in deep, slow breaths. From what she could see, he was alone.

The door to the next room opened and Volraag strode in, followed by a hooded man dressed in tattered clothes, hardly the escort of a nobleman. The tatters had once been many colors, but they had faded into pale shades of gray and brown. Seri paid him little attention. She found herself growing furious at the sight of Volraag. He had betrayed her trust and murdered dozens of innocent people!

Then the hooded man dragged in a third: Tezan. Seri stifled a gasp. He threw Tezan onto the floor in front of Lord Varion, who barely moved.

"Did you enjoy my surprise, Father?" Volraag asked.

"Eh? That was your doing in there?"

"Yes. Turns out our 'King' here was just a wild magic user who was channeling magic from others. I just took away his source of power."

Lord Varion laughed, but ended up coughing. He did not look well at all.

Volraag walked to the desk and picked up some papers. He flipped through them without paying much attention. Tezan muttered something no one could hear, but stayed on his hands and knees. The tattered man stood by the door. Lord Varion noticed him for the first time.

"Who is this?"

Volraag appeared to ignore him. He set the papers down and looked off toward the center of the citadel. "As I recall it from last year, your power will come rushing back to you probably in about five to ten more minutes. Lord Tyrr should be getting his back right now. It happens in the order that you gave them up."

"Yes, that's the way it works. Volraag, who is this man and why is he here?"

"Him? He works for me. And he's here because your time is up, old man."

"What?" Lord Varion's voice rose. "What are you talking about?"

"I'm saying that I'm tired of waiting for you to die." Volraag finally looked directly at his father. "I'm tired of watching you abuse this incredible power you have, year after year." He took a step closer. "The wrong people have too much power in Antises. It's time to change that."

Volraag gestured to the hooded man. "Do it."

The stranger stepped forward, and as he did, his hood fell back. This time, it was Dravid who barely contained a gasp. Seri glanced at him, then back at the drama below. The stranger's skin was gray and... peeling? Only one condition made someone's skin appear like that: leprosy.

Lord Varion had the same thought. "You bring a leper into my chambers? What is wrong with you, boy?"

The leper slipped behind Lord Varion's chair before he could turn. A cord of some kind appeared in his hands. He looped it around Varion's neck and pulled.

Lord Varion gasped and his huge hands tried vainly to pull the cord away. The leper pulled tighter and Varion's eyes grew wide. Inarticulate sounds came from deep in his throat.

Dravid touched Seri's shoulder and she looked up. He gestured below as if asking if they should do anything. Seri lifted her hands helplessly. What could they do? What *should* they do?

Volraag watched impassively. Tezan looked up from the floor and a look of horror flooded his face. "What are you doing?" he cried.

"I would think that would be obvious," Volraag answered. "By now, my half-brother should also be dead, leaving me as the rightful Lord of Varioch and heir to its power. Trust me. I'll do far more than my father ever did with it."

"You can't kill someone like that!" Tezan said.

The leper yanked harder and Lord Varion's feeble attempts to escape stopped. His arms dropped to his sides.

"It appears that I can," Volraag said.

The leper held the cord tight a moment longer, then let go. He checked Varion's breathing. "He's dead," he said in a raspy voice that sent chills down Seri's back.

"Excellent. Any minute now, the power will come to me." Volraag faced in the direction of the Inner Sanctum and closed his eyes. "I've waited so long for this."

Silence descended on the room. The leper moved to stand next to Tezan. Volraag waited with his eyes shut and hands spread to his sides. Seri and Dravid watched.

Nothing happened. Minutes ticked by.

"Perhaps you made a mistake," Tezan said, sarcasm dripping from his words.

"Shhh," Volraag breathed. "We must wait for good things to come to us."

Still nothing happened. Seri couldn't be sure, but it seemed that more than ten minutes had gone by since Varion's murder.

Finally, Volraag opened his eyes. "As unlikely as it seems, Kishin must have failed," he said. "This complicates matters." He turned and looked down at Tezan. "Fortunately, we have you, sire."

Tezan looked anxiously at the leper and back at Volraag. "I... I can be useful to you," he said, licking his lips.

"Yes, you can." Volraag looked to the leper. "Bring him. It's time for the next stage of the plan."

• • • • •

Nian moaned and started to pull himself up. Marshal had barely noticed his presence. The priest felt the back of his head and then his nose. "Owww. What happened? Who was that?" Then he noticed Marshal and Aelia. "Oh."

He shifted nearer, leaning on one arm while he stretched the other toward them. "Marshal, I can't imagine what you're going through right now. The eidolon--"

"Stop."

Nian's eyes widened and he almost fell, barely catching himself. "You... you spoke! The curse is lifted?"

Marshal turned to look at him. "Yes," he said.

Nian's mouth hung open. "P-praise Theon," he whispered. "I didn't... I doubted. I'm so sorry."

A gust of wind came out of nowhere and brushed Marshal's hair back. Nian felt it too, and looked around in confusion.

Marshal looked up at the open sky. In an instant, something struck him. He felt it like a sudden pressure over every inch of his body. In a moment, it pushed into him, then swirled around, congealing within his chest. The pressure was now inside, pushing out. As it grew, he realized it was power, power like he already possessed, but so much stronger. And it kept growing. Another wave of the outside pressure hit him and pushed inside, followed by another.

Marshal's hands began to shake, followed by the floor around him.

"What's happening?" Nian asked. Marshal couldn't answer. The power grew and grew and grew. He felt like he was going to explode.

And then he did.

Marshal threw his arms up and power erupted out of him. He screamed, a raw, visceral sound that combined his grief, anger and confusion all together in a roar almost immediately drowned out by the rumble of stones shattering. The roof of the temple exploded outward, sending shards of rock and dust in every direction. The waves of power Marshal continued to spew outward pulverized what was left.

As he lowered his hands, the power continued to flow, ripping massive tears down both walls. Chunks of stone tumbled both inward and out. Nian scrambled out of the way.

Finally, the eruption stopped. Marshal remained on his knees next to Aelia, though his whole body continued to tremble. Silence descended, but only for a brief moment. With a groan, the entire front half of the temple folded in on itself and collapsed. A cloud of dust bloomed outward, obscuring anything outside.

Nian stood shakily and looked around. "The power..." He looked down at Marshal. "Did that just... happen?"

Marshal nodded. Then blinked as he realized he had done so instinctively, without having to think about what a nod meant.

"Lord Varion must be dead," Nian said, almost to himself. "That's the only thing that makes sense."

He took Marshal's hand and pulled him to his feet. "And that makes you, my friend, the new Lord of Varioch." He looked around at the destruction. "But the priests might not be too quick to confirm that, I'm thinking."

Marshal opened his mouth. "I... I don't..."

"Marshal!" The shout came from outside. "Marshal! Are you there?"

Marshal looked around as his thoughts became more ordered. The assassin was nowhere to be seen. But another enemy waited outside. He balled up his fists and started forward. It was time to end this.

(((77)))

"Which way are they going?" Seri asked.

Dravid craned his head to see Volraag as he left the room. "I think… they turned right."

"Let's go!"

Seri crawled as fast as she could. She had no idea what Volraag's next phase might be, but the man had already killed dozens, including his own father. With that strange leper working for him, he seemed capable of anything, defying the Laws of Cursings and Bindings.

Another strange wave of power washed over them. Seri almost felt like it pushed her against the far wall of the tunnel. It had a direction to it. If she weren't so mixed up in her directions, maybe she could tell--

"West," Dravid said. "It came from the west."

Rasna or Varioch, then. The Masters had said it indicated a curse being lifted. Was this second wave another curse being lifted, or a continuation of the first?

No time to think about it now. Seri hurried on until she found another vent. She made room for Dravid and peered down. Which Lord's room was this?

Lord Rajwir and Lady Ajaw stood almost directly below the vent, locked in a passionate embrace. Seri jerked her head back in embarrassment. If anyone was safe from Volraag, it was these two. Lady Ajaw's bodyguards no doubt waited just outside the door.

Seri yanked on Dravid's sleeve and hurried on to the next vent. If the rooms were set up in geographical order, as things had been in the Inner Sanctum, this would probably be Mandiata. She looked down.

A dark-skinned scribe hastened away from a massive chair facing the wall. Seri couldn't see the occupant, but the tiger pelt thrown across the back of the chair made it clear that this was Lord Sundinka of Mandiata.

"Should we do something?" Dravid whispered.

"What can we do? Yell at him to watch out?"

"Maybe?"

"By now he's got his power back. If we just yell, he's more likely to attack us, once he figures out where we are. I don't think he'll appreciate us spying on him."

A thump came from the exterior room. Seri looked back down in time to see the door open and Volraag enter, followed by Tezan and the leper. The assassin was cleaning blood from a dagger.

"I said I needed rest, Bouba," Sundinka said without looking.

"I apologize for the intrusion, Lord Sundinka," Volraag said. "I have some rather urgent business."

Lord Sundinka came to his feet slowly and turned. His eyes took in the three men. "What is this? How did you get in here unannounced?"

"Start your work," Volraag said to Tezan. He turned to the leper. "You know what to do."

The leper turned and rushed at Lord Sundinka. Seri gasped, but her eye was drawn to Tezan, who raised a hand toward Lord Sundinka and appeared to be concentrating.

"Fools!" Lord Sundinka's rumbling voice was drowned out by his own magic that erupted out from him before the leper could reach him. His chair shattered, the leper was thrown across the room, and the tiger pelt fluttered through the air. Volraag caught it and held it up almost absently.

"This is very pretty," he said. "Surely you didn't kill this beast yourself, my Lord?"

"What perfidy is this?" Sundinka held up his hand, palm outward, toward Volraag. "Have you gone mad?"

"Perfidy. Now there's an interesting word," Volraag said. He lifted the tiger pelt up and looked it over with a critical eye. "I suppose that is a good word for what's been happening throughout Antises lately."

"What are you talking about?" Lord Sundinka breathed heavily, clearly exhausted.

Volraag lowered the pelt and looked at Lord Sundinka. "The rule of the Lords has been, altogether, a dismal failure, don't you think? The wrong people have held the power, and everyone else has suffered." He looked at Tezan. "We're here to change that. Tezan?"

Tezan had been holding one hand aimed at Lord Sundinka all along. Now he gasped and aimed the other at Volraag. Sundinka winced suddenly. "What... what are you doing?"

Tezan's wild magic power! The woman on the boat said he could steal power and give it to someone else! Seri activated her star sight and took in a frightened breath. Sure enough, she could see power flowing in a massive rush from Sundinka into Tezan. And now, it was flowing back through Tezan's other arm and into Volraag.

The new Lord of Varioch closed his eyes and inhaled deeply. "Ahhh. Now this is more like it."

"My power! You cannot take my power!" Sundinka charged Volraag with a roar. The leper appeared out of nowhere and stabbed upward into the Lord of Mandiata's chest. His head fell back with a whimper and he twisted falling off the dagger onto the floor with a heavy crash.

"Almost..." Tezan said.

The leper stood over Sundinka and waited. The Lord reached toward him, arms shaking. The last of the power flowed out of him into Tezan and then to Volraag. Tezan dropped his arms and staggered. He fell against the wall and slumped to the floor. Volraag began to laugh. It was the coldest sound Seri had ever heard.

At a nod from Volraag, the leper stabbed Lord Sundinka again. He stiffened and his arms fell. The leper withdrew his dagger and began to clean it again.

Volraag pointed at Sundinka's body and gestured. A burst of power shoved the Lord's body into the corner of the room. "Now this is more like it!" Volraag cried. He laughed again.

Seri and Dravid looked at each other. Lord Sundinka was right. This was madness. Someone had to stop Volraag. But how?

Volraag kicked at Tezan's leg. "Come on, your highness," he ordered. "Two down, four to go. Five if you count my half-brother, but he'll have to wait for now."

"Give me a moment," Tezan said. "I need to rest before I use the power again, if you want it to work."

"Fine. Take a break." Volraag flipped the tiger pelt over his own shoulders and admired it again. "I may just keep this."

Dravid pointed, and he and Seri hurried away. They scrambled back toward the exit.

"We have to stop him!" Seri said. The next room in the geographical order would be Arazu. Volraag might kill Lord Enuru and Lady Lilitu!

"We need help!" Dravid said. "The two of us can't stand against a

Lord's power, not to mention those other two."

Seri nodded. "You find Jamana and he can get Master Korda," Seri said. "I'll find Master Hain."

"Why do we need to find them?" asked a voice behind her. Seri almost slammed her head against the tunnel's ceiling in shock before she realized it was Ixchel's voice.

"What are you doing here?"

"Finding you. Not too difficult. What's going on?"

"No time to explain."

Dravid climbed out of the exit as quickly as he could. Seri followed him. She handed him his crutch and he set off down the hall. Ixchel jumped smoothly down beside Seri.

"Wait. Can I ask you to help protect someone else?"

Ixchel frowned. "I am here to protect you," she said.

"Yes, but my Lord is about to be killed. He needs someone to protect him right now!"

Ixchel's face showed little reaction. She drew her sword. "You want me to go to Lord Enuru's chambers?"

"Yes, I'll be there as soon as I can, with more help. Watch out, though. Volraag is coming, and he has a Lord's power. He also has an assassin of some kind with him. Try to slow them down. I'll be there soon!"

Without waiting for Ixchel's answer, Seri turned and raced down the hall. Where would Master Hain be at this time?

• • • • •

Marshal climbed over the fallen stone and looked down into the temple courtyard. Immediately, he found himself the focus of attention. A crowd had already gathered at the gates, attracted by the temple's fall. At Marshal's appearance atop the rubble, they erupted in shouts, both of dismay and exuberance.

Marshal's attention, however, was drawn to the courtyard itself. His eyes locked on to Victor's flail, lying alone in the dust almost directly below him. He spun to the left. Victor and Talinir stood there, swords drawn, facing down five of the shadow creatures now, all who also wielded shadowy blades. The two parties had backed away from each other, apparently after some lengthy fighting. Both his friends sported several cuts and injuries. The eidola appeared unharmed.

Anger welled up in Marshal. He felt the blood rushing into and through the scars on his face. These creatures had been following him around everywhere, even in private moments. They had attacked his friends. They had killed his mother. With all that had happened, he needed somewhere to focus his emotions. This would do.

Marshal leaped off the rubble. As he did, he released a burst of power downward. Unlike earlier, the power felt the same in both hands. The blast tore apart more stones, and launched him high in the air. He wobbled in the air, but maintained his balance. As he approached the ground, he released a smaller burst that slowed his descent somewhat. He still hit hard and stumbled forward several steps, before regaining his balance. He stood between his friends and the eidola.

"Impressive," Talinir said. "I am assuming that you have a full Lord's power now."

Marshal nodded and stared at the shadow creatures. His own sword was buried somewhere in the rubble, but he felt no need of it. His power was enough now. He turned to the central eidolon, who carried a larger sword than the others. It twisted suddenly in a mock bow.

Marshal scowled. What was this about? Why were they even here?

Before he could do anything else, the ground rumbled. Marshal looked about in surprise. The tremor had not come from him. A second tremor followed almost right away.

"Marshal?" Victor said tentatively.

He had no time to respond. The earth shook with a ferocity that far exceeded his own power. The cries of the crowd outside the gate turned into screams. Marshal fell to his knees. The rubble of the temple shifted. Portions of the outer wall collapsed. In the distance, he saw a two-story building crumble in upon itself.

A crack opened almost immediately in front of Marshal. He watched as it widened, rocks and dirt pouring into the gap. Then the dirt erupted back out. Something dark pulsed within the crack. The trembling of the earth slowed almost to a stop. Marshal got to his feet and stared at the crack. The darkness trembled.

And then it shot up into the air, a wall of darkness edged with dancing, multi-colored crackles of light. It formed a square around eight feet long on each side. A blast of cool air expanded from it.

As Marshal watched, the darkness swirled and became clear. The wall became a portal, a doorway into a landscape far different from the temple courtyard. With a shock and a sharp pull on his heart, he recognized the Starlit Realm he had visited in Intal Eldanir. The

Otherworld waited only a few steps away, and it called him.

•••••

Seri spotted Master Hain down the hall right before the earthquake struck. But that made no sense. The Passing had taken place. Zes Sivas should have stabilized, even without the King's power.

None of that mattered in the moment. The ground trembled, then erupted in a cataclysmic shaking that far exceeded any of the previous quakes. Seri fell to her hands and knees, but kept trying to crawl forward, to reach Master Hain. The hallway floor buckled behind her and heaved her forward, even as parts of the ceiling began to fall.

Master Hain was beside her in a moment. He knelt on the trembling floor, holding his hand straight up above them. As rocks fell, they shattered apart from his power. Pebbles and dust rained down on both of them. Seri shielded her head.

Why was this happening now? It didn't make sense!

A chunk of rock the size of a dinner plate slammed down next to Seri. Master Hain was having difficulty. It felt like the entire citadel was collapsing around them.

At last the trembling subsided. Master Hain stood slowly, keeping his arm up and looking around for any further danger. Seri caught her breath and joined him.

"This is... wrong," Master Hain said in a low tone. "It should not be happening now." He looked down at Seri. "Are you all right? I should check for others in need."

"No time! We have to save Lord Enuru!"

He frowned. "What is--"

"I'll tell you as we go!" Seri grabbed his arm and pulled. "Hurry, Master! He's already killed two Lords!"

Master Hain demanded answers and Seri gave them as they hurried back toward the Lords' quarters. Every direction they went, they ran into devastation. Debris of all kinds clogged the hallways, forcing them to take alternate routes or climb over fallen stone and wood. Rays of sunlight pierced through gaping holes. As they climbed one particularly difficult pile of debris, Seri looked up through four floors of the citadel above her head.

The area of the Lords' quarters seemed to have suffered less damage than elsewhere. They moved much faster upon reaching it. Seri picked up the pace.

She rounded a corner and stopped, trying to grasp the situation before her.

•••••

Marshal felt a sudden rush. He jerked to the side barely in time to dodge an eidolon's blade as it flew past him and darted into the portal. The other four chased after it, leaving Talinir and Victor behind.

The last one, the leader, paused after stepping into the portal. He turned to face Marshal and his appearance altered. His stature grew to a height that seemed implausible, ten or eleven feet tall. The shadow receded away from him, revealing his skin and clothes. Marshal gasped, then blinked several times because the gasp actually made a sound. That had never happened before. The eidolon was one of the Eldanim.

But no. Even as he appeared that way, his skin shifted to a blackness that somehow seemed darker than the star-filled sky behind him. It was as if his skin were absorbing light and color, rather than reflecting it. He threw back his long, white hair and laughed. The light of the stars glittered off the warpsteel sword in his hand.

"Come, Marshal! Will you pursue us into our world?" he called.

Marshal stared at the strange being and his bizarre appearance. For some reason, he remembered the long shadow he had seen back in Efesun. Had that been cast by one of these creatures?

Victor and Talinir appeared next to Marshal. "We can take him together!" Victor said.

"No," Talinir said. "We should not venture into the Otherworld. Marshal, are you all right?"

Marshal ignored him and took a step closer to the portal. The stars called to him. He couldn't see many of them through the portal, but those that he could see stirred that burning desire within. With a force of effort, he focused his eyes on the eidolon who stood waiting for him.

"Why?" he asked, his voice thick and breathy.

"You-- you spoke!" Victor exclaimed.

"Why follow us?" the eidolon said. "Because it's the only way you'll find out why we've been watching you. Why your mother died."

"You… killed."

"The curse was lifted!" Victor said. "But that means… Aelia…"

Marshal looked back and forth at his two companions. Talinir's injuries looked superficial. He shook his head. "Do not do this," he said. Victor, on the other hand, bled profusely from a thick gash on his right thigh. Marshal put a hand on his friend's shoulder and looked him in the eyes. Victor's eyes reflected a mixture of joy and sorrow. Apparently, Aelia's last words to him had revealed her intention.

"Help Nian," Marshal said slowly. He pointed to the temple. "With my mama."

Victor nodded, his eyes welling up. Marshal released him and turned to Talinir.

"It is folly to pursue them there," Talinir said, offering an outstretched hand. "Let us all help with your mother, Marshal. We--"

Marshal grabbed Talinir's outstretched hand and yanked him off-balance. Then pushing the warden forward, he took both of them through the portal.

It vanished behind them.

(((78)))

Ixchel and one of her fellow Ch'olan warriors fought together against the leper assassin. Another warrior already lay dead at his feet. Tezan cowered behind Volraag, who seemed to be trying to find a way past the melee. The door to Lord Enuru and Lady Lilitu's quarters had been shattered, along with much of the stone around it. It seemed likely Volraag had done that, rather than the earthquake. Only a few cracks in the walls and ceiling gave any indication of the earthquake here.

"Cease this madness!" Master Hain thundered.

Volraag turned almost casually to face them. "Ah, one of the Masters. I wondered how long it would take."

"Prince Volraag! Stop, please!" Seri cried. "Zes Sivas is falling apart! Help us!"

"Lord Volraag, if you please, Seri. My father is dead, making me the Lord. And I owe this all to you. I was hoping I'd get a chance to thank you."

"Thank me? You're killing people! Stop this!"

Volraag's face hardened. "The wrong people have held the power and Antises has suffered. Once I have consolidated all of the power in myself, I will correct this." Behind him, Ixchel actually ran up the wall and vaulted off her sister warrior's shield over the assassin's head. His blade cut a gash in her shield as she flew over him.

"It doesn't work that way," Master Hain said. "Come. It is not too late to stop this. We can work together and solve things."

"You Masters have been just as foolish as the Lords," Volraag countered. "Your time is over. Zes Sivas itself is throwing you out, it seems."

The assassin backed against the wall as Ixchel and her companion came at him from both sides. He wielded blades in both hands, blocking their attacks.

"It will throw us all out if we do not come together," Master Hain said. "We can--"

"The time for talk is over!" Volraag leveled his hands at Master Hain and unleashed his power. Master Hain narrowly managed to get his own power up in time to blunt the force of the explosion that came at him, but was shoved back against the wall nonetheless.

Seri blinked and the corridor filled with color. Master Hain warped together dozens of separate beams. Tezan's personal light would have seemed bright in any other circumstances, but it paled compared to Volraag, who exploded with a veritable maelstrom. And behind him…

Lord Enuru appeared at the doorway, his hand clasped tight by that of his wife. "Die, usurper!" he cried. A cacophony of light erupted from him. Volraag spun and tried to throw up his own defenses, but was a split-second too late. Enuru's power caught him and spun him back.

Throwing out power in every direction, Volraag crashed into the wall and then through it! He came to a stop, still on his feet, outside the citadel. Clouds of dust around him filtered the sunlight into dozens of beams that confused Seri's vision.

The sword fight halted temporarily at this. Other than the sound of falling, tumbling rocks, all was quiet. Master Hain pushed away from the wall. Lord Enuru looked warily into the dust cloud.

Volraag's chuckling broke the silence. "Tezan!" he called. "Would you step out here, please?"

Tezan glanced fearfully from Lord Enuru to Master Hain. "You do not have to go with him," Master Hain said.

The would-be King shook his head and scrambled over the rocks into the sunlight.

"Fools," Volraag said softly. The dust around him cleared enough for Seri to see him raise both arms.

"Look out!" she screamed. But her voice was drowned out by the sound of Volraag's unleashed power destroying the building above them.

•••••

The balcony had not been harmed in the devastation that wrecked the temple or even the earthquake that followed. Kishin sat alone in the corner, unseen by Marshal or the priest throughout it all.

The explosion of power had been stunning, but he had barely noticed. His attention was focused solely on his own hands, which he turned back and forth repeatedly, as if expecting something to change.

Pure, undefiled skin covered his hands. Light brown, like the day before the curse had fallen on him.

Impossible. The word kept running through his mind, a refrain that wouldn't stop. Impossible.

His fingers trembled as he lifted them up to touch his face. He felt his cheeks, his forehead. They felt smooth, unblemished. He felt higher and found hair. He had hair again! He pulled on it and felt pain. It was real.

His mind denied it. It could not be true.

In desperation, he ripped his raggedy cloak off and tore his tunic open. He stared at the healthy skin on his chest and stomach. He tore one of his pant legs open to see more. Everywhere he looked, he saw only purity and health.

Impossible! Totally and completely impossible! It could not be true!

He staggered to his feet and walked to the balcony's railing. He stood blinking in bright sunlight. It took him a few moments to realize the light didn't hurt. He could look around in the brightness without the usual agony.

No. No, no, no.

Curses could not be lifted. The world did not work that way.

Yet here he stood.

He stood as a living contradiction. It was impossible, but it was true. It was wrong, but it was right. It was an abomination, but it was a miracle.

Kishin had born the ravages of his curse for twenty years. He was Kishin the Leper Assassin, Kishin the Untouchable. He owned this as the very definition of his being. It was all he knew, all he believed.

"Tell me your curse," he whispered. He had no answer to his own question. Who was he now?

He heard murmuring voices. Of course the destruction of the temple would draw a questioning crowd. His presence would raise more questions. Better to avoid them all.

Kishin the cleansed took his first step into an unknown world, a world in which he had no idea how to live.

•••••

"What have you done?" Talinir almost screamed. He stared around them, his mouth open in horror. Surprised, Marshal looked up at him. The Eldani warden had grown to at least nine feet tall. His appearance no longer seemed wrong to Marshal's eyes. Unlike their opponent, Talinir's skin had not changed. He staggered and collapsed, still staring.

"Hahaha! Welcome to the other side, Talinir!" cried the eidolon. "Welcome, my brother!"

"You are Durunim! You are no brother of mine!"

"Not directly, perhaps, but we will be soon. I am Curasir and as I am, you soon shall be."

For the moment, Marshal ignored them. He stood in the Otherworld at last. It was all he had longed for since his first awakening there at Intal Eldanir. The glorious stars filled the sky, shining their multi-colored hues across the landscape.

And now Marshal saw that landscape. It was not at all what he expected. When he had come to be healed, he had been lying in a bed, seeing only the stars and their unfathomable beauty. Now he saw all of the Otherworld, stretched out before him from the top of the high hills of Reman.

Except Reman did not exist here. He saw no sign of the city, or any other city. Instead, devastation ruled the hills and everything around them. At one point, it was clear this had been a forest of some kind. The remains of fallen trees criss-crossed the ground intersected sporadically by a small number that still endured. Most of these seemed lifeless, falling apart. A few clung to life, but only a handful of leaves remained to them on their highest branches. Here and there, craters of various sizes pock-marked the countryside. Smoke drifted from some of them. In the distance, he saw some large creatures moving slowly.

How could this be? How could a world possess such beauty in the skies above and such horror on the ground below?

The eidolon or Durunim or whatever he was spread his arms wide. "Do you not care for our world, Marshal? Is it not to your liking?"

Marshal looked back at him. "I… I do not…"

"You don't understand? Of course not. Do you want to tell him, Talinir, or shall I?"

"I can't be here," Talinir said softly. "This is not right. Not like this."

"I will, then." Curasir gestured broadly with the sword. "This world once teemed with life as yours does now, Marshal. But your people, you humans, came to Antises and destroyed it."

Destroyed?

"When your mages bound all the magic together in their King and Lords, they stripped most of the magic from this world to do so. Your world holds together at the cost of this one!"

"That's not entirely--" Talinir began.

"Quiet, Eldani! If you spent more time here, you would know the truth, also. This world is ravaged because of humans."

Marshal only knew the basics of the history of Antises. He had no idea if Curasir was telling the truth or not. But it still did not answer the questions that mattered to him.

"Why me?" he said.

"Your power." Curasir took a step closer. "You hold the key to restoring everything. We have been watching you for years, waiting for this time, when you would come into your own. My masters are eager to meet you."

"Your restoration would destroy Antises!" Talinir said, struggling back to his feet.

"Only this world matters to me!" Curasir said. "Marshal, you've seen the beauty here. You've felt its pull. Imagine what it could be like, what you could make it!"

•••••

Time seemed to slow as Seri spun away from Volraag and crouched to shield herself. Her mind raced through the facts. Volraag's power was going to collapse this entire section of the citadel down on top of them. Master Hain and Lord Enuru might be able to protect them like before, but they didn't have time to prepare. Her heart felt a sudden pull toward Ixchel, the Binding in action. But she could think of only one way to escape the massive stones falling toward her head.

Her star-sight showed light beams of every possible color all around her, coming from Master Hain, Lord Enuru, Volraag, and Zes Sivas itself. She grabbed one of the darkest purple beams she could find, the most powerful in her experience, and did something she had never done before.

Master Hain had taught her that using magic with a living thing involved "feeling" the life of that thing and weaving or forcing the magic in between the life itself. Since the awakening of her senses on that one momentous morning, she had felt the life of Zes Sivas itself. Day by day, her connection to the island and its power had grown, both in power and intimacy.

With both eyes wide open, Seri took the magic and forced it between the life of Zes Sivas itself. A scream shattered against her ears, though she wasn't sure if it came from her own throat or from the island. Seri ripped the magic apart, wrapping it around herself. Purple fire and darkness enveloped her. She blinked.

And found herself in the Otherworld.

Cautiously, Seri rose to her feet. No one had come with her. She had acted almost entirely on instinct and saved herself, but abandoned everyone else. Surely they would be all right. Master Hain could protect himself. Ixchel was near Lord Enuru, who could do likewise.

The stars - those immense, beautiful stars - shone as before. She stood, not within a hallway, but atop a pile of rubble. The citadels of this world, if citadels they had been, had been destroyed long before. As always, she saw a thin column of smoke weaving its way into the sky somewhere nearby.

The air was still. Seri heard nothing and a quick look around showed no movement, either. No sign of the beast that had threatened her the last time she had seen this place (or had she actually been here then?).

Her racing pulse began to slow. Despite the ruins about her, Seri felt at peace here. She took a deep breath and smelled the smoke. That was odd. It smelled… different. From experience, she knew smoke could smell many ways, depending on what was being burned, but this smell defied her senses. The closest she could come was burnt cinnamon, but even that seemed way off the mark.

Curious, Seri set out across the rubble, moving toward the smoke. It wasn't far, from what she could tell, somewhere near the coast on the northwest side of the island.

The beauty of the stars began to pull at her. In her previous visions, she had seen them, of course, but not like this. So many colors! The magnitude of some of them! Her heart seemed to swell within her breast. An unknown emotion grew with it, forcing a tear from her right eye. She brushed it away angrily. Why would she cry? It made no sense.

The smoke came from beyond the next pile of debris. The unstable rubble made her climb difficult. As she crested the top, she shoved over a flat stone and caused a small avalanche down the other side toward the smoke.

The sound of another rush of movement answered it. "Who's there?" a voice called.

Seri looked down and saw a man looking back at her.

(((79)))

Marshal bowed his head and took a deep breath. Since stepping into the Otherworld, he had felt strange sensations all throughout his body. When Lord Varion's power had become his, only a few minutes ago, it had coalesced into a seething, roiling fury within him. But now, he felt as if the magic were permeating every part of him, growing and growing. He had no doubts Curasir was telling the truth about his abilities. Given the right training, he could probably change this place. Part of him wanted to, to make it a place worthy of those stars.

But at what cost? If what Talinir said was true, the earthquake was only the beginning of the troubles Antises would face. More than that, these… Durunim had killed his mother. Nothing else mattered right now.

The ground shook beneath Marshal. This time, he knew he had caused it.

"Don't waste this opportunity," Curasir said. "If you don't help, we have others we can turn to. You will be cast aside, forgotten. Your value, your purpose, is with us."

"I am… valuable."

"Yes. Yes, you are."

The ground shook again.

"I have… a purpose."

"A glorious purpose. Let me show you."

"I am… loved."

Curasir frowned. "Well, yes, I suppose…"

Marshal screamed and unleashed his power directly at Curasir. The towering Durunim was thrown back down the hill and tumbled several times before righting himself. To Marshal's shock, he laughed and launched himself into the air.

"Idiot. This is the Starlit Realm. My power reigns here!"

Curasir came down and swung his sword in Marshal's direction. Power not his own slammed into him, driving him back and rattling his bones.

Curasir landed a few feet away. "Come, Varion's son. Show me your power," he taunted.

Four Durunim warriors rushed at Marshal from all sides.

•••••

"Who are you?" the man demanded. He seemed equally as shocked to see Seri as she was to see him.

He stood well over six feet tall, gangly and perhaps malnourished. His clothes hung in tatters, and his graying hair long and unkempt. His age was hard to construe, but Seri guessed him to be at least late middle aged, perhaps older. Seri took a step closer, then stopped with a gasp as she caught a better look at him. Blotches of pure darkness appeared on various places on his pale skin, some around the size of a coin, others much larger. They looked like Curasir's skin had appeared when Seri saw him within the heart of Zes Sivas, a complete absence of color.

The man held a rough wooden spear aimed at her. The smoothness of its haft spoke of long usage. On the ground beside him, a low fire burned, the source of the smoke at last.

"I'm Seri. What-- who are you?"

The spear tip lowered. "How did you get here? What is going on?"

"I want to know the same about you. I didn't know anyone lived here. Have you been here long?" Seri felt a bit annoyed at his questions. After what she had been through!

"Long enough not to trust anything," the man said. "You're clearly not one of the Durunim, but you shouldn't be here, unless..."

He paused and looked her over thoroughly. Seri felt self-conscious under his gaze. She had the feeling she was being evaluated for something. At the same time, thoughts of home began to push back to the forefront of her mind.

"Listen, I don't know who you are," she said, "but I need to get back. The Lords are under attack. Two are dead already."

He nodded. "Two already. That makes sense." He glanced toward the west. "And the fight over there has already begun too."

Fight over there? Seri was curious, but she needed to get back. "Why can't I see the magic on this side?" she said to herself. She tried blinking a few times without any change.

• • • • •

Marshal blasted one of the Durunim away with his power. The ease with which he did so surprised him. Had he grown attuned to it that quickly? A second one swung a massive sword at him, which he ducked with ease. Being three feet shorter than the other combatants had its advantages.

To his right, he caught brief glimpses of Talinir. The warden was a blur, battling two, even three of the Durunim at once. He seemed to be holding his own.

Curasir pointed his sword at Marshal again. As the power exploded toward him, Marshal leaped up, blasting the ground with the full force he could muster. The impact launched him skyward with a speed that took his breath away.

"Marshal!" Talinir's shout barely registered on his ears.

As he hit the apex of his flight, he sucked in huge lungfuls of air. At this height, the giant stars looked almost close enough to touch. Again, his heart ached at the glorious sight. If only he could just lie down again and look up…

A blast of power struck him in the back. It wasn't strong enough to do any damage, but it threw him off balance and he tumbled head over heels as he plummeted towards the ground.

"You're in my world, human!" Curasir called. "You cannot hope to beat me!"

• • • • •

The stranger took a step closer. His movement drew Seri's eyes to his feet: shoeless, rough, and dirty. How long had he lived here? She looked up and found him studying her intently.

"Your eye…" he said.

"Yes, I have a star in it. I can see magic. Sometimes."

"That must be why you're here," he said. "You can help him!"

"Help who?"

A rumble echoed across the sky. Seri looked to the west and saw a distant figure leap impossibly high into the air, silhouetted against the stars. A second figure flew after the first. She couldn't see much from this distance, but they appeared to be fighting somehow. Magic?

"Yes, there!" the stranger cried. "He's there. You have to help him!"

"Why should I?" Seri asked. "I don't know who that is. I don't know you. Why should I listen to you?"

The stranger took a deep breath and planted his spear in the ground beside him. He faced Seri with a stern gaze.

"Because I'm the King of Antises!"

(((80)))

Marshal had no idea if he could beat this enemy. He had no idea what he was even doing here. At this point, however, he was a little more concerned with stopping his fall. He threw bursts of power out, hoping to stabilize his tumbling, but with nothing for them to push against, it did little good.

Instead of resisting, he turned into the fall, eventually righting himself to the point he was falling face-down. The ground, twisted and broken, rushed to meet him. Now he could use his power. He pointed down and blasted at the ground, hoping to slow his descent as he had back at the temple. He was falling much further and faster this time, but the principle was the same. He slowed and turned feet-first.

By the time he came to a rough landing that jarred all his joints, he had carved out a new crater in this devastated plain. He climbed a few steps to look out. His arc would have taken him out over Lake Litanu, wouldn't it? But Marshal saw no water in any direction. Could this land be devoid of water, also?

He had no more time to think about it. Curasir blasted into the ground a few feet away, using a similar technique to his own landing.

Immediately, Marshal unleashed his own power at his opponent. He marveled again at the simplicity of using his power, but winced, as well. His hands and forearms pulsed with pain, much like the first time he had experimented with this power, weeks ago.

Curasir held up a hand and used his own power to block Marshal's. The earth erupted around him, flinging dirt and rocks in every direction. The longer Marshal persisted, the more the air filled with dust and debris. With a final growl of frustration, he stopped. The pain in his arms was growing. There was a limit to how long he would be able to continue this fight.

Curasir looked completely unfazed by any of it. "You have such potential, Marshal," he called. "So unlike your mother, or even your grandfather. Both of them had to be removed to make room for you, of course. You are the one that matters, the one that can change everything."

Marshal knew Curasir was taunting him, but he didn't care. The mention of his mother unlocked new resolve and rage within him. He screamed incoherent syllables and erupted with even more power than his last attack.

Curasir launched into the sky this time, dodging the attack and flying in an impressive arc further out over the lakebed. Marshal growled and threw himself into the air in pursuit.

●●●●●

"You're what?" Seri stared at the stranger, mouth agape.

"I'm the King of Antises," he repeated. "I've been here a long time, but I don't know how long it's been in your world. Time doesn't quite work the same way here, I think."

Seri was full of questions. Which King was he? How many generations since the last real King? How had he gotten here? Why hadn't he returned? Then again, how could she take his word for it? Hadn't she just uncovered a false King?

"How can I be sure you are who you say you are?"

"There's no time!" The self-proclaimed King looked back to the west. The ground trembled.

Seri looked too. Whoever the combatants were, they were throwing out tremendous bursts of power. She could see that much even without her star-sight.

She turned back and found the King standing right beside her. She gasped and stepped back. How had he moved so fast?

"Listen to me!" he pleaded. "I know you can't fully understand. But there's a man fighting over there--" He pointed westward. "—who is the key to saving everything and everyone."

Seri glanced that way again. "I don't know what I can do," she said. "If I had my star-sight…"

The King suddenly had his hand in front of her face. "*Curinir!*" he said firmly.

Seri felt a tingle swirl around her left eye. She blinked several times.

When the King removed his hand, she could see... everything. Beams of light swirled about, emerging from the ground below and re-entering it. The Otherworld had suddenly become infinitely more colorful.

"Out there." The King stood behind her and pointed over her shoulder.

She looked at the fighters again. With the star-sight, they now dominated the landscape, two miniature suns throwing swirls of light at each other. She had difficulty making out much more than that at this distance. They had to be several miles away, at least.

"I can't tell--" she began.

"Look closer."

As if her eyes reacted to the King's command, she suddenly felt like as though she were only a few hundred yards from the combatants. She could see them clearly.

One of them was impossibly tall and immediately familiar. "Curasir!" His skin appeared as it had the last time she had seen him on this side - dark, absorbing all colors. At the back of her mind, she connected it with the splotches on the King's skin. He glowed with tremendous power, rivaled only by his opponent.

The other appeared human, a young man. His power glowed with such brilliance Seri couldn't tell anything else about him. He clearly possessed a Lord's power, and... something else. That was odd. No other power had ever glowed in that particular way, though it was difficult to make out. She started to turn toward the King, wanting to see his power.

He grabbed her head on both sides and aimed it back at Curasir and the boy. "Look at them!" he commanded. "Look at the sources of their power!"

•••••

Marshal slammed into the ground again. His landings were improving, but every time he did, it jarred all of his joints. He didn't know how much longer he could keep this up.

Another blast from Curasir struck him before he was ready. Something cracked inside and he wheeled about before slamming into the side of the new crater he had just created. He rolled over and saw the towering form of Curasir striding toward him. He lifted a hand and blasted power outward. Curasir appeared to casually deflect the blast with his sword. Apparently, he could use it for more than channeling his own power. Marshal wished Talinir had taught him that trick.

Curasir pointed the sword at him. "Come, let us end this. You have no hope."

"Nyargh!" Marshal tried to blast again with similar results. His power seemed to be weakening along with his body.

Curasir shook his head. "You just got your tongue and that's the best you can do? Pathetic." Curasir hit him with a blast of power that slammed him back into the dirt. Marshal groaned and tried to get back up. Curasir hit him again.

"Now that your mother has done what was needed, with my help, we can proceed with your true purpose. You can join us willingly, or we will just take you. Your compliance is desired, but not necessary. I would prefer that you work with us. It will be glorious, Marshal. Glorious."

While Curasir spoke, Marshal concentrated on focusing all of his power into his left arm. Thus far, he had been blindly releasing bursts of power without any real thought. Maybe a more concentrated burst would accomplish more. He gritted his teeth and lifted his arm.

The power erupted from his hand and Marshal screamed in agony. He felt finger bones breaking. The blast caught Curasir by surprise and knocked him off his feet. He dropped his sword as he was thrown back through clouds of dust and stone. He tumbled out of Marshal's sight.

With a moan, Marshal tried to get to his feet. The pain in his side blossomed, he stumbled, and fell again. He tried to catch himself with only his right hand and failed, striking his head on a rock. The pain of impact paled in comparison to the agony that cascaded through his broken hand merely from brushing it against the ground.

He rolled with a whimper and saw Curasir's sword only a few feet away. Holding his left hand against his chest, he crawled on his remaining hand and knees toward it. Blood poured down his face and mixed with tears that fell outside his conscious control. His shredded clothes provided no protection to his knees that scraped on the rocky ground with every movement. He choked on the thick dust and tried to spit.

The sword was so close. He could make out something carved into the gold on the pommel, a flying creature of some kind.

"I'll take that." Curasir reached down and picked up the sword just as Marshal reached for it.

•••••

Seri frowned and looked again. As she had already seen, the young man's power came from within, like the Lords, even though there was something else to it she could not identify. Curasir, however... He was drawing power from somewhere else. Hundreds of beams of light streamed into him like a giant umbilical cord, moving with him wherever he went. She followed the cord from Curasir until it passed almost right past her.

"He's drawing the power of Zes Sivas to himself!"

"Exactly. He's been killing the Masters to free up more of the island's power." The King's voice sounded grim. "But you can do something about that."

She probably could. But should she? "I don't know the boy," she said. "I know Curasir, and I don't trust him, but how do I know the other guy is any better?"

The King spun Seri's head around and she found herself looking him directly in the eyes. Power like she had never seen glowed within them. Why didn't he act himself? Why...? "I cannot reveal myself here," he whispered. "The danger is too great. But you can act. You can save him."

(((81)))

Marshal rolled onto his back and tried to stop crying. Everything hurt so much.

Curasir's silhouette blocked out the stars above him. "I believe that's enough now," he said. "It was a valiant effort, but you've lost. You can't even fight any more." He glanced up as if hearing something. "Come, the tunaldi will be investigating if we stay here long. In your condition, you wouldn't last long against one of them. Now, one last time. Will you give me your power?"

Marshal fought to control his breath. His power swirled about inside him, as if it didn't know what to do after being used so much. It felt so wrong, so unfair, to fail so completely now. After all they had been through, the journey, the Eldanim, the assassin, and then… Aelia. All of it to bring him here to be defeated, his power used to destroy Antises? Was this the purpose his mother had wanted for him?

"No," he whispered. No. She had loved him, had wanted to give her life for him. He had a greater purpose somewhere. He could feel his power building up again, not that it had helped so far.

• • • • •

Seri turned back to Curasir's power flow. She reached out and grasped the most powerful beam of light and pulled it away. But there were hundreds! She couldn't do that to all of them. Instead, she took the one beam, looped it over all the others and pulled. The pressure against her was enormous. Almost immediately, she felt some kind of resistance feeding back into her own body, draining her strength. She staggered and almost let it go.

"You can do this!" the King urged.

Seri pulled as hard as she could and dragged the beams of light back down, re-channeling them all back into Zes Sivas and cutting off the power from Curasir. The impact of the power striking the ground threw her backwards. She felt two strong arms catch her.

"Well done," the King's voice whispered. "With such actions, the world changes…"

He said something else, but Seri couldn't make it out. The effort of cutting of Curasir's magic, after everything else she had been through in the past few hours, had been more than her body could take. She slipped into unconsciousness.

● ● ● ● ●

"No?" Curasir repeated. "Very well." He aimed his sword at Marshal one last time.

Nothing happened.

Curasir lifted the sword and looked at it, as if it had done something wrong. "Odd." He pointed his other hand at Marshal and again, nothing happened. He growled and looked to the east. "That girl. That foolish girl. How did she even get here?"

Marshal had no idea what he was talking about, but clearly something had gone wrong. He closed his eyes. He didn't dare focus his power through his other hand. But maybe that wasn't necessary. Why even use the hands?

Marshal let himself go limp against the crater's floor, opened his soul, and gave Curasir his power.

The magic exploded out of his entire body in one enormous burst, more powerful than anything he had done, more majestic and enormous than anything he had even imagined. Curasir, caught in its thunderous outpouring, skyrocketed into the air and vanished from sight. The impact pushed Marshal back into the dirt, grinding him down.

As the power faded, so did his strength. He wondered where Talinir was and whether he was all right. He thought of Aelia and wondered what she would think of all this. Would she be proud of him? Marshal couldn't be sure, but one truth he did know. Through his dust-clogged throat, even as he felt sleep descending, he whispered, "I am loved."

(((82)))

Seri woke and found herself lying on green grass near the water's edge on Zes Sivas. It seemed peaceful for a moment, and then the sound of many voices overlapping filled her ears. She got to her feet and looked around.

The setting sun illuminated an island in shambles. Most of the outer wall had fallen. People milled about inside and outside its remains. One broke away and ran toward her. She recognized him. Jamana.

"Seri-Belit!" he cried. For once, she didn't mind at all hearing her full name. Seeing his magnificent grin more than made up for it. She smiled in return and was about to answer, but Jamana reached her and swept her up in an enormous hug. Behind him, she saw Dravid moving toward them as fast as his crutch would allow. Others followed him.

"Where have you been?" Jamana demanded, letting her go. "We have been searching everywhere!"

"I've been... in another world," she said as Dravid arrived. He tried to shift his crutch out of the way, but Seri ignored it and hugged him, anyway.

Ixchel strode up, followed more slowly by Adhi. Her bodyguard looked her up and down. "You look well," she said. "If you are going to travel to other worlds, you should take me with you. I cannot protect you from here."

Seri couldn't help it. She giggled. Ixchel wasn't impressed by the idea of another world; she only considered how it would affect her job.

She looked around at her friends. They looked somewhat battered. All of them had bruises here and there, but no one looked significantly injured. All of them looked at her in expectation.

"When Volraag caved in the citadel, I sort of… transported myself into the Otherworld," she said. "I don't know how long that's been, or even how I got back, really."

"It's been hours!" Dravid said.

"What happened, then?"

Dravid shifted his weight. "I found Jamana and Master Korda and we were on our way back to help," he said. "That's when the earthquake hit."

"Master Korda protected us," Jamana said. He pointed toward the citadel. "That building is not safe any more, I am thinking."

"Especially after Volraag blasted it!" Dravid said. "He brought down the throne room and everything!"

Seri looked to Ixchel. "Did everyone that was with you get out okay?"

Ixchel's face was as impassive as ever. "One of my sisters died at the hands of that assassin. I do not know what became of him."

"And the others? Lord Enuru and Lady Lilitu? Master Hain?"

"The Lord and Lady are fine," Dravid said. "Master Hain is… ah…" He glanced at the others.

"Master Hain is not well," Jamana said, his smile fading. "We had to dig him out of the ruins."

"I need to see him!" Seri said. "Take me!"

Jamana gestured and they all began to walk together. In her head, Seri couldn't help but try to map out all of the new Bindings that would have been created through all of this mess. She knew she felt a new one of her own, toward Master Hain. She could tell they were getting closer to him.

"Volraag is gone," Dravid said. "He left while we were digging everyone out."

"Master Ganak met him at the dock," Adhi inserted. "He warned him never to come back, I think."

"What about the next Passing?" Seri asked. "If his power is not returned…"

"Things do not look well," Jamana said. Then he grinned. "But you are alive! And have traveled to another world! This is a good thing. A very good thing. You must tell us all about it!"

"I will," Seri promised. "But first, I must see Master Hain."

As they walked, Seri heard more news. At least twelve people had died in the earthquake, but more remained missing. The Masters and remaining Lords had all survived mostly unscathed, with their powers to protect them, but the rest of the citadels' inhabitants were not so lucky. Several apprentices had perished as well. Lords Tyrr and Rajwir had already departed the island, concerned over the possibility of war with the new Lord Volraag.

The devastation to Zes Sivas was extensive. As Jamana had said, the Citadel of Mages was no longer safe. Much of it remained intact, but extremely unstable. The Inner Sanctum was buried under tons of rubble. The Masters were using careful applications of their power to shift debris, looking for survivors and needed supplies. The Citadel of Kings had fared somewhat better, but the throne room and surrounding areas had been destroyed by Volraag.

When Seri saw Master Hain, he appeared to be dead. His face, what she could see, was covered in bruises. His right arm and both legs had been bound up with splints. His chest trembled as it rose and fell in labored breathing. His left eye was swollen shut, but his right eye brightened at the sight of her. She knelt by his side. Jamana gestured for the others to back off and give them privacy.

"I knew…" Master Hain's voice contained an alarming gurgle to it. "I knew you were alive." He lifted his left hand and Seri took it gently.

"I- I transported myself to the Otherworld," she said.

Master Hain nodded slightly and coughed. "I suspected. Tell me. All."

Seri pointed to her own eye. "It began with this," she said. While her friends waited, she carefully explained everything that had happened with Curasir, her star-sight, her discovery of Tezan, and her foolish decision to trust Volraag.

"I should have come to you," she said, a tear trickling down her cheek. "I was afraid."

Master Hain's hand tightened ever so slightly around hers. "Tell me… about today."

As twilight deepened, Seri recounted what she and Dravid had seen, Volraag's plan, and her own actions. She swallowed hard and began to tell about her adventure in the Otherworld. At her mention of the stranger's identity claim, Master Hain jerked spasmodically and coughed over and over. Seri found some water and helped him drink. Before he could ask any more questions, she hurried through the rest of the story and finished with waking up back on Zes Sivas.

"I can't be sure he actually is the King," she said, "but he… felt like it, if that makes sense."

Master Hain swallowed. "Can you… go back?" His voice seemed

weaker than before.

"I don't know," Seri said honestly. "I can try, but I'm not entirely sure what I did to get there."

Master Hain pulled weakly on her hand and she bent closer. In an even quieter voice, he whispered, "Tell all to Master... Korda. No one else. Ask his advice." Master Hain's eye closed.

He was silent so long, Seri thought he had fallen asleep. Then he opened his eye and whispered again, "Whether I... live or die, Lord Enuru will have... to appoint a new Master. Before that... I promote you. You... are a full mage now."

"I- I haven't even been an apprentice yet!" Seri protested.

Master Hain shook his head slightly. "Full mage. So you... can travel. You will need to..." His voice trailed off and he did not speak again.

Seri waited a few moments, then stood to her feet. The sky had grown much darker while she knelt. All around, people lit fires and torches in order to keep working. She looked back at the other acolytes. She now outranked them all. It felt strange to think it. She had come to this island to become a mage. Never in her wildest dreams had she imagined it happening this fast, let alone traveling to the Otherworld, fighting against one of the Eldanim...

She took a deep breath and looked up. A handful of stars already shone in the twilit sky. She turned back to Jamana.

"Take me to Master Korda."

• • • • •

Seri, mage of Arazu, stood on the dock of Zes Sivas in her blue robes, watching as a rowboat approached. She chuckled when she recognized Hauk, the boatman who had brought her here months ago.

Dravid leaned against a pylon behind her. "So... west, then?" he asked.

She nodded. Master Korda had listened intently to her entire story and wearied her with questions long into the night. She had foregone sleep even longer to write a lengthy letter to her parents. She couldn't help wondering about their reactions to her promotion. In the morning, Master Korda instructed her to attempt the journey to the Otherworld again. She was unable to duplicate the feat. Master Korda did not act surprised. Instead, he tasked her with finding the mysterious boy she had helped in the Otherworld.

"For I suspect you will find that he has returned to our world, as well," the big mage told her. "Whoever he is, he has much power and will need guidance and protection. Find him, and bring him here."

More than that, the Masters all insisted a curse had been lifted somewhere in the West. For some reason, they saw this as even more important than all of Tezan and Volraag's machinations. Master Korda said something about the end of all curses. Seri couldn't even imagine what that might mean.

So many other questions remained unanswered, especially about Curasir. Perhaps he had killed the two Masters to absorb their connections to Zes Sivas and gain the power he needed for that battle in the Otherworld. But that did not explain his interest in Seri, or his connection to Lady Lilitu and her mysterious power.

Ixchel snorted. "Westerners are weak," she said. She eyed the approaching boatman suspiciously.

Seri smiled. At least two of her friends were able to accompany her. Without Master Hain to train him, Dravid had no reason to stay. And Ixchel insisted she would follow wherever Seri went. Master Korda would not permit Jamana to travel yet. As an acolyte, he would be needed. The remaining Masters planned to rebuild the Citadel and had begun sending messages to each of the six realms, asking for aid. Seri wondered if they would be able to make much progress before another earthquake struck. Regardless, there was much work to do.

"Rasna or Varioch?" Dravid asked.

Seri hated the thought of going anywhere near Volraag. But he had spoken of a brother, someone who now possessed Lord Varion's power. Was he the one she had seen?

"Varioch," she said. "But we won't go to the capital."

Dravid nodded. "I wish a Master were going with us," he said.

Seri agreed. She hated the idea of being the one in charge. But Zes Sivas needed all of the Masters right now. And Master Hain… She had visited him one last time this afternoon. To her disappointment, he had not regained consciousness. The healer did not have much hope for his recovery, either.

Hauk pulled the rowboat up to the dock and tossed his rope to Dravid. The acolyte caught it, but nearly lost his balance in the process. The boatman glanced over at Seri.

"Ah, I remember you," he said. "Had enough, eh? Didn't think they'd let a woman…"

Ixchel knelt on the edge of the dock and pointed her sword at Hauk.

"You are speaking to my mistress, Seri-Belit, Mage of the Realm," she said, a fierce look in her eyes. "And you will show her the respect she is due."

Seri smiled. Regardless of the journey's end, she had no doubt it would be interesting.

(((83)))

"This will never do." Marshal was sure he heard a voice speaking through a haze of pain, but he didn't recognize it. "If you go back here, you'll drown." After those confusing words, he heard nothing more, at least not clearly.

He slept for hours. At times, his pain pulled him partially awake. Someone did something to his hand that caused it to explode in agony, but even that wasn't enough to restore him to full consciousness. He drifted off again in a few moments. Someone moved him, that much he knew, but not much more.

Only once did he wake enough to have a coherent thought. "Talinir!" he called.

"Rest," the unknown voice responded. "I'll try to find him later."

Marshal opened his eyes the barest fraction and caught a glimpse of a grey beard. Then his eyes rolled back and he slept again.

When he finally came to himself, the coolness of the air against his face felt strange. Everything had seemed warmer since he crossed into the star-lit realm, though he hadn't noticed before now. His eyes opened slowly and looked up at the stars. They twinkled across the sky, normal size and color. The moon's sliver was barely visible near the horizon. Back in the regular world.

He sat up and winced. His entire body ached, but the sharp pains in his side were the worst. Shouldn't his hand be hurting more? He lifted it up and saw thick bandages wrapped around his entire left hand and upper forearm. He could tell multiple splints within the wrappings held his bones in place. Someone had worked hard on that. The mystery voice?

He finally looked at his surroundings. He sat on the shore of a swift-flowing river. Lights from a large city shone from perhaps a mile away behind him. It was hard to tell in the dark, but it looked like Reman.

Marshal felt fatigue overtaking him again, though not to the degree he had experienced lately. This felt more like the simple tiredness one would expect after a busy day. He lowered himself back down and watched the stars for a few minutes. His heart ached for the beauty of the stars in the Otherworld, but his mind now pushed back against that. It wasn't the perfect world he had thought it to be. Thinking about that, he slipped off to sleep again.

"It's about time!" The loud cry startled him awake some time later. He opened his eyes and blinked against the bright sunlight.

He heard movement and rolled to see. Victor scrambled down the bank toward him.

"Do you know how long this stupid Binding has had me running in circles?" he demanded. "It kept wanting me to swim out into the lake!"

He stopped as he finally saw Marshal's appearance. "Whoa. What happened to you?"

Marshal shook his head and pulled himself back up to a sitting position.

"Did you… did you lose your voice again?"

"No," Marshal said. The word sounded so strange coming from his mouth. He wondered how long it would take him to grow used to speaking. He also realized his mouth was parched. He moved down to the water's edge and tried to drink.

"Oh. Well, that's good, I guess." Victor looked around. "Where's Talinir?"

"I think… I think he's still there." Marshal waved vaguely with his left hand and then winced. Scooping water up with one hand to drink wasn't easy, either.

Victor knelt beside him. "You look horrible. Here." He handed him a water pouch. Marshal took it gratefully.

"I don't know what you've been doing all this time," Victor went on, "but you've missed a lot here. There was quite the uproar over what you did to the temple. Most people think the earthquake destroyed it, but those few dozen that saw you there keep trying to tell the story of the scar-faced man with magic powers."

Victor scooped up some water and splashed it on his own face. "Then the prince came back, except he says he's Lord Volraag now. His father's dead. Which is why you got the power, I guess. But get this: he has power too! How did that happen? I thought you got it all!"

"I don't know," Marshal said. He handed the pouch back to Victor. "How… long have I--"

"How long have you been gone? It's been three days, Marshal. Three days since you and Talinir jumped through that crazy doorway and left me behind." Victor sounded hurt.

Three days. Had it been so long? Had it been so short? It felt wrong either way. "My… mama?"

Victor let out a breath and his shoulders relaxed. "Nian took care of everything. Come on. I'll take you there." He took Marshal's hand and pulled him to his feet.

• • • • •

A simple stone marked Aelia's resting place amidst a small grove of pine trees. Her name and that of her father were its only decoration. Marshal knelt beside it and rested his hand on the stone's smooth surface.

"Why?" he whispered. He knew the answer she would have given, the answer she gave. But it still made no sense to him. He wasn't worth this. No one was.

"Did you, uh, beat that eidolon thing?" Victor asked.

Marshal nodded. It didn't seem like much, but at least he had accomplished something. He wondered what Aelia would have thought of that.

"She loved more than any woman I've met."

Marshal looked up at Nian, who strolled into the grove.

"How did you know we were here?" Victor asked.

"I am… not very welcome at the temple lately," Nian said. "I've been staying nearby and keeping a watch out for you. I knew you'd return eventually."

Marshal snorted and looked back at the stone. Nian placed both hands on his shoulders. Marshal tensed up instinctively, then tried to relax.

"I'm glad to see you made it back, Marshal. Those who venture into the Otherworld do not always return."

Victor toyed with his flail. "What was it like over there?"

"Dark," Marshal said. "But beautiful."

"What will you do now?" Nian asked.

Marshal shook his head. He had no idea.

"We should walk back into Reman and demand they recognize

Marshal as the true Lord!" Victor said.

"No." Marshal looked up. "I can't."

"Sure, you can. You're the rightful heir. Your mom told me all about it, and… It's part of why she got your curse lifted." Victor looked from Marshal to Nian. "Isn't it?"

"I don't--" Nian began.

"I can't do it!" Marshal said. He put his right hand on the ground. A slight tremor radiated out from him. He looked up at the other two. "That was as strong as I can get."

"What happened? You tore the entire temple apart a few days ago!"

Marshal shrugged. "I think… I did too much."

"You overextended yourself?" Nian asked.

Marshal nodded.

"Then you just wore it out. It'll come back, right?" Victor again looked hopeful. "Right?"

"I don't know." His lips felt tired. Too much talking.

Nian moved around opposite Marshal and the stone. "This is what I can say of Aelia's purposes," he said. "She believed you had a great purpose in this world, Marshal."

This he knew. She had repeated it almost every day of his life.

"And I'm… valuable."

"Yes. All of Theon's children are valuable. But your mother showed how incredibly valuable she believed you to be."

"I'm not worth it."

"Is anyone?" Nian knelt and faced Marshal. "You now have to face the life she died to give you. You have to live in a manner to make it worth it!"

Marshal's face twisted in agony. "How?"

"How can anyone? You make a difference where you can. Rumors are spreading that our new Lord Volraag murdered his father. Both Varioch and Rasna are preparing for war. The earth itself is shaking. All of Antises is waiting, looking for hope in these dark times. You…. You had a curse lifted!" Nian stood and spread his arms. "That has never happened in all our recorded history! I've long heard it said that once one curse is lifted, it will set Antises on the path to the lifting of all curses. You, Marshal, are a symbol of hope itself!" He paused and added more quietly, "Of grace itself." He reached a hand down to Marshal.

Marshal ignored it and stood on his own. In his mind, he saw the little girl with the twisted arm in Efesun. "Until all curses are lifted," he whispered. He looked once more at Aelia's stone, then turned to Victor.

"Let's get started."

For more information on Antises,
upcoming books, and more,
visit timfrankovich.com

(Join the mailing list and receive a free short story,
featuring the origin of Kishin!)

If you enjoyed this book, please post a review!
There's no better way to spread the word.

Acknowledgments

While I have had many stories in my head throughout my life, this one has an odd history. I've always wanted to write epic fantasy, but my earliest attempts were all far too derivative. It took me years to find the right combination of characters and plot.

One day at college, a friend and I were discussing our respective interests - for me, it was writing and fantasy; for him, it was music and theater. We playfully toyed with combining the two into the first epic fantasy stage play. We got as far as one opening scene where the villain, Volraag, gloats over his plan to obtain all the lands' magic and combine them into the Heart of Fire. We named the land Antises and the central island Zes Sivas. Then we argued over the hero's name (the villain's half-brother!). He suggested a combination of our two names, which I thought sounded silly. And that was as far as the collaboration went. After graduation, he and I drifted apart. I have no idea where he is now, but I hope this book finds its way to him sometime.

After I got serious about writing a few years ago, I wrote one book that I now regard as practice (it may see the light of day, revised, at some point in the future). Then I turned to my true love, epic fantasy. But which of the epic fantasy stories that have filled my brain since childhood should I use? As I dug through old notes on my computer, I came across one named "Heart of Fire." I read over the notes we had brainstormed, and as I did, new ideas entered my head. I sketched out a brief outline, calling the hero Marshal now (named after my friend). I realized that this had the makings of something truly epic in length and scope.

* * *

But the story still needed much more. I conceived the secondary storyline, taking place on Zes Sivas, but it needed a second protagonist. And so Seri was born. Her story wrote itself more than any character I've ever created.

I am deeply indebted to Stephen Tallman and Allen Perkins, my beta readers. Your reactions to the characters and their trials helped shape many of my revision thoughts. I also gained enormous insights from editor Mica Kole, whose developmental analysis helped me nail down some weak points in the story and revise numerous key points.

My sister, Cindy, always wanted to read everything I wrote while we were younger, giving me needed motivation. The seeds of some of these plots and characters were planted in some of those earliest scribblings.

The guys who have been a part of my tabletop gaming group - John, Justin, Mark x3, Lance, Jimmy, Derek, Ernie, Carson - have been a constant source of inspiration, whether they knew it or not. Some of them show up under other names in various parts of my writing.

I can never repay my wife, Denise, for allowing me to spend far too many hours sitting in front of a computer screen. You are the best ever, oh love of my life!

The highest praise belongs to my Creator, who made me in His image as a sub-creator, giving me the desire to do things like this.

Obviously, there is much more to tell in the story of Antises. Keep track of the news on timfrankovich.com, my mailing list, Facebook author page, Twitter, and whatever other wacky social media gets invented between now and the next book…

About the Author

Tim Frankovich has been exploring fantastic worlds since third grade, when he cut up a grocery sack and drew a Godzilla-meets-superheroes story. Since then, he's gotten a little bit better at the writing part (not so much with the drawing).

His goal as a writer is to transport readers to another world, make them care deeply about characters in dire situations, and guide them deeply into life itself.

At the moment, he is probably suitably conscious somewhere in Texas with his beloved wife, awesome four kids, and a fool of a pup named Pippin. *Until All Curses Are Broken* is his first novel.

The following is a preview chapter of
Until All Bonds Are Broken,
the sequel to *Until All Curses Are Lifted*

"Watch out for the Curse Boy," Titus warned.

Victor scowled as little Marshal trotted up beside him. Though all three boys were eight years old, Marshal hadn't kept up with the other two's growth spurts. He seemed much younger. Plus, the curse and all.

"You're going to follow us if we don't let you come, aren't you?" Victor asked.

Marshal's face twisted as he seemed to be thinking hard. Then he nodded.

Victor sighed. "All right. Come on."

"Do we have to?" Titus asked. "He's just going to be in the way."

"If we don't, he'll follow us and we'll probably get in trouble. If we let him come, we can keep an eye on him."

Titus rolled his eyes and pushed past Marshal onto the trail. The three boys set off, following the well-worn path through the mountainous terrain. All of them were accustomed to this part of their quest, having spent their entire lives on the edge of the mountain pass known as Drusa's Crossing.

"It's the left turn," Titus said.

"I know, I know," Victor grumbled. Of course it was the left turn. The right turn led to the river where they did all their fishing. That was the path they always took, the path they were supposed to take. The leftward path led somewhere else, somewhere higher.

Victor took the lead and turned left, pausing only long enough to glance toward the right and make sure no one could see them. It would be just his luck if his father - or worse, his mother - chose this exact moment to wander down the path.

He felt a strange thrill as they moved out of sight of the trail's fork. They were truly in the unknown now. No parents. No adults at all.

"My older brother took me up here a few weeks ago," Titus said. "It's not that far now." He had to remind them this wasn't his first time up the path.

The trail led up a rough incline that proved challenging for the boys, especially the shorter Marshal. In places, they had to scramble up onto rocks using all four limbs. One day, Victor vowed, he would be able to stride up these rocks with single steps. Why did growing up have to take so long? He had so many things he wanted to do, especially once he got out of this tiny village.

Marshal slipped on an angled rock, but recovered before his knee hit the ground. Victor glanced at him. The smaller boy smiled. Without the ability to speak, Marshal struggled to communicate in even simple ways. Victor felt sorry for him, but if he showed any sympathy, it would open him up to the mockery of Titus and the other village children.

"Right up there!" Titus said.

Victor pulled himself up the last step. He wobbled and managed to stand up straight. He almost lost his balance as Titus pushed his way up beside him. Both boys held on to each other as they moved to make room for Marshal on the narrow ledge. The smaller boy pushed in-between them.

The view was spectacular. From this slim vantage point with their backs to a rock wall, the boys could see for miles. Behind them, Mount Cassius soared another two hundred feet or more before it reached its final peak. The climb from here would be almost impossible, even for a well-trained adult.

"We're almost as high as you can get!" Victor said. His mouth remained open as he looked from side to side. Aside from the path they had scrambled up, the ground dropped off rapidly all around them. The rocky slopes cascaded down toward the valley far below.

For the first time, Victor felt uneasy. He could understand why their parents did not want them climbing this high. The ledge was very small, and a fall from this height… he doubted anyone could survive that. Maybe this hadn't been the best idea.

Marshal pointed insistently at something to their left. Victor peered in the indicated direction. "It's… it's home!" he exclaimed. Amidst all the trees, a single thatched rooftop could be seen peeking out from an area that leveled off and curved mostly out of sight behind them. It had to be one of the houses in Drusa's Crossing.

"Whose roof do you think that is?" Titus asked.

Victor squinted. "Might be Marshal's," he said. "His cabin is the furthest out."

"That's on the opposite side," Titus disagreed. "This is the other end of town."

"Wouldn't that be too close to the actual pass?" Victor furrowed his brow. The climb had twisted back and forth several times, making him unsure of their actual facing.

"No, because if we were facing the other way, we would be looking into Ch'olan. People are strange there."

"You only say that because your brother does."

"It's true! Some of them wear feathers!"

Marshal yanked on a spiraling root as thick as his arm. Loose dirt and pebbles rained down on all three.

"Watch it!" Victor griped.

"Dumb Curse Boy." Titus feinted a lunge at Marshal, who wavered, a look of panic crossing his face. He grabbed at the root again.

"Stop that!" Victor said. "We should go down. It's too dangerous up here."

"Coward."

Victor's face felt hot. "What did you say?"

Titus waved his arms. "We came all the way up here for this, and you want to go down because you're scared! I expected that from Curse Boy here, but not you!"

"You can't call me a coward!"

"I already did!"

Victor balled up his fist and stepped around Marshal toward Titus. "If we weren't up here, I'd teach you a lesson!"

Marshal grabbed at Victor's arm, but he shoved his hand away.

"I'd like to see you try it." Titus snorted. He turned and deliberately dropped down on his behind before sliding off down onto the trail. "Whenever you're ready."

Victor took another step. As his right foot touched the ground, he knew he had done something wrong. His stomach plummeted and he felt a strange feeling wash over his entire body. The gravel and dirt gave way under his foot and he lost his balance.

"Victor!" Titus screamed.

Victor pivoted as he began to fall. His eyes swept past Titus' shocked expression, past the wall of the ledge, and past Marshal, who looked... determined? Before Victor even realized what was happening, a thick root, the one Marshal had been yanking, looped over him.

In desperation, Victor grabbed at the root. He slid three feet and came to an abrupt halt. His knees banged against the rock. The root wrapped beneath one of his armpits. He seized it and looked up.

Marshal held on to both ends of the root, his teeth gritted and legs braced. Victor couldn't grasp how he hadn't been yanked down along with him.

"Ahhh!" A cry finally escaped Victor's lips. He scrambled against the sheer rock wall, trying to gain a foothold of some kind. Marshal continued to hold on, but couldn't pull Victor any higher. Titus shouted something incoherent.

Leaning on the root that encircled him, Victor released it with one hand, reached up and grabbed it a few inches higher. He pulled, legs still searching for anything at all to brace against.

Marshal looked back over his shoulder at the root's source. Victor followed his look. One end of the root extended from the ledge's wall about three feet above Marshal's head. The other curved around out of sight. Marshal nodded. He released the side whose end wasn't visible, and bent down, still holding onto the other side of the root. His outstretched hand didn't come anywhere near Victor, but he did take hold of a lower spot on the root and pulled.

Victor also pulled and managed to scramble up a few more inches, grabbing a higher spot.

Titus attempted to get onto the ledge to help, but between Marshal and the spot Victor had collapsed, he couldn't find room. He slid back down onto the trail.

Inch by inch, Victor repeated his earlier movements, slowly working up the root. His arms felt like they might give way at any moment from the strain.

"You can do it!" Titus called.

Victor's fingers brushed against Marshal's. The silent boy dropped onto his stomach and reached as far as he could, still holding the root with his other hand. Victor swung himself upward and reached. Marshal grasped his hand, but couldn't hold it. Victor slipped loose and screamed as all his weight hung from one hand. It slid another inch and splinters cut into his palm.

He swung himself up again, not sure if he could make it. This time, Marshal caught his hand and held on. They hung there for just a moment. Then Marshal began to pull. Victor pulled back, then lunged upward to catch a higher spot on the root with his other hand. A few moments later, Marshal pulled his hand up over the lip of the ledge. In just a few more moments, Victor struggled onto the ledge himself and lay still. Safe.

"Theon's pillars!" Titus said. Standing down below, his face was almost even with Victor's, lying on the ledge. "I can't believe... Theon's pillars!"

Victor turned his head and leaned on his elbow. It shook with fatigue. He looked back at Marshal. "Thank you."

"Who would have thought? The Curse Boy saved your life!" Titus looked from one to the other, then his eyes widened. "He saved your life," he repeated. "That means..."

Victor let his head drop down onto the rock again. "Devouring fire!" he whispered.

●●●●●

Victor looked across their meager camp at Marshal, sound asleep. Though he had been immensely grateful to the other boy for saving his life, for ten years he had resented the Bond it created between them. That resentment included Marshal himself.

Who would have ever guessed that Marshal would drag him off on this grand adventure they were having now? Sure, it had hurt to leave behind his home, friends, family. But that faded over time. He could barely remember Careen's face now. He frowned. That wasn't right. But he had gotten to fight monsters, meet magical beings, and learn how to wield a sword. He wouldn't trade all this for the world itself.

When Marshal disappeared into the Otherworld, the Bond between them had become a painful thing. When Marshal was in any kind of danger, Victor always knew, always felt a pull, sometimes practically physical in nature. But this had been different. The pull couldn't pinpoint a direction most of the time Marshal was gone. At times, Victor had felt pulled in every direction. It felt like his insides were going to explode out of his chest. He couldn't sleep, barely slept.

But now Marshal was back. The danger was past. The Bond had faded away. Victor felt immense relief to have his friend back. Because that's what Marshal was now: his friend. A better friend than he'd ever had. And now his curse had been lifted! The possibilities for them now were infinite. Marshal might very well become the Lord of Varioch! And Victor...

He lowered his head. During Marshal's Otherworld venture, the other thing had faded. But now, now that was back. Victor hadn't mentioned it to anyone yet. He had no idea what to think. But being around Marshal for so long was changing him. That had to be the reason.

Victor lifted his hand before his face and watched.

His fingers vibrated.

The story continues in
Until All Bonds Are Broken

www.ingramcontent.com/pod-product-compliance
Lightning Source LLC
Chambersburg PA
CBHW021952120726
47898CB00001BA/87